Amish Brides
Collection

Samantha Bayarr

Amish
Brides
Collection
Samantha Bayarr

Contains these 4 Books

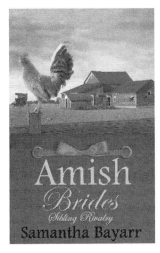

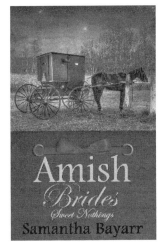
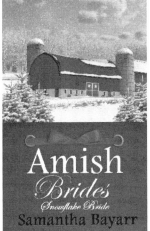

Livingston Hall Publishers

Inspirational Books of Distinction

Amish Brides

Book One: Sibling Rivalry

Samantha Bayarr

Amish
Brides
Sibling Rivalry

Samantha Bayarr

Table of Contents

[CHAPTER 1](#)

[CHAPTER 2](#)

[CHAPTER 3](#)

[CHAPTER 4](#)

[CHAPTER 5](#)

[CHAPTER 6](#)

[CHAPTER 7](#)

[CHAPTER 8](#)

[CHAPTER 9](#)

[CHAPTER 10](#)

[CHAPTER 11](#)

[CHAPTER 12](#)

[CHAPTER 13](#)

[CHAPTER 14](#)

[CHAPTER 15](#)

[CHAPTER 16](#)

[CHAPTER 17](#)

[CHAPTER 18](#)

CHAPTER 19

CHAPTER 20

CHAPTER 21

CHAPTER 22

CHAPTER 23

❧Sibling Rivalry❧

CHAPTER 1

"Is he dead?"

Lavinia Miller set her gaze in the direction of Willow Creek where her sister pointed to the *Englisher* who lay face-down on the muddy embankment. The gentle current of the creek washed over his feet as they hung over the edge, forcing them to sway. If not for the length of his body anchored safely ashore, he'd have likely drifted down to the next county. The very possibility of the man lying there dead made Lavinia tremble with an unnatural fear. A fear that only comes from witnessing death first-hand.

She stiffened her upper lip and narrowed her brow with defiance. "There's only one way to find out!"

Bethany shook her head furiously. "You won't get me to go over there to look. I ain't touching a dead body."

Lavinia knew all too well the feel of a dead body as the life drained from it, but she pushed back the memory.

"No one said anything about touching him, you chicken! If he's dead, we'll run back to the barn and call the law. They can come take care of him."

If their father was here, he'd most likely tell his daughters to stay back and let the law handle it, but Lavinia felt a sort of morbid curiosity that had suddenly taken charge of her.

She *had* to know if the man was dead.

Lavinia swallowed back fear as she grabbed hold of the willow branches that hung over the embankment, using them to leverage herself to avoid slipping in the mud. Recent rains had raised the level of the creek enough to soak the grassy area along the bank to where each step she took caused her to sink. Rich, black soil stuck to the bottoms of her black, lace-up shoes and splattered the hem of her dress. Laboriously lifting each foot against the slight suction of the mud made for a long walk of the short distance between her and the *Englisher.*

"Wait!" Bethany called.

Lavinia stopped abruptly, whipped her head back toward her sister, heart pounding. "Don't scare me like that. You made me think there was a snake or something coming after me!"

Bethany rolled her eyes. "What if he's dangerous?"

Looking back at the *Englisher,* who was now only a few feet from her—still face-down in the mud, Lavinia shook her head. "How dangerous can he be like that?

"He could be faking! What if he's faking?"

Lavinia stared at the lifeless man. "Why would he be faking?"

"So, he can attack or *kill* whoever finds him!"

"That's *narrish.* If he wanted to do that, he would probably hide behind a tree instead of pushing his face in the mud, wouldn't you think? He looks hurt. And who knows how long he's been lying there. He could be dead!"

Bethany rolled her eyes again. "I doubt it. We'd probably be able to smell him by now. Besides, I don't see any buzzards pecking at him!"

"That's horrible!"

"Maybe. But it's the truth!"

Lavinia sighed impatiently and continued on the muddy path toward the stranger. The gurgle of the rushing creek muffled most of the sound this close to the water, and Lavinia wondered if anyone would be able to hear her if she should need to scream for help. The closer she came to the man, the faster her heart hammered against her ribs. With her sister's words rattling her confidence and her history with death so close to her, she approached him warily.

The late afternoon sun warmed her back, sending a bead of sweat trickling down the bodice of her dress. If not for the breeze drifting from the chilly creek, she'd probably faint from the late October heat. Swiping at her dampened brow, she bent over the man to check if he was breathing. As far as she could tell, he wasn't moving. The bird's song in the willow trees overhead and the flow of creek water rushing by intruded upon her ability to hear him breathe. Since he was face-down, she was unable to detect the rise and fall of his chest. On impulse, Lavinia nudged at his heel with the toe of her shoe.

He rolled over and sputtered, barely breathing—but breathing nonetheless.

Startled by his alarming reaction, Lavinia jumped backward, ready to run if he posed a threat.

Groaning, the man looked helpless and in a lot of pain, though he didn't open his eyes.

"Looks like he ain't dead!" Bethany hollered from the safety of the willow tree.

Thank the Lord, Lavinia thought, as she blew out a sigh of relief.

Kneeling beside the stranger, Lavinia leaned back on her haunches and pulled the man's head into her lap. Using her apron to wipe the mud from his face, she felt warmth radiating from him like a surge of static electricity. The hot sun had surely warmed him, but there was more to it than that. With compassion, Lavinia gently caressed his temples, smoothing back his dampened, mud-streaked curls. Running her hand along his strong jawline, the stubble that peppered his smooth, sun-kissed face prickled the tips of her fingers.

Though he looked to be a little worn and dirty, she couldn't help but notice how handsome he was.

Her subconscious allowed the steady flow of the creek to occupy her thoughts as she breathed out the simplest of prayers.

Please Lord, let him be alright.

"What are you doing, Lavinia?" Bethany called from behind the willow tree, where she'd been hiding her face.

Ignoring her sister, Lavinia continued to stroke the man's face, allowing her fingers to make a trail through his auburn curls and willing him to open his eyes. His breathing, though a little labored, was steady.

He groaned again, his eyes fluttering.

"Are you in pain?"

No answer.

"Can you tell me your name?"

Still, no answer.

Whoever he was, he certainly did not look Amish, though Lavinia couldn't think of a single reason he'd be walking along the bank of the creek dressed the way he was. His muddy shirt, a blue button-up, most likely his Sunday attire, hugged strong arms and a muscular chest. It was still slightly tucked into the narrow waist of his black dress-pants.

Beside him, curiously, lay a black hat that resembled an Amish hat—perhaps from another community. Not far from him, she noticed a backpack wedged in the reeds closer to the creek.

He clutched his left side as he let out another deep groan. Slowly moving her hand over his, Lavinia palpitated his ribs lightly, noting him wince from the pain. Unbuttoning the middle buttons of his shirt, she slipped her hand into the opening, glancing at the bruises and swelling over the area where he couldn't tolerate her touch. Though they didn't feel broken, his ribs were most likely cracked, and that could be just as serious. She would never be able to move him unless she bound his ribs, or she might risk breaking them. Unpinning her apron, Lavinia wrapped it around his torso and knotted the ends at his right side.

"You shouldn't be touching him," Bethany called from the safe distance of the willow tree. "Do you want me to get *Daed?*"

Lavinia shook her head, not wanting to take her eyes off the man—this beautiful man that she hoped would wake up.

She cradled his head once more and his lashes fluttered as he suddenly looked up at her with chocolate-brown eyes.

Reaching up with muddy fingers, he covered her hand that cupped his jaw and sent her a pleading look.

"Can you tell me your name?" she asked.

"N—Nate."

"I'm Lavinia and I'm going to help you."

He smiled weakly and closed his fingers over hers just before his eyes closed again.

Panic ran through her veins like icy creek water.

"Don't leave me," Nate whispered.

I wouldn't dream of it, Lavinia thought.

Turning toward her sister, Lavinia hollered impatiently. "Come over here and help me get him up."

Her voice seemed to startle Nate. He turned his head toward her, allowing her to feel the knot on the side of his head. Thankfully, he didn't seem to be bleeding from anywhere that she could see. She suspected he'd traveled some distance, and had likely walked down to the creek to get a drink because he didn't seem dehydrated, and she hoped it would help him recover.

"I already told you I ain't coming over there. I'm going back to the barn to call for an ambulance."

"*Nee,*" Lavinia begged. "Please help me get him up."

She had already been down that road and she would not let history repeat itself.

Bethany began to trudge through the mud toward them, muttering complaints under her breath. Lavinia tuned her out, putting her full attention on the handsome stranger. She wouldn't let her sister call for an ambulance. She would do everything she could to prevent it, even if it meant threatening to tell their *daed* some of the secrets Bethany had recently confided in her.

Calling for an ambulance hadn't helped Daniel.

She'd watched helplessly while her twin had bled to death waiting for that ambulance, when the community doctor could have gotten to him faster. Lavinia had panicked at the sight of all the blood and had made the call from the barn when Daniel had caught his wrist on the barbed-wire fence.

The pain and guilt she carried with her from that day haunted her even now that two years had passed.

Daed would certainly make the same call for an *Englisher.*

No, there would be no ambulance for *this* man.

As long as Nate was breathing, Lavinia would devote herself to caring for him and nursing him back to health.

CHAPTER 2

"Why can't *you* take his cold, wet feet?"

"Stop complaining, Bethany, and just help me—please!"

Lavinia looped the insides of her elbows in Nate's armpits and hefted him up until his head rested against her ribcage. Assessing him to be around six feet tall, she wasn't surprised at the weight of his muscular frame. It wouldn't be easy toting the dead-weight of a semi-conscious man the distance to their farm, but Lavinia was as stubborn as could be. She'd managed to talk her sister into putting him up in the loft above their barn, safe from their father's strict supervision.

Since Daniel's death, their *daed* had mostly kept to himself, but he constantly reminded them of the rules of his *haus*. Lavinia knew it was because he feared harm would come to them if they were out of his immediate sight for too long, but she also knew that with a farm to tend to, he couldn't watch them every minute and didn't have the time to enforce the rules the way he would prefer.

Bethany stumbled and dropped Nate's feet. He let out a deep groan and pulled his hand toward his ribs as Lavinia stopped abruptly to prevent his head from slipping away from her.

"You need to be more careful carrying him," Lavinia reprimanded. "If his ribs are broken they could pierce one of his organs and he would bleed to death."

"It ain't my fault he's so heavy! You act like I meant to drop him."

Lavinia narrowed her gaze on Bethany, but held her tongue to keep from letting on just how irritated she was with the girl. She knew she couldn't move Nate without her sister's help, which put her in an unfortunate state of dependence on her. Bethany would be certain to find a way to use this *favor* to her advantage as it suited her. Bethany was a selfish girl, but lucky for her, Lavinia loved her despite it.

For this reason, Lavinia patiently waited for Bethany to resume hold of Nate's feet so they could continue walking to their barn. Until then, Lavinia let her mind drift to memories of her last moments with Daniel. She bent down and rested her chin on Nate's head, swallowing back tears. Was she doing the right thing? What if she couldn't save him? Would his death be her fault too? Surely *Daed* would blame her the same way he blamed her for Daniel's death. She would never forget the look in her father's eyes that day.

He hadn't looked at her since.

Bethany hoisted Nate's feet onto her sides and pushed out a disparaging breath. "I'm ready. Let's go before I drop him again!"

Lavinia gladly broke from her reverie. She had spent the past two years trying not to think of Daniel, but her twin was suddenly plaguing her thoughts. She convinced herself that each stride they conquered was one step closer to saving Nate. If they could just get him comfortable in the loft, he would heal from the wounds that encumbered him. Saving Nate wouldn't bring back Daniel, but it would serve as penance for her foolish decisions that day that her father claimed had contributed to Daniel's demise. Decisions she vowed never to repeat.

A few more steps put them behind the barn. "Go see where *Daed* is. He needs to be *gut* and busy at whatever he's doing so we have enough time to get Nate up the stairs."

"How do you know his name?" Bethany demanded through gritted teeth.

"He told me."

"When did he tell you? He's knocked out."

"He told me before you came over to help me move him. What does it matter? Just go see where *Daed* is— please!"

Bethany cast her sister an angry look before leaving to do her bidding.

Alone once again with Nate, Lavinia sank to the grass and rested his head in her lap. She pushed back his curls behind his ears wondering what it would be like to have such a handsome man for a husband. Lavinia knew better than to hope for such a thing. Not only was she responsible for Bethany and her father and their farm, she was as Plain as a woman could be—especially compared to her sister, who had never had any trouble gaining the attention from the boys in the community.

Please, Lord, bless me with a man such as this to love me, Lavinia whispered.

She felt foolish even asking for such a prideful prayer, but she meant it with all her heart.

Bethany came back around the back side of the barn. "*Daed's* under the big oak tree in the yard taking a nap."

Lavinia noted the direction of the barn's shadow. "Is it that late already? We need to hurry before he gets up and wants his supper and I don't have it ready for him before evening chores."

"I agree," Bethany said. "Let's get him upstairs to the loft. I'll stay with him while you make the evening meal so *Daed* won't get suspicious."

Lavinia felt a twinge of jealousy toward her sister, who had no idea what real responsibility was. Being nearly five years her senior, Lavinia had been taking care of Bethany since she was four years old—since *Mamm's* death. But now the girl was almost eighteen and she was still too dependent on Lavinia.

Truth be told, Lavinia had only herself to blame. She'd catered to her sister and had not enforced the teachings that an Amish woman should know to do by this age. For Lavinia, it had always been easier to do the work herself than to struggle with getting her sister to do her fair share.

Though she'd taken on the role of *mamm* to Bethany, she wasn't her *mamm,* and could not get her to do much without an argument. Rather than having *Daed* discipline her by taking the strap to her back-side, Lavinia had allowed her sister to rebel too often to help her to be responsible this late in her life. Now it would be up to Bethany to mature enough to understand the importance of learning the skills needed to be a married woman. Lavinia knew Bethany was nowhere near being ready for such an important role; she was too busy enjoying the attention of every young man in the community to settle for just one. It angered Lavinia that Bethany couldn't even be responsible for herself, and suddenly, she wanted to take responsibility for Nate!

"Perhaps *you* should make *Daed* his evening meal for a change. I do all the work around here while you flit around making whimsical play of your life instead of being responsible!"

Bethany scowled. "I do plenty of chores around here!"

"Not without an argument."

Bethany dropped Nate's feet causing him to clutch his side and groan. "If you think I do nothing around here, then you can take him upstairs yourself while I go tell *Daed* you're hiding an *Englisher* in the loft. You aren't too old for *Daed* to take you out behind the barn for a *gut,* sound lashing like our cousin's get from their *Daed.*"

Lavinia was fuming, but dared not show her anger to her sister. She needed her help *and* her loyalty at this moment. For reasons unknown even to herself, she wasn't willing to let Nate depart from her life without a fight. She supposed it stemmed from the losses she'd suffered—especially with her twin's recent death. Whatever the reason, she felt that *Gott,* Himself had a hand in it somehow.

For that reason alone, she would have to tread water with her sister's immature temperament, and succumb to the girl's whims. It filled her with a deep resentment toward her sister, but she pushed it down, just as she'd been doing most of her life. Because of Bethany, she had not been allowed to enjoy her youth enough to appreciate it. She'd been a mother and caretaker of her sister and her father since she was a mere child herself, and her *mamm's* death had in a way cheated her out of a life as well.

Lavinia sighed impatiently. "Please help me get him upstairs and stop using threats to get your own way. Since you've helped me get him this far, *Daed* will know I didn't get him here by myself, so we will *both* get a sound lashing. You can either work *with* me and we can get him upstairs before *Daed* wakes up and sees him, or we can stand here and argue a little longer and get into trouble. It's your choice little *schweschder*."

Bethany narrowed her gaze on Lavinia. "I'll help you get him up there, but not for *you*. I'll do it for Nate. After all, he's pretty handsome."

Lavinia held her tongue even though she would enjoy giving her sister a sound lashing herself.

CHAPTER 3

Lavinia rushed through the cooking, knowing that every minute she spent preparing her *daed's* evening meal meant another minute Bethany was spending alone with Nate. She'd wanted to be there in case he woke up—in case he asked for her.

Jealousy rose in her again at the thought of Nate making a connection with Bethany if he should wake, especially since she felt she'd already made one with him. She felt foolish for not wanting Nate to like her sister, but she'd never had the chance to be so close to a man before, and Bethany had been on so many dates, she'd made her way around the young men in the community more than once. Lavinia, on the other hand, had never had even one date. She'd been too busy being the responsible one while Bethany sneaked out of the *haus* so many times it ceased to bother her anymore.

Her father came in before she could set everything on the table and grumbled without looking at his daughter. "Supper's late."

"I'm sorry *Daed*. I must have gotten behind in my chores."

He took the plate she offered without looking up. "Where is your *schweschder?*"

"She's probably picking apples and lost track of time. I'll fetch her right away."

Her father tasted the stew without praying first, his long, wiry beard dipping in the bowl as he lowered his head to take another bite.

Lavinia escaped through the kitchen door before he could say another word. If he found out she'd lied to him, he'd surely take the switch to her back-side. She ran to the barn and up the outside staircase to the loft apartment that had always been intended for Daniel to use during the first year of his marriage, but sadly, he'd never gotten the chance. It pricked her heart to think of the things her *bruder* would never be able to do, such as marry and have *kinner*. It filled her with guilt. She supposed it was one of the reasons she didn't date. There was a part of her that thought she didn't deserve to be happy since Daniel wasn't able to do those things either.

Lavinia pushed down the guilt over Daniel's death and quickly made her way up the stairs to the loft. Entering the small bedroom, Lavinia covered her mouth to prevent the gasp from escaping her lips. She watched in shock as Bethany bent over Nate, whose bare chest lay exposed. From what she could tell, the girl had torn a bed-sheet into long bandage strips and used them to bind his ribs. She had just finished tying the last strip when she noticed her sister staring blankly at her.

She smiled proudly.

"He woke up for a minute, but he passed out when I moved him to wrap his ribs."

Lavinia rushed to Nate's side, leaning close to check his breathing. "You should have waited for me to come back. You could have seriously hurt him by moving him yourself!"

Bethany waved a casual hand at her older sister.

"Why are you yelling at me? I got him all fixed up."

"Did you check his ribs to be certain they were set before you wrapped him?"

Bethany shook her head. "I don't know what you mean."

"Exactly!" Lavinia scolded her. "Now I'm going to have to cause this poor *mann* more pain by undoing the bandages to be certain his ribs are in the correct place, and then rewrap him."

"I'm sorry. I was only trying to help."

"*Daed* wants you at the supper table," Lavinia said through gritted teeth.

"But…"

"Just go! I need to fix this the same way I take care of everything for you."

Bethany fisted her hips angrily. "What is *that* supposed to mean?

Lavinia took a step toward her sister. "It means you need to grow up and start thinking of someone other than yourself. You are almost eighteen years old and you don't even know how to cook or do laundry or…"

"I help you with all those things!"

"Hanging up one dress and then running off does not earn you the skills needed to be on your own. What would you do if I wasn't here to do everything for you?"

Bethany shook her head knowingly. "That's not going to happen. Where would you have to go, *schweschder?* We *both* know you will most likely end up a spinster."

The comment prickled down Lavinia's spine like the sharp quills on a porcupine.

"And so shall you be," Lavinia retorted. "Unless you learn the skills you need to keep a husband."

Bethany cocked her head sideways and smiled.

"I *know* what keeps a husband happy!"

Lavinia let a gasp escape her lips at her sister's brazen words. "You should confess that evil from your mind at once! If the Bishop—or *Daed* heard you speak of such things you'd be shunned for sure and for certain."

"Maybe if you'd take down that wall you've built around yourself and go on a date for once in your life, you might just know what I'm talking about."

Lavinia's eyes widened. "You've done *that* on a date?"

Looking over at Nate, Bethany shushed her sister. "Of course not! I'm talking about kissing!"

Sadly, Lavinia had never been kissed, and didn't hold out much hope for such a thing. Her thoughts turned to Nate and wondered if the kiss she'd placed on his forehead counted. She supposed only if he'd kissed her back would it have counted. The very thought of it sent a warmth through her veins that surged toward her toes.

She let her gaze wander back toward Nate, who lay sleeping on the bed, oblivious to their rather brazen conversation. It was inappropriate to speak of such things in private, let alone to be speaking of them within earshot of a man. Some women in the community would talk of those things during quilting bees or work-bees, but Lavinia had only ever listened. This was the first time she'd participated in such bold talk.

Lavinia narrowed her gaze at her sister. "I imagine you've kissed every single *mann* in this community."

Bethany smiled. "You've imagined correctly."

"That's shameful!"

"What is shameful, dear *schweschder,* is that *you* haven't kissed even one of them!"

Lavinia couldn't deny the pitiful truth in her sister's statement any more than she could deny her yearning for such an experience. Looking over at Nate once more, she swallowed down the lump that choked her, knowing that such a man as handsome as he would *never* find her attractive enough to kiss.

Nate's hand reached for hers, startling her out of her reverie.

"Water," he said, his dry lips parting slightly.

Though his eyes remained closed, Lavinia was happy he'd reached for her rather than for her sister. The glare Bethany shot her let her know her sister didn't feel the same as she did.

Lavinia poured water into a glass from the pitcher at his bedside and scooped her hand under his head to assist him. She placed the glass to his lips and tipped it just enough to allot him small sips. He looked up at her with weary eyes. Lavinia couldn't help but notice the pain in their chocolaty depths.

"I need to check the bandages around your ribs," she said cautiously. "It might hurt a little, but I think *mei schweschder* may have forgotten to set your ribs before she bound them."

He nodded his consent and Lavinia set to work undoing the damage her sister had done to this poor man.

The screen door to the loft slammed behind her and she knew Bethany had left in a huff. She didn't care. She was glad to be rid of her. Bethany had always been selfish and immature, and this situation was proving to be no exception. She pushed back her disappointment in her sister and concentrated on tending to Nate's injuries.

Wincing, Nate let her know every time she put too much pressure on his sore ribs. She hated hurting him, and repeatedly apologized, but didn't feel it was enough for the torture she was certain she was putting him through. Thankfully, none were broken clean through, but she could feel two spots that were cracked. Pressing them tightly into place before binding them, Nate let out a low groan, noting his discomfort.

"I'm only doing what's necessary to assure proper healing of these ribs," she quickly said in her defense.

"I know you're doing the right thing," he said gently. "But sometimes doing the right thing can be…downright painful."

His accent sounded familiar, but his choice of wording seemed "put-on", she thought. She wondered if he could indeed be Amish, but his clothing and speech would suggest he was either an *Englisher,* or *posing* as one.

CHAPTER 4

Nate looked up at Lavinia as she finished binding his ribs. He felt guilty for deceiving her, but he also knew keeping his privacy was necessary in order to conclude the soul-searching endeavor he'd set himself on. He wanted more than anything to let her know he was Amish, to confide in her how much he battled the decision to get baptized, but he feared she might be inclined to persuade his decision in one direction or the other. And he hadn't yet decided for himself.

Even though his cousin, Adam, expected him to bring in the harvest, he wasn't ready to leave this Angel of Mercy just yet. Her gentle, loving care made him crave more of the same. Surely such a lovely creature as she had a beau, but he could hope she didn't—couldn't he? He focused his gaze on the dark blonde tendril that waved across her smooth, pink cheek as she leaned over him tightening the strips of cotton cloth over his ribs. Her deep green eyes were filled with caring, but seemed lonely. Could it be she didn't have a beau after all? He knew it was selfish and foolish to hope for such a thing—especially since he barely knew her, but he couldn't help himself.

"If you're hungry, I made some lamb stew."

He quickly nodded. Lamb stew was one of his favorites.

She knew she would have to wait until her father went about his evening chores before she could bring Nate anything to eat, but she hoped to impress him with one of her best supper dishes. She knew it was foolish to think such things, but she'd heard many of the women in the community talk of *gut* food being the *way* to a *mann's* heart, and she aimed to find out if that was true.

As she finished tying the last of the cotton strips across his ribs, she tugged at the quilt at the end of the bed, wishing she didn't have to cover up his bare, muscular torso. But she had to accept that keeping him warm would help him heal and keep infection at bay.

Nate took note of Lavinia's rosy cheeks as her gaze trailed up his chest and settled on his arms and shoulders while she slowly tucked him into the quilt. He was tempted to flex his muscles to impress her, but he resisted, knowing it might embarrass her. Instead, he watched her study him as if she was storing away in her memory the sight of him without his shirt on, and he welcomed her to look as much as she wanted. When her gaze lifted and their eyes met, he remembered her kissing him, and couldn't help but wish he could kiss her back.

He'd never felt that before, though he'd been on his fair share of dates.

Most of the young women in his community were only concerned with having a husband, and were not concerned with falling in love. He, on the other hand, intended only to marry for love. His parents had married for love, and they were the happiest pair he knew. Too many folks in his community had troubled marriages and were estranged from each other due to their lack of compatibility—or even love for one another. Many of his friends who had married at a young age just for the sake of marrying were already miserable, and would have to endure a lifetime with the mate they'd chosen for *physical* reasons of desire rather than from true love. If asked, they would deem *him* to be the foolish one, but he knew what he wanted, and that was a mutual love that could endure the test of a lifetime.

"So where did you travel from, if I may be so bold as to ask."

"From a farm in Ohio," was all he dared say.

"So, then you know how to plant and harvest?"

"I've lived on a farm all my life," he admitted.

She set a curious gaze on him. "Where were you headed?"

"To work on a farm in this area."

"So, you've already found work, then?"

"In a manner of speaking." He looked her straight in the eyes, wondering if she intended to question him until she managed to get it out of him who he was and what he was up to.

"And the ribs...no one *hurt* you, did they?"

Nate shook his head. "I was on the railroad bridge and the train was headed toward me too fast, so I had to jump. I'll take a few cracked ribs over being flattened by a train any day!"

"Does your *familye* live in Ohio?"

He nodded.

"You ask a lot of questions."

She giggled, sending his heart aflutter.

"*Mei daed* always said I was a curious child."

His look softened. "You are anything but a child now."

Her cheeks heated. Was he *flirting* with her? She dared not hope for such a thing, but she almost couldn't help herself. Perhaps he was only flattering her since he was at her mercy and depended on her to take care of him until he regained his strength and his ribs healed some. Was he worried about the care she would give him? Perhaps he felt as if she'd brought him here against his will, which, in a way, she had. He was in a strange place with people he didn't know, and had no idea if she meant him any harm. She felt sorry for him and felt the need to offer him an *out*.

"We have a telephone in the lower part of the barn if you'd like me to call someone for you—so they know you are alright—and where you are."

He smiled. "That won't be necessary. I should be well enough to travel in a few days or so, and I can be on my way then if you want me to."

She didn't want him to leave. If she had her way, he'd stay and help work *her* farm. Perhaps he could even help to bridge the gap between her and her father and restore the closeness they shared before Daniel's death. It saddened her to think of Nate leaving already when he'd only just gotten here. "Those ribs could take a while before they heal—depending on how badly they're cracked."

He couldn't help but smile. It seemed she was as eager for him to stay as he was to be here with her. She was a true angel, and the most beautiful of women he'd ever encountered. "You're probably right. In the meantime, I think I will enjoy having you care for me. But please, don't let your sister do any more doctoring on me."

They both laughed, and he clutched his ribs, holding them until he stopped laughing.

"She means well," Lavinia defended her sister, even though she knew better.

She didn't want Nate to think they were careless or would hurt him. She would have to keep a closer eye on her sister when she tended to him in her absence. But perhaps, she would have to engage Bethany in a few more chores to afford her a bigger window of time to care for Nate herself. It would be tricky to maneuver around her *daed's* regular schedule. It was possible that she could give the excuse that she was only trying to give the girl more responsibility to teach her what she needed in order to find a husband. After all, the girl was almost of marrying age, and perhaps her father would appreciate her help in preparing Bethany for her future.

Nate patted her hand, sending a surge of warmth through her. "I'm sure you're right, but I prefer your gentle touch to her rough treatment."

Lavinia smiled shyly. She knew he was only complimenting her first-aid skills, but she didn't care.

A compliment was a compliment.

A warm evening breeze scented the loft with freshly mowed hay, and the cricket's song added to the romance that thickened the air between them. Lavinia wished she could hold onto this moment as long as she could, knowing she may never have another one like it as long as she lived. If it were up to her, Nate would fall in love with her, and bring happiness to her life again. Though nothing could fill the voids of her lost mother and twin brother, having a husband would help to heal the hurts that kept her sad. She already felt this man's kindness. She didn't need to know who he was to feel that *Gott* had brought him into her life for a reason. And she aimed to find out just what that reason was—if she could keep her father and sister from messing it up for her.

Lavinia cleared her throat. "I can get you that stew now if you're ready."

Nate's mouth began to water at the thought of it.

"I was born ready!"

"I won't be but a minute. I hope you like lamb stew and buttermilk biscuits."

"They are my favorite!"

Lavinia was pleased to hear that it was his favorite. It was hers too!

Giggling like a young girl, Lavinia left him, excitement filling her at the thought of feeding him her best cooking. She would serve him and dote on him as a *fraa* would, hoping he would give her the consideration she desired from him—even if he *was* an *Englisher.*

CHAPTER 5

"What are you doing, *dochder?*"

The deep rumble of her father's voice startled Lavinia so profoundly, she dropped the bowl of stew she'd dished up for Nate. The contents splattered onto the wood floor of the kitchen, while the large, ceramic bowl seemed to shatter into an endless splay of pieces.

Though the hot stew burned her ankles where it splattered onto her bare skin, she didn't dare complain in front of her father. Instead, she scrambled to pick up the pieces of broken pottery and then mopped up the stew with a dishrag. All the while, she ignored her father's question, hoping the distraction of the mess would allow her enough time to think of a reasonable answer.

Feigning distraction would not buy her much time, especially since she could see him tapping his boot impatiently on the wood floor. It was something he'd done to show his irritation since she was a child, and she knew her time against his patience was limited. Soon, she would have to give an answer whether she was ready for it not, and whether he was ready to accept it or not. Lately, he was not accepting of whatever she had to say, and so she didn't think it would matter what she said—as long as she said *something*. Any answer was usually better than saying nothing.

She had tried avoiding answering only one time in her life, and it was not a lesson she would risk learning the hard way a second time. Even a lie at this point would be better received than ignoring him. If there was one thing her father did not permit from his *kinner,* it would have to be ignoring him.

"Why are you serving up supper this late? You should be washing the dishes and turning in after you finish. Why didn't you take your meal with Bethany earlier?"

"I was too overheated from the day's chores to eat earlier, so I thought I would have a little of the stew now before tucking away the rest for your afternoon meal tomorrow."

Her voice cracked several times as she spouted off the lie to her father, and she hoped he was too tired to notice. It was her *tell* whenever she wasn't being completely honest, and she'd been that way since she was a child. Instead of calling her on it, he merely grunted and turned toward the stairs. The sun had retired more than an hour ago, and he would retire now too so as to be well-rested to start his day early. He'd kept the same predictable schedule for as long as she could remember. He was a creature of habit, and she was grateful that he would stick to his routine now and leave her alone.

Truth be told, she had grown tired of his prying and disapproval of her every move in recent years—ever since Daniel's death. Her twin's parting from this world had changed her world in too many ways that caused her to despise her present life. There were even times when she'd thought her *daed* would have preferred if *Gott* would have chosen to take *her* instead.

It saddened her to think of her life with such disregard, but her *daed* had all but shunned her since that day. Her father blamed her for Daniel's death. He'd said as much after the funeral when he'd told her he would never again be able to look upon her face as long as she lived. It had made her feel as though they should have put her in the ground right alongside her *bruder* because she'd become dead to her own father from that moment on.

Standing at the bottom of the stairwell, Lavinia listened for her father's bedroom door to close before she dared to dish up another bowl of stew for Nate. As soon as he'd finished in the bathroom and was seemingly tucked into bed, Lavinia felt she could finally breathe easy. She didn't know why she'd become so afraid of her father in recent years, but she supposed it had stemmed from him taking out his anger over Daniel's death onto her. He had become selfishly filled with anger to the point it had destroyed his relationship with her. Lavinia was in mourning too, but he didn't seem to care about *her* loss. She and Daniel were connected, as all twins were, and she'd suffered the loss of a part of herself that she just couldn't explain to anyone—especially when she didn't even understand it herself.

Deciding she should wait until her father fell asleep, Lavinia listened carefully for the soft snoring that would let her know her father was down for the night. As the whistles and sputters began to resonate through the house, she relaxed. Only now would she feel safe leaving the *haus* and entering the loft to feed the handsome *Englisher.* Thankfully, Bethany would soon be gone, and would not return until the wee hours of the morning, leaving Lavinia alone with Nate.

Giddiness rose in her causing her to tremble lightly at the thought of spending time alone with the handsome stranger. She had to admit, though, that if he wasn't injured the way he was, and incapable of overpowering her, she certainly would not spend any time alone with him. In his current state, as an injured man, his dependence on her made him somehow seem *safer* in her eyes. Her father would certainly disagree if he knew about Nate's presence in their home, but if she could help it, he would *never* discover her secret.

Trusting Bethany with the secret was a whole other story, and she was not ready to face *that* fight that was sure to rear its ugly head soon enough. For now, she would enjoy some time with Nate without the threat of her sister betraying her.

Lavinia balanced the tray with a large bowl of stew and extra buttermilk biscuits, along with a pitcher of fresh lemonade as she climbed the stairs to the loft. Before she even reached the top step, she could hear her sister giggling and flirting with Nate. She steadied the tray and listened for a moment. She was not happy to hear that her sister was alone with the *Englisher*.

Jealousy rose in her. Why must she compete with her younger sister for everything? It just wasn't fair. Bethany came by her beauty honestly; she was the lucky one that closely resembled their mother. Lavinia, on the other hand, could pass for her brother if she donned a pair of trousers and a straw hat, and cut her hair. She just didn't stand a chance if her sister got in her way.

It would seem Bethany intended to do just that.

"I hope you don't think I'm rude," Nate said. "But I'm too tired for company tonight."

You tell her, Nate!

"I promise I won't stay long," Bethany begged.

Can't you take a hint, dear schweschder?

"If you don't mind, I'd like to get some rest so I don't have to burden your family for too long."

"You're not a burden at all, Nate. In fact, I'm glad you're here. You're a refreshing change from the immature boys in the community."

Stop throwing yourself at him so shamelessly, little schweschder!

"Please, Miss…"

"Bethany. *Mei* name is Bethany."

Lavinia couldn't help but giggle at her sister's tone. She was obviously irritated he'd forgotten her name.

"Surely you understand, *Bethany,* that I need my rest so I can be up and on my feet as soon as possible. I have a job waiting for me that I am unable to do unless I get the rest I need to heal. If I can't work, I won't be able to support myself."

"*N-Nee,*" Bethany stuttered. "I understand. Do you need anything before I go?"

Please say no, please say no!

"Uh, no. Thank you. I'll see you tomorrow."

"Goodnight, then."

"Goodnight, uh…"

"Bethany!"

"Right. Goodnight, Bethany."

Good night dear schweschder!

Bethany nearly ran Lavinia over as she exited the screen door. She clenched the tray to keep from wearing the contents as Bethany brushed by her without saying a word. She stomped down each step angrily, while Lavinia suppressed the urge to laugh at her sister's tantrum. She was obviously put out by Nate rejecting her offer to keep him company.

To Bethany, it was a crisis, but to Lavinia, it was an opportunity.

CHAPTER 6

Lavinia stood outside the screen door, trying to work up the nerve to enter the loft after overhearing Nate ask her sister to leave. For a moment, she debated whether she should enter or not, but then she remembered he'd asked for the stew. She regretted taking so long in getting his supper to him—perhaps he was now too tired to eat it.

If he's not up to having company, I'll leave the tray with him and go home then.

Anticipating the squeak of the screen door before she opened it, she tried pulling slowly on the handle, but that only made it worse.

"Who's there?" Nate called from the bedroom.

"I'm bringing your supper," Lavinia said as she stepped inside the small kitchen. "May I come in?"

"Please do," he begged. "I'm starving!"

Lavinia was happy to hear that at least her stew was welcome. Time would tell if Nate would welcome her company for any longer than it took to serve him the stew. As she entered the small bedroom, Nate tried to sit himself up in the bed, but was failing miserably.

"Smells heavenly, but I'm afraid you might have to stay and help me eat it. I'm not sure if I can sit up enough to feed myself!"

Lavinia's heart did a somersault behind her ribcage. She relished the idea of spoon-feeding this man more than she probably ought to. She set the tray on the bedside table while she took note of Nate's struggle to gain a semi-sitting position without hurting himself.

"Let me help you," she offered.

He took the hand she offered. "Thank you, Lavinia."

Her gaze locked with his only for a moment, but it was long enough to see kindness in his eyes. But there was something else. Something that drew her into them. Something that resembled *love.*

He remembered mei name!

Only moments ago, he'd forgotten her sister's name— or had he? Had he *forgotten* as a means to get rid of her? Lavinia certainly hoped it was so.

She couldn't help but smile as she continued to gaze into Nate's eyes.

He cleared his throat. "I'm ready."

Lavinia felt warmth radiating from her spine to her cheeks. She was certain her face had turned several shades of red as embarrassment coursed through her.

"I'm sorry. Um—I'll just—well, here. Let me put this napkin under your—chin."

Lavinia fumbled with the linen trying to place it near his neckline without touching him. She didn't understand how she could suddenly be so terrified to touch him. She wanted desperately to crawl into the crook of his arm and sink into him, but the fear of rejection eclipsed her desire.

Nate gently pulled her hand into his, guiding her shaky fingers to set the linen napkin into place. Her hand fit nicely in his, and she allowed his grasp to linger over hers.

"Is something troubling you?"

His question startled her, causing her to yank her hand away.

"*Nee*—no. I'm just a little tired is all."

She would never admit to the sudden tension she felt around him that stemmed from attraction to him.

"I think I detect a little worry in your beautiful, green eyes."

What? He thinks I have beautiful eyes!

Deep down, Lavinia knew better than to put any stock in such prideful compliments. *Ach,* she suddenly didn't care. Being humble and proper hadn't gotten her anywhere in life except lonely and alone. If this *Englisher* wanted to take her away from all that, even if only for the duration of his stay in the loft, she would gladly encourage him!

"*Nee,* not worry, but perhaps a little apprehension. You are an *Englisher,* and you speak more boldly than I'm used to."

She thinks I'm an Englisher! Should I tell her the truth?

"Don't tell me none of your other *boyfriends* ever paid you a compliment."

"I've not had time for dating. *Mei mamm* passed away just before *mei* tenth birthday. *Mei schweschder*--sister, Bethany was only four at the time. I've been like a momma to her, and I've taken care of *mei daed* and twin *bruder*—brother up until he died two years ago."

Lavinia hung her head with sadness at the mention of Daniel.

Nate put his fingers under her chin and lifted until her eyes locked on his adoring gaze. "It seems to me it's time to start taking care of *you.*"

"Amish are not the same as *Englischers.* We take *familye* responsibility very serious. I have a duty to *mei daed* and *schweschder.*"

"Seems to me your sister is grown, and a bit selfish and immature, if I may speak boldly. As for your dad, he isn't incapable of caring for his own needs. What would they do if you married?"

"I don't think that would ever happen. But in those situations, an Amish husband would help me to care for *mei familye.*"

"What if *I* wanted to marry you?"

Lavinia felt her heart slam against her ribs. "I assume you ask that for the sake of argument?"

Nate shrugged. "What if I was serious?"

Lavinia reached up and prodded the knot on his head. "Perhaps you hit your head harder than I originally thought. You must be suffering from a concussion. How is your vision? Is it blurry?"

"There is nothing wrong with my vision—but I wouldn't mind seeing double. Two of you would be quite nice!"

Lavinia sighed playfully. "Will you be serious for just a minute?"

"I am being serious!" he scoffed. "Life is too short to hold your tongue when you have something important to say. I'd consider myself lucky to be able to marry a woman like you."

"A woman like *me*? What do you mean by that?"

He reached up and stroked her cheek. "The sort of woman who is beautiful—inside and out."

Lavinia tucked her chin shyly, but Nate lifted it with his fingers until her gaze met his again.

"Why would you want to marry me? We are from two different worlds. Besides, you've only just met me!"

"We aren't so different, you and me. But first, answer something for me; what do you suppose your family would do without you here to serve them?"

Lavinia giggled as she pondered his question. "I suppose they would probably starve to death wearing dirty clothes!"

"That is exactly my point. Don't you think you should teach them to fend for themselves? You can't be a servant to them for the rest of their lives. *You* deserve to have a life too."

"By marrying you?" she asked jokingly.

He took her hand in his and kissed the back of it. "Why not?"

She snatched her hand away. "Because unless you're Amish, then *mei daed* will never allow it."

He used her hand to draw her close to him.

"What about what *you* want?"

She splayed her hand over his chest, enjoying the feel of his warm skin and the curly hairs beneath her fingers just before she pushed away from him. "It doesn't matter what I want. It only matters that I follow the rules of the Ordnung."

Nate crossed his arms over his chest defiantly.

"That is exactly why I left."

"What's exactly..." she paused to look him over once more before finishing her sentence. "Wait—you're Amish, aren't you?"

"*Jah,*" he admitted. "But until I met you, I knew exactly what I was going to do."

Lavinia wasn't certain if she was overjoyed that he was indeed Amish, or angry that he'd kept the truth from her. She supposed all that mattered was that he finally told her.

"And what is that supposed to mean?"

"I was planning on hiding out at *mei* cousin, Adam's, farm until the harvest was over. I figured that would give me enough time to see if I was ready for the baptismal classes—to make a decision if I was going to stay or go to live among the *Englisch.*"

"What does any of that have to do with me?"

He took her hands in his and gently caressed them. "Because until I met you, I had mostly decided I would leave. But now I would like to stay and court you, especially if the possibility of marrying you exists."

"Surely you've had other opportunities in your own community."

She silently chided herself the minute the words left her mouth, but she needed to know if he was serious.

"*Jah,*" he admitted. "There were plenty of opportunities handed to me, but none that I cared to accept."

Lavinia pushed down the giddiness that tried to overtake her. "Why would you want to court me instead of someone like—someone like *mei schweschder?*"

Why can't I keep from putting mei foot in mei mouth?

Nate squeezed her hands fondly. "I've had my fill of offers from selfish, spoiled girls like Bethany. I want a *fraa* who will put me first, just as I would put *her* first. I want a beautiful, giving woman—like *you.*"

CHAPTER 7

Lavinia stood abruptly, allowing her gaze to focus on Nate's bare chest. "I'm not certain we should be here alone—without an escort. If you are serious about courting, *mei daed* will never agree to it if he thinks we've acted improperly."

"The girls in my own community in Ohio put a light in their windows at night, and the guys come around and take them courting in their buggies until the wee hours of the morning. Don't they do the same here?"

"*Jah,* Bethany leaves the *haus* nearly every night. She is a wild one. If *mei daed* were to ever find out, he would not approve, but I make excuses for her behavior and cover for her."

Nate caught Lavinia staring at him, and tucked his hand in hers. "You haven't told me if you would consent to being courted by me."

Lavinia blew out a discouraging sigh. "You've only just met me. You don't really know enough about me yet to make that kind of decision."

He squeezed her hand. "I know all I need to know about you. I heard the kind words from you when you rescued me, and the prayers you said for me. You are a humble servant who has been taken advantage of by your *familye*. Perhaps *you* are the one in need of rescuing."

Lavinia couldn't help but agree with him, but she would never admit to such a thing. In as much as she would enjoy this *mann's* company, she could not accept his proposal of courting—especially if it could lead to marriage. She had an obligation to her *daed* and Bethany, and to the memory of her dear *bruder,* Daniel.

Nate tucked his hand under her chin and lifted gently to set her gaze back on him. "What has you so worried? Is it because you don't know *mei familye?* I will be happy to introduce you to *mei* cousin, Adam. I think we are close to the Troyer farm, *jah?"*

Lavinia stiffened. She *knew* Nate. He hadn't visited their community in some years, but she remembered him. Adam was friends with Daniel, and the three of them spent an entire summer working the neighboring farms after the big hail storm that took out the early crops. There a lot of replanting that year. Working bees had kept Lavinia busy with the women in the community to keep the working men from going hungry.

Nate smiled. "You're thinking of the hail storm. I do remember catching fireflies at dusk and sipping lemonade that a certain young lady made for me."

"I made it for the *menner* who were working to replant the fields."

Nate pushed out his lips and smiled. "My mouth is still all puckered up from that tart lemonade given to me by the prettiest girl in the whole county."

Nate pulled her close and placed his puckered lips against hers.

Caught off guard, Lavinia was too stunned to return the kiss. The next one, however, she eagerly took pleasure in.

He deepened the kiss, consuming her with his every breath. His impulsive passion seemed to employ a responsive urgency in her. He wanted her—every bit of her.

Lavinia's flighty heartbeat didn't interfere with her insatiable hunger for Nate's sweet, warm kisses. All thoughts focused on the feel of his lips against her mouth, her cheeks, and her neck. It was making her dizzy with delight, but she was powerless to stop him—not that she wanted to. She was ready to give herself to this man who made her feel more alive than she'd felt her entire life. She was a part of him already, and no ghosts of the past could separate them.

Bethany washed down the last bite of snitz pie with a big gulp of milk as she watched angrily from the kitchen window for her older sister to leave the loft.

What is she doing up there?

More than half an hour had passed since Bethany had brushed by Lavinia as she'd exited the small living space above the barn where they'd hidden the handsome *Englisher*.

He *was* handsome.

And Bethany had her intention set on him.

She tapped her foot against the wooden floor, becoming angrier with each tap.

How long would she wait for Lavinia to exit the loft?

Another possibility suddenly crossed her mind. What if he'd hurt her sister*?* Their *daed* had warned them about trusting *Englischers* too many times to remember.

But Nate was injured.

What if he was faking?

After all, he'd asked *her* to leave, claiming to be too tired for company. Surely, he wouldn't be entertaining Lavinia—would he? Bethany's anger and jealousy turned full-circle, and recycled itself in her mind, bringing her such angst she couldn't escape the kitchen fast enough. She quickly conquered the distance between the *haus* and the barn, climbing the stairs lightly so as not to alert the *Englisher* and interrupt possible cover-up of his wrongdoing against Lavinia.

Bethany fully intended to catch the *Englisher,* but wanted to remain quiet in case her sister was in trouble. The element of surprise could mean the difference between saving Lavinia and getting caught in the man's trap along with her sister.

She tiptoed up the last few stairs and peeked inside the screen door.

They were nowhere to be seen.

All was quiet—too quiet.

Bethany's heart beat rapidly at the thoughts that flashed through her mind of Lavinia lying dead on the floor while Nate hovered over her with a weapon in his hands. Just because he was handsome didn't mean he wasn't capable of being a dangerous *killer,* did it?

Focus, she chided herself. *Lavinia could be in danger.*

Carefully opening the screen door only enough to squeeze through, Bethany was relieved she'd managed to slip through without the hinges creaking. She shook as she padded quietly across the linoleum floor of the small kitchen toward the bedroom door. She paused before looking in the room, momentarily wondering what she would do if she should catch him hurting Lavinia.

Lord, help me to save mei schweschder if she should be in trouble. Give me strength to deal with whatever I find behind this door.

Nothing could have prepared Bethany for what she saw as she peered around the doorframe. Too stunned to speak, Bethany stood there observing Nate and Lavinia engaged in a steamy sequence of kisses. At first, she wondered if the way he was holding her was possibly against her will, but it was soon evident that Lavinia was an all-too-willing participant in the inappropriate scene unfolding before her eyes.

Anger rose in her. She'd wanted to explore that very option with the handsome *Englisher*. But here was her older sister—her very *plain* older sister gaining the attention from the very man who'd just rejected *her* less than an hour ago.

Jealousy filled her.

What did Lavinia have that Bethany didn't have? What did he see in her? She was shaped like a boy, and could easily pass for their brother, Daniel. Bethany had gained enough attention from the local boys to *know* she was physically desirable. Lavinia, on the other hand, had never been on even one date.

What if *that* was the appeal? What if her innocence was what attracted him to her? Perhaps, then, her sister was indeed in danger of being compromised by this *Englisher*. She had to put a stop to his plot against Lavinia before he compromised her.

She cleared her throat, but neither of them stopped mauling each other.

Clearing her throat again, she shuffled toward them, making them aware of her presence.

Lavinia jumped up from the edge of the bed, leaving the shirtless *Englisher* feverishly wiping his mouth in her wake. Holding her hands up to her obviously angry sister, Lavinia sent Bethany a pleading look.

"I can explain," she quickly offered.

Bethany pursed her lips. "What is there to explain? I clearly saw this stranger—this *Englisher* taking advantage of you!"

"That's not true," he said in his defense. "I'm not a stranger, and I've asked Lavinia if I can court her."

Bethany took an aggressive step toward Nate and gritted her teeth at him. "It sounds to me like you've done this before. Courting Lavinia? You really expect her to believe such lies? You saw her as a vulnerable opportunity—nothing else. I'd be willing to bet you make a habit of taking advantage of innocent girls!"

"You're right. Because this isn't the first time I've broken a few ribs and gotten lucky enough to be stowed away on an Amish farm by an unsuspecting woman such as Lavinia!" he scorned her. "Listen to how *narrish* you sound."

Bethany gasped. "And now you mock us by using the Amish language against us?"

Nate was growing impatient with Bethany's accusations. "I used the word because I *am* Amish!"

Bethany looked at Lavinia to confirm the lie he was telling. Right on cue, she defended him.

Bethany turned and walked toward the door. "I don't want to hear any more of these lies. I'm getting *Daed.* Surely *he* will settle this—*mann-to-mann!"*

CHAPTER 8

Lavinia chased after Bethany as she ran down the steps that led to the loft. The screen door slammed behind her, and she worried Nate would think her to be uncivilized for her abrupt reaction to her sister's threat. When she caught up with Bethany, Lavinia looped her fingers in the crook of her sister's arm, forcing her to stop running from her. "I'm not going to tolerate the disrespect you've shown me any longer. You are nothing short a spoiled *boppli* and I won't allow you to threaten me. If you want to tell *daed,* I'll be telling him what *you* do every night when you sneak out of the *haus.*"

Bethany pulled in a breath and narrowed her eyes. "You wouldn't dare!"

Lavinia grabbed Bethany's arm and began to pull her toward the kitchen door. "Let's go tell *daed* everything and then we'll both fall under the ban!"

Bethany began to cry. "Please don't tell. I don't want to be shunned. I can't take care of myself out there in that big world without you and *daed* to take care of me. You're right! I've been acting spoiled for a while now—since about the same time Daniel went to Heaven. I didn't think you cared about me anymore because you're always so moody."

Lavinia pulled Bethany into her arms. "Of course, I still care about you! All we seem to have anymore is each other. Since *Daed* lost Daniel, he won't forgive me for not saving him, and that has made me feel sad."

Bethany sniffled. *"Daed* doesn't blame you. It wasn't your fault. You called for an ambulance. You did everything you could to stop the bleeding, but *Gott* reached down from Heaven and took him from us."

"*Daed* doesn't see it that way. He doesn't even look at me anymore, and he barely speaks to me. I think he stopped loving me."

"*Ach,* Lavinia, he still loves you. Don't talk like that. I think he's just sad is all."

Lavinia hung her head. "He doesn't forgive me any more than I forgive myself. I shouldn't have called that ambulance. I panicked. All that blood…"

Her breath caught in her throat and she suppressed a strangled sob. "I didn't mean to let him or *Daed* down. I wish I could have taken Daniel's place. *Daed* would have been better off."

Bethany grabbed Lavinia by the arms and gave her a gentle shake. "Don't you ever let me hear you talk like that again! I don't know what I would do without you."

"You don't care about me any more than *Daed* does. You both take me for granted and take advantage of *mei gut* nature."

Bethany let go of Lavinia's arms and pulled her into a hug. "I'm sorry I've let you take all the responsibility around here. I promise I'll learn how to cook and all the other things I ain't *gut* at."

Lavinia sniffled. "I love you, dear *schweschder.*"

Bethany gave Lavinia a squeeze. "I love you too. I'm sorry I don't say that to you often enough."

Wiping her tears, Lavinia looked into Bethany's eyes with a seriousness she'd never shown before.

Bethany waved a hand at her and scoffed.

"Don't worry. I ain't gonna tell *Daed* about Nate, but I gotta know; is he *really* Amish?"

"*Jah,* he's Adam Troyer's cousin."

Bethany waggled her eyebrows. "So, you *really* are going to court him then?"

Lavinia shrugged. "I don't have time, and besides, I'd feel guilty."

"Those kisses I witnessed didn't look like they were full of guilt. What do you have to feel guilty over? *Daed* and I can take care of ourselves."

Lavinia shrugged.

"What is it, dear, *schweschder?*"

"I would feel bad going on with my life and being happy when…when Daniel can't enjoy his life anymore. He'll never get married or have *kinner,* so why should I be able to?"

Bethany furrowed her brow with concern. "He may never get married or have *kinner,* but he's in Heaven. He's not missing out on life. Maybe he's missing it on this earth, but he has eternal life now. He's not unhappy, and he wouldn't want *you* to be unhappy either."

Lavinia smiled. "When did you get to be so wise?"

"Because *you* raised me!"

They both giggled and Lavinia pulled Bethany into a sincere hug. "I'm sorry for the things I said to you—about you being spoiled."

"You shouldn't apologize for telling the truth. I *have* been acting spoiled. I've let you do all the work around here, and that hasn't been fair to you. I'm sorry for that. I'll try harder from now on."

Lavinia blew out a sigh of relief. "That would be *wunderbaar!*"

"So, what are you going to do about Nate?"

Lavinia shrugged. "I don't know what I should do."

Bethany laughed. "When a *mann* that handsome asks to court you—you give him your consent!"

"But…"

"Don't make excuses, Lavinia. He looked serious about you. And you deserve to be happy. Don't worry about *Daed;* I'll take care of him for a change. In the meantime, go to Nate and tell him you will consent to courting him. If you don't, someone else will. He's a handsome catch."

Lavinia knew in her mind that it was the logical and right thing to do—for the sake of her future. This was her chance to really be happy, and Bethany was right about Daniel. He would want her to be happy. Nate certainly made her feel like the happiest woman in the entire county—maybe even the history of mankind—if such a thing was possible.

Giggling with giddiness, Lavinia turned around and started toward the stairs to the loft. She turned and paused to wink at her sister.

"Go and be happy—promise me you'll be happy."

Lavinia smiled brightly. "I intend to."

Lavinia made fast tracks to the stairs that led to her future—a future filled with happiness with a very handsome, Amish *mann* who wanted to court *her*.

CHAPTER 9

Lavinia stepped into the room where her potential *betrothed* lay snoring lightly. She gently placed her hand upon Nate's bare chest, feeling the gentle rhythm of his heart that beat in perfect tempo with her own. She couldn't help but smile as he covered her hand with his, but remained asleep. She definitely wanted this man. She wanted every part of him. But in the back of her mind, all she could hear were her father's reprimands the day of Daniel's death. The very reprimands that filled her with too much guilt to live her life to its fullest potential.

Though she tried to block out his angry words, she couldn't help but drift back to that dreadful day…

Lavinia hung precariously over the top of the split-rail fence watching her twin *bruder* repair the barbed wire at the top of the chicken pen.

"Look at that one, Daniel," Lavinia squealed. "It looks like a *mann* holding an umbrella—with a big roaring lion ready to leap out at him."

Daniel took his attention off his work and looked up into the sky to humor his twin. "They just look like clouds to me, but if you say so, then I believe you can see *things* in those clouds."

"You have to use your imagination, dear *bruder.*"

Daniel took another look. He couldn't bear to disappoint his sister. "Well since I'm older—and wiser than you are, I'll leave the imagining to *you.*"

"*Ach,* you are only older by twelve minutes! That doesn't automatically make you wiser."

Daniel tightened the wire and connected the end to assure the chickens stayed *in* and the foxes stayed *out.* "Of course, it does. I'm too old to indulge in silly *girl* games of watching the clouds. Don't you have some laundry to hang on the line?"

Lavinia sighed. "If I didn't know better, I'd think you were trying to get rid of me."

"That's *narrish.* I wouldn't dream of trying to get rid of my favorite twin!"

Lavinia furrowed her brow. "You say that all the time, but you know I'm your *only* twin."

Daniel chuckled. "That's why you're *mei* favorite!"

"*Nee,* you patronize me!"

"Don't let *Daed* hear you using big words like that or he'll know about those unapproved books you've got hiding in the loft."

Lavinia gasped. "How did you know about those books?"

"I know more than you think I do."

"And you haven't told *Daed?*"

"*Nee,* I figured if he found out he'd put you under the ban, and I, for one, would not be able to live even one day without listening to your musings. They keep me grounded where I belong."

Lavinia lifted her head, feeling a little woozy as the blood rushed back to her brain all at once after hanging upside down for so long. "What do you mean?"

"You don't think I've wondered what life would be like out there—in the world? I've flipped through a few of those books myself, and though I found nothing wrong with the content, the Elders and *Daed* would see it differently."

He could see he had Lavinia's full attention, and momentarily wondered if he should continue to talk about such a risky subject.

"I've got an obligation to this *familye* as the eldest son, and that's a big responsibility. You and Bethany have the advantage of leaving the community and searching out another life—away from here, if you should choose to do so."

Lavinia's eyes widened with every word her brother spoke. "You've thought of *leaving* too?"

"*Jah,* I have."

There. He'd said it. Now what?

"Let me backtrack a minute for you. Back to before—before *mamm* left us. Life was *gut* then. *Daed* was happy and life on this farm was something special. With *mamm* gone, each year became more and more difficult. Suddenly you were raising Bethany, and I was doing the work of two *menner. Daed* shut down and barely functioned for some years. We were only *kinner* at the time and didn't understand, but that kind of life makes a child grow up fast—too fast."

Lavinia reflected on his statement, knowing that what he said was painfully true.

"There is a whole world out there to explore, and if all you ever do is experience it through your books, then that is better than the stifling existence we've come to accept here in this community. You can't be Bethany's *mamm* forever. Soon, very soon, you will meet a *mann* who will love you and want to raise a *familye* with you. That is the *familye* you should raise."

Lavinia didn't believe a word he was saying. She knew how plain she was. All her friends had begun courting over a year ago, and some were already married, but she hadn't been asked on one date yet.

"*Ach,* I'll probably end up a spinster."

"If you do it will be the fault of our *daed* who has put the burden of *his* responsibilities on us. I'd like to marry someday too, but I doubt it will happen for me. You and Bethany have a chance to marry if I am the one who stays to take care of *Daed.* If *Daed* would have accepted help from the community as he should have, or even remarried for our sake, then you would have had a real childhood and so would I have. We would have had normal chores of a farm, and been able to enjoy our growing years instead of having the responsibility of taking on the role of *parent* to our *daed* and a *boppli* at such an early age."

"But even I know how much *Daed* missed *mamm.* He still does. I hear him talking to her at night when he's praying just before he goes to sleep.*"*

"Jah, and I feel bad about that, but as painful as it was for him to accept, he should have been the parent instead of allowing you and me to step into that role."

Lavinia tipped her head back again, hoping the distraction of the clouds would put an end to the very serious conversation she and Daniel were having, but it didn't work. "Perhaps if I am the one to stay, then *you* can marry and have a *familye. Daed* built the loft for you to live in when you find a *fraa."*

Daniel scoffed. *"Daed* forgot one important thing."

"What's that?"

"Time."

Lavinia scrunched up her face. "Time for what?"

Daniel furrowed his brow. "Exactly *mei* point. There is never enough time to live our lives. No time at the end of the day to meet someone, much less to find the time to court."

"We mingle with enough of the youth at work bees and whatnot, but you're right. We haven't been to one Singing despite the many invitations from our friends. Why do we always make excuses instead of just attending one?"

Daniel wiped his dampened brow with the back of his shirtsleeve. The back of his neck was red from the sun, and Lavinia knew he needed a cool drink soon before he collapsed from the heat. She didn't want to go inside just yet. The clothes on the line still had at least another half an hour before they would dry in the humid, summer heat. She had come to realize Daniel was right about the lack of joy in their everyday lives.

Right at this moment, all she wanted to do was to get lost in the formations of the clouds. She hung upside down again, her grip on the edge of the fence slipping. "Help!"

Daniel stepped toward her, hoping he could catch Lavinia and prevent her from toppling to the ground below, but instead, he tripped and fell against the taught, barbed wire fence, his wrist catching a barb. His flesh tore open as he slid to the ground, the pain unbearable. He let out a series of rumbling groans as he struggled to clasp shut the gash he just couldn't see around the uncontrolled flow of blood at his wrist.

Lavinia fell backward off the fence rail and landed on her shoulder, hearing a crack accompanied by instant pain when she hit the hard-packed ground below. She rolled to her other side, struggling to regain her footing. Her hand went up to her obviously broken collar bone, her knees felt weak and her stomach heaved from the pain. She could hear Daniel groaning, but momentary disorientation kept her from him.

Lavinia finally turned toward Daniel.

Panic filled her at the expanse of blood covering her *bruder* and the soil around him.

Tucking her arm to her side against the pain in her collarbone, Lavinia bolted toward Daniel and fell to her knees beside him.

"What do I do?"

Daniel shook and shivered. "You need—to—tie it off—to stop—the bleeding."

Tears filled Lavinia's eyes and she shook so violently with fear that she struggled to tear off her apron, the pain of her broken bone making it a struggle. Ripping the hem brought unbearable pain, but she needed to strip the cloth enough to tie off Daniel's bloody wound. With shaky hands, she ignored her own pain and wrapped the heavy linen strip around his wrist three times, knotting the ends over the strip that was already saturated with blood.

"It's not helping," she cried.

Daniel was weak, his eyes turning a hazy grey.

"Go—to the barn—call an—ambulance."

She pushed herself up with one arm and staggered to the barn, her chest heaving with fear.

At her father's work table, she picked up the receiver and hit 9-1-1.

"9-1-1, what's your emergency?"

Lavinia relayed Daniel's condition and her address all in one sentence, tossing the phone down on the tool bench without bothering to hang up. She stumbled back to the yard where she'd left Daniel, his lifeless form bringing terror to her every step. By the time she reached him, she was numb.

She dropped back to her knees beside him and began tearing another couple of strips of cloth from her apron, tying each piece in vain. Before she could even tie the ends, the blood soaked through the material. She tied another strip above the wound, hoping that would keep the blood from draining too quickly. He might lose his arm from the break in circulation, but at least it would spare his life—wouldn't it?

Daniel looked up at her with an unexplained urgency. "Promise me—that..."

Lavinia shook her head madly. "Don't try to talk. Save your energy. I can hear the sirens. They'll be here in just another minute."

Daniel coughed and shook, his ashen features sinking. "Promise me—you'll marry—and have your—own *familye.*"

Tears poured down her cheeks at his words. She didn't want to promise such a thing. She knew what a promise like that meant and she was not ready to give up on her brother's life. The ambulance barreled down the dirt drive toward them.

She could see it.

Her brother would be safe. He was going to be just fine—wasn't he? She looked down at Daniel, his lashes fluttered against a set of eyes that had turned dark. Eyes she no longer recognized. Eyes with barely any life left in them.

She choked back a heavy sob threatening to force its way out.

"Promise—me," he said with a weak urgency.

She reluctantly made the promise, but it was too late.

He was already gone.

The memory of the sirens screaming in the driveway tormented her. If only she'd gotten him that cold drink instead of hanging upside-down over the fence rail. The ambulance had come, but they were too late.

None of it mattered now. She was alive and he was—dead and gone.

Her hand resting against Nate's warm flesh made her replay the promise she'd made to Daniel. She'd promised to marry and have a *familye* of her own.

Was that possible with Nate?

Could she allow Nate to court her knowing it could end in marriage?

Bethany had given her blessing, but what would her *daed* do if she tried to leave his *haus* to cling to Nate? Would he ever give his approval, or would she forever be scorned in his eyes, unworthy of any happiness?

Nate stirred, looking up at her with soft, loving eyes. He pulled her into the crook of his arm, holding her tightly against him. Suddenly, her *daed's* approval no longer mattered, and neither did his harsh words.

CHAPTER 10

Nate reached up and tenderly brushed away a tear from Lavinia's cheek—a tear she didn't know was there.

"What has you so upset? Did it go that badly with your *schweschder?*"

Lavinia paused to reflect on the very mature conversation she'd had with Bethany. "*Nee,* it went as opposite as it could have. We settled a lot with that argument. Funny, but we'd never argued before—ever."

"Then what is troubling you so much it's caused you to cry?"

Lavinia couldn't look at him.

"I was thinking of *mei bruder—mei* twin."

Nate nodded knowingly. "*Ach,* Daniel. I heard of his death from *mei* cousin. The three of us hung around together the summer I stayed to help with the replanting. That's how I knew of *you.*"

He picked up her hand and held it to his warm cheek. "I remembered thinking that entire summer that you worked way too hard for a girl your age. You worked alongside the women in the community and never once participated in any of the youth activities. I so wanted you to come out with us just once to a Singing or a bonfire outing, and I even looked for you, but you never showed up. Daniel knew that I liked you then, but he told me you would never give me a second look because you were too serious about your responsibilities. He was right."

Lavinia's heart caught in her throat, keeping her from responding. Nate liked her back then? How had she missed that? Daniel had been right about one point he'd made the day of his death; she had become her *mamm* from the time she was just a girl herself.

She sat up and looked him in the eye. "We were fifteen then, why didn't you say something to me?"

He looked into her questioning eyes, her voice choked with emotion.

"I was awkward at that age. It was easier for me to admire you from afar, than to be rejected up close and personal."

Lavinia felt sorry about Nate's youthful angst.

"I suppose I most likely would have rejected you then. I was too serious at that age. I felt I had to keep up with the other women in the community as Bethany's *"mamm"* in order for them to take me seriously. I hope you understand."

Nate used her hand to pull her back toward him.

"As long as you don't reject me now, I'll recover."

She wouldn't dream of rejecting him. He was going to be easy to love. She already did love him. It amazed her how much change her heart had gone through in just a few short hours. Her sister had finally decided to grow up and release her from the responsibility of raising her, and Lavinia had finally released the burden of guilt she'd been carrying around for the past two years over Daniel's death.

Most importantly were the feelings she'd developed for Nate in such a short time, and the impact those changes in circumstances would bring to her life. She was about to begin living her life, and she'd never felt freer in her spirit.

Lavinia looked into Nate's tender, brown eyes. There was love for her in those eyes, and she felt it like the warmth of a sunny day. How did she get to be so lucky?

Then it hit her.

"I'm curious about something…"

He went to kiss her, but she stiffened.

"What is it?"

"Why are you wearing *Englischer's* clothing and why did you let me think you were an *Englisher?*"

"I suppose I was trying it out—in case I decided to leave my community for good. I didn't intend to stay here and I certainly didn't intend on falling in love with you all over again."

"All over again?"

Nate winked at her. "I had it bad for you that summer. I didn't want to leave here without telling you, but Adam talked me out of it."

Lavinia looked at him lovingly. "I wish you would have told me."

He smiled, his dimples inviting her to kiss him.

"I wish I would have told you, too. But at least you know now."

"Since you didn't intend on staying here, I can have Bethany go over and let Adam know you are here so he can arrange to take you to his farm to care for you."

He pulled her closer. "Now wait a minute. Don't I have a say in this? I'd much rather *you* take care of me than Adam."

Lavinia enjoyed hearing that Nate needed her, and even wanted her to care for him. She liked this vulnerable and needy side to him, and she would be more than happy to pamper him while he stayed.

"I'd like that too. But for now, you need your rest."

Lavinia went to get up, but Nate held her playfully.

"Please don't leave yet. Part of the enjoyment of having you take care of me is so I can spend more time with you."

There was longing in his eyes, a longing Lavinia was powerless to resist.

"I suppose since we *are* courting now, I can stay for a while."

She propped his pillows behind his head so he could comfortably lean against them in a semi-sitting position. He held out his arm for her to cuddle him.

"I don't want to hurt you if I lean against your ribs."

He smiled. "*Ach,* I'm tough. Besides, I had some ibuprofen in my bag and I took a few when you went after Bethany, so it's started working on the pain. I don't think I cracked any of the ribs. I think they're just bruised."

Lavinia sat down gingerly beside him for two reasons; she didn't want to injure him, and she was still a little in shock that this *mann* was *hers.* She giggled inwardly as she cuddled up in the crook of his waiting arm. Each breath she took matched his, as did the giddiness of her heartbeat. If this was a dream, she didn't ever want to wake up. As far as she was concerned, his strong arms and protective love would be all she would need for the rest of her days on this earth. Safety engulfed her in those arms. She thought for sure and for certain she could almost live in those arms.

"Tell me, my sweetheart; have you ever thought of leaving the community?"

Her gaze followed the trail of his body until it rested on his eyes. She couldn't tell him how many times she'd thought of leaving, or how many times she'd set out to leave. Even if she hadn't gotten further than packing her suitcase, she didn't want him to know why.

The reasons only brought shame to her heart, shame for resenting her *mamm* for going to Heaven and leaving her to raise Bethany and care for her father. If Nate discovered the grudge she'd harbored in her heart all these years, he might find her thoughts to be wicked, and she didn't want to say or do anything that would cause him to change his mind about courting her. She'd only just found him, and had just found out he'd cared for her so much in their youth that his feelings easily renewed.

Certainly, thoughts such as those were best carried with a person to their grave.

"Doesn't every youth in the communities think of leaving at some point?"

It was all she could say at the moment. She'd since-then changed her mind and had even released her *mamm* from the wrongful grudge she'd had against her, so it was probably for the best if she didn't start off her relationship with Nate on a sour note. Her heart was no longer hardened; he'd even changed her in the short time he'd reentered her life. She wanted to be the sort of woman he could be proud to have at his side for the rest of his life, and if that meant she had to rid herself of all that was not holy, she would ask *Gott* to renew her no matter how painful it might be.

"*Jah,* I suppose they do, but I figured you would probably want to leave a little more than most since you had to be a *mamm* to Bethany, and a servant to your *daed.*"

Lavinia lowered her gaze, shame overtaking her. Nate lifted her chin to force her gaze back on him.

"There is no shame in not wanting to be in a role you aren't supposed to be in. I was in a similar spot myself until a few weeks ago when *mei* younger *schweschder* married. *Mei mamm* and *daed* were killed in a buggy accident just over eight years ago, and I was left to finish raising Amanda on my own. I farmed *mei daed's* land and took care of her. She's eighteen now and just married, so I was suddenly all alone in that *haus.* I'm twenty-six years old and don't know what to do with myself. I left a few days ago because I wondered what would become of me at my age."

Lavinia had wondered the same thing of herself. She had no idea he'd suffered the same fate she had. She was only three years younger than Nate, but too old not to be considered a spinster by the community.

"I felt resentment, when after a series of miscarriages, *mei mamm* finally had Amanda. She was her entire world because she was so happy to have a second *boppli,* and a girl, no-less. I was already eight years old, and didn't want more *kinner* to have to share *mei* parents with. But that first time she held my hand and said my name, asking if I'd help her milk our cow, I was happy to be her big *bruder.*"

So far, Lavinia could relate to everything he was saying. Should she tell him so?

"But then right after the accident, the resentment came back, but this time it brought with it a deep bitterness and anger disguised as mourning for *mei* parent's death. I told myself I would get over it, but the feelings of resentment only deepened, and that terrified me because I loved Amanda very much and didn't want to dislike her. Truth is, I just wanted our old life back, when both my parents were with us and I thought life couldn't get any better. But as time wore on, it all went away, and I accepted my role as caretaker for Amanda, but that didn't mean I didn't still feel cheated out of the life *mei* friends seemed to be enjoying."

Listening to Nate talk filled her with confirmation that her finding him on the bank of Willow Creek was no coincidence. *Gott* had put him in her path for a reason—to have each other to understand and help each other through the pain of losing loved ones, and the burden they shared for having to care for their sisters in place of a parent.

She *had* to tell him.

She knew it would ease both of their pain.

"It's almost like you're telling me my own life story. I understand the feelings you've experienced because I've felt them too. In case you didn't hear the heated argument between

Bethany and me, it's almost a mirror image of what you're telling me."

Nate chuckled and pulled her tight against his shoulder. "I heard the two of you arguing and that's why I'm telling you all of this. We can help each other through our feelings, even though coming here has already changed a lot for me. When Amanda married, I felt more relief than I have for years. I thought to myself *finally, I can get away from all this and live my life the way I want to*. But now that I'm here with you, I realize that distance was not what I need to heal; it was *you*."

Tears filled Lavinia's eyes and she didn't wipe them away before they warmed Nate's shoulder. She listened to the beat of his heart that matched her own.

"I believe we were meant for each other," was all she could say, but it was enough for them both to know there would never be a truer statement.

CHAPTER 11

The cricket's song lulled Nate into deep relaxation, but it was Lavinia's company that soothed his weary soul. This was the life for him, not a troubled existence among the *Englisch.* He certainly hadn't been thinking straight when he'd left his farm in Ohio, but now that he'd reunited with Lavinia, he was glad he had.

A warm breeze blew in from the open window and played with the blond waves that had escaped Lavinia's *kapp.* He delighted in the feel of her in his arms as if she was always meant to be there. He could get used to this. It was the easiest thing in his life in so many years, and he already couldn't imagine his life without her.

She shifted in his arms, her breathing slowed. She had fallen asleep. Though he hated the idea, he would have to wake her soon in order to avoid the appearance of improper behavior. If he wanted to get the blessing of the Elders and her *daed* to marry her, he would have to keep things between them on an approved level.

He pressed his face in her hair and breathed in the smell of lavender and oatmeal. He recognized the scent as being the same blend of natural ingredients his *mamm* used to make homemade soap. He'd continued to use her recipe to make it for himself, but he preferred the plain oatmeal—especially for shaving. His sister, Amanda, used to pick the flowers from their *mamm's* garden so she could add them to her soap to make it a little more feminine, but he never liked it—until now. Smelling it in Lavinia's hair put a warm feeling in him he didn't ever want to lose.

∽⊶

Lavinia stirred, looking up at Nate, who slept soundly next to her. She felt momentarily anxious at the reality that she'd fallen asleep in Nate's arms. She hadn't meant to, but she was so exhausted from the previous day's chores and the excitement of her new courtship with Nate that she'd suffered a lapse in judgment.

If he wasn't so comfortable and trustworthy, she'd have probably used more caution, never letting her guard down. But now it was nearly dawn, and her *daed* would be expecting his morning meal. She didn't want to leave Nate, but if she didn't slip back to the main *haus* soon, her father would catch her, and that would certainly be the end to her life in the community.

She lifted herself from the crook of Nate's arm, kissed him gently on the cheek and padded her way out of the loft. Being careful to keep the hinges of the screen door from squeaking so the noise wouldn't wake her *boyfriend— betrothed,* she stepped out onto the top step of the small porch and into the cold, morning air.

It was almost November, and the near-wintry breeze that ruffled the hem of her dress made her shiver with the reality of the change in season. No longer would she enjoy the hot days of Indian summer, but she now had the warmth of a new love to keep the chill from her. But in his immediate absence, all she could think about was putting on a pot of hot *kaffi* to warm her outsides to better match her insides.

Lavinia headed down the stairs of the loft with caution, being aware that her father could be anywhere this time of the day. The sun cast only enough twilight to light her way to the *haus.* Normally by this time, her father was tucked away safely in the barn busy with the morning milking. If caught, she could reasonably dash toward the chicken coop to make him think she was out to gather the eggs for an early start to the morning meal.

Thankfully, she managed to make her way to the kitchen unseen, where the smell of baking banana bread filled her senses. Panic rose in her until she spotted Bethany inside the pantry with a load of canned apples, flour and various spices in her arms.

"What are you making, little *schweschder?"*

Bethany blew at a tendril of sandy-brown hair that trickled over her forehead, her stained apron making her look as if she'd stayed up all night cooking.

"Ach, I'm going to make an apple pie for the evening meal. I've already started breakfast. I thought I'd try my hand at doing your job since I'm going to have to once you and Nate are married."

Lavinia giggled. "You're getting ahead of yourself, Bethany. We haven't officially begun to court yet, so we won't be getting married *this* wedding season. But I do appreciate the effort."

Bethany slumped against the doorframe of the pantry. "You mean I did all this for nothing?"

Lavinia crossed the kitchen floor and relieved Bethany of the burden in her arms before she dropped everything and there was a mess for her to clean.

"It wasn't for nothing. Learning to cook is *never* for nothing. It is a skill that all Amish women must master in order to make them an eligible catch for the best *mann* in the community."

Bethany blew out a discouraging sigh. "You got the best *mann* in the community. I've dated all the rest, and believe me, they don't even compare. I've considered giving up on the *menner* in this community."

Lavinia's eyes widened. *"You,* give up on dating? Do you feel alright little *schweschder?"*

"Ach, don't tease me. I'll have you know that I stayed home last night because I was so discouraged."

Lavinia set the food down on the counter and put the back of her hand to Bethany's forehead in jest.

"Ach, this *is* serious. You don't even have a fever!"

Bethany swatted Lavinia's hand away. "This is serious. Don't make fun of me. I'm worried I'm going to end up a spinster."

Lavinia smirked knowingly. "Up until a day ago, I was worried about the same thing. But you shouldn't worry. I *never* thought my life could change so fast, but this just goes to show you that you never know when *Gott* is going to choose to bless you."

Bethany rolled her eyes. "I've managed to find fault with each of the *menner* in this community. Where am I going to find another *mann* as wonderful as you've found?"

Lavinia smiled as her thoughts turned to the change in Nate from lying on the bank of Willow Creek unconscious, to so lovingly cradling her in his arms all night. "I *did* just sort of *find* him, didn't I?"

Bethany frowned. "I'm happy for you, but you can wipe the smile from your lips when you're around me, because I'm just not happy."

Lavinia took a stainless-steel mixing bowl from the cupboard and began the pie crust. "You don't need a *mann* to make you happy. We make our *own* happiness in this world."

Bethany handed her the butter and salt. "That's easy for you to say since you *have* a *mann.*"

Lavinia sighed with worry. "I don't have him yet. You've forgotten that *Daed* hasn't given his approval yet."

"You are well beyond the age of approval, Lavinia. Besides, you'll be lucky if you get more than a grunt out of him."

"Thank you for calling me old, little *schweschder.*"

"Ach, is that all you heard? Me calling you old?"

Bethany began to shake a fair amount of salt into the crust mixture, and Lavinia couldn't stop her before it was too late. "Now I have to throw this batch away and start all over again. The recipe calls for just a pinch of salt. How many times have I shown you how to make a pie crust?"

Bethany hung her head. "I'm sorry. But couldn't you just make two crusts and then we won't have to throw it away."

Lavinia thought for a minute. "I suppose if we double the recipe, we can make apple turnovers instead. But you will have to take the extras with you when you go to visit the Troyer farm to let them know Nate is here and that he's going to recover here with us."

Bethany furrowed her brow. "That's sort of risky, don't you think? If *Daed* finds him in the loft, we will have a *lot* of explaining to do."

Lavinia added more flour and butter to the bowl, her arm already aching from the blending. "That is what Nate and I decided. He will stay with us until he recovers. It will give us a chance to get a head start on our courting."

"When do you plan on presenting it to *Daed?* How are you going to explain how you already know each other?"

Lavinia hadn't thought that out.

"I suppose he will come over with Adam after he's recovered and we will play it off as if we've just met. He can ask *Daed* then. Or—we will do like most of the youth and see each other secretly, and *Daed* will never have to know until we are ready to be published for our wedding."

Bethany laughed. "Now that's taking things *way* too far."

"Perhaps," Lavinia agreed. "But I'm not even certain any of it will matter, as *Daed* doesn't acknowledge me anyway. I might even have to get married without him present."

Bethany's eyes bulged. "You wouldn't!"

Lavinia dropped the fork in the bowl and focused a serious gaze on her sister. "Perhaps I need to shock him into ending his bout of ignoring me."

Bethany shook her head and pursed her lips.

"Don't let him ruin this for you. If it was me, I'd do what was right and *gut* for *mei* future with the *mann* I was destined to marry. *Gott* brought him to you, and you shouldn't let this life get in your way."

Lavinia resumed cutting the butter into the flour, recalling inwardly the last conversation she'd had with Daniel. "I practically promised the same thing to our dear *bruder* just before he let go and let *Gott* take him to the great farm in the sky."

Bethany nodded knowingly. "That's a promise I aim to help you keep."

CHAPTER 12

Lavinia watched in shock as her *daed* made a show of spitting out his first bite of banana bread into his napkin. He looked up sternly, disapproval furrowing his brow. It was the first time he'd looked directly into Lavinia's eyes since Daniel's death.

The look in his eyes terrified Lavinia.

"What's wrong with this bread, *dochder?*"

He hadn't called her by her given name in two years. The tone of his voice sent shivers of emotion through her.

"Is there something wrong with it?"

"It tastes like you rubbed it on the underside of a skunk." His deep baritone filled the small kitchen with anger.

Lavinia and Bethany each lifted their slice of the bread to their mouths and took a daring nibble while their father watched with much anticipation. They immediately tucked their napkins beneath their lips to catch the vile-tasting bread.

Lavinia jumped up from the table nervously, snatching the bread from each plate and taking it to the counter. She quickly grabbed biscuits from the pantry and tossed them into the still-warm oven. "These biscuits will take no time to warm, *Daed*. I'm sorry about the bread. The buttermilk must have gone sour and I didn't realize it."

Bethany stood up abruptly, her chair crashing to the floor behind her. "Why do you cover for me like that, dear *schweschder?*" She turned to her father. "I am the one who made the bread, and I did it to help Lavinia who works too hard on this farm, and I…"

He pounded his fist on the table, interrupting her tantrum.

"Silence, *Dochder!*"

Her father's voice rumbled in her, rattling her to her very core. It was the first time he'd referred to *her* so informally. He'd been that way toward Lavinia for the past two years, and now, he'd included Bethany in his raging disassociation.

Bethany's face turned up, anger flaring in her eyes. "I was only trying to help."

She threw down her napkin and walked toward the kitchen door. "Nothing is *gut* enough for you, is it?"

Lavinia watched in shock as Bethany let the screen door slam behind her. She swallowed the lump of fear clogging her throat while her gaze travelled to her father. He was busy shoveling the remainder of his eggs in his mouth as if nothing happened, but she could see lines of distress etched in his permanently stressed face.

Pulling the warm biscuits from the oven, she crossed the room and set the plate in front of her father without looking at him. She feared if she made eye-contact with him again it could only have the worst of consequences for her. As for Bethany, she was certain her father would overlook her tantrum as always and not speak of it again. He'd lost control of his *familye;* that much was now evident to Lavinia. How that would affect her impending courtship with Nate remained to be seen. For now, she would carry on with him as planned, and be certain to keep it from her father at all cost.

Lavinia removed Bethany's plate from the table and set it on the counter. She reached for her own plate next, hoping her father wouldn't notice, but he startled her by grabbing her arm. He kept his head down toward his own plate, but after a few seconds of discomfort, he let go of her arm and resumed shoveling the last of his eggs onto his fork.

"Leave it. Sit and finish your meal."

Lavinia was afraid to sit, and she was afraid to defy her father as Bethany had more times than she could count. Lavinia had never stood up to her father. Why did her sister have more courage than she did? She envied her sister for that much, but she supposed she lacked the confidence needed for that sort of courage. Lavinia had never been that confident.

But with Nate in her life now, she was determined that she would start.

ॐॐॐ

When her father finally rose from his chair and exited the kitchen, Lavinia blew out a sigh of relief. Within minutes, Bethany whirl-winded into the kitchen and grabbed her plate off the counter, snatching a biscuit from the plate and stuffing most of it in her mouth.

"I thought he'd never leave."

Lavinia scowled at Bethany as crumbs spewed from her lips and onto the table. She swatted playfully into the air.

"Don't you have any manners?"

Bethany shook her head while making a show of the chewed-up biscuit in her mouth.

"*Ach,* little *schweschder,* act like a lady."

Bethany rolled her eyes. "You should take your own advice!"

Lavinia began to run water in the sink to wash the dishes. "What is that supposed to mean?"

Bethany wriggled her eyebrows. "It means that I had to start the meal this morning because *someone* stayed out all night with her new beau in the loft!"

Lavinia could feel the heat of embarrassment rising her neck and resting on her cheeks. "Speaking of Nate, I should get some food out to him. He needs to keep up his strength."

"I saw *Daed* hitching up the buggy to go into town, so you should be clear to take food up there in about half an hour. You could probably have enough time to visit with Nate before *Daed* returns for the noon meal."

Lavinia picked her hands up out of the soapy dishwater and flashed Bethany a pleading look. "Do you mind?"

Bethany let out a heavy sigh, throwing the back of her hand to her forehead. "First I have to cook, and now I have to wash dishes!"

Lavinia grabbed a linen dishtowel and dried her hands, twisting the towel and swatting at Bethany with it. "Don't be so dramatic. If you do the dishes, I can finish the apple turnovers."

Bethany jumped up from the table eagerly, bringing her empty plate to the sink and dumping it in the water. "You have got yourself a deal. I will take washing dishes over cooking and baking every time!"

Lavinia began to cut the rolled-out dough into squares, placing them on the cookie sheet. "You will have to learn some day."

"*Jah,* but I will never measure up to our *mamm.* But you're *gut* enough to run *mamm's* old bakery. Why haven't you ever done that? It just sits out there by the main road all boarded up like an abandoned old shack."

Lavinia whipped her head around, piercing Bethany with a discouraging glare. "Don't you remember why *Daed* boarded up the place?"

Bethany shook her head.

Lavinia lowered her head, a far-off gaze overtaking her. "I remember that day like it was yesterday. He caught us out there playing, and I'd started a fire in the stove. It was just before *mei* ninth birthday, but I knew what I was doing when it came to *mamm's* bakery. It was only a few weeks after she'd gone to Heaven, but no one ever cleaned out the place, and there was still flour and such in the cellar. I'd brought butter and eggs from the *haus* and decided I was going to make a batch of cookies. When *Daed* saw the smoke rising from the chimney, he'd come running from the fields thinking the place was on fire. But when he discovered us in there baking, he threw it all away and put out the fire in the stove, and then put us out in the yard. He didn't say a word, but I knew when he began to pull the planks of wood from the porch and used them to board up the doors and windows that he was mad."

Bethany stood there washing the same cup repeatedly, her full attention on Lavinia's story.

"Well by the time *Daed* finished hammering, I'd wet *mei* pants, but you threw a rock at the window and cracked it."

Bethany laughed. "I remember that!"

Lavinia finished placing a dollop of apple preserves on each square of dough, and then draped a square over the top and crimped the edges with a fork.

99

"I don't know how you remember that; you were barely four years old."

Bethany handed Lavinia the sugar and went back to scrubbing the pots and pans. Lavinia brushed each turnover with an egg-white glaze and sprinkled a generous portion of sugar on top before placing the tray in the oven. Then she grabbed a dishtowel and began to wipe the dishes dry while she waited for the turnovers to bake.

Bethany stopped scrubbing and turned thoughtfully toward Lavinia. "Do you suppose enough time has passed that *Daed* would let me open up that bakery?"

Lavinia gasped. "I don't want to be around when you bring up *that* subject. He will probably yell, or he might just ignore you and pretend he didn't hear you—he likes to do that a lot. But I can guarantee he will not permit it."

Bethany went back to the chore of scraping the skillet used to scramble the eggs. "I'm going to ask him anyway, and I'm not taking no for an answer!"

The kitchen filled with the warm aroma of cinnamon and apples. Lavinia breathed in, satisfied with the treat they would share with Nate's cousin, Adam, and his *familye*. They'd been distant neighbors forever, and Lavinia had even entertained *Frau* Troyer for several quilting and canning bees, but now that she was involved with Nate, she hoped to impress her future *familye*.

"*Ach,* I don't know how you can be defiant toward *Daed* and get away without a sound lashing behind the barn."

Bethany rinsed the skillet and placed it on the towel on the counter for Lavinia to dry, and then went about finishing the last of the cooking utensils.

"I know you think *Daed* is tough, but you need to know that he no longer has the strength *or* the will to enforce the rules he tries to lay down."

Lavinia looked at her sister curiously. "I think you are just a little on the side of being naïve where *Daed* is concerned, because he is certainly tough, and he *will* enforce the rules when pushed far enough. I, for one, do not want to push him to see just how far he can be pushed. But it seems you do, so let me know when you decide you are going to carry through with your *narrish* little plan, and I'll be certain I'm miles away from here."

Bethany giggled. "You are a chicken!"

Lavinia scoffed. "When it comes to *Daed,* I suppose I will always be *afraid* of him, but now that I have Nate, I will have *him* to step up in front of me and protect me."

Bethany laughed heartily. "You better hope he doesn't have to do any defending before those ribs of his heal."

"I have a feeling he would brave *Daed's* temper even with several broken bones!"

Bethany sighed. "You're lucky to have him. I have to admit, I was a little jealous."

Lavinia put a hand on Bethany's shoulder.

"Don't be jealous of me. Be happy for me."

"*Ach,* don't worry. It's isn't real jealousy. It's more of a sadness and loneliness."

"Well don't be sad either, little *schweschder,* because the right *mann* will come along for you, too."

"I wish I had your confidence."

Lavinia picked up the pair of crocheted pot-holders and opened the oven, letting the cinnamon-apple turnovers scent the kitchen with mouth-watering anticipation.

"It's funny that I always thought you had complete confidence in yourself, Bethany."

Bethany shook her head. "What you think you see is really a defense and an illusion. I *act* confident to make it *appear* that I am."

Lavinia chuckled. "I suppose I never thought about that. It's a pretty deceiving act you put on. Unfortunately, I don't even have enough confidence to *act* confident."

Bethany let out the stopper at the bottom of the sink and swished the suds down the drain. "I think we are getting way off-track with this conversation. I'm going to put on a dry apron while those heavenly smelling turnovers cool so I can get them over to your would-be *familye.*"

Lavinia's heart quickened its pace at the thought of it. Though she'd talked to Adam and his *mamm* plenty of times, she was suddenly nervous about the impending meeting. It would be as if she was meeting them all over again. The circumstances were different now. Suddenly she'd gone from being simply a neighbor to being *familye.*

She readied a tray of the leftover meal she'd been keeping warm in the lower part of oven to take it to Nate. Giddiness overtook her as she lovingly prepared everything just right. She'd been a servant all her life to her *daed,* but to serve Nate was a joy because he loved her, and her heart overflowed with love for him too.

CHAPTER 13

"Bethany, what's wrong?"

Lavinia felt dread traveling through her veins, churning up emotion like a waterspout over Willow Creek.

Bethany narrowed her gaze on Nate as she took her sister gently by the hand and guided her toward the small kitchen of the loft. Before they could exit the bedroom where Lavinia had been enjoying a leisurely breakfast with Nate, her path collided with a very beautiful young Amish woman.

Lavinia gazed into the woman's sea-glass, blue eyes and trailed over her shiny, flaxen hair. Her skin was flawless, like the porcelain dolls that are sold at the gift shop in town. Her slender hands rested on perfectly trim hips as her gaze stretched around Lavinia.

Tall, lanky and plain, Lavinia.

"Nate! I've been so worried about you!"

Nate's gaze darted between Lavinia and the young woman, shock rendering him momentarily speechless.

Please, Lord, Lavinia begged silently. *Don't let her be who I think she is.*

"Miriam, what are you doing here?"

"I went by and had *kaffi* with your *schweschder,* and she told me her husband is tending the animals for you through the remainder of the harvest because you plan to stay here. Why did you leave without telling me *goodbye?"*

"You shouldn't have come here, Miriam."

Nate looked past Lavinia at Miriam, who had brushed by her and was fast-approaching his bedside.

"Why wouldn't I come to you, my love?"

Her words dripped with honey, but her tone was soaked with vinegar. She pounced on the mattress beside him, startling Lavinia with her boldness. Nate, however, didn't seem surprised by her actions and ignored her.

Nate still had not looked at Lavinia, but she had heard enough. She wasn't going to stick around long enough for him to publicly humiliate her. The embarrassment she felt at having Bethany witness this was more than she could bear. She ran from the room, unable to handle the sight of *Miriam* sitting so close to the man she loved.

Nate called after her, but she was compelled to leave the loft.

She couldn't breathe.

Tears choked her almost to the point of suffocation. A myriad of emotions ripped through her, each twisting at her heart, wringing it out like the laundry on washday. Every breath she pulled in became more strenuous than the last as she struggled to make sense of her *relationship* with Nate.

Her feet prodded down the steps of the loft, propelling her into an automated state of mind, though her thoughts remained very much with Nate and the woman he *really* loved.

Had they had a squabble and he'd decided to put some distance between them? Or was the reality of it more grueling than Lavinia dared to imagine? She didn't want to think that she'd kissed another woman's betrothed, let alone that she'd fallen in love with him. She began to second-guess herself, wondering if her feelings for Nate had been nothing more than the makings of a *first crush*.

"Lavinia, wait," Bethany called after her.

Waiting wasn't a problem for Lavinia; moving was. Her feet felt planted in the earth like the tall stalks of corn growing in their field, only she didn't feel as graceful. Still, she wanted to bolt instead of facing Bethany.

"I think you should know that I told Adam to pack up Nate and take him back to his farm. He should be here soon with the buggy. I suspected as much about this Miriam Schrock. I'm so sorry Lavinia, but it's better you find out now, than to take up with a liar and a cheater like Nate."

Lavinia's breath caught in her throat as she stifled a sob. She would not cry over this man.

The hinges of the screen door squeaked the presence of Miriam. Lavinia looked up at the graceful beauty as she trailed pretentiously down the stairs toward them. Lavinia's first instinct was to run, but her legs still felt wobbly. Besides, it was best to get this over with and put her silly notions of a future with Nate behind her so she could go back to her life.

Ach, what life?

"I suppose I should thank you for *helping* my Nate," Miriam began in a condescending tone. "But I think it's best you know of my involvement with him in order avoid any more *confusion* on your part. I can certainly understand you developing a *crush* on the *mann. Ach,* surely you must know he was only being kind to you because you were helping him. You can't possibly believe he would prefer *you* over me. You live so simple here it's obvious you take Plain living to an extreme. After all, if you weren't wearing a dress, I'd have wondered if you were a *mann*!"

Lavinia's mind went numb and she tuned out the hurtful words. She couldn't hear any more of it lest she crumble inwardly like a dilapidated barn. If she didn't feel so numb inside, she'd have run to the next county before stopping, but her legs just wouldn't take her away no matter how badly she wanted them to.

Bethany pulled on Lavinia's arm, but she couldn't budge her from the spot she'd not yet moved from. "Let's go,

Lavinia. We don't have to stand here and be insulted by someone from another community. She thinks she's better than we are, but being from a different community and wearing fancy, colorful dresses doesn't make her any less Amish than we are."

If Lavinia would have been thinking a little more clearly, she'd have sworn she'd seen Bethany stick her tongue out at Miriam.

Miriam tipped her head to the side, swinging the loose flaxen hair from her *kapp*. *"Ach,* I'm not Amish at all. Turns out, I'm adopted! I'm an *Englisher.* And *that* makes me better than *both* of you."

Lavinia looked a little closer at Miriam's *perfect* skin, noting that she was wearing makeup. And though her dress might be acceptable for some other community, it seemed too fancy even for some of the rebellious Mennonite girls. Miriam was young, most likely Bethany's age, so it made sense for her to dress the way she was and to wear makeup, being that she was at the end of her *rumspringa.*

Bethany posted both her hands on her hips defensively. "We don't care what you *say* you are, but we know what we *think* you are! Your life is of no concern to us, so leave our farm and don't come back."

Lavinia looked at her little sister as if she'd suddenly become someone she didn't know. She knew Bethany was free-spirited, but she'd never heard her *fight* with anyone.

Normally, Lavinia would reprimand her for such behavior, but right now, she wanted Miriam to leave more than Bethany did.

"It doesn't matter what you think," Miriam said, flouncing her pale, yellow frock. "Nate wants to be an *Englisher* and that is what we have in common. *You* have nothing in common with him."

The snarly look Miriam sent Lavinia momentarily empowered her to harness the courage to fight this battle herself. Her lips parted, but the words stuck there like the bugs hanging from the strips of flypaper suspended from the rafters of the barn. Why couldn't she be as bold as Bethany?

"As soon as Nate agrees to leave the Amish, we will become *Englischers* together and he will forget all about the mistake he made in thinking he might want to stay here and court *you*. After all, why would he want someone like you when he can have me?"

The squeak of the screen door startled Lavinia out of the stupor in which Miriam's words had momentarily trapped her. Her gaze impulsively lifted to meet Nate's. Her heart involuntarily filled with pain the moment their eyes met.

"That's enough lies, Miriam," Nate called down to her.

Miriam pursed her lips and narrowed her eyes as if she was prepared to charge at Nate like a penned-up bull ready to fight. She looked up at him with a piercing glare in her eyes. "Perhaps you should take your own advice. You obviously didn't tell this poor *Tomboy* that you declared love for me the night of your *schweschder's* wedding."

"I did no such thing! You followed me around the whole night and wouldn't leave me alone."

Lavinia watched Nate grab the banister with determination, wincing with every step he took down the staircase toward them. For a moment, she was tempted to go to Nate and help him, but Miriam's words reminded her that he wasn't hers.

Behind her, the clip-clop of horse's hooves and the grinding of buggy wheels against the gravel driveway brought her back to reality.

Adam hopped out of the buggy without setting the brake and sprinted up the stairs to help his cousin down the rest of them. "I'm sorry about not getting here sooner, but I had to drop off *mei schweschder,* Libby, in town. I tried to stop Miriam from coming here, but she wouldn't listen to me."

Nate paused his journey down the steps long enough to glare at Miriam. "She doesn't listen to anyone. In fact, she doesn't even listen to reason."

Miriam planted her dainty hands on her dainty hips angrily. "You are the one who doesn't listen. If you did, you wouldn't have left without me. I'm the only one who understands how much you want to leave the community—we are meant to be together."

Nate chuckled. "I only left to get away from *you!*"

Miriam gritted her teeth. "You left because you're a coward who goes back on promises."

"I never promised you anything," Nate retorted.

"Having your way with me was an unspoken promise—a commitment to…"

Nate took an aggressive step toward her. "I never did anything except kiss you—once, and I wish I hadn't because when I realized what a shallow, self-absorbed person you were, I wanted nothing to do with you!"

Miriam pushed out her lower lip. "But I thought you wanted to live among the *Englisch* with me."

"You misunderstood me when I said I wanted to see what being an *Englisher* was all about, just as you misunderstood the kiss between us. When you showed up at *mei schweschder's* wedding, I told you I wasn't in love with you. I wish I'd never stopped to help you that day when your horse threw a shoe, and I wish I'd never impulsively kissed you that day either. You haven't left me alone since, and I don't understand why you can't get that I don't love you! I don't intend to have a future with you outside *or* inside of the community. You misunderstood my kindness for something else."

Miriam stamped her foot and let out an angry cry. "I didn't misunderstand anything. You should do the honorable thing and marry me."

Nate blew out a discouraging breath. "I'm not going to marry you over one kiss and a conversation about leaving the community."

Miriam leered at him. "*Ach,* it was much more than a simple kiss and we *both* know it."

CHAPTER 14

"Adam, fetch the Bishop. Bring him here so he can settle this once and for all," Nate demanded.

Miriam folded her arms across her ample bosom and pursed her lips. "Yes, Adam, fetch the Bishop."

Adam turned toward his buggy, but Bethany caught him by the arm. "Wait a minute. No one is bringing the Bishop here. Lavinia and I will have no part in the disagreement between the two of you. Go back to your farm Adam, and take these two with you."

She pointed disgustedly to Nate and Miriam while pulling on her sister's arm. "Let's get to our chores before *Daed* gets back from town. All of you need to be gone in the next few minutes."

They turned to leave, but Nate called after her.

"Lavinia, wait. Don't let Miriam's lies turn you away from me. I love you!"

Lavinia whipped her head around to face Nate, and Miriam stepped between them.

"You *love* her?!"

"*Jah,* I do," Nate said without taking his eyes off Lavinia. "And I want us to spend every night together just the way we did last night."

"You spent the night with *her?*" Miriam shrieked.

Nate blew out a heavy sigh. "*Jah,* I did. It was the most *wunderbaar* night of *mei* whole life."

Letting out a low-pitched growl, Miriam's eyes filled with tears. "So, you would take advantage of *two* women in the same week?"

"How dare you talk of *mei schweschder* that way!" Bethany screamed at her. "Get off our farm before I throw you off myself."

Lavinia glared at Bethany. As much as she wanted Miriam to leave, she would not tolerate violence or even the threat of violence.

Miriam ignored Bethany's threat and turned her attention back to Nate. "You made me believe you loved me!"

Nate shook his head "I don't understand how you can get all that from one kiss. I never took advantage of you."

By this time, Miriam was in a full-swing bout of fake crying. Lavinia recognized it since she'd heard Bethany do the same thing so many times.

"So, you admit to taking advantage of *her,* but deny your involvement with me! Why would you choose a woman who is so plain and boyish compared to me?"

Nate looked at her and scoffed. "There is no comparison. The beauty Lavinia has in her heart makes her the most beautiful woman in the world to me. *You,* on the other hand, are shallow and spoiled and self-centered. Not to mention how mean you are to others for no reason. I could never marry a woman who is so unkind to others when they have been nothing but kind to you."

"No one is ever nice to me!" Miriam complained.

Bethany stepped forward, kicking up a little dirt onto Miriam's pristine, white, canvas shoes. "Perhaps it's because you are just not a likeable person. You haven't been here more than ten minutes, and everyone here seems to be of the general mind to dislike you!"

"I don't care what you say. I'm not leaving until I get a chance to talk to your Bishop," Miriam insisted.

Bethany threw her hands up in disgust. "Adam, go fetch the Bishop. Let *him* tell her what a fool she's making of herself."

She turned to Lavinia and whispered in her ear.

"When Daed gets home, we are in for a sound lashing. You might be banned for your involvement with Nate. Miriam will surely tell even if you don't confess it yourself."

"But I haven't done anything wrong," Lavinia whispered back. *"I don't have anything to confess."*

"Ach, we both know it doesn't matter that you're innocent, Miriam will obviously lie and say anything she has to in order to make you look like you're in the wrong instead of her being the one at fault for wrong-doing. People like Miriam don't care about the truth because only the lies can be used as weapons, and they thrive on hurting others."

Bethany pulled her into the house while Adam went down the road to fetch the Bishop. They had chores they needed to get to, and if their *daed* returned in the midst of the chaos, they'd be in trouble for a lot more than the scene taking place in the yard. He was a very particular *mann* about how his *haus* was kept. In fact, he was very particular about everything, and they knew he would make the situation with Nate and Miriam *his* business—especially if it involved his daughters.

Once inside the kitchen, Lavinia looked out the window at Nate, who was leaning on the banister of the stairs while Miriam flailed her arms. She could hear the woman screaming at him from inside the *haus,* but Nate ignored her. Lavinia said a silent prayer that the Bishop would be able to get Miriam to tell the truth—that is, *if* she was lying about her involvement with Nate. Lavinia didn't want to think that he could be capable of taking advantage of the girl. Miriam *was* beautiful, but as soon as she opened her mouth, she became as ugly as Nate described.

Was it possible that he could look past her physical beauty and not find her attractive in the least?

Lavinia could see the ugliness, but she doubted a man would have an easy time looking past the obvious physical beauty. She wanted so much to believe Nate's explanation, but she didn't understand why a woman as beautiful as Miriam would lie about such a thing. It would seem she could have any man she desired, so why waste her time with one who claimed he didn't love her? Perhaps she was simply *narrish,* and there was *no* other explanation for her one-sided fixation on Nate.

Bethany nudged Lavinia. "So, do you believe him?"

It was a fair question, and certainly one that deserved an answer, but Lavinia wasn't ready to give her opinion just yet. She studied Nate's body language as Miriam continued to berate him.

He leaned his head against the railing and remained seated on the landing, eyes closed, his left hand pressed against his ribs. She knew he wasn't in as much pain as he was pretending to be, which meant he was ignoring Miriam and acting hurt probably hoping she would leave him alone.

She continued to watch, wondering how long it would take for Miriam to stop her rant. When Nate continued to remain quiet, her words became fewer until she finally gave up. He'd ended the argument simply by not giving her anymore to argue with him about. That is certainly the same way she would have handled Miriam. She knew that sometimes the best way to defuse an angry person was to remain quiet. It always worked with her *daed,* something Bethany had not yet learned.

Watching the way Nate handled the out-of-control Miriam, she realized that he *was* telling the truth. Already she knew his gentle spirit, and knowing that about him, he could *never* love such a mean-spirited woman as Miriam. Why couldn't Miriam see that? Was her anger blocking her from seeing that he wanted nothing to do with her? Lavinia could see it; anyone watching the two of them could plainly see he loathed her and regretted any involvement with her.

"Jah, I believe him," Lavinia finally said.

CHAPTER 15

Adam returned with the Bishop, but he didn't get out of the buggy. Instead, Adam hopped out and helped Nate into the back, while instructing Miriam to Join the Bishop up front. Nate paused at the back of the buggy to look toward the main *haus* as if to bid Lavinia *goodbye.*

The quietness of the kitchen made Lavinia shiver as she stared out into the empty yard where Nate had been only a few moments ago. Now, it was as if he'd never even been there. A deep sadness filled her, making her wonder if she would ever recover. She'd experienced nothing but loss in her life, and this was just too much for her.

Lavinia wiped her tears as she watched her father pull his buggy into the yard, his usual, anger-filled expression seemingly worse. Her heart filled with much trepidation at the possibility her father had run into Adam's buggy on the way up from the main road. Was it possible he'd spoken to the Bishop? He turned and looked toward the *haus.*

He knew.

Scurrying from the kitchen, Lavinia ran up the stairs to warn Bethany, who was gathering up the throw-rugs. Lavinia picked up an end of the large, braided rug in the hall and whispered in case her father had come into the *haus.*

"Daed just pulled up in the yard, and looks angry."

"He always looks angry," Bethany sighed. "But you don't suppose he knows, do you?"

Lavinia shook her head. "I think he had just enough time to talk to the Bishop at the end of the road. They had to have run into each other. The timing is too close."

Bethany dropped the rug. "Then he knows about Nate staying in the loft."

Dropping her end of the rug, Lavinia crumbled to the floor. "I don't want to face *Daed.* I don't want to have to explain to him how foolish I was to give my heart to a *mann* who is about to be forced to marry another woman."

Bethany crouched down beside her and put her arm around her shoulder. "No one said you have to tell him all of that! All we have to tell him is that we found him injured and we helped him. That's all. Nothing else."

"It's not that easy with *Daed,* and you know it. He's going to ask so many questions, you're going to think you're back in school taking a test in front of the whole class!"

Bethany leaned her elbow on her knee and rested her chin on her hand. She blew out a long, discouraging sigh.

"Stop that! I'm nervous enough without having *you* falling apart on me. You're the strong one—the one with enough guts to stand up to *Daed!*"

"Ach, I'm not so sure I can help you with this one," Bethany said quietly. "You might be on your own."

Lavinia narrowed her gaze at Bethany. "I didn't do *any* of this by myself! You were right there with me carrying Nate up from the creek and into the loft."

Bethany stood up and put her fists on her hips.

"It didn't take you long to use *that* against me, did it? If I didn't know any better, I'd say you tricked me into helping you so you didn't have to be the only one to blame for all of this."

Lavinia lowered her head in shame. "The thought did cross *mei* mind. But I'm sorry!"

Before she could answer, they heard creaking on the stairs. They looked at each other wide-eyed.

"Help!" Lavinia mouthed to Bethany.

Bethany rolled her eyes, and Lavinia knew she was on her own. She took a deep breath and braced herself for the worst conversation she was about to have with her father since Daniel's funeral.

"Bethany, go out to the barn and tend to *mei* horse. She had a long trip into town and back, and needs a *gut* rubdown."

Lavinia swallowed the lump in her throat, but kept her eyes to the floor. He was sending Bethany out of the *haus*—out of earshot.

This was not a good sign.

He was going to raise his voice for sure and for certain, and she was trapped between him and the stairwell. There would be no backing away from him should he decide to strike her. She prayed he would think her to be too old to administer a sound lashing.

"I ran into the Bishop on the way up to the *haus* just now. He tells me you helped a young *mann* from an Ohio community," he began in his usual, stern monotone. "It's my understanding that he stayed in the loft above the barn."

"*Jah,*" Lavinia answered without lifting her head. "He was hurt and unconscious so Bethany and I brought him here to recover."

"You brought a *mann* into this *haus*—into your *bruder's* loft without my knowledge. What if he was not Amish? He could have been dangerous, and I would not have known you were in danger."

"He told me he was Amish."

"When I saw him, he was dressed as an *Englisher*, and the young woman he was with was dressed the same."

"He's not *with* her. She chased him here, but he doesn't want to marry her!"

"Silence, *dochder*," his voice rumbled. "The Bishop stepped outside Adam's buggy and approached me so he could talk freely. The two *Englischers* are to be married if they intend to stay in the community."

"But he's not going to…" Lavinia started to argue, but thought it best to keep her thoughts to herself regarding Nate.

"Don't make me think you have an interest in that rebel, *dochder*."

"*Nee.*"

"As for the disrespect of your *bruder's* memory; I will not tolerate you spending any time in that loft. It was for Daniel, and he will never be able to use it because…"

"Because I let him die? Is that what you were going to say?"

"Don't be disrespectful to me, *dochder*."

"*Ach, mei* name is Lavinia! You haven't spoken *mei* name since Daniel's funeral when you blamed me for his death."

"You should have gone down the road to get the doctor. You took the coward's way out and called for an *Englisch* ambulance. It would have taken less time to get the doctor here than to wait for that ambulance."

Lavinia felt a thick sob catch in her throat. "I was afraid to leave him that long—there was too much blood."

"You should have done the right thing. Daniel would have wanted you to do the right thing."

Lavinia plucked an angry tear from her cheek.

"Daniel wanted me to have a happy life. Right before he died, he made me promise I would stop wasting *mei* life being a *mamm* to Bethany and a servant to you! He wanted me to get a husband and be loved for once in *mei* life instead of being wanted only as a servant and *mamm* to your *other dochder.*"

"He was *mei* only son, and *you* let him die!"

Lavinia broke into uncontrollable sobs. "I didn't let him die! He was the one who told me to call the ambulance."

His red-rimmed eyes glared at her. "*Mei* son would not have asked for such a foolish thing. It was *your* poor judgment that brought him to his end. He was a *gut buwe,* and he won't be able to carry on the *familye* name because you acted selfishly and put your own needs before his."

"I won't continue to rival Daniel for your attention *Daed,*" she said as calmly as possible. "Daniel is gone. He's with *Mamm* in Heaven and he isn't coming back. But I'm here and I can't live with your resentment any longer. Even if I don't marry, I think it's time for me to move on. I'll be packing *mei* things and moving to the B&B. I've been offered a job that comes with room and board. I didn't accept because of *mei* obligations here, but I can no longer stay where I'm not wanted."

She walked past him and he didn't say anything to stop her.

CHAPTER 16

Lavinia silently packed her small suitcase, tears running down her cheeks, a large accumulation of tears hanging precariously from the end of her nose and ready to drip onto her folded clothes.

Her father hadn't said a word to her when she'd told him she was leaving.

He hadn't tried to stop her.

He had been unyielding for too long.

It was obvious he no longer cared what she did, and at this point, Lavinia didn't either. Hurt and anger would drive her to prove to him she was worth more than her dead brother. More than being a servant and mother to her sister. More than a naïve pushover, and certainly better-suited for Nate than Miriam.

She wondered what was missing from *Miriam's* life that had made *her* so bitter. Was it worth even *trying* to figure out what drove Miriam? Funny, but it would seem they both had two things in common; neither of them had a mother—and they both loved the same man.

Albeit, Miriam's *love* for Nate was one-sided and very misguided, but in her own way, she seemed convinced her *love* for him was genuine. If Lavinia didn't know any better, she'd think Miriam's love was misdirected—almost like an attachment to fill a void in her life. Mourning the loss of a first love, perhaps, or even the loss of her unknown birth-mother. Whatever it was, it would seem as if the void in Miriam's life had caused her to have an unhealthy attachment to Nate.

It didn't matter what Lavinia thought. Miriam's life was her own. If only Lavinia could find a way to keep Miriam from taking out her unhappiness onto her and using that to try to destroy Lavinia's chance for a future with Nate. Lavinia truly loved Nate—unconditionally.

Sadly, it would seem Miriam had not learned to love that way. Her love was self-seeking and very conditional. Lavinia hadn't missed Miriam's change in attitude as soon as Nate rejected her. Suddenly, it seemed, she felt Nate *owed* her something—something she was *not* entitled to. And for that, she would punish him by forcing him to marry her.

Bethany poked her head in the bedroom door and scowled as she eyed the open suitcase spread across the bed. "What are you doing? You can't leave me here with *Daed!*"

"*Ach,* you don't need me anymore. No one needs me. No one *wants* me!"

126

Lavinia released a strangled sob.

Bethany crossed the room slowly, offering her sister comfort with a limp embrace. "I'm certain he loves you."

Lavinia knew her sister was referring to Nate and not her father. Normally, it would have been a comforting thought, but she feared it was too late to matter whether he loved her or not. Their love for each other would not be enough to prevent Miriam from working her best lies to keep them apart. But did she really have that power? As long as neither of them stood up to her, Miriam held all the control. Lavinia knew she wasn't strong enough to stand up against a woman as mean-spirited as Miriam, and Nate seemed to believe that keeping quiet would solve everything.

Did Lavinia have enough faith to wait this out and hope that *Gott* would intervene? It would seem she had no other choice.

"Have faith," Bethany said as if she could read Lavinia's thoughts. "You and Nate were brought together by *Gott,* and He will not let you be torn apart simply because this woman chooses to tell her lies to everyone who will listen. Sooner or later she will be found out for the spiteful, jealous liar she is, and then the Bishop will run her out of this community, and we will be rid of her for sure and for certain!"

"*Denki,* little *schweschder.*"

"*Ach,* it's the least I can do after I left you to be ambushed by *Daed.* I'm sorry about that. I heard what you

127

said to him about Daniel. You're not the only one competing against our deceased *bruder* for *Daed's* attention."

"*Ach,* little *schweschder,* I had no idea you felt the same way."

Bethany reached into Lavinia's suitcase and fingered the material of a blue dress she'd never seen before.

"What is this?"

Lavinia sighed. "I made this dress after Daniel died. I'd promised him I would marry someday, and sewing this dress helped me to mourn for him—as a way of keeping that promise. I had no idea I would ever really get married, and I certainly never thought I would meet someone as *wunderbaar* as Nate. But now—well unless *Gott* fixes this, I won't have any use for this dress."

"Then why do you have it packed?"

Lavinia giggled. "Just in case! Besides, if we are never coming back here, I don't want to leave it here because it reminds me of Daniel."

Bethany pulled her dresses off the pegs on the far wall of the bedroom they shared and stuffed them into Lavinia's suitcase without saying a word. There were four other bedrooms in the *haus,* but they had always preferred to share. It was the largest bedroom in the old farmhouse, and they had shared it since Bethany's second birthday. Her crib still sat in the corner of the room where their mother had placed it all those years ago.

To this day, Lavinia kept it dusted and the linens would get washed every few months to keep them fresh. There had never been a reason to move it. Their mother had put it there, and they had been content to leave it as a remembrance of her.

Now, it seemed, they would be leaving the crib and their mother behind, once and for all. It was too late to change their minds. They would leave their father and his bitterness behind them and start a new life.

CHAPTER 17

"Do you suppose Bess will take me in, too?"

"*Jah,* but together we will have to work for one salary."

Lavinia smoothed stray blond hairs from Bethany's cheek before she rang the bell at the front desk in the lobby of the B&B. The wide hallway of the one-hundred-year-old home boasted a wooden staircase that opened up to the floor above, and several sets of French doors opening to the parlor and formal living and dining rooms. The hardwood floors were worn with age, but still very shiny, and the area rugs were all freshly swept clean. Wood panels, thick with several years of paint, decorated the lower portion of the walls, and curved around the corner wall that led to a private room. It was the only main-level bedroom, and it was set aside as the proprietor's private quarters. This was indeed a grand old *haus* with a welcoming porch that stretched the length of the home and wrapped around on both ends. Lavinia could feel at home here, couldn't she?

"Why do we have to share a salary?" Bethany asked, interrupting Lavinia's reverie.

"She only needs *one* employee to cook and clean the rooms."

Bethany looked around at the expanse of the entry-hall. "For this place? This place has eleven bedrooms and more bathrooms than that! It's the biggest *haus* in this county. It would take a staff of at least seven to run this place properly."

"Bess and Jessup do a lot of the work, and Silvia works hard for this place. Her *schweschder,* Susie will be staying on and working with us if Bess gives us the job, so don't worry about how much work there will be. Whatever it is, we will do it together."

"But for *one* salary?"

"I will do the cooking and you can serve, but we will do the cleaning together. I'm certain she won't object to us sharing a room."

It was too late to turn back now. They stood in the lobby, suitcase in hand, prepared to work and live away from their father once and for all. Lavinia was determined not to let her father or Nate be the downfall of her state of happiness. She would have faith that her life would work out according to *Gott's* plan.

Bess strolled in though the swinging door of the kitchen, towel-drying her hands. She was getting on in years, and her hard work was beginning to show in the deep creases of her forehead that glistened with perspiration. She let her gaze fall to the suitcase in Lavinia's hand and looked at her curiously. "I thought you said you couldn't take the job? But even so, you remember it doesn't start until next month when Silvia gets married."

Lavinia swallowed down the lump forming quickly in her throat. She didn't want Bess to know her business with her *daed,* but she'd neglected to rehearse what reason she would give the older woman for why she was accepting the job. She *had* forgotten the job didn't start for another month. She didn't have the means to pay room-and-board for two for an entire month before the job became available.

"Perhaps…I made a hasty…decision in coming here," Lavinia stuttered.

She turned to leave, but Bethany caught her by the arm. "We will be needing a room then."

Bess paused to study the two girls standing before her. It was obvious to her they were in need for some reason or another, and it was evident they had no intention of sharing that information just yet. But needy they were, and being neighbors, she would help them as long as she could.

"Since Silvia seems busy lately with wedding plans, it seems I'm spending more time in the kitchen than I want to in order to pick up the slack. If you two can fill in for me, I'll give you a room in exchange for your help. But *only* on the condition that I don't have a reservation for the room. If I get full-up, you'll have to start paying for the room to hold it from a paying customer."

"Nee," Lavinia began.

"We'll take it," Bethany interrupted her.

Bess pulled a key-ring out of the desk drawer and reluctantly handed it to Bethany while Lavinia stood there in shock. "Are you sure this is what you want to do, Lavinia?"

She nodded automatically and took the key.

CHAPTER 18

Nate winced every time Adam's buggy hit a rut in the country road between his cousin's farm and Lavinia's. The sun was barely up, and the birds hadn't even begun their morning rituals yet, but Nate knew Lavinia would be up working hard the way she did.

Though he was still in a lot of pain, Nate was eager to see her and just didn't want to wait another minute. After the way he'd left things with her the day before when Miriam had made her scene, he felt he had to give her an explanation. He knew he'd be lucky if Lavinia agreed to listen to him, especially given the grave news he had to share with her. Unfortunately, he felt he owed her the truth of his possible fate before she heard it from someone else—namely, Miriam.

His introduction to the community Bishop had been grueling, to say the least. After hearing Miriam's *confession,* the Bishop had informed him if the girl's story didn't clear

134

him, he'd be forced to marry her or be shunned. He'd taken the classes for baptism already, and had agreed to take the baptism tomorrow, and then the wedding would take place right after. The *only* reason Nate agreed to take the baptism was because he hoped it would afford him the opportunity to marry Lavinia. He had *no* intention on marrying Miriam, even if meant he would be shunned. But Lavinia didn't know that yet, so he hoped she would give him the chance to explain.

"Are you sure you want to do this?" Adam asked him.

"*Jah,* I'm sure."

"Sounds like you have doubts. If you do, let me know before we pull into her driveway. Her *daed* is not the easiest person to get along with."

Nate chuckled. "I met him yesterday, remember? But I'm not going to see her *daed*—this time!"

Adam slowed his horse before turning into Lavinia's driveway. "You really think you're going to get out of this with Miriam so you can marry Lavinia?"

Nate nodded confidently. "I have faith that the truth will set me free."

Adam turned the horse into the driveway, but let him stroll down the lane, hoping the gentle clip-clop of his hooves would not alert Lavinia's father of their visit. They managed to reach the house, without being seen by anyone, but it looked as though no one was even home. With Adam's assistance, Nate slipped from the buggy and went to the kitchen door.

He knocked three times, but there was no answer. He turned around to get advice from his cousin, when Lavinia's father came toward him from the barn.

"She isn't here," her father said gruffly.

Wearing his Amish attire this time, Nate tipped his hat politely. "When do you expect her return?"

The man walked past without looking up.

"Don't know where she is," he said over his shoulder. "*Mei dochders* both packed their things yesterday and left home. I don't know where they are and I don't expect them back. I suppose you've put ideas in their heads about living among the *Englisch*. You had *no* right to come here and upset *mei familye* life the way you did. Go back to your own community and leave me alone. You've done enough damage here."

Nate turned around to face him. "If you're *dochders* left home, it might be because *you* have made them think you don't love them anymore, and Lavinia believes you blame her for her *bruder's* death. You need to forgive her—for her sake *and* yours."

Adam assisted Nate back into the buggy and then climbed in beside him. They looked one last time at Lavinia's father to give some sort of answer, but he just stared at them.

"Just so you know," Nate said. "I love Lavinia and would like to marry her. I have no intention of marrying that liar, Miriam!"

The man ignored them and walked in through the kitchen door and closed it behind him.

"That is one bitter *mann,*" Adam said as he clicked to the horse to set the buggy in the direction of home.

A deep concern set in Nate's thoughts. Where could they have gone?

ঔ৶৹

Lavinia dressed quickly after nudging Bethany to get up. Even though they'd gone to sleep too early, and had even missed out on the evening meal at the B&B, they needed to get up and start earning their keep. They should have helped to serve the guests the meal last night and helped to clean up, but they'd both been so overwhelmed from the dramatic events that took place yesterday, it's no wonder they slept for more than ten hours.

Lavinia pinned her apron and once again nudged at Bethany. "Get up. If we don't start working, we're going to have to start paying for this room."

Bethany stuffed the pillow over her head. "I don't care. I have money."

Lavinia snatched the pillow off her head.

"Where did you get money?"

She sat up sleepily and grabbed at the pillow, but Lavinia pulled it out of her reach.

"I'm not always out running around with boys like you think. I babysit for the Anderson *kinner.*"

Lavinia turned up her nose. "*Ach,* the ones that are always throwing rocks?"

"*Jah,* their poor *mamm* needs a break from them a lot since her husband is always working. Sometimes, she just likes to go get groceries by herself because they throw cans in the aisles and stuff like that. Plus, I sometimes help her do the wash."

Lavinia shook her head. "You do the wash at *her haus,* but you won't help me with it?"

"She has an automatic washer! You *know* how much I despise hanging clothes on the line."

Lavinia rolled her eyes. "They have one here, too, so you should be right at home with no excuses to do the wash."

Bethany pulled a paper bag out from under her pillow and dumped out the cash. "But she pays me *gut!*"

Lavinia dropped to the bed beside Bethany and ran her hand through the stack of bills. "This is a lot of money! What were you planning on doing with that?"

Bethany frowned as she stuffed the money back into the bag. "It's over five thousand dollars, and I was thinking about buying a car."

Lavinia giggled. "I always wanted to know what it was like to drive a car, but I never had the guts to do anything about it. If you want to spend your money on a car, I think that is a fine use of it. You obviously worked hard taking care of those out-of-control *kinner.* For that alone, you deserve something nice."

They both laughed. It was freeing to be able to laugh and share such things without having to look over their shoulder to be certain they were not overheard by their father—or worse yet—disturbing him in any way.

Bethany dragged herself from the bed and pulled her brown dress from the small closet in the corner of the room.

Fastening her *kapp,* Lavinia sighed as she looked in the mirror. She wished she could see herself the way Nate had claimed to see her. But none of that mattered anymore. This was her life now unless a miracle brought Nate back to her.

"I'll meet you downstairs in the kitchen," she said over her shoulder to Bethany. "Hurry!"

Bethany pulled her apron over her head. "I'll be there right behind you."

Lavinia closed the door and went down the service stairs to the kitchen. Silvia had already gathered the eggs and Jessup walked in just then with the morning milking, and exited without so much as a nod. For as primitive as they presented, they did use some modern conveniences that Lavinia noted. She'd never had an occasion to be in the kitchen before, and she was happy to see they had a large, industrial sink for washing dishes. They also had a nine-burner gas stove and a large refrigerator and freezer. She assumed they would have to in order to keep up with health codes, but Lavinia knew it would make things easier when it came to getting Bethany to do her fair share of the workload.

"Bethany will be down in just a few minutes," Lavinia said. "Where would you like me to start?"

Silvia looked up from kneading dough on the large, stainless steel island in the center of the kitchen.

"We don't usually start cooking until seven because guests like to sleep in a little. We have four guests—no, five. We just got in a young woman last night. She showed up in time to join us for the evening meal. A real pretty young woman from Ohio. She's getting married tomorrow—here. Bess agreed to hold the wedding at the last minute, so we have a lot of work to do to prepare for this wedding. We've never done a wedding on such short notice, but she only agreed to do it since we have you and Bethany for extra help now."

Lavinia's heart sank to her feet and she felt the blood draining from her face. Was it possible there was another beautiful woman in town from Ohio that was getting married tomorrow? She prayed it wasn't Miriam, because that would mean she was marrying Nate—*her* Nate.

Silvia went about her chores as if Lavinia wasn't even there. Carrying a stack of plates to the dining room, she nearly ran into Bethany as she entered through the swinging door.

Bethany entered the kitchen and rushed to Lavinia's side. "*Schweschder,* are you alright? You look as if you're about to pass out."

"Miriam is here!" she whispered to Bethany.

"*Ach,* are you sure?"

"*Jah,*" she said, tears filling her eyes. "And she is to be married tomorrow—to Nate."

"Do you really suppose she was able to convince the Bishop of her lies?"

"It would seem so. What am I going to do?"

Bethany handed her a napkin to wipe her face.

"We aren't going to do anything until we know for sure and for certain. And when we know, we will figure it out then."

"But *we* have to help with the preparations for her wedding because she's having it *here* and we work here now! I don't want to attend that wedding, much less be a *servant* for it.*"

If we must, that is what we will do," Bethany said sternly. "For now, you need to pull yourself together so I don't have to spend *mei* car money keeping a roof over our heads."

Lavinia swallowed hard the lump in her throat and wiped her face before Silvia returned and saw her in that state. Bethany was right. They had a job to do, and she would not jump to conclusions. She would trust that *Gott* would answer her prayer about Nate.

CHAPTER 19

Lavinia's fingers felt stiff from plucking all the feathers from the chickens to prepare for tomorrow's wedding. Perspiration rolled from the end of her nose and she swiped at it with her shoulder. Though it was a chilly morning, the blanching pot Jessup had set up over the fire-pit in the yard was making her too warm.

Her hands were raw from the blanching pot, and the laborious task of plucking some of the younger hens that had been selected because they were covered in pinfeathers, and those were not the easiest to remove.

Gott, please help me to do this task with a merry heart—even if it is for Miriam and Nate.

It was almost eight o'clock, and the guests would be expecting breakfast to be served any minute. It would be then that Lavinia would find out once and for all if Miriam was indeed the guest bride. She quickly let Jessup know she was finished blanching the first batch of chickens so he would gut them. She was grateful he'd agreed to do that task for her. It wasn't like she hadn't done it before for her own *familye,* but there would be more than thirty chickens to prepare for the wedding, and that was too much for her to handle on her own. The blanching and plucking alone would take another couple of hours. She'd already spent two hours preparing the first ten.

Brushing the loose feathers from the front of her, Lavinia went in through the service door to the kitchen to wash up in preparation for serving the morning meal. She hoped Bethany had fared well with working alongside Silvia in preparing the food. Cooking was *not* her sister's strong-suit, but Lavinia knew it would easier for Bethany than what *she'd* spent the morning doing. Bethany had never plucked a chicken—ever. So, Lavinia decided the best place for her sister would be the kitchen, knowing Silvia would have enough patience to give the instruction Bethany needed.

When Lavinia finished washing up, she could hear the guests gathering in the dining room. Bethany picked up the platter of various muffins and a pitcher of milk, while Lavinia hoisted a tray with three kinds of juice and several stemmed glasses, and together they took a deep breath to prepare for what they would find beyond the swinging door that led to the formal dining room.

"It's show-time," Bethany whispered just before Silvia walked in ahead of them carrying a large tray full of scrambled eggs, sausage and bacon.

Lavinia struggled to balance the tray she carried when her gaze focused on Miriam sitting at one end of the large dining room table. Almost immediately, Miriam flashed a look of disgust toward Lavinia, making her feel even more uncomfortable than she ever thought she could. She had nothing to be ashamed of. She was putting in an honest day's work. So why did Miriam's presence make her feel so unsure of herself?

Certainly, Miriam's over-confident demeanor was part of what made up her aggressive nature. Lavinia had already learned that Miriam had a way of *forcing* her way on people, and if they didn't do exactly what she wanted them to do, a punishment was sure to follow. Lavinia had already unintentionally crossed paths with the woman, and Miriam's very presence shook her confidence.

Miriam pinched the end of her nose dramatically when Lavinia stood near her to place the stemware and juice in front of her. "You smell like dead chickens. You're causing me to lose my appetite, and I must keep up my strength. After all, tomorrow is my wedding day, and I wouldn't want to have a bad wedding night with Nate."

Lavinia blew out an angry breath as she finished placing the stemware around the table, finding it very difficult to ignore Miriam's comment about spending her wedding night with the man *she* loved. Lavinia quickly exited the room, waiting until she reached the safety of the kitchen before she let out a strangled cry.

Gott, please don't let Miriam force Nate to marry her, she cried out. *I love him and I really believe you have blessed me to be his fraa. I pray that Miriam's lies will be found out in time. Help me to have faith.*

Bethany and Silvia trailed into the kitchen just then and rushed to her side.

"Why did you let her talk to you that way?"

Lavinia sniffled. "Because she is a guest here, and I am nothing but a servant. This is *mei* life now. I work here, and will for probably the rest of *mei* spinster life, unless *Gott* sees fit to change this situation around."

Lavinia sobbed even harder while Bethany filled Silvia in on what had happened. Pulling the end of her apron to her face to wipe it, Lavinia choked a little. She did smell bad. Miriam was right about that.

"That snooty girl doesn't have the final word," Bethany said. "*Gott* does."

"Miriam can't take something away from you that *Gott* has blessed you with," Silvia offered. "Have faith that *you* will be the one to marry Nate if it be *Gott's Wille.*"

"How am I going to get through that wedding tomorrow when *mei* heart is breaking?" Lavinia sobbed.

"This isn't over until the Bishop declares them as wed, so don't give up hope, dear *schweschder.*"

Lavinia stood up and wiped her face, and then crossed to the back end of the kitchen and took a clean service apron

146

from the pantry closet. "You're right. I'm not going to let her win. Her lies will *not* get between me and the man I love, no matter how many people she has listening to her lies. The truth will set Nate free from that evil woman!"

Bethany smiled. "I believe I'm starting to rub off on you a little bit, big *schweschder!*"

"*Ach,* I believe you're right," Lavinia agreed.

She wiped her remaining tears, and all three went back out to the dining room to finish serving, presenting a united front against Miriam's trickery.

CHAPTER 20

Lavinia shook as she prepared food for the wedding that was to take place in less than an hour. She hadn't slept more than twenty minutes all night, tossing and turning so much Bethany had gotten after her for not having more faith. It wasn't that she lacked faith in *Gott* to fix the situation, she lacked the confidence that the humans involved would not use their free will to create a different plan from *Gott's.*

She'd prayed for wisdom for the Bishop, and for Miriam to suddenly grow a conscience. She didn't have much faith in the latter. What she did have faith in was her love for Nate, and his love for her.

Love never fails, she kept telling herself.

As she finished working on the last of the celery casseroles, she wondered what had become of Bethany. She hadn't seen her in some time, and she'd made the excuse of putting the table cloths on all the tables at least twenty minutes ago. If her sister had run off and given up on this job already,

Lavinia was going to have a tough time supporting the two of them.

A high-pitched scream interrupted Lavinia's reverie. It sounded like Miriam. Several screams, accompanied by stomping down the front stairwell alerted the entire house that Miriam was upset about something. Lavinia exited the kitchen door to see what all the commotion was, when an angry Miriam ran into her.

She held up a dirty, blue dress and shook it in Lavinia's face. "Look what your sister did to my dress! I caught her putting chicken guts on my wedding dress!"

Lavinia looked beyond Miriam at Bethany who had strolled in behind Miriam, wearing an obvious look of satisfaction on her face.

"Tell her Miriam, why it is that you conveniently have that wedding dress with you! Tell *mei schweschder* how you planned this whole thing, and how you lied to force Nate to marry you."

"I will tell her no such thing! I only said that because I caught you trying to sabotage my dress. Well, naturally I went along with you because I didn't want you soiling my wedding dress," Miriam stuttered. "Now what am I supposed to get married in?"

Bethany stuck her tongue out at Miriam. "It doesn't matter because Nate isn't even going to show up. He doesn't want to marry you, he wants to marry Lavinia!"

149

Miriam stormed off in a fitful cry. "You'll be sorry—both of you!"

When she was out of earshot, Lavinia reprimanded Bethany for doing something so spiteful and childish.

"You're just a pushover," Bethany muttered.

"*Nee,* but *Gott* commands us not to repay evil with evil."

"*Jah,* you're right. Let's go finish preparing the food for her wedding so she can kick us some more."

"Honestly, Bethany, I don't know where you get your attitude from. Vengeance is for the Lord, not for us."

Bethany sighed. "I hate it when you're right."

Lavinia walked into the kitchen with Bethany. She didn't want to prepare the food for Miriam's wedding any more than her sister did, but she wouldn't let her know that. She would always have the attitude of being a mother to her younger sister, and for that reason alone she would suffer through being a *gut* example to her no matter how painful it was for her.

CHAPTER 21

Lavinia looked out the side window at all the benches set up in front of the gazebo. They were nearly all filled. Had the entire community come to witness this wedding? In the back, buggies filled the parking area and they were beginning to line up alongside of the long driveway leading to the *haus*.

Suddenly, her eyes focused on Nate, who was walking up the lane with Adam.

He was dressed for his wedding.

Panic filled Lavinia as reality set in.

He'd shown up.

He was actually going through with it.

Her hand clamped across her mouth as she stifled a sob. She couldn't fall apart. It wasn't over yet. He was a *gut* and honorable *mann*. But was he so honorable that he should go through with marrying a woman simply because she'd tricked him? Most likely it was so, and the sooner she faced it the

151

better off she would be. Like it or not, she had a job to do, and she would need to go in there and tend to the guests with a smile pasted on her face, or she might lose it.

The kitchen door opened just then and in walked her *daed*. "Hello, *dochder*—Lavinia."

Lavinia collapsed into the nearest chair, stunned at her father's presence. But more than that, it was the first time he'd spoken her name since Daniel's funeral.

"I know you're surprised to see me here," he began. "I wanted you to know that I don't blame you for Daniel's—for Daniel's *death.*"

He didn't look her in the eye, and she could tell he was having trouble getting the words out. She felt sorry for him. She loved him. More than that, she felt respect for him for the first time since she was a young girl, too young to realize his selfish ways and how they'd affected her life.

"I also want you to know that I'm sorry for expecting you to take on the chore of being *mamm* to Bethany. I should have married one of the women in the community so you'd have a proper *mamm* again and wouldn't have to raise your *schweschder,* but I loved your *mamm* so much I just couldn't bring myself to marrying another."

"Ach, I understand that."

She really did understand loving someone so much that she couldn't imagine ever loving anyone else. She loved Nate that much.

"The Bishop told me what happened with the young *mann*—*N*ate. I'm sorry for the outcome, but I've prayed things will work out for the two of you."

He'd prayed for her?

Tears rolled down Lavinia's cheeks as she slipped into her *daed's* waiting arms. "I'm sorry I left and took Bethany with me."

"I'd like you both to come home," he said in a loving tone.

He sounded different.

He sounded kind.

He sounded sincere.

"I'd like that too."

Lavinia felt relief wash over her. No matter what happened today, she and Bethany had a place to go home to.

CHAPTER 22

Lavinia couldn't take her eyes off Nate as she peeked out the service door. He looked so handsome. He'd asked to talk to her, but she couldn't bring herself to seeing him except from afar. She knew she'd broken his heart, but her heart was breaking just thinking of him going through with this wedding. Hadn't he been the one to say he wouldn't marry Miriam even if it meant he would be shunned?

What had happened to that declaration?

Surely if he intended not to go through with it he would have left her at the altar. Unfortunately, Nate was not that dishonorable. She prayed he only showed up to give Miriam one last chance to tell the truth.

"We have nothing left to do until it's time to serve the guests—*if* the wedding goes through, so let's go sit at the back and watch."

Lavinia whipped her head around and scowled at Bethany and Silvia. "Are you *narrish?* I'm not watching that *mann* marry that woman!"

Bethany hooked her arm sternly into Lavinia's and yanked her out the kitchen door into the yard. "That *mann* is the *mann* you love, and you will go watch to see if *Gott* has truly blessed you or not."

Lavinia allowed Bethany to pull her along, feeling so numb at this point, she didn't know if she would burst into tears or crumble into a million pieces.

As they walked toward the back of the benches, Miriam exited the side door nearest the gazebo.

"Miriam is wearing your wedding dress, Lavinia!" Bethany shouted.

Several members of the community looked toward the commotion, and Lavinia froze in place. She couldn't move, she couldn't think straight.

"I warned you that you'd be sorry!" Miriam said, contempt dripping from her words. She smiled maliciously. "Now you get to watch me marry the man you love—wearing *your* wedding dress!"

Bethany took an aggressive step toward her, but Lavinia and Silvia held her back.

"You are a miserable, evil person!" Bethany screamed at her.

Miriam smiled even wider. "Perhaps, but I'm about to be Mrs. Nathan Troyer!"

Miriam turned her back to them dramatically and walked to the gazebo where Nate and the Bishop waited for her. She took her place beside Nate and faced the Bishop.

Nate turned to Lavinia as she walked past the gazebo and winked at her.

Lavinia clenched Bethany's arm and smiled widely. "He still loves me, and he has a plan to get himself out of this mess!"

CHAPTER 23

Lavinia sat down on the bench automatically. With Bethany and Silvia on either side of her, she tried not to think and tried not to feel. She feared that if she gave in to her feelings she would break down and fall apart. If Miriam won this, as it appeared she had, then she would need to stay strong lest she lose her mind completely. She tried not to hope too much, tried not to expect too much. Even though Nate had given her the signal that he loved her, there was still the very large obstacle of Miriam's lies that stood between them. She prayed whatever he had planned would work.

Adam and Libby sank down on the bench beside them, and Libby nudged Bethany. "I still don't understand why *mei* cousin is marrying that girl. He doesn't even like her."

Bethany and Libby had been friends since they could crawl, but they hadn't seen each other in the past two days since she and Lavinia had moved into the B&B.

Bethany leaned over Libby and glared at Adam.

"You didn't tell her why Nate's marrying her?"

Adam shrugged.

"When Miriam showed up at *mei* cousin, Amanda's, wedding and got in that big fight with Nate, I knew then how much he hated her," Libby began. "She accused him of leading her on and making her think that he loved her. When he told her he wished he'd never kissed her in the first place, I thought I was going to fall on the ground laughing. She actually thought he loved her after only *one* kiss!"

"She still thinks it," Bethany said. "Except now, she's claiming Nate took advantage of her that night."

"That's not true," Libby said. "After Nate told her to leave him alone, I overhead Miriam on her cell phone talking to some guy asking him to pick her up. I followed her to the end of the road and watched her get into a car with an *Englisher.* She kissed him after she got in, and then they drove off. Miriam never came back to the wedding, and we both stayed over at Nate's *haus* that night."

Bethany grabbed Libby by the arm and yanked her to her feet. "You have to tell the Bishop this and stop the wedding!"

Adam pulled on Libby's arm and forced her back down gently beside him. "Stay here and wait."

Just then, a young man walked up to the gazebo.

"That's him!" Libby whispered. "That's the one she drove off with that night."

"*Ach,* are you sure?" Lavinia asked.

"*Jah,* I'm sure. I couldn't forget that spiky blonde hair of his."

The look of shock on Miriam's face as the young man walked up to her would not soon be forgotten by Lavinia. She watched in shock herself.

"R-Ray," Miriam stammered. "What are you doing here?"

The hurtful look in his eyes was disheartening.

"The real question is—what are *you* doing here?"

"I'm getting married as you can very well see," she said snottily. "How did you know I was here?"

Ray pointed to Nate. "He called me from your cell phone after you left it in his cousin's buggy. He told me how you lied and was forcing him to marry you."

"I didn't lie, and I'm not forcing him."

Ray shook his head. "I really thought you cared about *me*. You cared enough to spend the weekend with me, but not enough to marry me, obviously."

"I *never* spent the weekend with you! We're only friends."

"That's a lie," Libby shouted from the back of the community. "I saw you get in the car with him the night of

159

Amanda's wedding. You kissed him when you got in the car, and you never came back. Nate couldn't have taken advantage of you that night because *mei bruder* and I stayed at his *haus* after the wedding."

Miriam let out a low-pitch growl.

The Bishop then turned to Miriam. "If you intend to remain in the community, you must confess your transgressions."

She growled at Nate. "I have nothing to confess. I'm better than this. I'm an *Englisher!* I don't care if I stay in the community. You're all backward and primitive." She turned back to Nate. "I want my cell phone back. You had *no* right to go through it."

"I had *every* right. Your lies could have kept me from marrying the woman I love—Lavinia."

Miriam growled at Nate again, and then turned to Ray. "Let's go!" she demanded.

"I don't want to go anywhere with you! You're nothing but a liar." He stormed off toward his car, leaving Miriam dumbfounded.

The Bishop came forward and addressed Miriam. "If you will not confess, you must leave."

Miriam stormed into the B&B muttering under her breath that she would rather die than to give a confession just to stay in the community.

After a moment of shocking silence, the Bishop asked Lavinia to come up to the gazebo and take her place next to Nate.

"Members of the community," the Bishop began. "There will not be a wedding taking place between Miriam and Nate, as it appears she has lied about her involvement with him. However, it has come to *mei* attention that Lavinia and Nate have something they wish to confess to everyone."

He flashed Lavinia a knowing smile.

Lavinia looked at Nate. Had he already confessed to the Bishop he'd spent the night with her? They both knew it was innocent, but perhaps he'd neglected to leave that part out to afford the opportunity to marry her.

"Will you marry me?" Nate whispered to her.

"*Jah,* but Miriam took *mei* wedding dress."

"*Ach,* I don't care that you are wearing a maid's uniform. The dress Miriam has on is now tainted and I wouldn't want you to marry me in it. I want to marry you just the way you are."

Happy tears filled Lavinia's eyes as he kissed her gently before addressing the community.

"I must confess that I love this woman and would like her to be *mei fraa.*"

He hadn't told of their night together after all.

He *was* an honorable *mann.*

He loved her and wanted to marry her, and not because the community would force it on him. He would marry her because he loved her.

Are you eager to know what happens next for Miriam?
READ ON TO THE NEXT PAGES...

Amish Brides
of Willow Creek
Book Two: Second Chances

Table of Contents

CHAPTER 1

CHAPTER 2

CHAPTER 3

CHAPTER 4

CHAPTER 5

CHAPTER 6

CHAPTER 7

CHAPTER 8

CHAPTER 9

CHAPTER 10

CHAPTER 11

CHAPTER 12

CHAPTER 13

CHAPTER 14

CHAPTER 15

CHAPTER 16

CHAPTER 17

CHAPTER 18

CHAPTER 19

CHAPTER 20

CHAPTER 21

CHAPTER 22

CHAPTER 23

CHAPTER 24

CHAPTER 25

CHAPTER 26

CHAPTER 27

CHAPTER 28

CHAPTER 29

CHAPTER 30

❧Second Chances☙

CHAPTER 1

"It's gone!"

Bethany tore the quilt off the bed and tossed the pillows onto the floor. She flung items out of the drawers of the antique bureau and threw it all on the floor at her feet.

"What are you looking for?" Lavinia asked.

"Miriam stole *mei* car money."

"Let's not jump to conclusions," Lavinia said trying to calm her frantic sister.

"I'm not jumping to conclusions. I *know* she took it!"

Bethany continued to throw things around the room they'd shared at the B&B, when she came across the empty paper bag the money was in. She wadded it up in a ball and pounded it with her fist. "Miriam warned us we'd be sorry just before she took *your* wedding dress and tried to marry your new husband in it! Now she's stolen *my* money. I had over five thousand dollars in this bag."

"Perhaps you should have given more thought to your actions before tossing chicken guts on her wedding dress," Lavinia reprimanded.

"I only did it to defend *you!*"

"*Ach,* where did that get you? Now she's taken my wedding dress *and* your money."

Bethany tossed the wadded bag onto the bed.

"We need to go after her before she gets on the Greyhound Bus. Adam offered to drive her to the bus station to keep her from ruining your wedding. I'm sure he's gotten her there by now, but we can still catch her if she hasn't gotten on the bus back to Ohio."

"I have a feeling she's not going back to Ohio," Lavinia said calmly. "Especially if she did take your money. For all we know, she may not even be getting on a bus. Hopefully Miriam is long-gone by now whether she has your money or not."

Bethany sank to the edge of the bed. "*Ach,* do you know how long I've been saving that money? I worked so hard for that money, and now it's gone."

Lavinia didn't know how to comfort her distraught sister. She didn't even know how to get that kind of money back. It was more money than she'd probably seen in her lifetime.

"Let's get you home. Nate and I don't want to be out all night running you home."

Bethany sighed. "With you married now, Bess offered me the job here. Now that I am out of money, I think I'll take it. Besides, I'm still not ready to go home. *Daed* may have had a change of heart, but I need to know it's sincere before I commit to going back home."

Lavinia nodded knowingly. "I suppose I don't blame you. If this doesn't work out, you can always fall back on your other idea."

Bethany looked at her curiously. "What idea?"

"Because *Daed* has had a change of heart, perhaps now would be a *gut* time to approach him about *mamm's* bakery. Especially if you don't intend to go back home right away. Talk to him about it now, so that if he gets angry, you won't have to live with him."

They both giggled.

"It's definitely something to think about," Bethany said. "Maybe I should bring it up after you give him the news of his first *grandkinner.*"

Lavinia blushed. "*Ach,* we have only been married less than an hour, and already you have me pregnant? I honestly think I'd like to wait a year to have *mei* first *boppli* because I'd like to spend some time with *mei* new husband first."

Bethany giggled. "Well, I hear it takes about that long to have a *boppli,* so your plan will work out just fine for you!"

Lavinia swatted in the air toward her sister.

"That isn't funny. I meant I wanted to wait at least a year before even getting pregnant."

"*Ach, gut* luck with that!"

Lavinia shook her head. She wasn't going to admit that her sister knew more than she did when it came to men, but she was certainly eager to find out for herself. Lavinia hated to see her younger sister so discouraged, but she had a new husband waiting for her.

"Speaking of which, *mei* new husband is waiting very patiently for us. Are you going or are you staying?"

Bethany let out a breath of defeat. "I suppose I have no choice but to stay. But are you sure you don't want to help me try to find Miriam and *mei* money?"

"I think we should leave all this in *Gott's* hands. If she took that money, *Gott* will find a way to get it back to you."

"I pray that you are right, dear *schweschder,*" Bethany said, blowing out another defeating breath.

CHAPTER 2

Miriam lurched forward, straining desperately to heave panicky gasps of air back into her lungs. Her face stung and her thoughts pulsated in correlation with the pain that engulfed her. Warmth dripped down the side of her face.

Blood.

Her ribcage would not yield to the shallow puffs of air she dragged in. Why couldn't she breathe? She felt wet earth beneath her fingertips, though she didn't comprehend her immediate surroundings. She listened, but all she could hear was the sound of her own cries.

Something floated down whimsically beside her.

Twenty-dollar-bills.

Several of them.

It was the money she'd stolen from Bethany to teach her a lesson. But why were they sailing through the air? Each

170

bill assaulted her, whipping at her like sheets of rain in heavy wind.

What had she done?

Is Gott punishing me?

She clenched the bills, each one she could get her hands on. She scrambled across the ground gathering them with desperation.

Someone touched her shoulder.

Adam.

Her gaze focused on the commotion behind him.

An up-turned buggy, wheel still rolling.

She followed the trail of tire marks on the wet pavement to a small car that had careened off into the ditch.

They'd been hit by a car.

Miriam staggered toward the downed horse.

He lifted his head and struggled to get to his feet.

He was alright, just trapped beneath the harnesses that bound him to the overturned buggy.

Was *she* alright?

Her shoulder hurt. Her face stung. Her head pounded.

She let the money drop to her feet and lifted a hand to her face. She touched her cheek, running her fingers down a laceration the full length of her face. She pulled her hand away, bringing her wet fingers up in front of her to examine them.

Blood.

Lots of it.

"Miriam, you're hurt. Sit down."

It was Adam's voice she heard, but she wasn't comprehending what he was trying to say to her.

Was she hurt? She didn't know.

She guessed it would account for the blood and the pain she felt. Or did she? Her vision was dizzying, and it confused her.

Sirens interrupted her thoughts, if she really had any that made any sense. Looking down at the money swirling about her feet, she bent to pick it up.

She'd lost a shoe.

"I can't find my shoe," she said frantically.

"I'll find it for you," Adam offered. "But first, let the paramedics take a look at you."

People were talking to her, but she didn't want their help. She needed to find her shoe.

And she needed to find the rest of the money so she could return it to Bethany.

She still had Lavinia's wedding dress.

She would never have a use for it.

She would never love again.

Miriam succumbed to the dizziness, then all went black.

CHAPTER 3

Miriam tried to move, but everything ached. She fluttered her heavy lashes.

Someone was talking to her.

"We were unable to give you anything but non-narcotic pain meds because of the pregnancy," a female voice said while holding Miriam's wrist.

Miriam forced her eyes open, focusing on a nurse taking her pulse.

"W-what?" Miriam whispered.

The nurse let her wrist drop gently against the bed and made a note in her chart.

"I said, you might still be in a lot of pain because we can't give you anything stronger than Tylenol for the pain because of your pregnancy. We did an ultrasound and everything is just fine. That little one is tough to survive that accident." The nurse stopped to look at Miriam, who had said nothing. "You're about twelve weeks along. You did know you were pregnant, didn't you?"

Miriam closed her eyes.

She couldn't answer.

She was too ashamed to face the truth she had ignored until now.

She knew she was pregnant.

The test had come up positive.

It was the reason she'd tried to force Nate to marry her. She knew that if she were to marry the father of her child, an *Englisher,* she would lose the family she'd been adopted into. It was the only family she'd ever known, and she feared her actions had caused her to lose them. Without an Amish husband, she would have to leave the community.

It didn't matter now.

She'd already been banned.

She now knew she would not have been able to convince anyone that the child was Nate's. She was too far along. When she'd thought up the crazy plan, she'd had no idea how far along she was. Now, she had no idea what she was going to do with herself or even what she would do with a child. She was just a child, herself—barely twenty, and unwed. Tears ran down her cheeks from her closed eyes, as she listened to the nurse leave the room.

She was all alone.

And that was how she would be—even with a baby to care for. A million thoughts ran through her head. Her own mother had given her away. Had her mother been in the same bad spot she was in? Had her birth-mother made the same mistake she had made? She would have to do the same thing to her child that was done to her—she would have to give the child up to strangers to raise.

She had no other choice.

She couldn't take care of a child without a husband. She had no job and no money. The Amish family that adopted her would not help her care for the child. They would try to force her to marry the father of the child, but when they discovered he was an *Englisher,* that would be the end of her relationship with her family. It didn't matter because Ray would never marry her now that she had hurt him so badly.

She no husband, no job, no roof over her head, no money, and no hope.

Even the money she'd stolen from Bethany was gone—blown away in the streets after the accident. Her intention was just to borrow the money, and she was going to send it back to her after she'd gotten settled into a place and gotten a job. Now it was gone, and not only would she have to find a way to pay back that money, but she would also have to find a way to support herself now that she'd left home.

She could never go back now—she would be shunned if she wasn't already.

Where was she to go?

She needed a place to stay, but there would be no one in this community that would take her in after the Bishop ran her out of the community. Not to mention the fact she was pregnant out of wedlock.

What was she to do?

She couldn't go home to Ohio, and she couldn't stay here in Indiana. She certainly couldn't stay in this hospital too much longer. Sooner or later, even *they* would make her leave.

Tears filled her eyes. She'd made a mess of her life, and now she'd made a mess of the life of an innocent child just as her own mother had. She always told herself she would not grow up to be like the woman who had given her away, but here she was in the same predicament. Her child would suffer from her mistakes, just as she had suffered from her birth-mother's mistakes. It just wasn't fair. Was *Gott* punishing her? Had *Gott* had a reason to punish her own birth mother for the same reason?

Miriam placed her hands over her abdomen and sobbed even harder. "I'm so sorry I did this to you. I was trying to grow up too soon, and now I've made a mess of both our lives. I hope you understand that I can't take care of you. Please forgive me for wrecking your life before it really starts. I hope someday you can forgive me."

She was sobbing so hard she could barely get the words out, but they were too important not to say.

She wondered if her own mother had spoken the same words to *her* before she'd given her up. She would have liked to have known her mother, and especially the reason the woman had let her go. She'd always resented her birth mother for giving her up, and thought of her as a coward who took the easy way out. But she was beginning to understand that perhaps what her birth mother had done was the bravest, most responsible thing she could have done for Miriam.

If Miriam had her way, she would be married, and keeping her child would not be a second thought—it would be an automatic one. One that she wouldn't even have to consider because it would be a given that she would raise her child.

But now—well, now things were different.

She couldn't keep her child—that was the given.

CHAPTER 4

"Miriam, you have a visitor," her nurse said. "Do you feel up to seeing anyone?"

She didn't respond.

She didn't care.

With her back to the door, she continued to stare out the window at the cold, October wind blowing sheets of rain sideways. It was a miserable day to match her miserable mood.

Hearing footsteps, she pulled the bed-sheet over her face, hoping to hide the large bandage that covered her cheek from the corner of her right eye to just below her chin. She'd been told that her face had suffered a tear that had required thirty-seven stitches, and would most likely leave her scarred for life.

On top of everything else, she'd been stripped of the one thing she had always been sure of—her physical beauty. It was what she felt linked her to her birth-mother, from whom she was a mirror likeness. Her adoptive mother had given her a photograph when Miriam was young—before the woman had passed away giving birth to her own child.

Miriam had an older brother, her adoptive parent's natural child. Her adoptive mother had suffered many miscarriages since his birth, and was not supposed to have any more children, but she'd become pregnant again. Thinking she was out of the woods at full-term, she'd suffered unforeseen complications. She and the baby had both perished, leaving Miriam at the age of seven to be raised by her adoptive father and brother who was four years her senior.

Miriam wasn't up for any more pain or heartache. And she certainly wasn't in the mood for anyone to come and gloat over her misfortune. The only people she knew in this town disliked her, and they would certainly ridicule her over her present appearance.

She heard the padding of soft footsteps entering her room.

"Go away," she whispered.

"I was hoping to meet you sooner, and under different circumstances," a kind, female voice said quietly. "But I only just learned you were here in Indiana."

Miriam didn't respond. She assumed the woman would realize she'd walked into the wrong room and leave just as quickly as she'd come in.

"I'm Claudia, Ray's mom. With Ray back in Ohio with his dad, I thought this would give us an opportunity to get to know one another."

Miriam felt her heart make a sudden somersault behind her ribcage. What was Ray's mother doing here, and what did she want with Miriam? Didn't she know she and Ray had broken up?

"How did you know I was here?" Miriam asked the woman without turning around.

"Your friend, Nate called looking for Ray and explained you were here. He thought Ray might want to see you."

My friend, Nate? That's funny! He's never been a friend. If Nate sent word to Ray, then he must know I'm pregnant. She's only here because she knows about the baby.

Humiliation rose in Miriam. The last thing she wanted was for this woman to meddle in her business. It was tough enough on her to sort this out for the best interest of her and the baby. But now, she would have someone trying to influence her decision when her mind was already made up.

"You shouldn't have come. I'm sorry you wasted your time, but I'm giving up the baby and no one is going to make me change my mind. It's what is best for it. I don't know how to be a mother because I never really had one, and I certainly can't support a child—I have no money and no job and nowhere to even go when they kick me out of here."

The woman sat down in the chair beside the bed and placed a gentle hand on Miriam's arm. "I didn't know you were pregnant. I only came here because Ray had told me so much about you. He loves you very much."

"He doesn't love me anymore," Miriam said with a shaky voice. "I hurt him by trying to marry another man. Didn't he tell you what a mess I've made of everything?"

Miriam choked back tears that seemed to want to flow despite every effort she made to stop them. She felt the woman's hand patting her arm gently.

"He told me about that, but I figured you probably had a pretty good reason for doing what you did. Especially since Nate is such a good friend to you still that he would call to let Ray know how you were doing."

"He probably just wanted to humiliate me. He was probably hoping Ray would come and see me at my worst. I've got a huge gash in my face that is going to leave an ugly scar, and I'm knocked up and all alone. What better revenge could Nate find against me than the mess I've made of my own life?"

"When I got pregnant for Ray, I was alone and scared like I'm sure you are right now. I wasn't married to his father, and I was only seventeen years old. My parents tried to make me give him up, but I thought it was best to keep him and raise

182

him myself. I can't say it wasn't tough raising him alone. It certainly would have been easier if his father had married me, but he wasn't in love with me. He wanted another girl. He married her, and they were divorced a year later. But at that time, Ray's father decided to take an active role in his life. Even though we couldn't make it work as a family, we did manage to raise him together. He's better off for it, I think. Ray says so.

He knows I was a young unwed mother and faced with having to give him up for adoption. He says he's glad I kept him, but he also knows it wasn't easy for me. Did I make the right decision? There is really no way of ever knowing that because I don't know if he and I would have been better off if I'd let someone else raise him. Times were tough, but the love was always there. It sounds as if you've made up your mind, but if you should change it, I'd be willing to help you.

My parents didn't support my decision, and they let me do it alone. I believe if I'd had someone to help me through raising a child on my own, it might not have been such a struggle. But I would do it all over again if I had to. Keeping a child and raising it on your own is not an easy decision, and certainly not for one who is weak. It takes a strong person to handle that kind of responsibility."

"I don't think I'm that strong," Miriam muttered under her breath.

"Ray is that strong," she said.

"He doesn't want me in his life. No one does. I'm shunned from the community here, and I will be shunned from my own community if I try to return home. I only wanted to marry Nate because he is Amish and I didn't want to be alone and lose my adopted family. If I married an *Englisher* I would have lost them. But none of that matters now because I've already lost them. I have no family now."

"Since you are carrying my son's child; that makes *us* family," Claudia said in a comforting tone.

Miriam turned slowly in the hospital bed, wincing against the pain that still pounded in her head. Focusing on the woman sitting beside her, she noticed right away that Ray had the same coarse blonde hair, and his eyes were the same greenish-blue. She seemed young, but Miriam supposed that was due to the young age at which she'd had Ray.

Could she trust this woman? She almost didn't have any other choice. Still, she didn't want the woman taking an interest in helping her simply because she didn't want Miriam giving up her son's child for adoption. She couldn't raise a child when she had no idea of where she was even going to live, or how she was going to survive without a job. There would be no help from the community because of the pregnancy; that was for sure and for certain.

CHAPTER 5

Miriam stood in the bathroom of her hospital room staring blankly at her reflection in the mirror. Her eye was blackened, bits of green filling in the curve just under her lashes. Her eye itself was bloodshot, and her vision was a little blurry. Would she lose her eyesight? The doctor hadn't said anything to her about it, but he also hadn't told her how bad she looked either.

Though she wanted to see just how bad the cut on her face was, she reasoned with herself that what she didn't know couldn't hurt her. Once she saw what was under the bandage, there would be no way to take back what she'd seen.

She was already a little freaked out over what she *could* see. It was the part hidden under the bandage that terrified her the most. Her cheek was physically painful, and she figured that was not a good sign.

She continued to stare at the unrecognizable reflection staring back at her. She was never going to be the same in any way—no matter what lay beneath the bandage. Even if she didn't have the cut on her face, she feared what having a baby was going to do to her figure. She'd seen what it had done to several of the girls her age. She wasn't ready for her entire life to change.

Gott, I don't know if I'm ready for this, but I pray that you will give me the strength to get through it. Take away the selfishness and anger I feel right now. Help me to make the right decision for the baby that I'm carrying. And please put forgiveness in the hearts of those I've hurt with my carelessness.

Miriam winced as she lifted trembling fingers to the edge of the bandage that covered most of the right side of her face. She slowly folded down the edge, hoping to see something, but all she saw was more discoloration and bruising. She wiggled her face a little feeling the tug of the stitches that limited movement of the skin. It felt tight and stiff—almost unnatural.

What had they done to her face?

Closing her eyes, she tugged lightly at the bandage, pulling down toward her chin until she'd removed the entire piece of gauze. She was terrified to open her eyes—terrified to the point it was making her nauseous.

But she *had* to see—*had* to know.

No matter how terrible it was, she had to see what had happened to her in that accident. Slowly lifting her gaze, she blurred her vision and looked only in her eyes. She allowed her gaze to drift down her face, not comprehending what she saw.

She pulled a trembling hand to her mouth, shock rendering her speechless.

It was far worse than she'd thought.

She stifled a strangled cry, swallowing hard the reality of her reflection.

I'm hideous!

Thick black stitches pulled the sides of her cheek together, holding her skin so taught it caused her pain.

"Why did they have to use stitches that were so noticeable?" she sobbed.

She could see little holes along the cut where the thick stitching laced her face back together. Were they permanent? What if makeup wouldn't cover the scar? Was she doomed to look like this for the rest of her life? She was too young to have her life so ruined. How was she ever going to feel normal again?

She padded her way back to her bed and slumped down against the hard mattress—not caring about the pain it caused her. She hadn't even bothered to cover her face back up. What was the use in it? She was forever ugly. Might as well get the world used to seeing her now so they could gasp and get it over with.

She was numb with sadness and self-pity.

She was alone and pregnant—and ugly.

A knock to her door startled her. She was not in the mood for another visit from Claudia at the moment.

"Go away," she said sniffling.

"I came to see how you were doing," a male voice said.

Miriam turned halfway around to see who it was.

It was Adam.

He was the *last* person she wanted to see right now.

This was all *his* fault.

Miriam whipped her aching head around and pointed to her stitched-up face. "You want to see how I'm doing? *This* is how I'm doing! I'm scarred for life thanks to you!"

Tears ran down her face, and she winced as they stung her wound. "If you had been paying more attention to the road than to me, then that car wouldn't have hit us."

"I'm sorry. I was only trying to talk to you. I only—"

"I didn't want you to talk to me! I wanted you to leave me alone," she screamed at him.

"I was only trying to help you. I felt bad that you were being run out of the community. I wanted to help you find a way to stay because—"

"Because what?" she interrupted. "Because you thought I was pretty?"

"Well—*jah,*" Adam admitted.

She turned her face more toward him. "I'm not so pretty now, am I?"

"That cut doesn't change how beautiful you are."

"Are you kidding me?" she sobbed. "It changes everything!"

"It doesn't change anything in *my* eyes. But that wasn't the *only* reason I was hoping you would stay. I believe that everyone deserves a second chance."

"A second chance for what? I lied to trick your cousin into marrying me."

"I think I know why you did it," he said cautiously.

She pursed her lips and narrowed her eyes. "And why is that?"

"Because you're pregnant. If you marry an Amish *mann* you can remain in the community. But if you marry the *Englisher,* Ray, who is probably the *daed,* then you would fall under the ban."

"It doesn't matter now," she sobbed. "I've already lost my family."

"You don't have to," Adam offered gingerly.

"When my brother comes to take me back home, he will find out then, and he will return to our community without me."

"What if you stay here instead?"

Miriam flashed him a confused look. "I can't. The Bishop has banned me from this community. It's only a matter of time before my own community is sent word of my actions."

"You can stay here if you are married."

"Nate married Lavinia—or did you forget?"

"I will marry you," Adam said.

"Why would *you* marry me when your cousin refused?"

He hung his head. "I suppose I feel I owe you— because of the accident."

Miriam considered his words carefully. She was facing being homeless and pregnant and scarred for life with no possibility of ever marrying. She was desperate. Marrying Adam might just work. She didn't love him, but he didn't love her either. He was attractive, and a hard worker. There was real possibility there.

Could she go through with such a plan?

She'd been prepared to make the same mistake only two days ago, but she'd done that without even thinking. Now that she'd had time to think about it, she wasn't so certain it was the right thing to do. But the problem still remained of her pregnancy. If she married, she could keep her child *and* her family.

It saddened her to realize that this was what her life had become, but she felt she had no other choice.

Miriam looked up at Adam, tears pooling in her eyes. "Alright, I'll marry you!"

CHAPTER 6

"You must keep this bandage on your wound," the nurse reprimanded Miriam. "If it gets infected, it is more likely to scar."

"What does it matter?" Miriam mumbled. "It's going to be a terrible scar no matter what."

"Infection won't be good for the baby, and neither will the medicine we will have to give you. All that will be harsh on the baby's system. So, let's keep this covered up so we can avoid all of that."

Her nurse was a little short with her, but Miriam knew she was only trying to protect her and the baby. It was hard to think about that right now though. With the decision of marrying Adam weighing on her, she had little room to think of anything else at the moment.

Another knock sounded at the door.

Do people not understand I want to be left alone?

"Good afternoon," came Claudia's cheery voice. "How are you feeling today?"

Miriam looked over at her and grunted her answer.

"That good, huh?"

Miriam couldn't even force a smile, knowing the movement of her face would cause her pain.

"I saw you had company a little bit ago and thought I'd go down to the cafeteria for a cup of coffee until the young man left. But I couldn't help but overhear your conversation. I wasn't trying to eavesdrop, but I kind of did out of concern for you and the baby."

"Well then you already know that I agreed to marry Adam so I could stay in the Amish community."

"I wish I could say I understood what being part of an Amish community means to you, but I don't," Claudia admitted. "But you don't have to make that decision right away."

Miriam shrugged. "I should make it soon because I will begin to show in my pregnancy soon. My brother will be here in a few days and he will know. He will enforce the marriage in my father's absence or he will shun me."

Miriam began to cry all over again.

Claudia patted her gently, offering her a tissue from her purse. "I wanted to offer you another alternative to marrying Adam."

Miriam's ears perked up. She would listen, but she was pretty well determined to marry Adam. Even though she was torn between being Amish and *Englisch,* she feared losing the only family she'd ever known. Just because her birth mother was *Englisch,* did not mean she knew what it was like to be *Englisch.* All she knew was being Amish.

"I'd like to offer you a place to stay while you recover," Claudia began. "I have a guest room that has never been used, and I think you could be very comfortable there for however long you want to stay. I also have a gift shop in town, and I could use some help there once you are back on your feet in a week or so. I can give you a place to stay and a job for as long as you want them."

"What about Adam?" Miriam asked. "He will want to court me until we are married. Won't it be uncomfortable for you to see us together? I will want to court him even while I'm deciding for sure and for certain."

Claudia shook her head. "It won't be a problem for Adam to come *calling* for you. I will do everything I can to make him feel welcome."

Miriam looked at Claudia wondering if there was a *catch* to her offer, but she hadn't mentioned any house-rules for her. Perhaps she should ask if she expected anything of her while she was a guest in her home.

194

"Do you have any rules I should know about so I don't accidentally break any while I'm there?"

Claudia smiled. "You are a grown woman who is about to be a mother. I don't think it's necessary to put any strict rules on you. As long as we respect each other's space, I think we will get along just fine."

"I'm used to rules," Miriam said. "The Ordnung is nothing but rules." She patted her belly. "Obviously, I broke a few of them."

"I'm not here to judge you. I just want to help you and my grandchild to have the best possible outcome."

There it was—the *catch*. She had a vested interest in Miriam because of the child she carried. She prayed she wasn't making a big mistake by agreeing to stay with Claudia. But just like with Adam; right now, she had no other choice.

CHAPTER 7

"Why are you marrying that woman?" Libby asked. "She has done nothing but cause trouble for everyone here."

Adam followed his sister into the chicken coop. He knew what Libby said was right, but he felt obligated to take care of Miriam anyway. His carelessness could have caused the loss of her baby. As it were, the woman would have to live with a scar on her face for the rest of her life. Would she resent him for that? She would see it every day. Would she ever be able to forgive him? Perhaps not, but marrying her might make a difference.

"I owe her for what I did to her."

Libby shook her head with frustration. "It was an accident. You don't owe her anything. She owes Bethany a lot of money though. She is a thief and a liar, and she's hurt your cousin and his new *fraa*. What does Nate even have to say about your decision?"

Adam lowered his head. "I haven't had the nerve to tell him yet."

"*Ach,* that right there should tell you that you shouldn't marry her. Let her marry the *boppli's daed.*"

"I'm marrying her so she can stay in the community."

Libby adjusted the egg basket in her hand, reaching under another hen and feeling for an egg. "That is the wrong reason to marry someone. Don't you want to marry someone you love?"

"I could learn to love her," he said in his defense. "And she could learn to love me. We could have a *gut* marriage if we try."

"She's a selfish woman, *bruder,* don't kid yourself about that. She eagerly agreed to let you marry her for that very reason. She was only thinking of herself. She is what the *Englisch* call an opportunist."

"What do you mean by that?"

"It means she saw an opportunity in you, and she took it. But you handed it right over to her."

Adam felt under one of the hens and pulled out an egg, dropping it in Libby's basket. "She's not as bad as you think she is."

Libby narrowed her gaze on Adam. "Perhaps you should look beyond her pretty face and into her not-so-pretty soul."

Adam placed another egg into the basket. "That is not for you to judge. I think everyone deserves a second chance."

"I'm not convinced Miriam deserves anything from anyone, but you are right. That is not for me to judge. If it means that much to you, I will try to give her some consideration—but only because she is to be your *fraa* soon."

Libby had made her way to the end of the chicken coop and let herself out the door, Adam on her heels. "When is the wedding? Will it be quick and quiet, or will you be having an open wedding with the community?"

Adam hadn't thought that far ahead. His main concern was how his *daed* was going to divide his property so he would have a place to live with Miriam once they were wed. He didn't put much stock in the wedding itself as he did about supporting her and a *boppli* so soon. It wouldn't take but a few days to put up a basic house on the far end of his *daed's* acreage, but he also needed help from the very community that had shunned Miriam to get them started with their new life together. He worried the community would not be so willing to shower them with the usual gifts to set up their house, or food to start them off for the winter that was already on its way.

Adam shouldered out into the cold, November wind. Right on cue, as if the first day of November was required to turn to winter, the wind and icy rain assaulted him as he made his way to the barn for the morning milking.

Normally he spent the morning milking in prayer, but today, he had a lot of thinking to do. Perhaps marrying Miriam was going to be tougher than he originally thought. It was too late to take it back now. He'd made a promise to her, and he was a man of his word. He owed her, and if that meant defending her to a community that rejected her, he'd have to do whatever it took to change their minds about her.

His own parents hadn't been too happy about the idea of him marrying her. He had led them to believe he was the father of the child she carried, which wasn't easy considering Miriam had only just tried to marry his cousin less than a week ago. He didn't enjoy deceiving his family this way, but he felt an obligation to Miriam that they just wouldn't understand.

A cold draft whirling through the barn interrupted Adam's thoughts. Nate walked up to him and stared at him for a moment.

"I ran into Libby on the way in here. Is it true? You're to marry Miriam? After what she did to Lavinia and Bethany and me?"

Adam crouched down on the milking stool in front of Buttercup and began to milk her. "Don't make me defend my decision to you. My mind is already made up."

Nate leaned up against the stall. "I won't put you on the defensive end of my opinions, but I will tell you to be certain you know what you're up against. She's a handful, and if you're not sure about this, she could make your life miserable.

If you change your mind, I'm here. If you go through with it, I'm still here for you."

"I appreciate the show of support. I'm going to need it when the community finds out my plans."

"Have you thought about what you will do if you don't get the support of the Bishop and the community?"

Adam didn't have an answer for his cousin. He had no idea what he would do if pushed by the Bishop to choose between his obligation to Miriam and his commitment to the community. He hadn't thought that his offer of marriage could get him shunned when he'd made the offer to her. He supposed if it came down to it, Miriam would back out if it meant she would not be able to remain in the community. Wouldn't she?

CHAPTER 8

Miriam folded her things neatly and tucked them into the broken suitcase that Adam had salvaged from the wreckage after the accident. With trembling hands, she tucked away her parting instructions from the hospital.

Her parting instructions.

They had just released her and she still hadn't decided if she would accept Claudia's offer to recover at her home. Deep down, she knew she had no other choice. But she wasn't ready to leave the hospital, even though they'd told her repeatedly how lucky she was, and that there was no medical reason to keep her. If mental anguish counted, they'd keep her here forever. But unfortunately, her state of mind seemed to be the only thing preventing her from accepting the final diagnosis.

She'd tried to insist that more tests be run on her to be certain she hadn't suffered anything internal they might have missed. After all, being thrown from a buggy could have caused all sorts of damage to her internal organs. No matter how many questions she asked, and how much she pressed the hospital staff, they didn't agree with her requests for a more in-depth analysis of her complaints.

Now, after a week of being here, she'd gotten used to the busy noises of the hospital that never seemed to quiet. The constant bustle that made her aware that someone was always up watching over her had become comforting. She'd felt safe here—protected. Now, the very thought of having to travel by car to Claudia's house filled her with an uneasiness she just couldn't shake.

Her stomach knotted, she dreaded leaving, but she continued to pack the things they'd given her to take *home* with her. Adam had offered to pick her up, but she was more willing to ride in Claudia's car than in a buggy for now. She wondered if she would ever be able to ride in a buggy again. The thought of it made her shudder.

Right on cue, Claudia appeared in the doorway of her hospital room as if magnetized to Miriam's thoughts. She crossed the room and tucked her into a soft embrace. But for Miriam, who hadn't welcomed the awkward contact, anxiety and a suffocating feeling ensued.

Miriam struggled to escape the unnatural embrace Claudia had drawn her into. This was not normal for her—a mother's solace. There had not been any affection for her—no patience—no love, since her adoptive mother had passed.

It was something she dearly missed.

At her *mamm's* funeral, she'd flung herself across the primitive, pine box where her *mamm* lay all-too-silent, begging her *mamm* not to leave her.

Daed had scooped her up by her middle and dragged her off, balancing her against his side while she'd kicked and screamed like a squealing piglet. The last thing she'd remembered of that day was being tossed in the back of *Daed's* buggy with no one to hold her. The stern look of disapproval over her behavior separated them. There was no comfort for her—only stifled tears. There would be no respite from the pain and solitude that would become her life. It was that day that she'd accepted he wasn't her real father.

Claudia let her go and moved to pick up her suitcase. "Did you hear from your brother?"

"Jah—yes. He is going to be here at the end of the week, but my father is not coming."

Claudia patted Miriam's arm cautiously. "Do they know of your plans to marry *Adam*?"

Miriam nodded. "Benjamin is not as stern as my father, and so he is eager to attend the wedding. I didn't tell him the rest of the story. I figured that was best said in person."

She could tell Claudia wasn't happy with her answer, but she had only agreed to give her decision some added thought.

"Just because I'm marrying Adam does not mean you will not be able to be a part of the baby's life. Adam agreed to allow Ray the liberty of seeing the child."

Claudia didn't look convinced.

"The Amish are a peaceful people. It is what keeps me bound to this life. When I met Ray, I thought I was missing out on something because I never knew my birth-mother, who was an *Englisher*. I thought I wanted to be like her, but now—" she patted her abdomen. "Now that I'm pregnant, I want to change that for my child. I want to raise my child with Amish values."

"I'm trying to understand," Claudia said. "But I think you can raise your child with those values whether you raise it in an English household or an Amish one. The Amish is in your heart, not in your blood."

Miriam hadn't thought of it that way before. She'd spent the remainder of her childhood after her *mamm* died struggling to know where she fit in. Though she admired and craved the Amish lifestyle and values, the *Englisch* blood coursing through her veins seemed to stir up rebellion in her. Because of that, she feared raising her child in an uncontrolled environment away from the rules of the Ordnung.

"I don't want my child to repeat the mistakes I have made. I repeated the same pattern as my birth-mother, but I will not give up my child like she did. I'm certain she did what she thought was best for me, but I want to see what making the other choice will do for *my* child."

"But you were raised in an Amish household, and you still became pregnant out of wedlock. How do you think you can change that for your child?"

Miriam shrugged.

She didn't have an answer that was logical. The thing she feared most was dying when the child was young and leaving it behind to fend for itself the way her own *mamm* had done.

CHAPTER 9

Miriam stood in the doorway of the room in which she'd been welcomed to stay. In her mind, the arrangement was only temporary—until the wedding next week. Miriam was eager to get the wedding over with soon—before she began showing her pregnancy.

Claudia didn't seem to have the same sense of urgency that Miriam had. She still talked of Miriam working in her gift shop downtown, and had even made open plans for a homecoming dinner for Ray tomorrow evening.

Miriam wasn't so certain she was ready to face Ray, but she knew it was inevitable. If she had her way, she'd avoid him indefinitely, but she'd promised his mother that she'd give him the news of the pregnancy, and offer him the option to be a part of the child's life.

It would not be easy for her to stifle her feelings, but she'd convinced herself she was doing what was best for her child. She was confused, and very torn between doing what was right, and what she thought was best for her child. Deciding to be unselfish for a change, she opted to consider the best course of action for the child she carried. And that, she felt, was to remain in the Amish community.

Placing her suitcase on the bed, Miriam picked up a tailor-made, Amish doll tucked in front of the pillows. She turned it over, reading the tag boasting its manufacturer.

Made in China.

Miriam understood that Claudia was only trying to make her feel *at home,* but to her, the doll was nothing short of an insult. It wasn't authentic. It wasn't Amish-made. She sat on the edge of the fancy, store-bought quilt that draped the bed in more insult, and stared at the doll in her hands.

Mamm had taught her how to make dolls when she was only four years old. She and *mamm* had sewn a doll for each of her twelve cousins the Christmas just before she'd died. Miriam pulled at the taught stitching, ripping it without thinking. She looked up, noticing Claudia standing in the doorway, watching her.

"Forgive me," she said holding up the doll. "I didn't mean to rip it. If you have a needle and thread, I'll sew it. Or I can make you an authentic one instead."

"Authentic?" Claudia repeated.

"Made by the Amish."

She showed Claudia the tag in the back.

"This one was made in China. Wouldn't you rather have one made by the Amish?"

Claudia reached for the doll. "I suppose I never thought about where it was made. I sell them in my store, and I've never had anyone complain about it."

Miriam chuckled. "You sell those in your store?"

"Uh-huh, why?"

"Because I could make them for you, and you could make more money selling authentic Amish-made dolls. The material to make these is very inexpensive."

Claudia smiled warmly. "How about if I get you some material, and you can sell them at the store yourself. You can have all the profits from it because they will probably drive in additional business for me if I have *authentic* Amish-made dolls in my store."

"*Danki.* I could use some money with the baby coming. I can't expect Adam to take on all the responsibility. Besides, I owe someone some money."

Claudia looked as if she wanted Miriam to elaborate on her comments, but she wasn't willing to say any more than she already had. She'd already said too much.

She stretched and forced a yawn, hoping the older woman would get the hint.

Thankfully she did.

"I'll leave you to get settled in. Let me know if you need anything. Otherwise, I'll check in on you after a little while."

She shot her an awkward smile and exited the room.

Miriam knew she'd hurt her feelings, but she needed some alone-time if she was going to rehearse what she would say to Ray when she saw him tomorrow at dinner. Her stomach roiled at the thought of it, but it was a necessary meeting.

How had her life suddenly become so complicated?

In the course of one summer, she'd managed to compromise her virtue, become pregnant, and ended the season by becoming scarred for life. In retrospect, all of it had scarred her for life—not just the physical cut down her face. Her life was never going to be the same.

She wondered if she could ever love Adam the way she loved Ray. She was so numb from all the physical and emotional pain of the last couple of months, it was a wonder she could even think at all.

Her thoughts wandered to the first time she'd met Ray. He was so handsome, and Miriam was immediately smitten with him. He'd been so kind and understanding, she couldn't help but fall for him. No one in the Amish community had understood her except her *mamm*.

But Ray understood her.

He understood the pain she'd suffered when she'd lost her *mamm*. He even understood her need to find her birth mother. He'd been such a good listener, he'd nearly made her forget her troubles. And when he held her—that was when she'd forgotten everything, including her morals.

Ray had a way of helping her to understand herself. She trusted him. In fact, she'd trusted him with her innermost secrets. Things she'd never told anyone. Not because it was too secret to tell, but because until she'd met Ray, she'd had no real friends. She'd always had plenty of cousins around, but she could never tell them anything she didn't want to get back to *Daed* in some way or another.

Ray had been an exception. He had been more than a boyfriend. He had been a true friend to her.

She blew out a heavy sigh.

How was she going to live without him?

She hadn't thought that far ahead.

Hadn't thought about it even when she'd risked everything to try to trick Nate into marrying her.

Now that she'd agreed to marry Adam, she would lose Ray all over again, and it hurt more than she ever thought it could.

CHAPTER 10

Miriam trembled when she heard Ray's truck pull into his mother's driveway. Panicking, she crossed the room to the mirror above the long dresser and stared at her reflection. The bandage almost looked worse than the wound it covered. He would certainly find her as hideous as she found herself to be.

Why had she agreed to this meeting so soon?

She needed more time—more time to heal from the accident. Surely, he would understand she just got out of the hospital, wouldn't he? She moved closer to the mirror, examining the bruises that still surrounded her eye. Though the doctor had removed the stitches because the surgical glue had held the wound closed, the bruising and redness had not gone away, and the swelling remained. She knew she didn't want Ray to see the wound on her face until it was healed enough that she could pack a heavy layer of makeup over it.

For now, she would have to face him with the bandage on.

From the other room, she could hear muffled voices, and she worried Claudia would tell her son everything before Miriam had a chance to explain. But perhaps it would be easier for her if Claudia paved the way for her—smoothed out some of the lies she'd told. No, that wasn't fair to Claudia, who'd been just as kind to her as her son had always been.

Miriam wished she could turn back time.

Wished she'd never gotten in that buggy with Adam.

In truth, her mistakes had begun when she'd gone after Nate in a state of panic. If she'd have talked to Ray first, instead of thinking her only choice was to marry an Amish man, she might not be having to face him now in the state she was in.

Thinking back on her hasty decisions, if she'd had a trusted friend who would have sat with her while she'd waited for the results of the pregnancy test, she might not have acted out of panic. Ray was the closest thing she had to a friend. He probably would have sat there with her and waited. He would have understood. But now, he wasn't going to understand, or even concern himself with her feelings. He'd said as much when he'd caught her trying to marry Nate.

Once again, there would be no compassion for Miriam. No love. And no understanding.

She swallowed down a strangled cry as she looked into her own eyes.

Eyes that had deceived.

Eyes that had betrayed.

Eyes filled with remorse.

Unfortunately, there would also be no mercy for her now. She would have to face the consequence of her sins, and she would have to face them alone.

****

A light knock sounded at Miriam's door.

She pushed at the tears that dampened her eyes and crossed to the bed. Ducking into the quilt, she pulled it over her, hoping she could convince Ray she was sleeping and he would leave her alone. Perhaps his mother had told him everything and she would never have to face him.

But that wasn't fair.

To him—or to the baby.

She had to stop thinking of herself.

Ray would certainly reject Miriam, but he wasn't the type of man to reject his own child. There was no future for her with him, but he had a future with his child, and she owed him that much.

I need to grow up, she chided herself. *I'm about to become a mamm, and I need to put this wee one first.*

She wiped her face of the evidence of defeat and pulled the covers down from her head. She sat up in the bed and breathed in deep. Ready or not, she would face Ray and get it over with.

Gott, give me strength. Put forgiveness in his heart for me, and let him accept his child.

"The door is open," Miriam said with a shaky voice.

The door opened slowly, and Ray poked his head in cautiously. When his gaze fell upon her, he rushed to the bed and sat beside her, pulling her close to him.

"I'm so glad you're okay. If I'd known you were in the hospital, I'd have come to see you sooner. I only just learned of the accident a few minutes ago."

He held her out to look at her.

She was too shocked to say anything.

He pulled her back against his shoulder.

"I know I told you I never wanted to see you again, but I didn't mean it like *that*. Please forgive me for being so harsh. Don't be angry with my mother, but she also told me about the baby, and the reason you were going to marry Nate in the first place. But what I don't understand is why you would agree to marry another Amish man instead of trusting *me* to take care of you and our baby."

Miriam couldn't answer him.

She was too busy enjoying the feel of Ray's arms around her. Oh, how she loved him—still. She'd been fooling herself all this time. She couldn't go through with marrying Adam without it crushing her. She could never love Adam—she loved Ray, and would never stop. Miriam knew if she married Adam, she would forever mourn the loss of this man, whose arms she could never fall into again—not for as long as she lived.

Miriam began to cry.

Ray held her closer, stroking her hair the way he used to when she'd talk to him about missing her *mamm.* It made her feel comforted, loved, but most of all, it made her feel safe.

Why did Ray have to be so wonderful?

"I still love you, Miriam. I don't want you to marry Adam. I want you to marry *me.*"

Miriam choked on her tears and hiccupped.

"Don't do this, Ray. Don't make me choose between love and responsibility to my child."

Miriam pushed away from him, realizing there was one thing Ray would never understand about her. She was Amish, and he was *Englisch,* and it would forever separate them.

CHAPTER 11

Miriam selfishly allowed Ray to hold her for some minutes before she could bring herself letting him go. She would have to tuck her feelings for him away in her heart, only to bring them out when she was most in danger of making another bad decision.

Telling herself she could only allot a portion of his love to come through for the sake of their child, was her way of dealing with the loss she would suffer. It was something she would endure for the benefit of the baby so that he or she would not have to grieve the losses she did. Miriam wished she didn't have to make such sacrifice, but she would do it for her child. She would make certain this child had the best of both worlds, no matter what it cost *her*.

Ray lifted her chin to look at her. This made her feel uncomfortable and awkward.

"I'd like to see what happened to you, Miriam. Will you remove the bandage?"

The request caught her off guard. She didn't want him to see. She didn't want anyone to see. Wasn't the humiliation of this moment bad enough without adding rejection when he looked upon her face that would forever be disfigured?

Her reluctance did not go unnoticed.

He lifted the back of his hand and stroked her other cheek, warming her skin. "I love you, Miriam, and I don't want any more secrets between us."

What did he mean by that?

He kissed her forehead ever so gently. He was the kindest man she'd ever met, and here she was rejecting *him*. He wasn't rejecting her! What was she thinking? Was it possible that she could trust this man with more than she originally thought?

She, herself, had no idea what was under the bandage at this point. She hadn't seen it for several days—the day the doctor pulled the stitches out. It was so red and puffy. She was so discouraged by her appearance that she'd let the nurses change the dressing daily, while she waited impatiently for them to cover it back up. Though a small part of her was curious, a bigger part of her didn't care if she ever looked into another mirror and looked back at the reflection.

Resorting to remaining Amish would afford her the opportunity to hide behind a mirror-less society, and she hoped in time she would forget what her own reflection looked like. After some initial shock, the community would get used to seeing the scar on her face, and she would live among a people who would never tease her for her appearance. In the *Englisch* world, she could never hide such a flawed appearance.

Giving in to Ray's gentle curiosity, Miriam tugged at the top of the bandage, peeling it slowly down her face. The white, papery tape pulled at the baby-fine hairs on her cheek, but remarkably, the wound was not as painful as it was. It had been ten days since the accident, and even her nurse had remarked at the significant healing that had taken place in such a short time. Perhaps she would be lucky, and it had miraculously healed and there would be no scar for Ray to witness.

It was a stretch, she knew.

But hope, she did.

With her wound and her dignity now exposed, Ray looked upon her with more love in his eyes than she'd ever seen in them. He tucked her close to him and kissed the side of her face near her ear.

"I still love you, Miriam. And I still want to marry you. Having a line down your face does not change things in my heart. If nothing else, it puts us more on an even playing field."

She lifted her head from his chest. "What do you mean by that?"

"I still think you're just as beautiful, but now you have been humbled by God, and you aren't so full of yourself. You used to intimidate me because you acted as if you were too good for me because of your physical beauty. You're still just as beautiful in my eyes, but actually more beautiful, because God has removed the pride in you that always stood between us."

Did he just say I was more beautiful?

"*Ach,* you're confusing me."

"You don't need to hide behind the Amish community for someone to love you. If you want to live in an old farmhouse with no mirrors, then that is how we will live, if it means you will accept that my love for you has *nothing* to do with how you look on the outside. I've seen what is in your heart. You've shown that part of you to me—the part you keep hidden from everyone else. You can stay in the Amish community and hide your face, but you could never hide what is in your heart—not from me."

It was as if he was looking into her very soul and plucking out her pride and tossing it aside. He was right. She had been very prideful, using her outer beauty to get what she wanted. But with Ray, she'd let her guard down and shown her heart—her *true* beauty—according to Ray. It was something she would never be able to hide from him. She had to ask herself why she would even want to.

It was a question she just couldn't answer right now.

CHAPTER 12

Miriam bandaged up her face with the gauze and tape the nurse had sent her home from the hospital with. She had survived Ray seeing the wound, and had even taken a peek at it herself when he'd left the room to greet the family that Claudia had invited to see Ray, and to meet Miriam for the first time. She was surprised at the amount of healing that had taken place in just ten short days since the accident. It had given her hope that perhaps with a small amount of makeup, she could easily hide the line down her face to where no one would see it. She would have to wait until it was completely healed though. Even so, she still wasn't ready to expose her imperfection to the world just yet.

It filled her with shame that Ray knew her so well as to call her out for her feelings of vanity over the scar on her face. He knew her well—she'd give him that much. But it wasn't

220

enough to make her choose him over being able to hide away her imperfections in the Amish community.

Miriam adjusted her simple blue dress and checked the pins beneath her *kapp*. Soon, she would have to do away with her fancier dresses. She would miss them. But she couldn't wear them if she was a married woman in the community. Being single and in her *rumspringa* years, she could get away with a certain number of things, but that would be all over as soon as she and Adam were wed.

She wished with all her heart that she could marry Ray. She loved Ray. It would be easy to be his *fraa*. But with Adam, it would be a lot of work to get through a lifetime in a loveless marriage.

From the other room, Miriam could hear happy chatter from a room full of women. Occasionally, a male voice would give a quick answer, but for the most part, the conversation seemed to be dominated by the women-folk.

Though Miriam was used to attending work bees and quilting bees where sometimes one hundred or more women would gather, it was within a close-knit family community. Here, the women were all strangers. She would have to learn their names, and she wasn't good in crowds of *Englischers*. But with the scar on her face, she would have a new reason to keep her eyes cast downward.

These women will be related to mei boppli, she reminded herself inwardly. *I suppose I owe it to the wee one to at least learn to know them.*

That way, when her child talked of their *aenti* or *onkel* later in life, Miriam would at least have recollection of who was being referred to.

It is what is fair to the kinner.

She stiffened her upper lip, took in a deep breath and pretended she was about to sit down to dinner with her adopted father. He was almost more of a stranger to her than the women that waited for her on the other side of the door. At least with the women that were eager to meet her, she had some sort of connection with them through Ray. Her connection to her father was lost the moment the cord of life between her and her *mamm* was severed when they put her in the ground.

Miriam opened the door slowly, and was surprised to see Ray propped against the wall outside the door.

"I was hoping you wouldn't be too much longer," he greeted her with a smile and a kiss to her cheek. "I wanted to take you in there myself so you wouldn't feel so intimidated by my aunts and cousins. They can be a bit overwhelming until you get to know them."

Miriam's feet stopped working. Maybe she wasn't ready to go in there just yet. Maybe she could be excused since she just got out of the hospital.

"I'm feeling a little tired," she said softly. "Perhaps we can do this when I've had a little more time to recover."

Ray took her gently into his arms. "You'll have to forgive my mother and my aunts, but they know you intend to marry Adam next week, and they don't think they have enough time to *talk you out of it.*"

"Talk me out of it? So that is what this dinner is all about? To bully me into changing my mind?"

Miriam was furious.

Ray held her closer. "No! I told them to back off. I told them not to say anything to you. But they think that if they are welcoming enough and shower you with love that it will make you change your mind."

He kissed her forehead. "Just go along with it for me. They really want to welcome you into our family, and it would be a shame if my family couldn't spoil you just a little. You deserve it after everything you've been through."

Miriam didn't think she deserved anything from Ray *or* his family. She'd rejected them all, yet they were about to welcome her into their family. How would she ever be able to face them knowing she had no intention of becoming a member of their family?

"I don't know if I can deceive them like that."

"You won't be deceiving them. You don't have to become family with them to be their friend. I know you could use a few friends. Let them get to know you, so that later down the road they can tell our child they know you, and they will have good things to say about you."

Funny, *Miriam* didn't have anything good to say about herself right now.

"I will meet them. But I won't let them spoil me. It would make me feel too guilty."

Ray kissed her quickly on her lips, catching her off guard. "You won't regret this, I promise. Thank you for doing this for me. It means more than you know."

It meant a lot to her too.

She just didn't know it yet.

CHAPTER 13

Miriam looked around the room at the sea of gifts Ray's family had brought for her and the baby.

Guilt welled up in her throat, choking her.

How would she ever repay these people? They hadn't even let her help clear the table after dinner. Her debt seemed to be spiraling out of control just as her life was. If not for Ray sitting closely beside her, doting on her, she would have fainted for sure and for certain.

Embarrassed by the attention everyone was showering her with, she was grateful Ray hadn't left her side since he'd brought her out of *her* room. She wasn't used to this much attention, nor was she used to sitting around and letting others do the work that needed to be done. But they refused every offer of help she shot their way. She had not been raised to be pampered. She was raised to work hard and do whatever needed to be done until the work was finished. Unfortunately, in the Amish community, there was *always* work to be done.

Perhaps in time they will let me do my fair share of the work around here.

Between her and Ray, they had opened countless gifts that included cloth diapers, little t-shirts, bibs, toys and rattles, a silver cup, and several baby blankets and sheet sets for a crib. There were even a few envelopes boasting hefty sums of money.

The final gift, a rather large box, contained an elaborate wooden crib. It was beautiful, but it was way too fancy to use in an Amish household. It brought to Miriam's mind her own baby crib and the blankets her *mamm* had sewn for her when they'd adopted her as a newborn. It saddened her to think of the quilts her *mamm* must have spent hours sewing for her. But by marrying Adam, her *daed* would most likely let her use those things for her child. The crib had been in the family for three generations, and normally, Benjamin would have first rights to such a family heirloom, but he was yet unattached. It was the only hope she had of getting her father to let her to use the crib.

By the time everyone went home, Miriam felt so overwhelmed, she was ready to go to bed. It wasn't that she didn't like every one of his family members, she was just feeling ready for some quiet-time alone to think.

Ray had other plans for her.

"I have a surprise for you," he said, taking her hands. "I was going to wait until tomorrow to show you, but I don't think I can wait that long. If we're lucky, we'll get to see it before the sun goes down completely."

Miriam fastened her seatbelt in Ray's truck, feeling the bile making its way up her throat. She swallowed hard against the acid that threatened to spill from her mouth. She'd ridden in Ray's truck plenty of times, so why was she so nervous? Perhaps it was the *surprise* he claimed he had for her. She couldn't take any more surprises right now. She needed calm and normal routines—not upheaval and surprises.

But what if it's a gut surprise?

That was likely not possible, and she knew it. Ray was too excited about this surprise for it to be anything but more pressure for her to choose him and reject Adam.

Miriam watched the flicker of the quickly-setting sun filtering through the trees as they drove down a long dirt drive toward Willow Creek. At the end of the road sat an old abandoned farm house and a barn with a collapsed roof on one side. Split-rail fencing corralled an overgrown area of land in front of the creek.

Ray parked the truck and turned to her. "We're here. What do you think?"

"The sunset over the creek is beautiful," she said warily.

"No. I mean, about the house and the barn. Isn't it great?"

She was afraid he was talking about that.

She shrugged. "For what?"

She was almost afraid to know the answer.

"For you and me to live in, that's what!"

He was way too excited about this, and Miriam couldn't think straight at all. She couldn't even respond.

"This morning, while you were sleeping, I got on the internet and started looking at property for sale. I found this piece here and it's practically *free,* it's so cheap. My dad said he would loan us the money to pay for it, and he's going to set me up with my own construction business here. I won't have to go back there and work for him anymore. I can fix up the house and the barn myself. The best part about this, is that you can remain close to the Amish community, and we can raise our child on a farm like you were raised."

Ray looked at Miriam, who, by this time, had tears in her eyes. But they were not happy tears. They were tears of remorse. Tears of regret.

"Aren't you going to say something?" he asked softly.

"I wish it was that simple," she said, hiccupping.

Ray hopped out of the truck and jogged around to her side and opened the door.

He held his hand out to her and she took it reluctantly. "Let me show you," he said with a smile.

She could not resist that smile.

They walked up onto the front porch of the white-washed, clapboard house that boasted a rickety porch swing.

Ray pointed to the swing. "I can fix that. Imagine how many summer nights we would enjoy out here sipping lemonade and rocking the baby to sleep."

Tears ran down Miriam's face.

She could see it.

They walked in the through the broken front door and into the front room with dirty wooden floors and a brick fireplace on the far wall between two broken windows.

"I'll fix the door so it closes—and locks, so you'll feel safe. I can put in new windows, of course. You could make pretty curtains and make braided rugs for the hardwood floors. The upstairs has four bedrooms. And the kitchen—the kitchen has a huge pantry for all the canning jars I know you'll fill it with. Can you see us living here, Darlin'?"

Miriam could see it.

And that's what scared her the most.

CHAPTER 14

Miriam found a note from Claudia addressed to her sitting on the kitchen counter next to a large paper sack with handles. The letter stated she would be home early from the store, and that the bag contained all the items she would need to get her started on her new venture. The letter also boasted that Claudia had another idea to help her out, and that it was a surprise.

Miriam didn't think she could stomach anymore surprises. But her curiosity got the better of her. She peeked inside the large shopping bag to find all the materials she needed to make at least one hundred Amish dolls.

Finally, something I can do to start paying my way around here.

Miriam took the bag and her cup of coffee back to her room and laid it out on the bed to begin. As she started to cut the pattern she'd memorized when she was only a child, she realized she had no wedding dress in which to marry Adam. She didn't dare ask Claudia or Ray for such a thing, but perhaps she could ask her brother to get her some material to make one when he arrived for his visit on Friday. That wouldn't leave her much time to do the sewing, but perhaps she could wear her navy-blue dress and make only a new pinafore for the wedding.

Her own wedding dress had been left at the B&B, and even if recovered, was swathed in chicken guts. The blood would not come out of the garment after this much time had passed. The dress she'd taken from Lavinia was not recovered from the remains of the accident. And so, she was left with no other choice than to wear the plain, navy blue dress, unless she could talk her brother into providing her with enough money to get the material for a new pinafore.

For now, Miriam was content to make as many Amish dolls as Claudia's store could carry. Miriam was desperate for the money to pay back Bethany. It could mean the difference between her acceptance back into the community once she and Adam had the Bishop publish their wedding. A full confession would be required of her. She was, indeed, prepared to give the confession she should have given the day of the accident. She would do that on Sunday when she attended services with Adam and Benjamin.

Miriam began to sew the pieces together to make her first doll. She pondered the events of the past two weeks, wondering if things might have been different if she'd have just given the confession that was expected of her that day. What had she been thinking? She supposed she was thinking the same thing she believed now, but only then, she acted in haste.

Was she still acting in haste? Was she making the best decision she could for her and her child? Her own feelings couldn't be an issue anymore. She had to grow up and put her child first. But would that child understand having a stepfather in his or her life instead of a real father. She had not had her real father or mother in her life, and it was something she'd always craved, despite the love her *mamm* had showered her with.

It wasn't the same as the situation with her birth parents. At least her child would know his or her real father, unlike Miriam had. No, Miriam would make certain her child knew its real father no matter how hard it would be for her to never be able to live her life with Ray. She hoped that in time it would be easier for her to be around him. But now, in her current state, the pregnancy made her feel vulnerable and needy.

Truth be told, she wished there was another way, but she just wasn't brave enough to stand alone away from the only family she'd ever known. Perhaps with *grandkinner,* her *daed* would come around a little more, and she and Adam would have the support of his Amish community to help set up their life together as a married couple.

It was the perfect plan.

So why did everything about it seem so wrong?

Perhaps it was the love she still carried for Ray that was clouding her judgment. She knew she needed to ignore those feelings in order to stay on course. It would be difficult to ignore with him in the same house for the next few days until her wedding, but she would have to find a way to steer clear of him as best she could. And though he expected a final answer about the house, she'd tried her best to let him down easy and he hadn't taken the hint.

Unfortunate for her, there was no more time for subtlety. She would have to break Ray's heart all over again, and that nearly broke her spirit to even think about it. He needed to know she intended to go through with marrying Adam, no matter what.

She prayed he would understand, and that the hurt would be minimal—to both of them.

Lord, take away the love Ray has for me. Give him understanding and wisdom to accept my decision about marrying Adam. Take away the love I have for Ray and please stop my heart from breaking.

Miriam stifled a sob, but she couldn't prevent the tears from pouring down her cheeks.

If it be Your Wille, Gott, she added.

CHAPTER 15

Miriam stumbled sleepily into the kitchen, hoping to find some fresh coffee. She could smell it, but worried there wouldn't be any left since she'd gotten up late. She'd tossed and turned so much during the night over all the stress of Ray's announcement last night, that she hadn't fallen asleep until nearly four-thirty this morning.

Now noon, she was certain she would be alone in the house. Claudia would be at her store, and Ray was surely busy setting up his new business his father had promised to help him with. She shuffled up to the counter and pulled a clean coffee cup from the cupboard and held it under the spout on the coffee-maker. Fresh, *hot* coffee drained into her cup while her heart did a somersault behind her ribcage. If there was hot coffee, someone was home besides her. Looking up, she spotted Ray sitting at the small table just off the kitchen sipping a steaming cup.

I should have stayed in my room, she grumbled to herself.

"I was hoping you'd get up while I was here getting a little lunch. I've already put in a full day's work, but I suppose you probably had a little trouble sleeping last night with all the excitement of yesterday."

Miriam forced a smile, but quickly let it go when the expression cinched her wound. Her hand instinctively went up to her cheek, holding the bandage against the tightness. She wondered if she would ever be able to really smile again—but not just because she worried about breaching her wound. A sadness filled her at the sight of Ray, knowing that marrying Adam would never be able to fill that void in her heart.

He rushed to her side. "Are you in pain?"

She shook her head, unable to look at him without worrying she would cry.

"Are you ill? My mother told me you would probably get sick a lot in the beginning of your pregnancy."

She shook her head again, hoping she could convince him. She knew if she let on how she was feeling, he would take her in his strong arms, and she would be powerless to escape his loving embrace.

She wanted to be his *fraa,* but that just wasn't possible. But she could allow him to hold her, couldn't she? No, that could be too risky. She would never want to give him up, but she *had* to.

Lord, please give me the strength to resist this mann's love.

He closed the space between them, causing her to take an instinctive step backward.

"Come here, Darlin', and let me hold you. You're shaking."

She clenched her jaw to keep her teeth from chattering. Her nerves were causing bile to form in her throat. Her willfulness was ineffective against his persistence. He had her in his arms before she could put up her defenses. This was where she wanted to be; it was where she was meant to be. But she couldn't—could she? Should she?

His mouth found her neck as he leaned down to deepen the hug. Sweet kisses tickled her neck as he swept his lips over her jawline and to her cheek, where they suddenly consumed her mouth. Giving in to his passion, Miriam couldn't help but deepen the kiss. She couldn't stop herself. She wanted him for a husband in every way. She wanted to raise their child with him. She even wanted that *happily ever after* with him.

Reality made her heart skip a beat.

It made her throat constrict with tears.

If she didn't push him away, the reality would surely suffocate her.

It would pull her further down into the depression she'd settled into.

With a gentle nudge, Miriam separated from him. Her eyes closed, and her breathing came in jagged gasps.

"What's wrong, Darlin'?" Ray asked.

She held her hands up in front of her, eyes still closed. "I—can't."

She felt him making a subtle attempt at pulling her back into his arms, but she remained too rigid for him to embrace her without force.

"I want us to be a family, Miriam. That's why I went ahead and purchased that farm on Willow Creek this morning."

Her eyes flung open, and she stared him down.

"You did what?"

"My dad went with me this morning and he paid cash for the farm. He wrote up a mortgage for me to take over. I've been over there for two hours already taking inventory of all the supplies we need to fix the place up."

He looked at Miriam, who stared blankly at him.

"Well, aren't you going to say something?"

She hiccuped as she tried to pull in a deep breath. "You shouldn't have bought that place. Not for me. Not for *us*. I'm still planning on marrying Adam."

His face drained of all color.

"*Why?* " he asked, barely above a whisper.

"I *must.*"

Ray clutched her arms gently, desperation in his eyes. "But you just kissed me! I thought you—loved me."

She didn't dare admit her love for him. If she did, he would never let her go, and he had to. She needed him to release her from the guilt that plagued her. The guilt had taken up residence in her mind, embedding itself like a nightmare.

Who was she kidding?

This *was* certainly a nightmare, and one she couldn't wake up from.

"I still intend on marrying Adam. Please don't make me say it again. He will be taking me to Sunday service, and our wedding will be published then."

"If you think I'm going to stand by and let you marry another Amish man, then you don't know me at all."

Miriam narrowed her gaze on Ray.

"Another Amish man? I didn't marry the first one—but I *will* be marrying this one—and you won't be able to stand in my way. My mind is made up."

"Then change it, because I'm not letting you go," he said as he stormed out of the kitchen door.

Miriam watched him tuck his head against the wind as he walked out toward the wooded area behind his mother's house. She was momentarily tempted to take him his coat, which he'd left on the hook by the door, but she decided it was best to let him *cool off.*

CHAPTER 16

Miriam wiped a fresh tear to keep it from soiling the doll she was stitching by hand. Sewing the dolls was just what she needed to keep her idle hands busy until she recovered from the accident, but there was nothing that could keep her idle thoughts from turning to Ray. They'd had an argument, and Miriam had reasoned with herself now more than ever that it was simply not meant to be between the two of them.

The sound of buggy wheels grinding against the concrete driveway, and the hollow sound of the horse's steady, clip-clop as it drew nearer to the house, startled her from her depressing thoughts. She peered out the blinds to see Adam pulling his horse into the circle driveway.

Her heart thumped hard and fast. Not with excitement over her betrothed, but with dread. The kind of dread that fills you with the deepest form of regret and shame, it's too unbearable to live with.

Adam wasn't supposed to come for her until Sunday. Today was Wednesday. What could he possibly be doing here so soon?

Her first instinct was to go back to her room and not answer the door, but she knew she had to face him sooner or later. Best to get it over with so she could go about the business of making the dolls to pay back her debt to Bethany, and put aside a little for the baby. She couldn't afford the interruption right now, but this was all part of her growing up and taking responsibility for the mistakes she'd made.

Miriam jumped as the footfalls on the porch concluded with a ring to the doorbell. It startled her, as she was not used to hearing the sound of the *Englisher* device. It struck her as odd that Adam would ring the doorbell instead of knocking, but, perhaps he might think someone was home with her. Was it possible that he knew Ray was here?

A new thought occurred to her.

Worry suddenly flooded her thoughts as she wondered what would happen if Ray were to intercept Adam's visit and show his disapproval. She supposed it was an inevitable happpenstance, but that didn't mean she wouldn't avoid the opportunity at all cost.

Miriam lifted her still-aching body from the leather recliner and went to the door before the bell rang a second time. She pasted a smile on her face and swung open the door as if she was happy to see Adam. No sense in giving him a reason to back out of marrying her.

"Gudemariye," she said just the way her *mamm* had taught her when she was little. Miriam had, for the most part, spoken as an *Englisher* ever since her *mamm's* funeral, making every effort to lose her accent. It had been what had separated her from her adopted father and brother—her unwillingness to adhere to the Amish way of life.

Now, as she spoke to Adam, she intended to prove she would make a smart match for him in every way—right down to carrying on the use of their language to child she now carried, and any future *kinner* she would bear for him.

She felt suddenly dizzy and sick to her stomach at the thought of having the same intimate relationship she'd had with Ray. She couldn't imagine being that submissive to anyone other than Ray, whom she loved.

Adam leaned in and awkwardly kissed her forehead. It happened so quickly she didn't have time to react.

"Do you think you might be up to a buggy ride?"

Her heart quickened its pace and her cheeks flushed. She wasn't ready, but she supposed she had to start trusting him at some point. After all, he was to be her husband in only a few short days.

241

"*Jah,*" she said, suddenly feeling very *fake.*

"Where would you like to go?"

Miriam didn't have to think about it. If she was to remain in this community as Adam's *fraa,* there would be a lot of fences for her to mend. She would have to start with the hardest one—Bethany. She not only owed her an apology, she would have to settle her debt with the girl before she made her confession to the Bishop prior to the wedding.

After voicing her destination to Adam, they were on their way down the long driveway to the main road that led back to Willow Creek. She occupied her mind with the layout of the house Ray had bought for the two of them to pass the time it took to travel, and to keep her mind from getting anxious over being in Adam's buggy again.

In her mind's eye, she mentally furnished the home, while Ray started a crackling fire, where she would sit in the hand-carved rocking chair with their baby at her breast. It was only a dream, but it was a good dream—one that she shared with Ray.

But here she was, sitting beside Adam—her betrothed, thinking of Ray tinkering around the home he would fix up just for the three of them.

The three of them.

It had a nice sound to it. She could see him cuddling and cooing their baby, and then handing him or her back to its *mamm—her!*

No matter how many times she told herself, she still couldn't comprehend what it would be like to be a *mamm*. Claudia told her it would happen in an instant the first time she held the wee one, but she worried she lacked the natural instincts to care for a child. She was already convinced Ray would love their child, and she knew she had the same love in her heart, but she'd been raised by two men, and they weren't exactly the mothering types.

"We're here," Adam announced.

Miriam reluctantly let go of her daydream, ready to face the reality that had become her life.

CHAPTER 17

Miriam's heart drummed against her ribcage at the sight of the B&B. How had they gotten there so soon? She wasn't ready for what she was about to do, but she took a deep breath and stepped out of the buggy regardless. Her shaky legs refused to take her any further until Adam slipped his arm around her shoulder and gently guided her toward the house. Her first instinct was to shrug him off, but she was so shaky, she feared she might faint if not for his hold on her. It made her feel like an invalid, but she didn't care at the moment. Her only concern was how she would broach the subject of her debt with Bethany.

The front door swung open as she approached the porch, and Bethany stood there with a smug look on her face. Though she knew she deserved nothing less from Bethany, Miriam felt the sting of her disdain.

"I came to apologize," Miriam immediately offered.

Bethany planted her fists on her hips. "I should think so after everything you did to hurt *mei schweschder* and me."

You forgot to say how I deserve everything that's happened to me, Miriam thought.

"I'm truly sorry for what I did, and I wanted you to know I intend to pay back every bit of the money I took from you."

Bethany looked at Miriam to see if she detected truthfulness. She couldn't tell. "You mean, poor Adam, here, is going to have to pay back your debt after he marries you!"

"*Nee,*" Miriam said holding out a finished doll she held in her hands. "I'm making these for a store downtown that Ray's mother owns. She's letting me sell them and keep the profits."

Bethany examined the doll's fine stitching.

"How long do you think that will last after you marry Adam instead of Ray?"

"The offer was not conditional," Miriam said defensively. "It is for the *boppli,* not for me."

Bethany skewed her mouth. "I hope you're right."

Miriam pursed her lips, but held her tongue.

"I came to say my peace, and to give this to Lavinia. I don't imagine she is here anymore as she's married now, but would you give it to her with my apology?"

Bethany took the doll. "I'll give her the doll, but I think the apology should come from you."

Miriam nodded agreement. *"Danki."*

She looped her arm in the crook of Adam's elbow and allowed him to assist her down the stairs of the large, wraparound porch, and into his buggy. It was there that she realized just how long of a road it was going to be before the members of the community accepted her again. She'd really messed things up for herself here, but she hoped to redeem herself with her change in attitude, and the true remorse she held in her heart.

****

A knock at the door startled Miriam. She'd fallen asleep in the recliner with a half-sewn doll in her hands and hadn't heard anyone approach the house. The afternoon spent with Adam had stressed her out so much she'd worn herself out with worry. He'd been kind to her, and a perfect gentleman, but that was exactly the problem. He'd been so nice it had caused more guilt to build up in her over marrying him.

Miriam forced herself out of the recliner to answer the door, though she was in no mood to see anyone. But since it was Claudia's home, she figured that as a guest, she'd better see to the door in case it was something or someone important.

Surprise filled Miriam at the sight of Lavinia standing on the porch, her blue wedding dress draped over her arms.

Lavinia held the dress out to her. "I thought you might need this for your wedding. I cleaned it for you. There isn't a trace of mess after what *mei schweschder* did to it. Bethany gave me the doll you sewed for me. *Danki.* I'm certain you will make a fair amount of money selling them. Your stitching is very *gut.*

Bethany asked me to tell you that she doesn't expect the money to be returned to her all at once. You can take your time in paying her back a little at a time. We know you need the money for your *boppli,* and Bethany has changed her mind about getting a car with the money—after what *happened.* We are both very sorry for what happened to you."

A lump formed in Miriam's throat. She didn't deserve such kindness from either of them, but they had both extended it nonetheless.

"Won't you come in for some tea?" Miriam asked, opening the door fully and stepping back to let her first *guest* in.

"Danki."

Lavinia followed her into the kitchen after Miriam set her clean dress down on the sofa in the living room. She would fix her guest some tea, and hope to make amends with her. She knew they would probably never be friends, but they would be neighbors, and reside in the same community. Their *kinner* would be cousins, and for that reason alone, perhaps, just maybe, Lavinia might learn to forgive her eventually. For now, she would understand that the clean dress presented to her was a peace offering.

While Miriam and Lavinia sipped tea, and nibbled on fresh-baked cookies, they discovered they had just a bit more in common than they could have ever imagined. Miriam was surprised to hear that she and Bethany had also grown up without their *mamm*. Seeing how well-adjusted they were compared to her, Miriam decided that the two of them might just be a good example to her. They whiled away the afternoon with tales of mischief from their youth, and even shared a few laughs. It was refreshing to Miriam to see that life did not have to be so difficult. That perhaps there *was* a chance they could someday be *gut* friends.

CHAPTER 18

Miriam woke early feeling heavier at heart than she had ever felt in her life—even after her *mamm* had died. Her conscience bothered her about too many things to sleep. The house was quiet—too quiet. At least at her own home, she had chickens that would be clucking, roosters crowing and cows bellowing—all for their morning meal. Here, she had no one to care for, no one to rise for, and no one to feed—yet.

She rolled her hand over the small of her abdomen. She would be showing soon—too soon. Everyone in the community would know she was with child—if they didn't already. She wasn't certain how long a pregnancy could be hidden, especially after the gossip that had circulated about one of the girls she'd gone to school with. They weren't friends, but she'd heard she'd become pregnant before her wedding. It was all the youth in the community talked about.

Miriam wondered if *she* was being talked about the same way in this community, and if the members of her own community already knew. The gossip-mill among the Amish could be harsh at times. When someone in the community committed a sin, everyone knew. As long as there was a confession, there was forgiveness among the people, but she would forever be *used* as an example to the other youth.

Forever talked about.

Forever reminded of the sins of her youth.

Would it be the same among the *Englisch?*

Miriam could no longer take the silence that drove her thoughts. She *had* to get up—even if it disturbed Ray and Claudia. She *had* to do something besides lying here awake to contend with her thoughts. She needed to occupy her mind. Though she had several dolls already sewn, and more yet to be sewn, she needed something a little more challenging to do this morning.

Perhaps she could prepare the morning meal for the household. But Claudia had a modern stove that Miriam had no idea how to operate. Besides, it was still too early. The sun hadn't even made its appearance on the horizon yet, and no birds chirped in the trees outside her window.

All was asleep, and all was quiet.

She rose from the bed anyway and quickly made it up, pulling the fancy quilt over the ruffled sheets. She liked the modern things, but it wasn't something she should get used to if she was to be an Amish *fraa.* Marrying among the Amish meant primitive belongings and hard work from sun-up to sundown, and beyond that if there were *kinner* in the *haus.* Would Claudia be willing to relieve some of the burden of raising the *boppli* from her? She hoped it was so, even though she would be married to Adam.

In the kitchen, she surprisingly found the ingredients she needed to make bread. Locating glass loaf pans that seemed too clean to have ever been used, she set them on the counter with the rest of the stuff she'd gathered from Claudia's pantry. She went about mixing and stirring, occupying her mind from her troubles.

When Miriam was young, her *mamm* had taught her that making bread was the best way to solve almost any problem. In the time it took to prepare, most things could be worked out. And the kneading of the dough was not only *gut* for working out frustrations, it was *gut* for making the arms strong enough to do other chores.

Miriam had no idea if what her *mamm* told her was true, but simply being reminded of her soothed her more than she could have thought. Usually, thinking of her *mamm* had always filled her with bittersweet memories that made her heart ache, but at this moment, for some reason beyond her reasoning, it brought her comfort.

Hearing a faint noise, Miriam looked over her shoulder to find Claudia entering the kitchen. Her fluffy robe was tied in a knot at her waist, and she lifted a hand to rub the sleep from her blue eyes that matched Ray's.

"I'm sorry if I made too much noise and woke you," Miriam immediately offered.

Claudia waved a hand at her. "No worries. I have to do inventory at the store today, and I had to be up early."

Miriam glanced at the clock on the wall and made note that the window above the sink still hadn't illuminated any hint of the sun.

"Surely not *this* early. But if you wouldn't mind helping me figure out how to turn on your oven, I'd be ever so grateful."

Claudia chuckled. "By the looks of things, I'd say you had trouble sleeping."

"*Jah*—yes."

Claudia crossed to the stove and pushed a few buttons causing a series of beeps. "It's on. When you want it off, just push this button."

"*Danki*—thank you."

Miriam didn't know why she was reverting to speaking as she'd been taught in her growing years, but she supposed it was because of her uncertainty as to where she fit in. She was between worlds, and had no idea which she preferred at the moment.

Claudia moved to the coffee maker and began to make a fresh pot. Miriam was grateful for that. She needed a cup to soothe her shakes, and she had no idea how to operate the modern device.

"I remember when I was first pregnant with Ray, and how terrified I was. I didn't sleep much the entire pregnancy, come to think of it. But trust me when I say, you should get your sleep now, because once that little one is born, you won't get much sleep for the first few years of its life."

Miriam gulped down a lump of fear that suddenly entered her throat. "Years?"

Claudia cupped an arm around Miriam's shoulder and gave her a quick squeeze before returning to the chore of making coffee. "I didn't mean to frighten you. I didn't have my mother around to help me, or give me advice about mothering. The trick is to sleep when they sleep. If you don't, you'll be exhausted. But I will be there if you need anything, whether it be advice like that, or just to help care for the baby if you get overwhelmed."

"Even if I don't marry Ray?" she asked cautiously.

Claudia smiled. "Even if you don't marry Ray."

Miriam felt a burden lift from her as she kneaded the bread dough. Her *mamm* had been right. Making bread can help you work out a multitude of problems.

CHAPTER 19

Miriam pulled the dressing from her cheek and examined it in the bathroom mirror. Surprised at how much it had healed, she felt a little foolish for keeping the bandage on it for so long. The nurse at the hospital had given her instructions before leaving that stated she would only have to wear the bandage for a few days after leaving.

That time had since passed.

She quickly re-dressed the wound and went back to the kitchen, where dishes awaited her attention. She ran her hand along the bandage, wondering if she would ever feel it was ready to remain uncovered.

Part of her had kept it covered from Ray's view, even though he'd made such a fuss about telling her it didn't disgust him the way it did her. Mostly, she'd kept it hidden from herself. She didn't relish the idea of catching a glimpse of her scarred face every time she passed one of the many mirrors in

Claudia's home. Most Amish homes didn't contain even one mirror. She would make certain that there were none in the home she would share with Adam. She didn't want the constant reminder that she was less than perfect.

Now, the wound was a mere, pink line down her face that she thought could easily be covered with makeup. But she would not be living among the *Englisch* where such a thing was commonplace, and even acceptable. Among the Amish, worrying about outer beauty was considered a sin of vanity.

Miriam had been guilty of vanity most of her life. From the time she was very young, she knew she didn't look like any of her cousins, and was said to be much prettier than they were. It was talked about in hushed tones, but she was always aware of the chatter.

The girls in school had mistreated her out of jealousy, and it had turned Miriam bitter toward them, causing her difficulty in making friends. Because of this, she'd turned to seeking the attention from the boys, causing even more strife with her female competitors.

They wouldn't be jealous of me now, she thought.

In her opinion, being unwed and pregnant with a scar on her face qualified her for a little sympathy. But she wasn't looking to be pitied; she wanted acceptance. Ray's cousins and *aenti's* had certainly accepted her. She wondered, though, if it had been genuine, or if they had been kind only because she carried Ray's *kinner.*

Miriam finished wiping down the kitchen and putting away the rest of the morning meal, including the bread she'd baked, when Ray entered the room. He approached her from behind, catching her off-guard, tucking his face in her neck and slipping his arm over her abdomen.

"How are my two favorite people this morning?"

He made her feel a little awkward, but in a good way. She loved the gentle attention he showered her with, as though she was the most cherished thing in his life.

"You sound like you had a better night's sleep than I did."

He kissed her lightly and crossed to the coffee maker to dispense a single cup from the reservoir.

The warmth of his kiss remained on her neck, causing her to miss the contact between them. She knew it was wrong to accept the attention from him since she was promised to marry Adam, but she reasoned with herself it was acceptable since she was carrying Ray's child. She was so confused about her feelings she didn't trust herself to make the right decision at all. Most of her time, lately, consisted of arguing with herself as to whether she was making the right choice. One minute she would think it was a solid, sane option, and the next, Ray would do something to make her doubt her selection, as he'd just done.

"I *did* sleep like a bear hibernating in the winter, but probably because of all the hard work I've put into our house for the last couple of days."

Miriam cringed at his comment to include *her* in the ownership of the house he'd purchased. She wasn't certain if he was *trying* to put pressure on her and fill her with guilt about marrying Adam, but he couldn't possibly add to the amount she'd already piled on herself.

Ray sat at the table and sipped his steaming coffee. Claudia had left more than a half hour before, but the coffee she'd made had remained hot in the automated warmer.

"Would you like something to eat?"

Ray sniffed the air. "Whatever you made smells heavenly, and I'm starving."

Miriam removed the plate from the refrigerator that she'd just put away for him, and put it in the microwave. She pushed the buttons just like Claudia had taught her only a few short minutes before she'd left for the day, and told her it was *"Just in case my son wakes up and wants to sample your wonderful cooking."* She'd winked at her and told her, *"The way to a man's heart is through his stomach."*

But Miriam wasn't looking to win Ray's heart. She already had it, and she was throwing it away like a fool. It was another wrong in her life she would have to learn to accept.

As she placed the food in front of Ray, she took pleasure in watching him as he dipped his face toward the steaming plate and breathed in the aroma with a smile spread wide across his full lips. She could get used to spending her days cooking for him and submitting to him in every way.

He was easy to love, and leaving him was going to be the hardest thing she would ever have to do.

The clip-clop of a horse approaching broke the spell between them, sending Miriam's thoughts into sudden turmoil.

"I think your *boyfriend* is here," Ray muttered under his breath as he glared out the kitchen window.

Miriam didn't blame him for being upset, but his comment stung.

"He isn't my *boyfriend,*" she snapped.

Ray stood up and took his empty plate to the sink, letting it drop haphazardly.

"You're right. He's your fiancé—your *betrothed,* as *you* would say."

"Ray, please don't…"

"Don't what? You're carrying *my* baby, and I love you! Help me to understand why you're marrying *him?*"

Miriam stifled a sob that threatened to shake her vocal chords. "I don't expect you to *ever* understand, but if you really love me, you'll accept it."

"You're right about one thing. I'll *never* understand, but I won't *ever* accept it either." He walked outside and greeted Adam briefly as he shouldered past him to the unattached garage.

Miriam threw her shawl over her shoulders and went out to meet Adam. His timing couldn't have been worse, but she hoped that perhaps his appearance would help Ray to come to terms with the reality of her impending marriage. Only problem was, she, herself, needed convincing of the reality too.

"Gudemariye, Miriam," Adam said cheerfully.

It nauseated her to hear that from him. Only a few short moments before, it had been music to her ears to hear Ray's smooth baritone say the same thing to her—but only in *Englisch.*

"Good morning, Adam," she said sternly. "What are you doing here? I wasn't expecting you until Sunday for the service. My brother, Benjamin will be here tomorrow to tend to my needs, so you shouldn't have come all this way for nothing."

"You're sounding more and more like an *Englisher* the more I speak to you," he said impatiently. "As long as you don't talk that way once we are married, so as not to shame me within the community."

Miriam placed her hands on her hips defensively. "Shame you? In case you've forgotten, I *am* an *Englisher."*

"Jah, but you were raised Amish. And I pray that you will raise our *kinner* in the Amish ways, and teach them the language of our community."

Miriam narrowed her eyes at Adam. "First of all, this *baby* is *mine*—not *ours.* And second, I wasn't planning on having any more children, so you won't have any children of your own."

Adam's expression fell. "Perhaps you misunderstood me when I offered to marry you that I would be raising *your boppli* as my own."

"Let's not forget that you *offered* to marry me as penance for the accident you caused; I only agreed to marry you as a matter of convenience."

"Convenience?" he asked.

"Surely you don't think I could ever *love* you!"

Adam lowered his head, defeat shadowing his expression. "My offer to you was genuine. I intend to make an effort to love you, and I hoped you would do the same for me. I intended to be a *gut* husband to you."

"I don't need you to love me. All I need is your good name and your Amish heritage. Let's just leave it at that."

Adam removed his straw hat, revealing tightly-coiled, flaxen curls. Funny that she'd never really taken the time to look at him or get to know him. He was very handsome, and kind as could be, but would those things be enough to make her forget Ray? Suddenly she noticed the sadness in his blue-green eyes, his height and strength no longer able to carry the weight of the burden she'd put on his broad shoulders.

"I'm determined to make it work, even if you're not," he said. "Perhaps you should consider moving into the B&B until we are wed."

"Why would I do that?" she shrieked. "I'm perfectly happy here."

"I'm not certain that being around the *vadder* of your *boppli* is such a *gut* idea…"

"Ray is my baby's father," she interrupted. "He will *always* be the baby's father, and he will *always* be a part of *my* child's life, so you'd better get used to his presence in our lives now."

Adam cleared his throat nervously. He was no match for Miriam's fury where the *boppli* was concerned, and she could see it in his posture. But she couldn't take back what she'd said to him. It was the truth and it needed to be said now, before it was too late.

"I was hoping that he would only want to see the *boppli* once for his peace of mind, and then allow you and me to do the raising—in the Amish ways. If that is not how it will be, perhaps I will have to discuss it with Ray instead."

Miriam pursed her lips. "We have already discussed it, and I *told* you how it was going to be. Either accept it, or…"

She let her voice trail off. She didn't want to finish the sentence. Didn't want to give him and *out.* She needed him to marry her, but she also felt it was important that Adam understood she couldn't let Ray go—even if she was married to *him.*

"I will be here to pick you up on Sunday for the service. The Bishop is still requiring a confession from you that you never gave, and he's expecting one from me now."

Miriam pointed to the bandage on her face.

"You mean for this? I should hope so!"

She stormed off, knowing how unfair she was being to him, but she just couldn't look him in the eye another minute. Her harsh words crushed him, and she worried that he would now back out of their arrangement.

She secretly wondered if she didn't hope he would.

CHAPTER 20

Ray walked in through the kitchen, determined to catch Miriam before she had a chance to hide herself away in her room. After overhearing the heated argument between her and Adam, he deemed this to be his best chance to change her mind before things got so far out of control there would be no fixing it.

She would be vulnerable now, and emotional, so he knew he would have to treat her with an extra dose of patience and love. But he wouldn't pass up such an opportunity to salvage his family and his future with the woman he loved more than his own life.

His heart sank when he didn't find her in the kitchen, but muffled weeping told him he would find her in her bedroom. As he rounded the corner of the living room, the crying reached his ears at the level that let him know she hadn't bothered to close the bedroom door.

Thankfully, his hopeful assumption was correct.

He stood quietly in the doorway for a moment, watching her shoulders shake as she cried into one of the overstuffed pillows that decorated the bed. His first instinct was to go to her, but he wasn't sure he should risk pushing her to the point she rejected his comfort.

Deciding it was worth the risk, he closed the space between them and slipped down onto the edge of the bed next to her and gently pulled her into his arms. She buried her face against his shoulder and trembled as she let loose heartbreaking cries. He had no idea what she was going through. He only knew he loved her and would do anything to help her.

Disheartened by her sobbing, he smoothed her soft, golden hair, burying his face in the sleek tendrils scented with honeysuckle flowers. He'd missed the fragrance of the homemade soap she used on her hair that yielded the silky feel of it between his fingers.

"Everything is going to be alright, Darlin'. You'll see things aren't as bad as they seem right now."

"They...are that bad," she managed in-between sobs catching in her throat. "And they're only going to get worse."

He ran his hand down the length of her hair, which she'd let loose from the tightly-wound bun at the base of her neck.

"It doesn't have to be," he said cautiously. "Marry *me,* and let me fix this for you."

"You can't fix this any more than I can," she managed with one breath. "I'm beginning to think it isn't going to matter if I marry either of you."

He kissed the top of her head, breathing in the aromatic bouquet.

Lord, help me convince Miriam that I love her, he prayed silently. *Give her the strength to accept my help. Forgive us for the sins we committed, and bless us with the opportunity to make it right by getting married.*

He wasn't sure if God had heard him, but he prayed it with all his heart nonetheless. It had been a while since he'd talked to God. He hadn't exactly walked the straight and narrow path with Miriam. His heart weighed heavy with the guilt of the situation he'd put her in. He was determined to spend the rest of his days making things right with her, but it wasn't going to be easy if she continued to resist his efforts.

"I'm sorry for the things I said to you earlier," he said thoughtfully. "The last thing I want to do is add to the pressure you must already feel."

Miriam lifted her head from his shoulder. Though her eyes were red and puffy from crying, he thought she'd never looked more beautiful. He tucked his hand under her chin and lifted while he bent down enough to touch his lips to hers. He couldn't help himself. He loved her, and he wanted her to know it.

He wanted her to trust his love, and to trust *him*.

Delight filled him as she deepened the kiss between them. He held her like it was the last time he would ever be able to. He feared it would be, but he savored this moment and the sweetness of her lips as they swept across his. He wanted to love her for the rest of his life—if only she would let him.

She pushed away from him all too soon.

"This isn't such a *gut* idea," she managed, breathlessly. "I'm betraying my betrothed."

Ray jumped up from where he sat beside her.

"Betraying *him?* You will betray *me* if you marry him!"

She shook her head without looking at him.

"If you can look me in the eye and tell me you don't love me, then I will step aside and let you marry him."

Ray knew it was a risky ultimatum, but he had to know once and for all where he stood.

She remained silent, and he could see the pain in her eyes as she began to weep.

"You can't tell me," he said softly. "Because you still love me. At least you kissed me just now like you did. That wasn't a casual kiss—that was a kiss filled with love. It left me wanting, and I believe it did the same for you."

"I *have* to marry Adam," she managed in between sobs.

"You don't have to! You can marry me, but it seems you are too much of a coward to do what's right."

He knew his words were harsh, but he simply had no more words for her.

CHAPTER 21

Miriam shivered as she strolled into the kitchen. The thick robe Claudia had given her was wrapped tightly around her, but it wasn't keeping in her body heat. She hoped that a cup of hot tea would warm her enough to get some rest. It was already late, and she just couldn't get warm enough to relax, let alone, to fall asleep. The fancy quilt on her bed was made more for decoration than practical use. The quilts back home did their job to keep a body warm, even on the coldest of winter nights. Right now, she missed them more than ever.

She shivered again as she looked out the kitchen window at the light flurries swirling about in the lamplight just outside the window. The decorative light-post illuminated the flakes of snow, causing her to feel a chill to the bone. Winter was going to be rough if it was already snowing. November had only just begun.

From the cupboard, Miriam pulled out a teacup and the box of chamomile tea. She filled the tea kettle and lit the stubborn burner on the gas stove from the box of matches Claudia kept in a primitive tin canister on the counter. It reminded her of the sort of wares she might find in an Amish kitchen. Claudia's entire décor was country and antiques. It was a comfortable old farm house, and Miriam thought it to be not too much unlike her own family home.

A noise from the family room startled her. Miriam followed the noise, finding Ray at the hearth putting thick wedges of wood in a stack on the fireplace grate.

He looked up and smiled warmly when she entered the room. "I heard you walk past my room, and figured you were cold, so I came out here to start a fire to warm you up."

He already knows me too well.

Miriam swooned at the gesture. He was the kindest man she'd ever met, and it filled her with guilt that he was kind to her, despite her constantly rejecting him.

"*Danki,*" she said quietly. "It's snowing—come see out the kitchen window."

He followed her into the kitchen and stood behind her at the window above the sink. He wrapped both his arms around her, holding her close and tucking his face in her neck. She allowed him to hold her as they stared out the window at the snow that fluttered around whimsically, as if perfectly choreographed for an encore performance for their eyes only.

The whistle of the tea kettle caused Miriam to jump. Feeling suddenly awkward, Ray let her slip out of his arms and excused himself to finish building the fire in the other room.

Miriam pulled another teacup from the cupboard, still feeling the warmth of Ray's arms around her. It instilled in her a desire to return the kindness he'd shown her by serving him some hot tea. It was the least she could do for him after the way she'd treated him earlier.

Miriam longed to care for Ray in the manner that a wife would, but she couldn't. She wished he could understand how much she would always care for him despite the fact she would be marrying another man, but it was not something that would likely come to pass. There would most likely always be strife between them as they tried to raise their child together, yet separately.

Miriam finished fixing the tea and brought both cups into the family room with her. Ray's eyes lit up when he saw she had two cups in her hand, knowing one of them was for him. He put the wedge of freshly cut wood onto the fire before taking the cup from her and sipping from it.

Miriam sat down on the oversized sofa and sank into the depths of the cushions, hoping it would warm her up soon. Ray put the poker down and closed the metal, mesh grating in front of the fire. He looked back at her, wondering if he should dare to sit with her, when he noticed her teeth chattering.

"You're still shivering," he said with concern, as he lifted a quilt from the end of the sofa and unfolded it over her.

He climbed in next to her and pulled her close to him. Within minutes, Miriam's shivering slowed as did her chattering teeth. She sipped her tea without mentioning the closeness between them, and he wondered how long she would allow it *this* time. He knew it was wrong for him to think such a thing, but he also wondered if she would continue to maintain her closeness with him even after she married Adam.

It suddenly dawned on Ray that Miriam—*his* Miriam would be Adam's wife, and the man would most likely expect her to be intimate with *him*. The very thought of it felt like someone had put his heart in a paper shredder. How could he just stand by and let Adam take Miriam from him? He couldn't stand the thought of another man holding her or kissing her and *more*. Would she cuddle up to him the way she was with him now?

A lump formed in his throat as he smoothed her hair. "I love you," he said quietly. "I'll always love you. I don't want you to marry Adam. I don't like the idea of him holding you the way I am now. I don't want you to kiss him the way you kissed me earlier. I don't want to let you go."

He watched her expression change in the soft glow of the firelight. Reflections of the flames flickered across her face, illuminating the tears that began to pour from her blue eyes. He could see that his words were finally beginning to have an effect on her, and he hoped it would help to change her mind.

"Don't ruin this," she said, sniffling back the tears. "Let's just enjoy the time we have together and try not to make more of it than it is. Hold me and make me feel safe and secure, even if it's only for this moment."

As tough as it was to concede, he would not fight her anymore. He would let be whatever would be, and accept whatever the outcome—no matter how much pain it caused him. For this moment, he would be content to hold her without any pressure for more.

Miriam set her tea on the lamp table beside the sofa and rested her head on Ray's shoulder. She looked up at him as his eyes closed. His breathing soon slowed and she felt the weight of him relax against her as he began to fall asleep. She closed her eyes, feeling the most comfortable she'd ever felt.

"I love you, too," she whispered.

CHAPTER 22

"Miriam Schrock!" a familiar voice woke her with a startling revelation.

She knew that voice.

"If *Daed* could see you now, you'd be in for a sound lashing for sure and for certain. In fact, I'm not opposed to dolling it out myself."

Miriam felt movement beside her—panicky, jerky movements, as if someone was in a hurry to move out of the way of something—or *someone.*

Was she dreaming?

Her eyelashes fluttered as she struggled to focus—on Ray, who was already on his feet and off the sofa where he was just lying beside her. How long had she and Ray been there? Her gaze followed the light streaming in through the large window behind the sofa.

It was *morning,* and they'd *slept* on the sofa *together.*

Her focus turned to the one calling her name for the second time. It was Benjamin, but how had he gotten into Claudia's home without their knowledge.

"It's a *gut* thing your *mamm* let me in here so I could witness for myself the sinful life you have made for yourself," he was telling Ray as he wagged his finger at him.

She wasn't dreaming!

Ray began to apologize to Ben, making excuses about them falling asleep and not meaning to.

Her *bruder* wasn't buying into any of it.

He waved a hand at Ray. "Save your lies for the Bishop. He will decide what really happened here."

He turned to Miriam, who was still half-asleep and trying very hard to process what was going on, while catching her breath and willing her heart to stop beating so fast. She stood up, gearing herself up to back-talk Ben, when morning sickness overtook her. She clamped a hand over her mouth and ran to the bathroom, Ben on her heels asking her what was wrong. She barely made it to the bathroom before the mere contents of her stomach spilled into the sink. She coughed and sputtered while her brother stood behind her, waiting for an explanation.

"What's wrong with you?" he asked. "Are you *pregnant?"*

"Jah," Miriam admitted as she grabbed a tissue and wiped her mouth. She turned on the water to rinse down the bile without looking up at him, a lump forming in her throat.

"From this *Englisher?"*

"Jah," she said. "But I'm marrying Adam Troyer, an Amish *mann,* so I can stay in the community."

"That's *narrish!"* Ben replied.

"That's what *I* told her," Ray chimed in.

Miriam looked at the two of them in the reflection of the bathroom mirror. "Both of you stay out of this. It's *my* decision what I do."

Ray looked at Miriam with narrowed eyes.

"Why won't you tell your brother that I proposed to you—several times?"

Ray turned to Ben. "I want to do right by your sister, but she's insisting on marrying the Amish man."

"If she's marrying the Amish *mann,* why did I find the two of you *sleeping* together?"

Miriam pursed her lips. "Don't talk about me like I'm not here."

Ben looked at Miriam with disgust. "You wrote in your letter that you were getting married. You didn't tell me any of *this.* Put on a clean dress and pull your hair up in your *kapp.* You look improper."

"There was nothing improper about what you saw. We fell asleep on the couch—that's all," Ray said in his defense.

"Then how did you manage to get her pregnant if the two of you haven't acted improperly?"

Miriam began to cry, and Ray crossed the threshold of the bathroom to stand behind her. He boldly pulled her toward him and rested a hand on her head to calm her. "She hasn't done anything wrong. I pressured her into *sleeping* with me, so if you want to blame someone, blame me!"

That wasn't entirely true and Miriam knew it, but she kept her mouth shut. She let Ray defend her honor, impressed by the protection he was giving her. As for her brother, he wasn't exactly supporting her, and that was his job as her older brother.

"Why can't you just be supportive?" she accused Ben.

"I won't be supportive of your sinful ways. You need to go to the Bishop and confess."

"I'm going to Sunday service with Adam the day after tomorrow, and I plan on giving a full confession at that time. Until then, do not judge me, dear brother!"

Ben hung his head. "What would *mamm* say if she was here?"

The mere mention of her adoptive mother brought fresh tears to her eyes. Oh, how she missed her.

"She would hold me in her arms and tell me she still loved me and that she couldn't wait to hold *mei boppli* in her arms too. I expect this behavior from your *daed*, but not from you, Benjamin Schrock."

"He's your *daed*, too."

Miriam shook her head, tears running down her face. "No, he's not. And you're not my brother. I only came to be with your family because my mother was in the same situation I'm in now. I imagine she was just as scared as I am right now—at a time when I should be able to count on family, I have none. Claudia, Ray's mother, has been very kind to me and is very accepting of my *situation*. Even Ray has been more supportive than you are being. I'm marrying Adam so I can stay in the community, and keep my Amish heritage for my baby. Isn't that enough for you?"

At the mention of Adam and her impending marriage with him, Ray walked away, closing himself up in his bedroom.

Ben turned to her and issued her a warning.

"You're making a big mistake, and you should worry more about fixing it than about who is behind you. It looks to me like you have Ray, but you are hurting him with your *narrish* behavior."

"What are you talking about? I can't marry Ray, and I *won't.*"

"Fix this," he warned again. "When you come to your senses and realize that what you're doing is destroying a lot of futures, you let me know. In the meantime, I'll be at the B&B.

I got a room there for a few days, unless you give me no reason to stay."

Benjamin turned his backside to her and stormed out of Claudia's house, leaving Miriam to cry it out on her own.

CHAPTER 23

"What are you doing here, Adam?" Miriam asked impatiently.

"I came to take you to the B&B so you can stay with your *bruder,* Benjamin."

"I told you yesterday that I'm not leaving here until the wedding, so you're wasting your time."

Adam took a step closer and whispered to her. "I don't want *mei fraa* sleeping with another *mann.*"

"I'm not your wife *yet,* and if you don't stop bossing me around, I won't be at all. I did not sleep with Ray. We were on the sofa, and he cuddled me because I was freezing, and we fell asleep in front of the warm fire. We were talking—that's all."

"You are not acting like a proper Amish woman. You won't last very long in this community. You already have several strikes against you for the lies you told about Nate, and now this. You will have a lot to confess on Sunday."

"Perhaps you should be worrying about your own confession, and never mind about mine. You've managed to upset me again, and I don't want to talk to you. Go home!"

She was *trying* to push his buttons. She was beginning to wonder if she didn't want out of this marriage, but she couldn't be the one to end it. He would have to do that for her. She just wasn't brave enough.

Adam threw his hands up in disgust and ran down the steps of the porch and hopped into his buggy. One click to the horse and he was on his way. At the moment, she didn't care if he ever came back.

****

Miriam pulled her heavy coat around her, wishing she'd worn a scarf and mittens. She stuffed her cold hands into the small pockets of her coat, bending them against the stiffness to cover them from the wind. Light flurries bounced and swirled around her, catching in her eyelashes. She blinked them away, finding it increasingly hard to see in front of her as the snow thickened.

She didn't remember Ray's house being this far down the road, but she trudged along, the wind at her back, the hem of her long dress slapping against her wet calves. She had no way of gauging how far she'd already traveled, but surely, she was close. If she didn't reach her destination soon, she would be soaked to the skin from the slushy snow that clung to her. It formed ice around the top rim of her boots and the cuffs of her sleeves, and was beginning to weigh down the pleats of her dress.

The sound of Ray's truck behind her caused her to turn around and stop. She waited for him to pull the truck over on the shoulder of the road. He leaned across the seat and pushed the passenger side door open and she hopped in without saying a word.

He turned the heater in the truck up so it blasted heat through the vents on the dashboard. "What are you doing out here without me? It isn't safe. You could have been hit or gotten lost. Visibility is not good in this thick snow."

"I was coming to see you," she said through chattering teeth.

He turned down the lane toward the house he'd purchased on Willow Creek. "I had to go into town for supplies and I stopped by the house to check on you, but you weren't there. My mother said you walked down the driveway, but you hadn't come back, so I came looking for you. What was so important that it couldn't wait until I came home tonight?"

"It doesn't matter," she mumbled, feeling suddenly foolish.

He pulled up to the house and parked the truck, and then turned in his seat to look at her. "You came out here in this weather for nothing?"

"Well, mostly, I needed some peace and solitude so I could do a little thinking. I figured I could get that on the walk over here. After all, I'm pretty confused right now, and I hoped I could talk to you about it. And for the record, it was barely snowing when I left the house. I had no idea it was going to turn into a blizzard."

Ray flipped his wipers before turning off the engine. "It is really coming down. Let's get inside and build a fire. We can talk then."

Grabbing the plastic shopping bags in the center of the bench seat of the truck by their handles, Ray hopped out of the cab and walked over to the passenger side. He assisted Miriam into the house and took the bags into the kitchen.

"I bought some groceries. Would you mind putting them away for me while I start a fire so we can warm up?"

She went into the kitchen—*her* would-be kitchen, and put away the items into the pantry and the freshly-painted cupboards. She looked around at the pale-yellow walls and the white cupboards thinking it was just as she would have done it. The scalloped edge of the cupboard that wedged itself above the kitchen window boasted a yellow-checked curtain with perfect pleats. She opened the doors, noting the plates and cups were in the exact cupboards *she* would have put them in.

How did he know?

Was it possible these subtle likenesses were a sign that they were meant for each other after all?

CHAPTER 24

Miriam gazed upon the modern stove in Ray's kitchen, admiring the ease of its use as she made the two of them some hot cocoa. She could hear Ray in the living room tossing wood on the fire and stirring up the embers he'd obviously left from an earlier fire. Before long, the sound of popping and hissing filled her ears as the wood began to burn.

Carrying the hot cocoa into the living room, she couldn't help but admire the simple, antique furnishings he'd placed in the room. Tucked away in the far corner of the room, an Amish-made rocker sat so far back she hadn't noticed it until now. It caused a lump to form in her throat because it was an exact duplicate of the rocker her own *mamm* had rocked her in as an infant. Miriam set the cocoa down on the coffee table and went over to get a better look at the beautifully handcrafted piece.

She turned to Ray. "Do you mind if I sit here, or is this just for decoration?"

He gestured toward the chair. "No, not at all. Please sit in it. I bought it for you—well, for you and the baby."

Miriam couldn't say anything. She eased herself into the chair and leaned back, closing her eyes. She'd sat in her *mamm's* chair many afternoons with her eyes closed, imagining she was rocking with her. It was a game she often played in her mind that brought her comfort. Whenever she would find herself upset about something, or missing her *mamm,* Miriam would sit in that chair and rock until she felt better.

Now was one of those times, and this rocking chair was the closest thing she had to finding the answer to her problems—an answer that perhaps was right under her nose.

"Thank you for the hot cocoa," Ray said, interrupting her reverie. "What did you want to talk to me about?"

She looked at him blankly, uncertain of how to broach the subject. He'd been so kind to her that she didn't want to hurt him more than she already had.

"I know you don't want me to marry Adam. You've made that clear, but since *mei bruder* is here, it's more important than ever that I keep that *familye* bond and remain in the community. I will become Adam's *fraa* in only a few days, and I'd like to know how you want to handle the situation with the *boppli.*"

Her sudden change to the thick accent hadn't gone unnoticed.

She waited for him to protest, but he didn't say a word. He simply went about putting another piece of wood on the fire and poked at the coals as he stared at them. She could see his jaw clench, but he kept his focus on the task, not lifting his gaze from where he stared into the flickering flames.

"I'd like to still see you," he said without pulling his gaze from the fire.

"What do you mean?"

"Just because you're married to *him* doesn't mean you can't still spend time with me."

Miriam put her foot down on the hardwood floor to stop the rocker. "I've never been married before, but I doubt it's acceptable to *date* the *vadder* of your *boppli* when you're another *mann's fraa.*"

Ray whipped his head around and narrowed his gaze on her. "I don't see how it can be acceptable to marry another man when you are carrying *my* baby."

He had her there. She had no answer for that one. If she did, she probably wouldn't be in this predicament in the first place.

"You're right! It's not acceptable. It's not even logical. But I know it's what I *have* to do."

He crossed the room to where she sat, and knelt in front of her. "*Please* marry *me,* then."

Miriam cupped his handsome face in her hands. She hoped their child would inherit the sparkle in Ray's blue eyes, but more than that, his kind heart. She dipped her head toward him and pressed her lips to his.

He lingered there, sweeping his lips across hers.

He loved her, and it broke his heart each time she'd rejected him.

"You only want to marry me because of the baby," she said in-between kisses.

Ray stopped kissing her and stared at her with a stunned look on his face.

"What would make you think such a thing?"

Tears welled up in her eyes. "I brought up the subject of marriage to you after I found out I was pregnant, and you told me it would be a long time before you would be ready to get married."

"Is that why you tried to marry Nate?"

Miriam shook her head. "Amish marry early. The entire community helps the married couple, and help take responsibility for setting them up with a house and food and housewares."

Ray closed his eyes and let his forehead rest on hers. "I only meant I wasn't ready financially. But because things happened the way they did, I now have this house, and my new construction business, thanks to the help my father and mother gave me. My aunts and uncles gave us most of the furniture in this house. The *English* help each other too. In a way, the situation did me a favor. It made me grow up and take responsibility for myself. And now I want to be responsible for you and our baby—because I love you—not because I *have* to."

Miriam closed her eyes and breathed in the smell of firewood on Ray's skin. She loved him too, but did she dare tell him?

CHAPTER 25

Miriam hadn't even had a chance to talk to Ray before her brother was in her face, causing her anxiety about her poor judgment. Ray had excused himself to the barn so she could talk with Ben, but Miriam would have rather talked to Ray.

"Why is it that I come to see you at Claudia's *haus,* and I find you *here,* at Ray's *haus* instead?"

"I stayed here last night because of the weather."

"His *Englisch* truck won't drive in the snow?"

Miriam avoided his narrowed gaze on her and sat in the rocking chair. She leaned back and began to rock without saying a word.

Ben leaned down on his haunches in front of her and placed his hands over the arms of the rocker to stop it. His gazed followed the lines of the chair, inspecting it from the straight back to the rockers on the bottom.

"This is just like *mamm's* chair. Where did it come from?"

"Ray got it for me without knowing it was just like *mamm's.*" Tears welled up in her eyes. "He told me last night I could have it to take with me where ever I lived."

Ben stood up and crossed the room and leaned against the hearth for a moment, seemingly deep in thought. He picked up the poker and stirred coals before placing a new wedge of wood over them.

"It seems to me that Ray really loves you."

"*Jah,* but I need more than love. I need security. The kind you get from *familye* and the Amish community."

"It seems to me you have a *familye* right here, and all the security you need. Look at this *haus* Ray has gotten for *you.* He even went to great lengths to find an Amish-made rocking chair for you just like *mamm's,* without even knowing about hers. I imagine this *mann* would do just about anything for you, and you wouldn't even have to ask him."

Miriam resumed rocking. "Don't you think I already know all that? But I am torn. I want to do the right thing, but I am afraid to lose my Amish heritage."

"You can't have one foot in the *Englisch* world and one foot in the Amish community. You need to pick one or the other. You were born an *Englisher.* You are Amish only in your heart—along with *mamm.*"

"But I was brought up Amish," she argued.

Ben shook his head. *"Nee,* you were always an *Englisher. Mamm* knew it, and *Daed* sees it more now. I think that's why your relationship with him has suffered so much since *mamm's* death. You represent something she wanted so badly she challenged the rules of the Ordnung for."

"Are you saying *Daed* didn't want me?"

"Nee. I'm saying Amish don't adopt except within the community."

Miriam stifled a sob, choking down the lump in her throat. "I was facing having to give up my *boppli* for adoption, until I got the proposal from Adam. If I marry him, I won't have to do that."

Ben pulled her into his arms. "Don't cry little *schweschder.* Don't you see? You won't have to give up the *boppli* if you marry Ray either."

Miriam hadn't even considered that. Here she was, thinking marriage to Adam was the only way to keep her *mamm* from slipping away from her completely, and it was the only way to keep her *boppli.* Was it possible that she could have everything she wanted by marrying Ray? It couldn't be that easy, could it?

No.

If she married Ray, she would lose the community—and her only brother, who stood before her now trying to convince her to make a move that would remove him from her life.

"But I'd have to give up you and *Daed* if I marry an *Englisher.*"

He smoothed her hair, supporting her head against his shoulder. "You won't have to give me up. I'll support whatever decision you make. If *Daed* doesn't like it, I will have to visit you and Ray without him knowing. But I'm a grown *mann* capable of making my own decisions. *Daed* may come around in time, but until then, you will still have me."

His words brought some comfort, but additional worries. "What about the community?"

Ben walked her over to the sofa and sat down next to her. "When I talked to Claudia this morning, she told me about Ray's *familye* showering you with gifts for the *boppli.* You have a small community in Ray's *familye.* Why would you turn that away?"

Miriam stood up and paced the room.

"Because I want what's familiar. I *need* familiarity of *familye.* I'm not ungrateful for the beautiful store-bought quilts they gave me for the *boppli,* but it just isn't the same as the one *mamm* sewed for me."

Ben jumped up from the sofa and ran out the door, hollering, "I'll be right back," over his shoulder.

Before she realized, Ben was back inside the house, arms full of the quilt her *mamm* had sewn. She pulled it from him, burying her face in its worn folds and began to sob uncontrollably.

Ben steered her shaking frame toward the sofa and helped her sit down.

"If I'd known it was going to make you this upset, I wouldn't have brought it. I took it off your bed and brought it with me thinking it would bring you comfort while you recover from the accident."

Miriam lifted her face from the quilt. "I'm not entirely sad—I just miss her so much. I'm just crying because I'm so happy you brought me this. I didn't think I would ever see it again. It's the only thing I have of *mamm's,* and I was worried I wouldn't have it if *Daed* knew the *boppli's vadder* was an *Englisher.*"

"Now you have it—no matter what your decision is."

Miriam hugged the quilt to her.

If only her decision could be this easy.

CHAPTER 26

Miriam heard the doorbell ring. It was something she wasn't certain she could ever get used to hearing. She hadn't heard a car or a buggy pull up into the long driveway, so she was curious as to who could be there waiting on the porch. She considered not even answering, but she couldn't do that in case it was someone important looking for Ray.

He'd gone into town to finalize some details with his construction crew, and Miriam missed him already. How was she ever going to get through the rest of her life without him? She wondered if she should consider *dating* Ray after she married Adam, just as he'd suggested. Could she do such a thing, even though their marriage was one of convenience alone?

When Miriam opened the door, it wasn't the cold and snow that took her breath away; it was seeing Bethany and Lavinia in front of her that did it.

"Are you alright?" Lavinia asked her. "You look very pale."

Miriam put her hand to her forehead and blew out a heavy sigh. "I think I might have stood up too fast. I feel like I'm going to faint."

"As long as it isn't from seeing us," Bethany joked.

Miriam thought she wasn't far off the mark as she sat down in the rocker.

"I see you got the rocking chair. When Ray spoke to your *bruder,* he described the one you had back home, and relayed the information to Ray so he could get it. He was very particular about what he wanted to get for you. I thought it was so romantic."

Miriam was suddenly confused.

"But *mei bruder* has only been here for two days, and when he saw it, he didn't say he'd helped pick it out. I wonder why he didn't tell me."

"Ray and Adam picked it up from Caleb Yoder yesterday afternoon. The Yoder's make all the furniture in our community. They have three generations who work on the furniture."

Miriam's eyes widened at the comment. "Adam went with Ray?"

Bethany nodded.

Were the two of them conspiring against her in order to force her to choose between them, or had they become friends? Either way, the idea of them spending time together for *her* benefit made her feel a little uncomfortable. But perhaps it was for the best. After all, they would both be raising her baby. She would rather have them get along than not, but she wasn't certain she relished the idea of them being friends either.

"You *do* know I'm marrying Adam and not Ray, don't you?"

"*Nee,*" Bethany said. "We assumed you were marrying Ray since he's the *vadder* of your *boppli.*"

Miriam practically choked on Bethany's words.

"I suppose Adam was waiting until Sunday service to have our wedding published," Miriam corrected them.

Lavinia handed her a package wrapped in brown paper. "We made this for your wedding, but I'm not certain it will work now."

"*Danki,*" she said with downcast eyes.

Miriam took it, confusion filling her. She lifted the edge of the wrapping feeling a little awkward at opening a gift from two women who had plenty of reason to hate her—yet they didn't. Forgiveness and peace were the Amish way, but she never thought much about it until now.

From the folds of the plain, brown wrapping, Miriam pulled a white, sheer pinafore with a swirl design embroidered into the silky material. It was the most beautiful pinafore she'd ever seen.

"We made it long-sleeved for the change in weather," Bethany said.

"It's *wunderbaar,*" Miriam said. "But much too fancy for an Amish wedding. Unless your Ordnung is more liberal than mine."

"*Nee,* it isn't," Lavinia said. "But we were under the assumption you were marrying the *Englisher.*"

Miriam admired the simple elegance of the pinafore, her thoughts turning to Ray. She imagined the smile he would give her if he were to see her in such a beautiful garment. But in order for him to see her in it, she would have to marry *him.* Did she want to marry Ray? She liked the idea of it, but she was too afraid to even think about it.

"Try it on," Bethany urged.

"I'm so—grateful you made this—for me," Miriam stuttered, trying not to offend them. "But if I can't wear it to marry Adam in, there is no point in trying it on."

"Try it on," Bethany repeated. "We will need to make another one that is plain, but first, we will have to see if it needs to be altered."

"I suppose that makes sense," Miriam agreed, secretly eager to try on the elegant pinafore.

Miriam stood from the rocker, excused herself, and walked toward the bathroom. She turned back midway, remembering her manners, and addressed her guests.

"Would either of you like some hot *kaffi,* or cocoa?" she offered.

"*Nee,* we can't stay long," Bethany said.

Lavinia stood and closed the space between her and Miriam, startling her by pulling her into a sincere embrace. "We only wanted you to have this gift from us, and to let you know that you *do* have friends here—no matter who you marry. After all, we have plenty of *Englisch* friends."

Miriam was filled with shock to her very core.

"You want to be *my* friend?"

"*Jah,*" they said in unison.

Tears welled up in Miriam's eyes. "I don't deserve your kindness. I've been so mean to you both."

"All is forgiven," Lavinia said gently, giving Miriam one last squeeze.

"You are the most beautiful woman I've ever known," Miriam said through choked-back tears.

Lavinia looked at Miriam curiously. To be called beautiful by a woman as beautiful as Miriam was the highest form of compliment she could ever get. But she quickly squelched her prideful thoughts, her crimson cheeks threatening to give her feelings away.

Within minutes, Miriam stood before the mirror in the bathroom at Ray's house—her house—if she wanted it. She admired how the pinafore hugged her narrow waist. Ray would certainly adore her in such a beautiful garment. She knew better than to give in to feelings of vanity, but at the moment, all she could think about was Ray, and the look that would surely cross his face when he saw her in this. Her desire for him to see her was almost more than she could suppress. At the moment, all she wanted was to indulge in the feeling of adoration Ray would certainly have for her, and it felt comfortable. It felt right.

CHAPTER 27

Miriam wrung her hands, waiting for Adam to pick her up for the Sunday service. She'd donned her best pink dress, her *kapp* was set just right on her head. Her apron was neatly pressed, her hair twisted the same way she'd seen Bethany and Lavinia wear theirs. The last thing she wanted to do today was to offend anyone in the community, and her appearance was critical.

Today would be a day of confession and remorse, and hopefully, forgiveness would follow. Her goal was to redeem herself in the community, and she was finally ready for whatever the day would bring. No matter what the outcome, she had to make things right with the community and clear her conscience.

As she exited her bedroom at Claudia's house, she passed Ray in the hall. His arms were full of boxes she supposed he'd packed from his room there. She knew he'd been slowly moving things into his new home, but she hadn't expected to see him this morning—especially not this early.

He leaned in and kissed her on the cheek.

"You look very pretty this morning. All that for me?"

Miriam's heartbeat doubled its rhythm, causing her to put an anxious hand to her chest for comfort.

"Adam will be here to take me to Sunday service in a few minutes."

No sooner had the words slipped off her tongue than regret filled her. Ray walked past her, but not before flashing her a hurtful look. When would she ever learn to control the filter between her brain and her mouth? For someone who'd decided she was going to stop hurting him, she was not off to a very good start.

Ray exited the front door. Miriam watched him toss the boxes into the snow-covered bed of his white truck that was very much in need of a good washing. A dirty layer of road-salt trailed the length from bumper to bumper, and mud clung to the tires. He leaned against the tailgate of the truck, his brow furrowed so deep, she could see it from the window from where she watched him. He was obviously not happy to hear she was still attending the service with Adam, but at the moment, this would be her only window to accomplish what she needed to do.

Though she was tired from lack of sleep, she was eager more than ever to get this over with. She'd stayed up with

Claudia until well into the wee hours of the morning talking. In the end, she'd admitted to Claudia that she still loved Ray, and always would.

Miriam's decision was an easy one, and now it was time to put into action what was in her heart.

Adam's buggy pulled into the driveway. He hopped out and approached Ray. The two shook hands and exchanged brief pleasantries, while Miriam squirmed at the sight of it. The only consolation for her was that this unpleasant situation was all about to end.

Miriam threw her thick, wool coat over her shoulders and walked bravely out toward the two men, neither of them sure of their fate with her. She tried not to make any direct eye-contact with Adam, but it seemed Ray had the same intention for her.

She stopped short of Adam's buggy and turned to Ray, who hadn't left the tailgate of his truck. "Can we talk when I get back? I had intended to talk to you this morning, but I stayed up so late with your mother talking last night that I overslept."

Ray shrugged at the implied chip on his shoulder. "I don't see that we have anything to talk about. I asked you not to go to this service, and you've made up your mind to go no matter how I feel."

She took a step toward him, but noticed the apprehension in his expression. "I *have* to go to give my confession."

"I don't understand why."

"I don't expect you to understand, but I hope you will support my decision," she said.

Ray didn't want to hear what she had to say. She'd made up her mind, and he would have a hard enough time trying to live with her merciless decision, without her rubbing it in his face. There are certain things you just can't take back once they are said.

Flaunting Adam in front of him was nothing short of cruel, and he wanted no part of it. He was hurt, especially since he had been so sure he'd been able to get through to Miriam. He thought she loved him, but it was apparent she did not. He was confident she would choose him, but it was evident he was wrong about that too.

Miriam closed the space between them when Ray didn't answer. "I'm sorry, but this is something I have to do. But I'd like to talk to you after I get back."

His jaw clenched. "I won't be here."

"Would it be alright if I came over to your house when I return?"

Ray looked off into the distance. "I'll be working on the barn all day. I don't think I'll have time to stop what I'm doing except to make a trip into town to the lumber store if I need to. Other than that, I'll be up to my ears with trying to patch the roof before nightfall."

Miriam knew now was not the time to get Ray to understand why she had to go to the service, or why she had to do what she felt she had to do in order to be able to live with herself. And she certainly was not about to have a detailed discussion about it in front of Adam. But she didn't want to leave things like this. She needed peace in her heart to prepare for what she felt was going to be the toughest decision she would ever have to make. In as much as Ray's support of her decision was critical to her well-being, Miriam suddenly realized she was not going to get it.

CHAPTER 28

Miriam listened to the rhythmic clip-clop of the horse's hooves as they passed yet another farm, while waiting and hoping Adam would start a conversation with her. Even if it was only small-talk, it would be better than nothing. She couldn't waste the entire ride to the Yoder farm waiting for an opportunity to tell him what she needed to say. She had to say it *before* they arrived for the service. If not, she would lose her nerve.

She shivered a little, adjusting the heavy quilt to keep the bits of snow from gathering over her lap.

Adam saw her shivering and tucked his arm around her.

She gently pushed him away.

"If you're worried about being seen like this in front of others in the community, they will accept it once they hear the Bishop publish our wedding today."

Miriam bit her bottom lip, fear welling up in her.

It's now or never. I won't get a better opportunity than this. Lord, give me strength.

"The Bishop won't be publishing our wedding, Adam. I can't marry you."

She felt him become rigid in the seat next to her, his hands tightening on the reins.

"I was expecting you to say this. I'm not surprised, but I'm disappointed."

Miriam turned so she could look him directly in the eye. "Why would you be disappointed? You only offered to marry me as penance for the accident. I forgive you for the accident, and I let you off the hook for having to marry me."

Adam glanced at her and then put his focus back onto the country road that was luckily devoid of traffic.

"What if I don't want to be let off the hook? What if I still want to marry you?"

A lump formed in her throat. "You don't *need* to marry me, and I don't believe you would *want* to marry me either. Don't you want to marry for love instead of obligation?"

Adam tried to put his arm around her again and she scooted away from him and shrugged his arm away.

"I could learn to love you."

Miriam sighed. "You shouldn't have to force yourself to love me. Love is something that comes naturally when you meet the one you are to marry. It is so far beyond your control that you can't keep it in no matter what, and you don't want to because all you want to do is be in that person's presence."

"I like being around you," he said defensively.

"You don't love me, and I don't love you. If we are to marry, that is what I would want for you *and* for me."

He turned to her, the horse following an instinctive path down the road without a lead. "We will take the time to court, then."

Miriam shook her head. "I don't have the luxury of time to court you. I'll be showing soon."

"Surely in a month you won't be showing enough to cause concern in the community. That would be enough time to see if we are compatible."

Miriam felt frustration rising in her. She wasn't getting through to him by being gentle with her words. She would have to shock him with reality.

"I don't want a marriage with someone I'm merely compatible with. I want to be married to someone I love. I love Ray that much, but I didn't realize it until I was faced with losing him."

Adam's expression changed.

She could see relief in his eyes.

"I am happy for you that you love Ray. I was still willing to marry you if it was necessary, but I understand now it won't be. If not for your honesty with me, I would have gone through with the marriage."

Miriam tilted her head against his shoulder.

"You are a *gut* friend, Adam. I will always be grateful to you for being willing to help me and the *boppli,* but it's time I grew up and accept what my fate is. I belong with Ray."

Adam gave her a quick, friendly squeeze. "I agree. But I suppose I need to take you back now—back to Ray. There is no reason for you to go before the community to give a confession since you will be living among the *Englisch* then."

"*Nee,*" she said. "Now it is more important than ever that I give that confession."

Adam looked at her curiously. "I don't understand why you would put yourself through that when you don't have to. A confession, especially a public one, can be nothing short of torture."

Miriam swallowed a lump of fear, pushing her worries aside.

"*Jah,* but I have made friends that I want to keep, and I can't do that if I don't make things right. I need to clear my conscience of the terrible things I did. I took advantage of your guilt over the accident and was willing to let you marry me out of guilt—all for my own selfish reasons—most of which I've made up in my head. I came close to ruining Nate's life with Lavinia, and now I could have ruined your life if I'd have let you go through with this fake marriage.

I have hurt too many people with my lies, and I want to be the sort of honorable person my friends can respect. The kind of person that learns from mistakes and makes every effort never to repeat them. I want Ray and *mei kinner* to be able to respect me, too. More than that, I want to be able to respect *myself,* and I won't ever be able to do that if I don't change my heart and do what's right."

"I'm proud to call you *friend,* Miriam," he said in a most sincere tone.

Tears welled up in her eyes at his words of comfort. It was just what she needed to give her the strength to face the community.

CHAPTER 29

Miriam twisted at the long tendrils she'd freed from her prayer *kapp*, waiting for Ray to answer his door. She didn't know why she felt the need to ring the bell, but after the way she'd left him two hours ago, she feared she'd ruined her chances with him.

Lord, please put forgiveness in Ray's heart for me the same way you did for the Amish community. Danki for blessing me with the words I needed to convey my remorse for my sins against them. Bless me with the same words now to make amends with the mann I love.

Ray opened the door, looking surprised to see her. "I didn't really expect to see you back here."

Trying not to cry, Miriam fought to find her voice. "I told you I needed to talk to you, but I had to address the Amish community first—to make amends."

Ray took a step back. "Well come in out of the cold and snow."

Miriam waved off Ben, who'd driven her, and watched as he steered Adam's buggy around the circle drive and down the dirt lane to the main road. After, she followed Ray into the house. She paused before sitting on the sofa, wishing she could sit in *her* rocking chair just once more—in case Ray rejected her and sent her on her way.

"Would you like some coffee or cocoa to warm you up a bit?" he asked as he stoked the fire.

"No—thank you." Miriam stood up nervously and walked over to the hearth and held her cold hands out toward the warm flames. It was something to occupy herself while she gathered her thoughts.

"I came to apologize for the way I've treated you, but I beg you to listen to why I did what I did. I'm not trying to make excuses for my behavior, because I take full responsibility, but I need you to know the reasons behind it." She looked up at him to be sure he hadn't lost interest.

"First, and most importantly, I want to say how deeply sorry I am for not trusting you with the news of the baby. I got scared when I found out I was pregnant, and after the accident, I was even more terrified when they confirmed the pregnancy because it meant I had to make some hard decisions."

Ray guided her back to the sofa and wrapped a quilt around her shoulders. "I wish you would have included me in those decisions. Maybe then we wouldn't be in this mess."

"I was afraid if I didn't stay in the Amish community, I would have to give the baby up for adoption the way my mother did to me. The Amish community was the only place I felt safe. But now I realize, Ray, that you would do anything you could to make me feel safe and to be sure we didn't have to give up our child."

"I would think my constant proposals and this house would be enough to make see that I would do anything for you and our child."

Miriam wanted to ask if he would still have her, but she didn't dare at this moment.

"I know, and I'm sorry for that. If only I'd trusted you more, things could have been different."

Discouragement furrowed his brow. "I told you the moment I found out that I would raise our baby with you. Why didn't you believe me?"

She could see the hurt in his eyes.

"It wasn't that I didn't believe you, after a long talk with your mother last night, she helped me to realize I have what she calls "trust issues". And even though I had never heard of such a thing, her explanation did make the most sense of anything I was feeling."

Ray chuckled. "I can see that. My mother can talk circles around anyone, but she only does it because she cares."

"I adore your mother, and I pray that I will still get a chance to be her daughter-in-law." Miriam knew it was a risky thing to say, but she couldn't take it anymore. She *had* to know if there was still a chance for her and Ray to be together and raise their child.

Ray pulled her into his arms. "I think I can arrange that."

Miriam was almost too afraid to hope she wasn't dreaming this moment with him.

Suddenly, Ray jumped up from the sofa and slid down on one knee in front of Miriam. "I suppose I should officially *ask* you."

Tears of joy threatened to choke her, but she swallowed them down, trying hard to contain her emotions.

Ray took her hand in his and pressed a kiss on the back. "Miriam, will you bless the remainder of my days by becoming my wife—my *fraa?*"

"*Jah,*" she said as tears spilled from her eyes.

Ray leaned up and pressed his lips to hers. It was the kind of kiss that could only be felt with the love that filled her heart for him. He was loyal to the very core of his being; how could she not love him? He was everything she needed and more—much more. She hungered for this man's love, but she would be hungry no more. He was hers; mind, body, and soul. Her heart would always belong to him, but at this moment, all she wanted to do was to claim his soft lips.

She swept her mouth across his, her hands to each side of his strong jaw. His whiskers prickled her fingertips, the feel of his manly flesh arousing delight in her. She would love him for the rest of her days and never let him go.

CHAPTER 30

Miriam fidgeted while Claudia's hairdresser piped baby's breath in-between her curls to form a flower "crown" around her head. The woman had made up Miriam's face conservatively, and surprisingly, the makeup covered the scar on her face completely. She stared at her reflection, noting how beautiful she looked, but she couldn't help but think how much she'd changed on the inside—where it counted the most. She was happy with the person she was now—a feeling she'd never experienced before. Claudia had complimented her on the progress she'd made, and she had to admit she was finally proud of herself for her accomplishment in that area.

When the hairdresser was finished fussing over her, Miriam let her out of the room at the B&B, and then slipped the silky pinafore over her head that Bethany and Lavinia had made for her. Though it wasn't traditional Amish, it wasn't traditional *Englisch* either. It was sort of a mixture of both, but she liked the fact that it was Amish-made. Made by two new friends who had come to see her marry the man she loved.

Claudia entered the room and presented her with a beautiful bouquet of yellow roses, sheer, white ribbons hanging from it that matched her pinafore.

"No *English* bride can be without a bouquet to hold at her wedding. It helps to hide your shaky hands!"

Claudia hugged her soon-to-be daughter-in-law just before she left the room.

She hadn't thought of the traditional bouquet, but she would be happy to carry it. Happy because Claudia had been thoughtful by presenting it to her.

Her brother poked his head into the room just then. "They tell me you need someone to *give you away.*"

"Jah," she said, feeling a little choked up at the offer. "I would like that very much *mei bruder.*"

"I know it's tradition for a *vadder* to do this job, but I will gladly step in for him since he couldn't be here. I'm not certain if he will ever come around, but I will always be your *bruder,* no matter who you marry."

Miriam didn't want to cry today.

She wouldn't.

She would be happy that her adoptive brother was with her, happy with the new family she was about to gain, with the friends she had earned through her change of heart, and with the man she loved more than anything, who was about be hers for the rest of her life.

After a quick hug, Ben took Miriam's hand and led her out into the large meeting room of the B&B, where her wedding would take place in only a few moments.

As she took her place at the doorway, the traditional *Wedding March* was played on the piano. With her arm tucked in the crook of her brother's elbow, Miriam stepped along the blue rug between the rows of chairs toward her new husband.

Miriam's eyes locked onto Ray, her handsome husband-to-be. The dark grey suit he wore hugged his six-foot frame, his blond hair pushed up in front just the way she liked it.

Ray was her goal, her future.

His smile washed away every last fear she had left in her. There was no doubt in her mind she was doing the right thing. She was confident she would have a good life with Ray, and that he and his family would take care of her and their baby just as well as even the largest Amish community would. She knew she wasn't losing the community; she had friends now that would support her. She couldn't help but think that she and her baby would have the best of *both* worlds.

Though Miriam would live and raise her baby in the *Englisch* world, she would forever remain Amish in her heart.

THE END

READ ON TO THE NEXT BOOK

Amish Brides
of Willow Creek

Book Three: Sweet Nothings

Table of Contents

CHAPTER 1

CHAPTER 2

CHAPTER 3

CHAPTER 4

CHAPTER 5

CHAPTER 6

CHAPTER 7

CHAPTER 8

CHAPTER 9

CHAPTER 10

CHAPTER 11

CHAPTER 12

CHAPTER 13

CHAPTER 14

CHAPTER 15

CHAPTER 16

CHAPTER 17

CHAPTER 18

CHAPTER 19

CHAPTER 20

CHAPTER 21

CHAPTER 22

CHAPTER 23

CHAPTER 24

CHAPTER 25

CHAPTER 26

CHAPTER 27

CHAPTER 28

CHAPTER 29

CHAPTER 30

❧Sweet Nothings❧

CHAPTER 1

"Fire!"

Panic rose in Bethany as she screamed for help, but no one came to her rescue. Flames licked the undercarriage of the overhead vent that spanned the length of the twelve-burner gas stove in the kitchen of the B&B. Smoke billowed above the flames, most of it spiraling up into the vent.

A strangled cry escaped her throat, her breath heaving.

With trembling hands, Bethany wrapped her fingers around the curved, brass handle of the ancient fire extinguisher and tried to release it from where it was clamped against the wall.

It was stuck!

It was an antique; probably as old as the one-hundred-year-old B&B.

Grease sputtered and popped from the flaming frying pan on the burner. Splatters stung the exposed flesh on her arms, triggering her reflexes to flinch with each blistering pop.

The blaze grew higher, backing her away from the stove. A million thoughts came in spurts, uncomprehending, and unresolved. Every possible resolution represented an additional obstacle. Her greatest one, being that she couldn't get close enough to the stove to turn off the gas without risk of serious burn.

Bethany tried to free the fire extinguisher once more, but it only jiggled. The more she pushed, the looser it came from its binding, metal strap.

Time was running out, but at the same time, seemed to be standing still.

She could taste the adrenaline in her mouth. It was sticky like sap coating her tongue. Her heartbeat muffled all noise as her entire focus rested on freeing the fire extinguisher.

One last shove to the side, and down it came onto her foot with a thud. She let out a brief cry, but the terrorizing force of urgency moved her arms automatically to heft the cumbersome brass canister with one hand and grip the rubber tubing. Pointing it upward, she aimed at the base of the fire and emptied the canister before it registered in her mind that the fire had been extinguished.

Bethany took in a deep breath, her breathing slowed, her heartbeat relented. The sound of the smoke detector reached her ears just then, and she realized the noise had been strangely muffled before. As if her other senses had momentarily shut down to accommodate her *fight or flight* reflex long enough to extinguish the flames.

"What happened in here?" came Jessup's stern baritone as he rushed up behind her and turned off the gas burner. The door from the butler's pantry swung back and forth with the force of his entrance.

Bethany turned around, unable to speak. She simply held up the empty fire extinguisher and pointed to the oversized cast-iron pan full of unusable fried chicken. The stockpots of mashed potatoes and gravy, and the loaves of freshly-baked bread on the warmer were also now inedible.

She'd ruined dinner for seven guests and four employees. It would be hours before the mess could be cleaned and a new meal could be prepared. The realization of the mistake flooded her mind all at once.

"It was an accident," Bethany managed.

She knew it was an excuse she'd given over and over to her boss, and she knew by the look on his face he would not show her any mercy this time.

"I'm sorry," she attempted to offer through tears.

Jessup walked over to the stove and surveyed the damage. Aside from grease splatters and a scorch of soot on the wall and stove, the only real damage was to the meal that his guests expected. He would have to feed them cold meat with day-old bread from the pantry they usually reserved for morning toast, and if he was lucky, there was enough fruit to make a salad to go along with the *chow-chow* that remained unharmed in the icebox. Luckily, the pies had already been placed in the butler's pantry awaiting the fresh-brewed coffee for after the meal.

Bethany crossed to the window and lifted the sash, hoping to release some of the smoke. She hoped her gesture would show her boss she was willing to fix the situation.

"*Sorry* isn't going to serve my hungry guests," Jessup reprimanded.

She crossed to the stove to attempt a clean-up, wishing she hadn't convinced Bess she could handle the kitchen on her own while the older woman had gotten off her swollen and tired feet for a while. Bess had gotten her nearly to the end of the meal before she decided she couldn't stand on her aching feet another second. All Bethany had to do was let the chicken reach a golden brown, and then remove it from the pan. The strainer spoon she'd used to scoop the drumsticks out of the pan had slipped from her fingers, and splattered the grease into the burner she'd neglected to turn off before sifting the chicken from the fryer. If only she'd written down the instructions before Bess had retired.

"*Sorry* hadn't made the sheets you turned pink go back to white again. And it hadn't cleaned the slippery buttermilk from the floor that you'd spilled before Mr. Brown slipped on it and twisted his back. But I will tell you that *I'm not sorry* that I'm going to have to excuse you from your position of employment here."

Bethany was stunned.

She let the broom drop from her hands and walked in a slouched posture back to her room to pack her things.

Only problem was; she had nowhere to go.

CHAPTER 2

"It's not fair!"

Bethany stamped her foot against the worn porch of her mother's old, dilapidated bakery that stood at the forefront of her father's farm.

"I'm leaving again, but *this* time, I'm *not* coming back!"

She'd meant it as a threat to her father, who'd allowed her mother's bakery to remain abandoned and uncared for, for too many years to count. Only problem was, Bethany was desperate now and had nowhere else to go. The threat was a gamble, she knew, but desperation to get her way was her driving force.

She'd been *let go* from the B&B after she'd nearly burned down the entire kitchen, and now she was asking her father for the impossible, and to put her in charge of feeding and serving guests.

She'd hidden her suitcase behind the barn to keep her father from knowing she no longer resided at the B&B, but it would only be a matter of time before he learned the truth from the gossip-mill among the community.

"I'd like you to come home," her father said gently. "But you haven't shown me you are responsible enough to run a bakery."

It was an excuse to keep her from invading her *mamm's* space, she knew, but she wasn't about to let her *vadder* off the hook. "I have been working at the B&B for over a month now. I can cook and do wash, and I've even learned how to serve guests. That would almost be the same as serving customers at the bakery."

She was stretching the truth, but she hoped he wasn't any the wiser. If he'd already heard of her domestic fumbles at the B&B, then her arguments were all in vain.

"Jessup was just telling me how well you were doing when I ran into him in town yesterday," her father said.

Bethany's heart beat so hard she could feel it in her toes. Had Jessup told her father the truth, or would he have spared the man's feelings, and told him she was a good worker to spare her father from embarrassment? That's what it was. She was an embarrassment to her father, and the whole community knew it but him.

But Bethany knew, and the only way to prove otherwise would be to run her mother's bakery successfully. But in order to do that, she needed her father's permission—or did she?

The more her father rattled on about the many unrealistic reasons she could not use her mother's bakery, the more she realized he was still not over her *mamm's* death. Although Bethany, herself, had been too young to remember the sort of details Lavinia always shared with her, she couldn't imagine how many more memories their father had stored away about her. He had not moved on, never remarrying, and now Bethany was suffering for it.

What she needed was to find a diversion for her father—something to occupy his time so immensely that he would have no time to keep track of her if she was to return home. She knew paring him up with someone would be next to impossible even though it was the most logical solution. Not because there was any lack of widows in the community, but because he was well aware of their existence and had refused their advances too many times to count. Most had offered pies and casseroles, and even though he'd accepted the meals with open arms, they'd closed just as quickly when the offers arose for more.

If there was a way around his stubbornness, Bethany was determined to find it.

The familiar clip-clop and whirring of buggy wheels reached Bethany's ears. Just up over the rise, the bobbing head of a horse came into view. As he pulled the buggy up the small crest, she noticed the wobbling wheel of *Frau* Yoder's buggy.

She was a widow!

"*Daed,* look at *Frau* Yoder's wheel," Bethany said a little too excitedly. "Shouldn't you stop her and help her fix it?"

Her father pulled at his long, wiry beard that was mostly grey. "*Jah,* I suppose that would be neighborly, but she could probably make it to Henry Graber's farm and he can fix it for her. She'd be better off in his care since he's the buggy maker."

He was always making excuses to avoid the widows in the community. It annoyed Bethany at this moment more than it ever had before. She knew fixing the widow's buggy wheel was not going to make them fall in love, but Bethany could certainly find a way to make it work for her benefit.

They had to start somewhere, didn't they?

Frau Yoder was the sweetest of all the widows in the community, in Bethany's opinion, and for an older woman, she was still very attractive. Some of the other widows in the community had aged beyond their years, and had stopped taking care of themselves. But not *Frau* Yoder. She was still very active in the community, and she made the best shoofly pie for miles around.

Frau Yoder slowed her buggy, bringing it to a halt at the crossroad where Bethany and her father were standing in front of the bakery.

She smiled brightly at Bethany's father.

"*Gudemariye,* Jacob and Bethany," the older woman said.

"*Gudemariye, Frau* Yoder," her father said.

Bethany smiled a greeting.

She couldn't help but notice that the widow had addressed her father by his given name, but he had been far too formal in return. She knew it was his way, but she was going to have to encourage him to change. She'd never tried before, and she had no idea if it was plausible, but she was more determined than ever to find out.

"I couldn't help but notice your wheel is a little wobbly," Bethany said cheerfully. "If you pull it up to our barn, *mei vadder* can tighten it for you."

"*Danki,*" the widow replied, without giving Jacob the opportunity to retract the offer.

Her father cleared his throat in a manner which Bethany knew was disapproving of her offer to the widow, but if she hadn't extended the kindness, he would have let her leave, and that did not fit into Bethany's plan for the two of them.

Gott had just dropped an opportunity in her lap, and she was not about to refuse a blessing so great.

CHAPTER 3

"Won't you *kume* in out of the cold and have some hot *kaffi* while *mei daed* fixes your buggy wheel?"

Bethany would have preferred the setting to be a warm, sunny day so they could sit on the swing and sip lemonade while they watched her father repair the buggy wheel, but perhaps the snowy day was a blessing in disguise.

Frau Yoder followed Bethany into the house, where she lit the stove for a fresh pot of coffee. She knew that the time it would take her father to tighten the buggy wheel would be accomplished at about the same time the coffee would be ready, and perhaps, she could coax him inside to join them.

The widow set her coat on the back of her chair instead of placing it on the peg near the kitchen door where Bethany had hung hers. Was she supposed to offer to hang it up for the older woman? If so, the window for such an offer had passed. She shrugged it off and went about getting three cups ready, determined that her father would join them.

"I hope you weren't in a hurry," Bethany said, breaking the silence between them.

"Nee," the widow said, fussing with her gloves that she'd set on the table. "I was on my way home when the wheel began to wobble. I worried I wouldn't make it to the Graber farm, so I'm grateful your *daed* was able to fix it for me."

Bethany smiled. "It was as if *Gott* put us out there at the road at just the right time to help you."

"Jah, tis true. I will have to bake a shoofly pie for your *daed."*

"Jah, he would like that very much," Bethany said eagerly. "It's one of his favorites, and I don't know how to make them."

The widow smiled gently. "I don't suppose you do, or you'd probably still be working at the B&B."

Bethany nearly dropped the coffee cups she was arranging on the serving tray. "If *you* know, then *mei daed* surely knows I've been relieved of my employment with the B&B."

The widow chuckled. *"Nee,* your *vadder* doesn't pay much attention to the community chatter. He keeps to himself, so I think you're safe there."

"Perhaps if you were to teach me how to bake shoofly pie, it would help me."

"My shoofly pie recipe won't help you get your employment back at the B&B."

Bethany smiled. *"Nee,* but it might help me convince *mei daed* to let me reopen *mei mamm's* bakery."

The widow's eyes bore a soulful look. "I'm not certain there is anything that will get Jacob to give up his attachment to that bakery. It will likely cave in on itself before anyone steps foot in it again."

"Perhaps if I fixed it up as a surprise, but he would need to be distracted." Bethany looked at the widow sheepishly. "If he was busy with *courting* someone, he might not notice, and by the time he noticed, he wouldn't care because he'd be in *lieb."*

"You are quite the dreamer," the widow said with an undertone of condolence. "But I have to admit, I wouldn't mind stepping into that dream with you."

Bethany turned around and looked the widow straight on. "You like *mei daed?"*

"Jah," she said, blushing. "Perhaps...*nee,* it's too *narrish* to even consider."

Bethany scooted to the table and leaned on her elbows, intrigued at the possibility of a *plan* that might work for both of them. "I'm all ears!"

The widow cast her eyes downward, but Bethany could still see the deep blush that had mixed with her expression. "I've wanted to court Jacob for years," she said with a far-off look in her eyes. "I've tried many a time to get his attention, and so has most of the widowed community. He's quite a *catch,* your *daed* is."

Bethany giggled. It was funny to hear that these women should see her father in such a romantic light. She couldn't help but think if they knew the *real* man behind their romantic notions, they might think twice about him. The first time he would come in from slopping the pigs and neglect to wash his hands before he sat down to eat, they might run for the hills. Bethany giggled again just thinking about it.

"What is so funny?"

"I was only thinking that *mei daed* has gotten sort of set in his ways, and I think he would be a lot of work for an unsuspecting widow like yourself. I don't think you know what you're getting yourself into. He eats the way pigs eat their slop, and sleeps in his dirty clothes after a long day, and worse! Are you sure you're up to adapting to that? He's too old to change."

The older woman smiled knowingly. "He isn't too old. He can still be molded."

Bethany chucked. "That seems like a lot of work to me, but if you're sure, then I'm up to the challenge too. I'll help you however you see fit. As long as it gets him out of the way so I can fix up the bakery and ready it for business, I imagine I'm up for most any challenge that comes my way."

Bethany hoped she wasn't getting a little too confident and getting ahead of herself, but for the first time in two days, she had more hope to hold onto than she thought possible.

CHAPTER 4

"*Daed,* please join us for a cup of hot *kaffi.* You must be very cold after fixing *Frau* Yoder's buggy wheel."

Bethany set the cup in front of him, giving him no other alternative but to sit with them. If she knew her father, he would suck down the coffee as fast as he could just so he could leave. As far as Bethany could help it, she wasn't about to let him.

Making a grand gesture of looking at the clock in the kitchen, Bethany crossed to the sink and dropped her cup in. Then she walked over to the pegs near the door and pulled her coat and mittens down.

"It's getting late, *Daed.* I need to get back to the B&B so I can help prepare the evening meal."

It was the only thing she could think of to say, and she regretted the words as soon as they left her lips. She had nowhere to go, and it was snowing. Perhaps Lavinia would take pity on her and give her a place to sleep for the night. She could always start over with her father tomorrow. Perhaps then he would see reason to letting her move back home and reopen the bakery.

Her father flashed her a pleading look, while the widow Yoder sent her a knowing smile. She winked at the older woman as she put on her coat. She hated the idea of walking to Lavinia's farm in the snow, but it was better than staying here and watching her father squirm. Though Bethany thought it to be rather funny, she wasn't going to stick around to witness it for herself.

Once she escaped the thick of the kitchen dramatics, Bethany found her suitcase behind the barn and brushed off the layer of fresh snow that had accumulated on the top. Her gaze lifted to the loft apartment above the barn, wondering if the risk of being caught in there was worth getting out of the cold.

She decided it wasn't.

The walk to Lavinia's house was going to be a long one, but perhaps it would afford her the time to think of a plan for her immediate future.

Bethany trudged up the driveway toward the main road, following the path of trodden snow from *Frau* Yoder's horse. The main road would not be as easy to navigate due to cars creating a thick slush on the shoulder of the road where she would need to walk. She prayed that buggies traveling the same road had provided enough room for her to avoid oncoming traffic in safety. She had cut through the woods along the bank of Willow Creek on the walk over, but it was now late afternoon, and she feared it would be too dark in the thick of the trees.

As she approached the crossroad, gentle clip-clopping reached her ears. She stood and waited for the buggy to come up over the rise, praying it was a neighbor she could trust not to blab to her father if she should ask for a ride. Whoever it was, was traveling in the direction of her sister's farm, so the only possible worry would be her father discovering the truth.

An unfamiliar horse and buggy came into view before she was able to distinguish the driver. Late afternoon sun shone on the lone occupant, making it difficult to determine who it could be. Perhaps it was someone from a neighboring community. It would certainly make it easier on Bethany if she could encounter someone who would not have the opportunity to reveal her shenanigans to the gossip mill in her own community.

A stranger might be the best thing for the situation. Perhaps she might even have enough nerve to give the driver the wrong name if he or she was willing to give her a ride down the road a ways. As she stood there anticipating, the sun filtered through the trees, allowing flickers of light to reflect off a familiar face.

It was Benjamin Schrock.

Bethany felt panic well up in her like a sudden gust of wind, ready to tip her off balance at the slightest move. But move she must. She couldn't have him seeing her with a suitcase in hand. He would know she'd been fired and was now homeless. It would embarrass her that, even if she could get her feet to propel her forward, he would offer her a ride.

She wouldn't care if it was someone like Adam, but Bethany had taken notice of Benjamin when he'd walked Miriam down the aisle at her wedding. She'd spent the entire wedding swooning over him. She'd studied him so much that day, she would recognize his strong jawline even in the dark. From this distance, she could make out his handsome features enough to be certain it was him driving the horse toward her.

It was too late for her to go back down the lane to her father's house. He'd spotted her and tipped his hat toward her. She stood there, frozen in place, but not because of the cold.

Benjamin pulled the buggy alongside her.

"You look like you're leaving town. Can I offer you a ride somewhere?"

His sultry baritone and mesmerizing blue-green eyes momentarily hypnotized Bethany.

"Are you alright, Bethany? How long have you been out here?"

He knows my name!

She knew he was looking for an answer, but she couldn't keep her mind on task. What had he asked her?

Benjamin threw down the reins, jumped from the buggy and was at her side before she could comprehend what was going on.

Now she was really embarrassed.

Think fast. What should I do?

Bethany shuddered and chattered her teeth. "I think I've been out here for so long, it's possible my brain might have frozen over for a second," she swooned dramatically.

Benjamin tossed her suitcase on the floor of the buggy and put his arm around her, urging her forward.

"Let's get you up here under the lap quilt with me so I can get you warmed up.

That's exactly what I was hoping for!

Bethany allowed him to assist her into the buggy, where he tucked her into the lap quilt and kept his arm around her, keeping her close to him.

"Where can I drop you?" he asked as he picked up the reins with his free hand and set the horse in motion.

She didn't give an answer.

She was right where she wanted to be for the moment, and she wasn't about to let it go just yet.

CHAPTER 5

Bethany stood on the porch of the Widow Yoder's home, waiting for her to answer the door. She shivered a little from the long walk over, remembering how nice her ride to Lavinia's house had been yesterday afternoon with Benjamin's arms wrapped around her. How she wished for the warmth of his arms now as snow swirled around her ankles. The porch needed shoveling, and she wondered if the widow had anyone to help her with such simple tasks. Perhaps her father would come in handy for the widow more than she'd originally thought.

When the door swung open, the widow pushed a shovel into her hands. It threw Bethany's thoughts into reverse. She was expecting to begin her lessons on making shoofly pie.

She wasn't here to shovel.

"You can start with the porch and work your way to that sidewalk. When you finish, make certain the back stoop is shoveled, and a *gut* path to the barn. It isn't easy for me to maneuver around in this snow, and I'm not going to get through another winter doing it myself."

Bethany was stunned.

She didn't mind helping the widow, but the woman had promised to teach her to make pie.

"Well, what are you waiting for?"

"I thought perhaps *mei daed* could do this stuff. I thought we were going to make pie."

The widow shook her head. "You work for me, now. This *haus* needs a *gut* cleaning, and I'm in need of someone to do it for me. We'll bake pie when the work is done."

Bethany leaned the shovel toward the house and let it drop against the clapboard siding. "You expect me to clean your house for you just so you will teach me how to make pie?"

"Jah," she said with a smile. "I can't entertain your *vadder* in *mei haus* when it isn't clean enough. The rugs haven't had a good shaking in a long time, and the whole *haus* is full of dust. I'm getting too old to climb those stairs well enough to clean all those rooms upstairs."

Then you're too old to marry mei vadder, Bethany thought.

"I'm not going to clean your entire *haus* just so you will teach me to make shoofly pie."

The widow smiled again, this time with a hint of impertinence in her eyes. "It isn't so you can learn how to make pie. It's too keep your *vadder* distracted so you can work on your *mamm's* bakery."

It would seem that *Frau* Yoder had her over a barrel. To Bethany, it felt more like domestic blackmail. She begrudgingly withdrew the shovel and walked back down the stairs to clear the snow that had accumulated to her ankles. She would do the work required, but only because she had no other choice.

What had happened to that sweet little old widow she'd had coffee with only yesterday? The difference in her was like night and day. Unfortunately, Bethany wasn't in a position to argue with the woman. If she didn't do the widow's bidding, the woman wouldn't do her part in keeping her father occupied long enough to allow Bethany the time it would take to clean the bakery and get it ready to open. Distracting her father was vital to Bethany's plan.

After a few minutes of shoveling, Bethany surveyed the long path that led back to the barn. It would take her all day to shovel all of it, and by the time she finished one end, she'd have to start all over on the other end. The snow was coming down so thick, it would surely add another several inches to the walkways before she finished. How clean would be clean enough for the widow? Would the woman expect her to stay out here all day before allowing her to come in and bake a pie? What about the widow's involvement? She needed to ask the woman what her plans were to keep her father out of the way, and just when she intended to fulfill her end of the bargain.

Bethany fumed as the shovel hit a patch of ice and dropped to the ground unexpectedly. She looked up at the house, realizing that the widow was standing in the front window watching her struggle. How long had she been there? The woman waved, and Bethany returned it with a scowl, letting the old woman know of her angst—not that she cared. She almost seemed to be enjoying it.

Turning her back to the widow, Bethany tried to ignore the woman, who seemed to hold her future in her hands. She knew if she didn't do exactly as the widow instructed, her chances of opening the bakery would not be likely. On the other hand, if she was going to be too busy doing the widow's house-work, she would be too exhausted to get the bakery cleaned up and ready for business.

A sudden thought occurred to Bethany. What if the widow turned on her and told her father she'd been fired from her position at the B&B? If she did that before Bethany had the chance to show her father what she could do with the bakery, it would be all over for her.

Bethany shoveled faster and more vigorously. She had to get this chore done so she could move onto the next one before the widow changed her mind about helping her.

This was going to be a long, hard road to travel, and her already sore back was going to pay for it.

CHAPTER 6

"How long do you think we should leave your *dochder* out there?" *Frau* Yoder snickered, as she watched from the warmth of her front window while Bethany struggle with the snow shovel.

Jacob tugged at his long, wiry, graying beard and sighed. "I suppose for as long as it takes for her to learn her lesson."

"From the look of it, she might freeze to death before that happens," the widow said, closing the curtains.

"*Mei dochder* has to be taught that she can't manipulate her elders," Jacob said sternly. "When she gets too cold, she will give up and realize what she's doing is not worth the effort."

Outside, Bethany had furiously worked to clear the walkway, and had nearly made her way to the barn, where her father's horse and buggy were safely stowed away from her sight.

"What if she doesn't?" the widow asked. "She seems pretty stubborn."

"*Jah,* that she is, but only time will tell."

"In the meantime, how about a piece of shoofly pie and a cup of *kaffi* to warm you up? I'm certain you're still cold from fixing the hinges on my barn door. That wind was something awful last night, wasn't it? I thought that door was going to blow clean-off."

"*Jah,* winter has set in for sure and for certain."

Jacob watched his daughter from the kitchen window. He thought about how much she had her mother's determination in her. Perhaps he should reconsider her request to open the bakery. If only she'd inherited her mother's natural ability to bake. The poor girl couldn't bake her way out a flour sack. If she could, she might have been able to keep her employment at the B&B.

Jessup King had reluctantly told Jacob of his daughter's release from his employ at the B&B after she nearly burned down the kitchen from her inability to cook. Jacob felt so sorry for his daughter, he hadn't had the heart to tell her he knew she'd been let go. The stubborn girl certainly needed some positive direction in her life, and he hoped the widow's influence would make a difference. He knew working for Jessup King could not have been easy on Bethany. Although he was a fair employer, he was a stern man.

Jacob's gaze focused on Bethany, who'd nearly finished the chore in record time. He would have done the shoveling himself if not for her showing up at the most opportune time. He'd just come in from fixing the barn door when she'd shown up. Although he didn't like the idea of deceiving his daughter, he realized it was a necessity to chip away at her rebellion.

Jacob sipped the last of his coffee and raised from the chair about the same time Bethany headed toward the front porch. "That's my cue to leave before I get caught here. I'll be back later to pick you up for that sleigh ride. *Danki* for the *kaffi, Frau* Yoder."

"I thought we agreed that if we are going to keep each other company, that you would call me by my given name, Anna."

Jacob smiled. "Alright, *Anna*. I will see you this evening."

Anna blushed, though her name sounded foreign coming from a man, but she smiled as she let Jacob out the kitchen door. She watched him disappear into the barn while Bethany knocked on the front door for the second time.

My, but she's an impatient girl.

The widow couldn't help but feel sorry for Bethany. If she'd had a daughter, she'd have taught her how to make her shoofly pie.

Perhaps it's time for mei mudder's shoofly pie recipe to be handed down to someone.

The widow went to the door and welcomed Bethany with a stern smile. She couldn't be too soft on the girl, or the lesson Jacob wanted her to learn would not be taught.

Bethany stomped her feet on the porch before entering the widow's home. As she crossed the threshold, she heard a buggy in the driveway that she'd just shoveled. She turned to see who it was, when the widow whisked her inside and closed the door. The woman oddly steered her toward the fireplace in the front room.

"Let's get you warmed up," she said as if in a hurry. "You can't make pie with cold hands."

"I think you might have company," Bethany said.

"Nee, I had to have *mei* barn door repaired after last night's storm nearly blew it off its hinges. He is leaving now."

Bethany hadn't remembered seeing a buggy in the driveway when she'd been shoveling, and the widow was acting a little strange. Was she up to more than Bethany thought she was? She shook off her suspicions as the fire roared in front of her. It felt good to get out of the cold and snow, but she worried the widow was only letting her warm up long enough to go back out and shovel the driveway again after she'd had a chance to warm up.

"Would you like some *kaffi?* Or perhaps hot cocoa would be better for a girl your age."

My age? Does she think I'm twelve?

"*Danki,* but I would prefer *kaffi.*"

"*Nee,* I think cocoa would be better for you," the widow insisted.

Then why did you even ask?

"Do you know how to make *gut* cocoa, dear?"

Your "sweet little old widow" routine isn't fooling me. You're up to something, and I aim to find out what.

"*Nee,* I suppose I don't know how to make *gut* cocoa," Bethany said in her sweetest voice.

It was no use fighting the woman. It was a battle she would not win. Since Lavinia had refused to get involved with her scheme to reopen her mother's bakery, she had no other choice but to rely on the widow to teach her basic baking methods. Unfortunately, Bethany feared she would probably be making more *crow* than shoofly pie.

CHAPTER 7

"How is it that I'm lucky enough to find you out here two days in a row?" Benjamin asked.

Bethany shrugged, feeling embarrassed that she needed a ride again. But the snow and wind were cutting right through her, so she wasn't about to turn down a ride from the man. Her teeth chattered and she shivered as he assisted her into his buggy.

Wait, did he say he was lucky to run into me again?

Bethany smiled, her teeth chattering so furiously, she almost couldn't close her mouth.

Benjamin pulled two lap-quilts over her and hugged her tightly to him for a few minutes. "If you're going to keep walking in this weather every day, I wish you'd tell me where I can pick you up, and I'll be happy to give you a ride."

"I'm w-working for th-the w-widow Y-Yoder," she said as best she could around her chattering teeth.

"Now that I know, I can't be responsible for you freezing to death. I'll pick you up every day about this time so you won't have to walk. I've been working odd jobs in town until I can find a permanent position somewhere. I'd like to stay close to *mei schweschder* at least until after she has her *boppli*."

"The w-widow l-lives at the end of th-that l-last turnoff if y-you w-want to p-pick me up th-there."

Benjamin pulled her closer and tucked his warm face against hers. "It's settled then. Right now, let's get you warmed up."

Bethany was more than comfortable in his arms. In fact, she couldn't help but think this was something she could get used to.

Benjamin leaned down and picked up a thermos from under the seat, poured hot cocoa into the cap, and handed it to Bethany. Grabbing the cup with both hands, she lifted it to her face and blew on the cocoa to allow the steam to warm her cheeks. She sipped the steaming liquid, feeling the heat permeate her insides. Soon, her teeth stopped chattering, and her muscles began to relax.

The widow had worked her to the bone today, and she was so exhausted, she fought to keep from dozing off in the comfort of Benjamin's arms. Though they hadn't conversed too much, there was an obvious, mutual attraction between them.

"What sort of work do you do for the widow?" Benjamin asked, breaking the silence.

He lifted the reins and set the buggy back in the direction of Lavinia's house where he'd dropped her off the day before. She didn't want to go back there, but at the moment she had no other choice. Her back hurt from the stiff mattress in her sister's spare room. Her own bed would feel perfect right about now, but the painful reality of her circumstances kept her from going home.

"Today, I shoveled her driveway again, and the walkway *twice,* and began working on cleaning the upstairs of her *haus*. But I'm only doing it so she will teach me to bake shoofly pie. I worked so hard the last two days, that we didn't even have time to start the pie."

Benjamin looked at her curiously. "Shoofly pie?"

"*Jah,* she was supposed to teach me to make it—for *mei mamm's* bakery."

"Your *mamm* has a bakery?"

"*Jah*—well, not anymore. She's gone on to be with the Lord. But *mei daed* won't let me reopen her bakery, so I thought that if I could surprise him with learning how to bake a pie he would give me a chance."

Benjamin let loose the reins and allowed his horse to slow his gait through a patch of deep slush.

"It takes much more than learning to bake a pie to run a bakery. You have to be able to fill special orders, and have cake-decorating skills. Not to mention, having a wide variety of baked-goods. You can't run a bakery with one kind of pie. You wouldn't have many customers. Besides, the business aspect of running a bakery takes inventory and book-keeping skills."

Bethany blew out a discouraging sigh. "How do you know so much about running a bakery?"

Benjamin chuckled. "I suppose it sounds pretty silly hearing about running a bakery from a *mann,* but in the off-season, I help *mei aenti* run her bakery."

Bethany's ears perked up at the mention of his experience. "*Nee,* I'm impressed."

"*Danki.* The women back in my community have spent a fair amount of years teasing me for it."

Bethany wouldn't dream of teasing him about it. She saw his experience as an opportunity to get her father to change his mind. But how was she going to convince Benjamin to help her? She had no money to pay his wages. Perhaps, he would consider doing it as a favor in exchange for the debt his sister owed her.

"How many years have you been baking?"

He gave the reins a gentle tug to keep his horse from splashing through the slush. "I've been working for her since I was about ten years old."

Bethany smiled. "You have more than enough experience to teach me how to run *mei mamm's* bakery. If I learn the whole business, *mei daed* will *have* to give me permission to open it back up."

Benjamin scowled. "You mean you're doing this behind your *daed's* back?"

Bethany's expression fell.

"Only until I can prove to him I can do the job. It's only because he is so stubborn he won't trust me."

"I don't blame him."

"What?" Bethany squealed.

"I wouldn't trust *mei dochder* if she was going behind *mei* back to do something I had forbidden her to do. It's obvious you *can't* do the job if you don't even know how to bake shoofly pie. And I won't help you deceive your *vadder.*"

Bethany turned to him, hoping she could change his mind, but his jaw clenched and his eyes remained forward as he halted the horse.

They'd reached her destination and the end of their conversation.

CHAPTER 8

"Why are you here?" Bethany asked impatiently.

"I gave you my word I'd drive you home," Benjamin retorted. "Just because I don't agree with your plan to ambush your *vadder* doesn't mean I won't keep my word to you."

Bethany pursed her lips. If he wasn't so adorable, she'd have walked home just to spite him. His disagreement with her plan had been a thorn in her side ever since yesterday. His harsh words had kept her awake most of the night, and all day she'd struggled to keep on task as she'd endured another long day of the widow's torture.

All of it over shoofly pie.

Was it worth it?

Her first answer would be yes, but after a long day to think about what she'd gotten herself into, she was beginning to second-guess herself and her plan. It was more than a matter of pie. It was her future independence, and her ability to support herself when she became an unfortunate *old maid,* enduring the whispers of her peers behind her back. Some would be sympathetic, but most would likely agree with Benjamin.

Ah, Benjamin.

It would seem he was her only prospect of avoiding the painful reality of becoming an *alte maedel*—old maid. But even Benjamin had suddenly turned on her, as did the widow and her own father.

Was it possible that she just wasn't meant to open her mother's bakery? At this point, she didn't care. She needed something to relate to her mother, and the bakery was what she wanted. Lavinia, the only mother she'd really known, was now newly married, and that left Bethany all alone and full of regret.

Regret over her early rebellion.

Regret that she'd taken Lavinia's instruction for granted.

"Danki, " she said humbly as Benjamin assisted her into his buggy.

His horse whinnied, puffs of icy air rolling from his large nostrils as he seemed to protest the extra passenger. Though she was dainty, Bethany's added weight would put an added strain on the gelding as he trudged through the slush and muck on the shoulder of the country road that would take her to her sister's house.

"I don't understand the unusually heavy snowfall we've had so far. Winter has barely just begun," he said, breaking the awkward silence between them.

"Jah, it would have been a *gut* day to stay inside and bake a shoofly pie," Bethany grumbled.

Benjamin chuckled. "She still won't teach you?"

"Nee," Bethany complained. "She has put conditions on my lessons every day. And each day so far, there has not been enough time for me to learn to bake after I finish all her chores. Not to mention the fact that I'm too exhausted."

"Perhaps the widow is pulling the wool over your eyes."

"Jah, don't think I haven't considered that. I did ask her to keep *mei vadder* occupied while I worked on the bakery to get it cleaned up, but so far, he hasn't been over there. I've been there working every day and haven't seen him even once."

"You are trying to pair your *vadder* with the widow?"

Bethany nodded.

"That is dishonest."

I don't remember asking you for your opinion.

"Don't you think that if your *vadder* wanted to court the widow he'd have done it by now? Or at the very least, begun to court her on his own without your interference?"

Her face heated with anger. "He would never ask her if I left it up to him. He is lonely, and needs someone to care for him because I don't want to be the one who has to."

"That sounds selfish. Not everyone wants to be married," Benjamin said sternly.

"Sure they do," Bethany argued. "You don't want to get married?"

Benjamin slighted his gaze at her and raised an eyebrow. "Not really. All of the women I have met are selfish—like you."

Bethany fumed. Why was he insulting her? She hadn't done anything to him. Unfortunately, her own sister had called her selfish recently, as did her sister's new husband, Nate. Perhaps there was some truth to their statements, but Bethany was getting desperate to stay out of her father's home—out of the sad reality of becoming an old maid.

It would seem it was to be her fate.

Even Benjamin didn't like her.

It would seem the bakery was her only hope.

Benjamin slowed the horse as they came upon her father's home. Turning into the lane, Bethany could feel sudden panic gripping her heart that beat heavy against her ribcage.

"Why are you pulling up to *mei daed's haus?* I'm staying with *mei schweschder,* where you've dropped me off the past couple of days."

"I think you need to go home," he said sternly without looking at her.

Bethany blew out an angry breath. "That isn't up to you to decide. You are not *mei vadder.*"

"Nee, I'm not. But someone needs to make you accountable for your actions. I think you should talk to your *vadder* and tell him of your plan before you begin it. Tell him the deal you made on his behalf regarding the widow so he can decide for himself. I know I wouldn't want someone pushing me into a relationship with someone I didn't choose."

"What does it matter?" she squealed. "You don't plan on marrying, so why should my decisions about *mei daed* bother you? It doesn't affect you or your decisions one way or the other."

"It does affect me," he said as he tugged hard on the reins to stop his horse.

Turning in his seat, Benjamin drew Bethany into his arms and pressed his lips against hers, his breath heaving passionately. Stunned by his sudden transformation, Bethany slowly succumbed to his kiss, clarifying her desire for him.

All too soon, the kiss had ended just as abruptly as it had begun.

"Go home," he said, still delirious from her kiss. "Make things right with your *vadder.*"

Bethany stepped out of the buggy and into her father's yard. Confusion clouded her mind. She could still feel the tingle of Benjamin's lips against hers. It reached all the way to her toes, dizzying her. She stood there, unable to speak, as she watched his buggy pull away from her and head back toward the main road.

CHAPTER 9

Bethany shivered, suddenly realizing she hadn't left the spot where Benjamin had dropped her off several minutes ago. She'd watched his buggy until he'd pulled out onto the main road, still in shock from the kiss he'd surprised her with. Her cheeks warmed just thinking about it.

"What are you doing here, *dochder?*"

Bethany jumped. She'd been so caught up with romantic thoughts of Benjamin that she hadn't heard her father walk up behind her.

"I'm tired," she said abruptly. "I've had a long day at work today, and tomorrow will be worse. I think I'm going to hit the hay early."

"There is beef stew you can warm up if you're hungry," her father offered.

She whipped her head around at his comment, knowing her father could not make beef stew.

"It came from the widow Yoder," he offered before she could question him.

Bethany merely nodded, glad to see that at least one of them was getting some benefit from the arrangement she'd made with the woman. Too tired to let it bother her anymore, she entered her father's house through the kitchen and shuffled toward the gas stove.

Lifting the lid to the still-steaming pot of stew, Bethany leaned in toward the pot and sniffed. Her stomach grumbled from not eating most of the day. She hadn't thought that the widow would deprive her during working hours, but she supposed the woman wasn't obligated to feed her. Since Bethany wasn't about to ask her, she opted to go hungry and work through the mid-afternoon meal. For this reason, she chose to eat the stew now rather than collapsing on her bed and sleeping like a rock.

She shuffled to the table with her bowl, noting the basket full of fresh biscuits in the center of the table. It would seem the widow was going all-out to win her father over. She wasn't making any progress with Bethany, but perhaps tomorrow would be the day.

Her day.

The day she would finally learn to make shoofly pie.

****

"Wake up, *dochder.*"

Bethany felt her shoulder jiggle. She groaned as she opened her eyes a little, unable to focus in the dimly-lit room.

Where was she?

"You fell asleep in your stew," her father said impatiently. "Go to bed."

Bethany lifted her head slowly from the table. She hadn't taken even one bite of the cold stew in front of her. She'd only laid her head down for a minute just to rest her eyes. How long had she slept there? She twisted and turned her stiff neck to loosen it up a little.

Her father turned up the flame of the gas lantern that hung above the table. If he was just coming in from his evening chores, then she would have likely just dozed off for a few minutes. But it felt *much* later than that.

Bethany glanced at the clock on the wall above the kitchen sink. It was ten o'clock!

"Where have you been, *Daed?*"

Jacob cleared his throat and averted her stare.

"I was out with the sleigh."

Bethany's eyes widened.

"With the Widow Yoder?"

"That is none of your concern, *dochder.*"

That means you were, Daed. And with you busy with her, it won't be long before that bakery is mine!

Jacob handed Bethany her suitcase.

Her heart sped up. "Where did you get that?"

"Benjamin went to Lavinia's *haus* to fetch it for you after he dropped you off earlier."

Bethany felt embarrassment warm her cheeks. If her father had seen Benjamin drop her off earlier, then he'd witnessed the steamy kiss between them. Would he punish her for such brazen behavior?

"I stopped him at the end of the road and he asked me to give it to you," her father went on. "He's a smart young *mann.* He explained to me how he told you to return home—after I asked him why he'd brought you here, and why he'd fetched your suitcase from Lavinia's."

Bethany was getting a little angry. "What else did he have to say?"

"He told me of your plans to open your *mudder's* bakery."

Bethany's expression fell. Why had Benjamin thrown her to the wolves like that? He'd kissed her like he loved her, yet he'd betrayed her confidence. Now she would never have a chance to run her *mamm's* bakery. Had Benjamin done it because he disapproved of Bethany's scheming against her father and the Widow Yoder?

Whatever the reason, it was obvious Benjamin didn't love her. How could he if he was so quick to betray her?

Bethany had no words for her father. Defeat filled her as she took her suitcase and headed toward the stairs. Now she was trapped in her father's house—doomed to become a spinster.

"Get some sleep, Bethany," her father called after her. "I expect to see you down at the bakery first thing after morning chores."

She whipped her head around to face him. Had she heard him correctly?

"Go on now, I need you well-rested. We have a lot of work to do before you can open the doors for your first customer."

Bethany giggled. Benjamin had come through after all. He hadn't let her down. Somehow, he'd been able to convince her father to let her open the bakery.

He *did* love her.

She felt giddy and in love all at the same time. Now, the only thing she had to worry about was learning how to make shoofly pie.

CHAPTER 10

Bethany shouldered out into the blizzard-like snowstorm, wishing she'd have been able to start her new project in the summer instead of the beginning of winter. At least she was grateful for her father's help. After all, he was the one who built the bakery in the first place. She hoped it wouldn't be too overwhelming for him to reopen the doors.

As she neared the end of the road, she noticed two buggies sitting in the small parking area. One of them looked like Benjamin's buggy. She wondered what he would even be doing there. Perhaps that since it was Benjamin's talk with her father that convinced him to let her open the business, he was there to help with some advice on how to get the place up and running.

Bethany stepped up onto the porch and walked cautiously through the door. It was odd to see the door without the boards that she'd grown so used to seeing. Her father had boarded it up only a few days after their mother had passed away, and it hadn't been open since.

She could hear her father inside the kitchen talking to Benjamin and another man whose voice she didn't recognize. Her intention was not to eavesdrop, but she just couldn't help herself. After all, this was her new bakery, and whatever was being said should be her business too. At least that is how she justified her reason for listening in on the conversation taking place in the next room.

"By the time Ray finishes repairing the porch and the windows, the place should be ready to start accepting customers," Benjamin was saying.

Ray? Did he mean Miriam's husband?

"I'll put in the initial order later today," Benjamin continued. "So we can begin baking as early as Monday of next week."

We? Why would Benjamin be ordering anything for my bakery?

Bethany was about to barge into the kitchen with all the fury of a grizzly bear when she overheard Benjamin thanking her father for hiring him to run the bakery.

Bethany choked back angry tears.

Why had her father hired Benjamin to run the bakery? This was supposed to be *her* bakery. But now it would be a thorn in her side. Benjamin had betrayed her just as she had originally thought. He'd secured himself a position in *her* bakery, and neither of them had even consulted her about it.

Bethany turned to leave, but was caught off-guard by Benjamin.

"There you are. We've been waiting for you," he said cheerfully. "We were just discussing the ordering schedule."

"I'm well aware of what you were discussing in there," she said angrily. "I have just one question. Who put *you* in charge of ordering for *my* bakery?"

"I did, *dochder,*" Jacob said sternly. "I hired him yesterday after hearing of your scheming ways to get me to open your *mamm's* bakery. Benjamin was kind enough to offer his experience since he's helped to run his *familye* bakery for the past fifteen years."

Bethany leered at Benjamin. "*Jah,* I'll just bet he did."

"That will be quite enough, *dochder,*" her father scolded her. "You have no experience, so I had no other choice but to put Benjamin in charge of the bakery."

"You put him in charge?" Bethany squealed. "I don't need to be watched over like I'm a *boppli.*"

"Nee, but you need instruction, and Benjamin has the experience to offer."

"Never mind, *Daed.* I changed my mind. I don't want the bakery anymore."

Bethany stormed out of the bakery, tears catching in her throat. Wind and snow assaulted her as she headed back toward her father's home, but Benjamin's betrayal had insulted her.

"Wait," Benjamin called after her.

She picked up her pace, but Benjamin's long strides caught up to her.

"Let me explain," he begged.

"I don't want to hear anything you have to say. You betrayed me!"

She tried to walk away from him, but slipped on the snowy path. He caught her in his arms, and he paused, looking into her eyes as she rested in his arms. He bent his head to kiss her, but she pushed him away.

"What makes you think I want you to kiss me after you betrayed me?"

"After we kissed yesterday I thought we were—well, courting."

"Well you thought wrong," Bethany shot back. "Why would I want to court a *mann* who would hurt me the way you have? You know how much *mei mamm's* bakery means to me, and you came in and just took over. There is not room enough for the both of us. I should have expected as much from Miriam's *bruder.*"

Benjamin stopped in the middle of the path and turned to her. "What is that supposed to mean?"

"Your *schweschder* stole *mei* money and now *you* are trying to steal *mei mamm's* bakery away from me."

Benjamin clenched his jaw. "I'm not trying to steal your bakery. I'm only helping until you learn for yourself. And I thought you forgave Miriam?"

"I don't believe you, even for a minute. Perhaps I shouldn't have been so quick to forgive her of that debt. Stealing is obviously a *familye* trait!"

Benjamin shook his head in defeat. "I'm sorry if you don't like me being a part of your bakery, but it was the only way your *vadder* was going to let you open it. Without me you wouldn't even have this opportunity."

"Is this the part where I'm supposed to be gratcful to you for stealing my dream and making it yours?"

He tried to grab her hand, but she pulled away.

"You have it all wrong. I did this for *you.*"

"Nee, you did it for yourself and your *schweschder's* husband, and if you're waiting for me to be grateful to you for stealing my dream, that is never going to happen."

Bethany marched away from him as fast as she could in the slippery snow.

It was obvious to her she'd mistaken love for an opportunist.

CHAPTER 11

Bethany walked slowly into the wind, keeping her head down as much as possible. Sleet stung her cheeks, despite having her hand above her eyes to shield her face, her other hand tightly gripping her collar. It was too late to wish she'd brought her umbrella. It might have made the short walk to the widow's house seem as if it wasn't so far. She would be soaked and half frozen before she reached the farm that bordered her father's property on the north side of Willow Creek.

Normally, whenever Bethany was upset about something, she would head down to the creek and do a little fishing, or she would run off with Libby. But Libby had left to visit with relatives in Nappanee two days after Lavinia's wedding, and she hadn't yet gotten a letter from her stating how soon she would return to Willow Creek.

So, today, Bethany was on a mission to get someone--anyone to help her, and she thought no one was better suited for the job than the widow. In Bethany's mind, the widow had the most to gain from any sort of arrangement that could be made—especially with her father's affections at stake.

When she reached the widow's house, she was so cold and her muscles so stiff, she could barely make her way up the porch steps.

Widow Yoder swung open the door and shook her head at Bethany. "You're late!"

"I'm n-not here to w-work," Bethany said, her teeth chattering uncontrollably.

The widow moved aside to let her in. "Well, if you aren't here to work, then, why are you here?"

Bethany crossed the room to the hearth and stood close to the blazing fire. Almost instantly, she warmed up enough to stop shivering as violently as she was. Soon, her teeth stopped chattering and she turned to the widow, who'd been standing behind her patiently waiting for an answer.

"Did you know that *mei vadder* hired Benjamin Schrock to run *mei mamm's* bakery?"

"Would you like some hot tea, Dear?"

"Not right now. What do you know about all of this?"

"Jacob did tell me last night that he'd hired the young *mann* to run the bakery. But I also know it was what made your *vadder* decide to open it back up in the first place."

Bethany peeled off her wet mittens and set them on the brick step in front of the fireplace, hoping they would dry before she would have to return home.

"You're so informal with *mei vadder* that you call him by his given name now?"

The widow shook her head, a worried look in her eyes. "I would have thought your *vadder* would have told you by now."

Bethany started to shake again, but not from the cold. "Told me what?"

The widow cast her eyes downward. "We are to be married at the end of the month."

Bethany's breath caught in her throat. "What?"

"I said…"

"I heard what you said," Bethany interrupted. "But that is too soon. I only just got the two of you together a few days ago!"

"*Nee,* your *vadder* and I have been seeing each other for a few months in secret."

"Why did you go along with my plan and act as if you had always wanted to marry *mei vadder* when you've been seeing him all this time?"

"Because I thought this would be an easy way for you to know about us."

"So then having me clean your *haus* and all that shoveling was just a preview of how hard I will have to work when you're *mei* step-*mudder?*"

"*Nee,* Jacob thought it was best to teach you a lesson to put an end to your scheming. I went along with it because he is to be *mei* husband, and as your *vadder,* I didn't question his parenting method."

Bethany cringed at the thought of the widow being her step mother. But as an adult, she would be pushed out of the home when they married. She was more desperate than ever. She *had* to get her hands back on her *mamm's* bakery, or she would never be able to support herself.

"This never would have happened if you'd have just taught me to make that pie!" Bethany cried.

Widow Yoder put her arm around Bethany and gave her a gentle squeeze. "Pie alone won't run a whole bakery."

Bethany shrugged the widow away and bent to get her mittens. "It would have been a start! Besides, you could have stood up to *mei daed* and taken my side. You could have told him you were going to help me. But you didn't. Instead, you lied to me and betrayed me just like Benjamin did."

"I am on your side, Bethany," the widow said gently. "I want to see you succeed with the bakery because I know how much it means to you."

Bethany shook her head furiously, tears dripping down her face. "You really have *no* idea at all."

Bethany walked toward the door, but the widow placed a hand on her arm.

"Let me drive you home in this weather."

"*Nee,* you only want to impress *mei vadder* by being nice to me in front of him. I'd rather walk."

"That's not true. I care for you, Dear."

Bethany chuckled, tears still streaming down her cheeks. "I had a *mudder,* and you'll never replace her no matter how hard you try."

"I would never try to replace her. I understand you are an adult now, and you don't need a *mamm,* but I would like it if we could be friends."

"Don't count on it," Bethany snapped. "I will do whatever I can to be out of *mei vadder's haus* before the two of you get married. I'd rather go begging Jessup King for *mei* job back at the B&B than to live with the two of you."

Bethany turned to walk out the door, when the widow picked up an umbrella out of a large piece of crockery and tried to hand it to her.

Bethany waved a hand at her and walked out.

"Keep it," she said over her shoulder. "I don't want anything from *you!*"

CHAPTER 12

Taking a shortcut through her father's field, Bethany walked swiftly in the furrow between the frozen remains of cornstalks. The sharp tips stuck out from the snow about an inch—just enough to help her avoid them. Stepping on them wrong could mean a cut to her calves, and she hoped to prevent that, if possible. Cutting through the field could be dangerous in the winter, especially because there was so much mud and ice to slip on.

The only other alternative was walking on the main road and having to pass Benjamin and her father at the bakery at the end of the lane that led to the house.

For her, it was not even an option.

Bethany chose to cut through the field rather than dealing with her earlier humiliation all over again. She needed time to think of a new plan to get her bakery back, and to get Benjamin out of it.

Stomping her snow-covered feet on the kitchen floor, Bethany didn't see Benjamin and her father until it was too late to run back out the door. It wasn't as if the idea didn't flash in her mind, but she would have surely made a bigger fool of herself than she had earlier when she'd run out of the bakery. Besides, she wasn't about to let the two of them run her off a second time.

Now she was trapped and had to face both of them. The two sat at the table near the kitchen window, sipping coffee. Benjamin looked up and smiled, his hazel eyes kind and inviting. His sandy blonde hair formed a flattened rim around his head from where his hat rested, and Bethany found it almost appealing that he was such a mess.

She wanted to confront her father about the widow, but she didn't dare say anything in front of Benjamin about it, fearing her father would threaten her with a trip out to the barn. She was much too old for a sound lashing, but it wouldn't stop her father from threatening it and embarrassing her in front of Benjamin.

She tried not to care about Benjamin, but she already mourned the loss of him in her arms, and the softness of his lips against hers. If only she could look past his betrayal, but at the moment, all she could see was him sitting with her father plotting to take over *her* bakery.

"*Kume,*" her father said. "Join us for some *kaffi*. It will surely warm you up. Did you go down to the creek to do a little fishing?"

Her father knew her all too well, and right now that bothered her.

"*Nee,* I went for a walk."

It wasn't a lie, but it wasn't altogether true either. Now, she didn't really care. Her only concern was thinking of an excuse believable enough to bow out of sitting with the two of them. She could not sit through small talk, and she wasn't ready to discuss the bakery and their betrayal.

"It's too cold for a walk," Benjamin said, jumping up from his chair. "Let's get you in front of the fire to warm you up. You look frozen half to death."

I would have gladly stayed outside and turned to an icicle if it meant I didn't have to see you and mei vadder right now.

Bethany forced a smile and allowed Benjamin to steer her toward the living room where a fire crackled and whistled in the brick fireplace. Her father was always putting damp wood wedges on the fire because he was too stubborn to keep a supply in the house where it had time to dry out.

At six foot, two inches tall, the man feared having spiders in the house from storing a small wood pile like most people did. She had argued with him too many times, saying that at the rate they burned the wood in the winter, it would have enough time to dry out a little, but not enough time to collect spiders. It was an argument she'd never won.

Once in front of the fire, Benjamin wrapped his arm around her and rubbed her arms to warm them up faster. He dipped his head down into her neck and breathed, his lips grazing across her skin just enough to send shivers straight to her toes.

Why does he have to be so persistent? He's trying to keep me from being angry with him, but it won't work.

Shrugging off his affections filled her with instant regret, but she needed to keep her perspective, and she couldn't do that if her mind was clouded with desire for him. She closed her eyes so she didn't even have to look at him. If she didn't get out what she wanted to say, it would be all over for her, and he would have the upper hand more than he already did.

"I need you to understand that the bakery is mine, and I feel you betrayed me by going behind *mei* back and talking *mei daed* into hiring you. Because you did that, I will not trust you again. You took what I told you in confidence and used it for your benefit. Now that we will be working together, we need to maintain a business relationship only.

Just because I'm now required to learn from you doesn't mean we have to be anything other than coworkers. You may be my teacher—for now—but you will never be my boss."

She took a deep breath and waited for him to object but he didn't. Though her eyes were still closed, she sensed his nearness. He closed the space between them and pressed his face into her neck.

She shivered from the excitement.

"I'll do whatever you ask me to," he said.

He kissed her neck lightly and walked away, leaving her more confused than ever.

CHAPTER 13

"Doesn't your *aenti* need you at *her* bakery?"

Bethany knew her tone showed irritation, but it was way too early in the morning to start her day off with being bossed around in her own bakery.

"I've sent her a letter to let her know I would not be there this season. I'm certain she has employed one of *mei* cousins by now."

Inwardly, Bethany grumbled, but she knew the only way she would be able to take over her bakery was to learn from Benjamin, and patience would be needed. Patience had never been one of her strongest virtues, and Lavinia had often warned her that her short temper would someday get the better of her. She hated to admit to such a thing, but it seemed her sister had been correct about that. She could feel the anger and resentment rising in her for Benjamin, and it had begun to mask the love she knew she had for him.

She looked into his hazel eyes, wondering if she could ever trust him enough to let the love she felt take over. Perhaps if she didn't feel so threatened by his presence in her bakery, she would be able to look past it. Lavinia would surely scold her for being prideful, but she couldn't change how she felt, and no amount of prayer had changed it either.

It would seem that she would simply have to work this out for herself.

Benjamin handed her one of the two brooms in his hand. "Let's get started. The sooner we get this place cleaned up, the sooner we can get the doors opened for customers."

Irritated, Bethany let the broom handle drop to the tiled floor. "Please do not boss me around like you own this place. This is *my* bakery, and I am perfectly capable of deciding for myself what needs to be done."

Benjamin leaned on his broom, intending to humor her. "Alright, you are in charge. From here on out I will do what *you* tell me to do. You are right. It's your bakery and you're the boss."

His reaction caught her off guard, but she relished his submission to her authority. She looked around the dirty kitchen feeling a bit overwhelmed at the layers of years' worth of dust and grime, wondering just where they should begin such an undertaking. Outside, she could hear Ray and his men hammering the new floorboards of the porch. The windows they ordered should be in tomorrow, and her father had taken the sign back to the barn to repaint it.

"Perhaps you could get the ladder and start wiping down those shelves while I sweep up some of this debris on the floor."

Benjamin merely nodded and crossed the room for the ladder. She stood there and watched him for a minute as he filled a bucket with soapy water. He seemed content to do her bidding, but she wondered how long that would last before he tried to take over again. Surely, once they began to bake, he would overpower her again and use his experience to rule over her again. For now, she was happy with the arrangement, as long as she had some control over how things came together.

Deep down, she felt bad, and knew that, as a woman, she should not be ruling over a man she desired to marry. But it was probably too late for all of that anyway. Too many feelings had been hurt and too many things had been said that could not be taken back. At this point, she determined that the relationship with Benjamin was over and so she would have to settle for his instruction so she could run her bakery once he was out of her life.

A lump formed in her throat at the thought of Benjamin leaving, but she pushed it down, reminding herself of his betrayal. It would be the only driving force behind her getting what she needed from him. His instruction would provide segue to her future with the bakery, and she would do well to keep reminding herself of that. She wished it didn't have to be this way, but it was too late to turn back the hands of time and undo all the hurt and betrayal that now festered in her heart as resentment.

After a while, Bethany grew tired of sweeping the large kitchen and went out to the lobby area, intending to sit at one of the tables to have a break. She wasn't used to all the physical work she'd been doing the past week between the widow's place and now the bakery.

She pushed her way through the swinging door from the kitchen to the dining room, but quickly retracted when she spotted Miriam sitting with Ray at the corner table.

"It was really kind of Jacob Miller to let you do this job to pay off my debt to Bethany," she heard Miriam tell Ray.

What?

Bethany fumed from behind the door, where she continued to listen to their conversation that had turned to talk of the unusual winter they had begun to have. She couldn't believe her father had agreed to let Miriam out of the debt to her without even consulting her first. She could use that money now to rent a place in town.

What was she to do now?

She couldn't live with her father and the Widow Yoder once they were married. There just wasn't enough room for her at Lavinia's house, and she wasn't about to move back to the B&B. Not only could she not afford to stay there, but she was also not about to humble herself to Jessup King and beg for her old job back.

That only left one place.

Her brother's loft apartment above the barn at her father's house.

Surely if he objected this much to her opening the bakery, her father would never permit her to live in the apartment built especially for her deceased brother.

No. She would have to endure living in the same house with her newlywed father and his widow-bride, both of whom disapproved of everything she did.

CHAPTER 14

Bethany stared out the frosty kitchen window at the snow, while she poured herself a cup of fresh coffee. It was going to be another cold day where she would be stuck inside the bakery, having to listen to Benjamin boss her around as if she hadn't a brain in her head at all.

After the first day, he'd tried repeatedly to give her advice, but she'd worn him down by reminding him that it was *her* bakery. She wondered, however, how long it would be before that would no longer do the trick.

The necessary repairs had been made and the inside was cleaned and ready for Ray and his crew to paint. A new coat of whitewash was needed for the outside as well, but it would have to wait until winter thawed out.

For now, the sign and the front door had been painted, and the new windows had been put in. Truthfully, Bethany barely recognized the place after all the improvements.

Lavinia had promised she would be stopping by later in the week, once they had begun to bake a few things. She'd agreed to come by and sample the confections, and Bethany was more eager than ever to impress her sister with her new skills. She'd studied all her mother's recipes late into the night, hoping it would transform her into the sort of baker her mother could be proud of.

Bethany straightened her *kapp* over her loosely-wound bun. She'd caught Benjamin watching her once or twice when she'd conveniently had to pull her hair down to re-pin it during the past two days. She purposely left it loose just so it would fall down a time or two during the day. It pleased her that he could be so easily distracted by her. This, she felt, gave her the upper hand when it came to the overall control of the bakery. She knew it wasn't right to take advantage of his affections in that way, but she was more than desperate to get him out of her bakery. If a little distraction was what did it, then that's what she would use as her weapon of choice.

It wasn't that she wanted to get away from Benjamin; she just didn't want him working with her—especially not as her boss in her own bakery.

"Benjamin tells me you are refusing his instruction," her father's deep baritone rumbled behind her.

Bethany jumped at the sound of his voice, but his statement immediately brought up anger in her.

"That is not true! He's just bossing me around, and I don't think it's fair. It's *my* bakery, not his."

Jacob pulled off his snow-covered coat and hung it on the peg near the kitchen door, crossing the room to the coffee pot on the stove.

"It's not yours either, *dochder*. That belongs to your *mamm*."

"Nee, mamm is gone, and I think *she* would want me to have it."

"Not if she could see what a mockery you have made of it. She would not be proud of you for the way you are rejecting instruction."

Bethany swallowed the lump in her throat, turning away from her father so he would not see the tears welling up in her eyes. His words stung, and she thought it was unfair of him to put words in her mother's mouth that way. It hurt her to think that her mother could be disappointed in her.

"You need to listen to Benjamin's instruction," her father continued. "He is very experienced. And you should not forget that if not for his offer to teach you, I would not have agreed to open the bakery for you. He deserves your respect and cooperation."

He didn't respect me enough not to betray my confidence, so why should I respect him? Especially when he's tattling on me as if we were schoolmates. It's obvious we aren't even friends. If he thinks I'm going to cooperate with him, he's going to wait forever. But I will let him teach me so I can get him out of my bakery as soon as possible.

It was obvious Bethany could not trust Benjamin. Not as long as he was under her father's employ. She would have to bide her time with him until she could learn enough to be on her own. It angered her that she was being forced to depend on him. She really liked him, and she thought he liked her too. But perhaps it just wasn't meant to be.

Her father took his cup of coffee into the other room to sit in front of the fireplace to warm up, leaving her alone to reflect on his hurtful words that still hung thick in the air.

If only Libby were back from Nappanee. The two of them could easily run the bakery. They'd talked about it for the past year, making plans and dreaming of making the most perfect confections that would cause the suitors to be lined up outside the door, waiting to ask for the hands of the two women who were well-known in all the surrounding communities as the best bakers for miles around.

Bethany determined she would write to Libby today and beg her to come home. If anyone could help her to get rid of Benjamin, Libby was the one who could do it.

CHAPTER 15

Bethany stormed into the bakery with such fury, she slammed right into Benjamin as he was walking through the kitchen door.

He caught her from falling backward, using the advantage to pull her into his arms. *"Gudemariye,"* he said cheerfully.

Bethany rolled her eyes, but didn't make a move away from him. "Is it?"

Benjamin smiled, his hazel eyes hypnotizing her. "Why wouldn't it be? The sun is finally shining after two solid weeks of snow and gloomy clouds, and I've got the prettiest girl in the community in my arms."

Bethany pursed her lips. "Don't be prideful, Benjamin."

Inside, she was trying not to smile at his comment. He had to know she was angry with him, as it would seem he was trying everything he could to divert her attention away from his recent betrayal.

Bethany tried to push at his chest, but didn't try hard enough to actually get away from him. Truth be told, she liked being in his arms.

"Let me go," she said, pretending to struggle.

He looked into her blue eyes, smiling, as his gaze traveled to her full, pouty mouth. "What if I don't want to? What if I want to kiss you instead?"

Her lashes fluttered, showing helplessness against his affection. Not wanting to miss his window, Benjamin bent his head and touched his lips to hers. She sighed vulnerably, giving into his hunger for her. He deepened the kiss, capturing her mouth as if to satisfy an insatiable love for her.

Forgetting herself, Bethany fell limp in his arms, allowing him to keep the kiss going. She no longer resisted him. She wanted his kiss to last forever—to make her forget she was mad at him. She wished it would take away the feelings of betrayal, the feelings of distrust she had for him. But it couldn't. It wouldn't.

Bethany pushed herself from him, still in a daze from his touch. "This isn't going to work."

"I thought it was working out just fine," he said, leaning back in for another kiss.

Backing away from him, she wriggled from his grasp and turned her back on him. "I can't continue to believe you like me enough to be kissing me if all you do is betray me to *mei vadder.*"

"*Jah,* I can see where that might be a problem for you," he said thoughtfully.

Bethany whipped her head around, a glint of hope in her sparkling blue eyes. "Then you'll stop doing it?"

Benjamin hated to hurt her, but she needed to be taught a lesson. If they were ever to consider a relationship beyond the wonderful kisses, he couldn't live with her unruly behavior and prideful ways.

"*Nee,*" he said. "I won't lie to your *vadder* just so you can continue to act like a spoiled, prideful woman. He agreed to open this bakery for you, yet you make a mockery of it as if it will run itself. You will run it into the ground and defile your *familye* name if you continue your unruly behavior."

Bethany leered at him, lips pursed, brow furrowed. "It's a *gut* thing I see now what you really think of me before I even consent to an engagement with you."

"I don't remember asking you!"

Bethany fumed. "I wouldn't consent even if you did ask!"

Benjamin tried to keep a straight face. "So, it's settled, then."

What just happened? Did he trick me again?

"Nee, it is *not* settled."

Benjamin crossed his arms over his muscular chest. She couldn't help but admire the contour of muscle that showed beneath the arms of his royal blue shirt. With the sleeves cuffed at his elbows, tan arms and strong hands invited her to embrace him, as did the slight smile across his jaw, peppered with two day's growth. She tried to imagine him with a beard—the beard he would grow if they were to marry. She was certain he would be even more handsome as the years wore on him. She imagined a life in his arms—his strong, waiting arms.

Could she go to him now? Probably not, after the way she'd just spoken to him. Unfortunately, she was caught between her anger for him, and feelings of desire for a future with him. In the forefront of her mind, her first concern was the bakery. Getting it away from Benjamin's clutches had to be her priority.

"What is left to settle? You are spoiled and refuse my instruction, and you no longer want to kiss me."

I never said I didn't want to kiss you anymore. But not at the expense of being called spoiled!

Bethany gritted her teeth. "I will accept your instruction. But we will keep a relationship that is strictly for the sake of the bakery."

She knew it was the only way she would get it back from him. She was at his mercy. She needed him to teach her, but she would not continue to let him play games with her heart. She wanted him oh so much, but she would not compromise her heart in lieu of her mother's bakery. It was everything to her.

Bethany looked at Benjamin. He was too handsome for words. If the bakery was everything to her, then what was to become of her feelings for him? Could she keep her feelings in check while spending so much time with him?

"It looks like we finally have an agreement," he said sadly. "You will be serious about learning how to bake from me, and will not resist my instruction anymore. In exchange, I agree not to kiss you anymore."

There is was. He'd decided for her—for both of them. What if she changed her mind about him? Was it too late? She'd enjoyed his kisses, but she knew she couldn't have it both ways. She had to choose. That meant rejecting her feelings for Benjamin and accepting his instruction. It was to keep her mother's bakery—to keep her mother in her heart.

If only she could have them both in her heart.

She looked at Benjamin one last time. She knew that to reject him, she would lose him. She swallowed hard the lump that formed in her throat, pushing down the love she already felt for him. She blinked away tears that threatened to spill down her cheeks.

"Agreed," was all she could say.

CHAPTER 16

Bethany watched Benjamin crack eggs and sift flour with such ease she didn't know whether to be impressed with his skill or intimidated by his perfection. He didn't even have to follow recipes. Even her mother had followed recipes. Hadn't she? The box full of recipes was proof of that. Wasn't it?

"Are you paying attention, Bethany?" Benjamin snapped at her.

She cleared her throat. "Of course, I am!"

He handed her the whisk. "Stir the cake batter while I prepare the remainder of the cake pans. Do I need to go over pan preparation with you again, or do you have it?"

Bethany rolled her eyes and nodded.

I'm not stupid! Stop telling me what to do! You think you're so perfect. I bet your precious cake batter wouldn't be so gut with eggshells in it!

Bethany looked over her shoulder at Benjamin, whose back was to her. She grabbed a handful of eggshells from the counter and crushed them between her hands, allowing the crumbles to fall into the batter. She stirred them in, hiding the evidence.

Suddenly, Benjamin was at her side, and she feared he may have seen what she'd done. If he had, he didn't say a word. He simply set the round pans to the side of the oversized stainless mixing bowl and took over as if she wasn't even there. Bethany stood to the side and watched him pour the cake batter into each pan that she'd greased and floured.

After placing them in the oven, Bethany took a moment to fix her hair near the sink in the back. Out of the corner of her eye, she could see Benjamin watching her, and that pleased her. She chuckled inwardly.

Keep on wanting what you can't have, Benjamin! You can't have me and the bakery. I'm going to force you to choose.

When she finished, she grabbed a fresh linen towel and dabbed at her neck. "Is it warm in this kitchen, or is it just me?" she complained.

She watched him clench his jaw.

She was getting to him.

"If you're too warm, why don't you open the back door for a minute; let some of that cold November wind in here. That should do it."

He walked past her, avoiding eye-contact.

Bethany crossed to the back of the kitchen and propped open the back door with the broom handle.

"If you're done cooling off, I could use some help filling these whoopie pies. The filling needs just a pinch more cinnamon. Would you mix that in really quick while I get the extra wax paper from the box in the back?"

Bossy, bossy, bossy! Perhaps a handful of pepper instead of a pinch of cinnamon might teach you to stop bossing me around in my own bakery.

She quickly mixed pepper into the whipped filling while Benjamin was in the back room. She giggled thinking of how much he would cough and gag when he tasted the whoopie pie filling.

Sabotage might just be the best way to get him out of my bakery! When he sees he's not as perfect as he pretends to be, he will give up and leave.

Now more eager than ever to ruin everything the man baked, she began to dream up in her head what she could do next. She would be diligent and write down the recipes as he made them, but she would leave out her *special ingredients* she would add after he was done. Then after they baked, he would be confused, and she could blame him.

He has some nerve calling me prideful. He's so full of himself, he thinks he's the best baker this side of Ohio.

She'd tasted the batter before putting in the pepper, and she had to admit she'd never tasted anything quite like it before, and she'd tasted a lot of whoopie pies in her days. He'd added some unexpected ingredients in there, ingredients that she hadn't remembered seeing in any of her mother's recipes. Perhaps he did have a knack for baking, but she wasn't about to feed his ego over it.

When they'd finished filling and wrapping about a dozen whoopie pies, she'd had enough practice. *Presentation is everything,* Benjamin had told her repeatedly. She'd bought plenty of whoopie pies around the community, and they hadn't wrapped them as fancy as he'd made her do them.

"Don't you taste-test them before you sell them?" she asked, hoping to get the chance to see him gag on his own confections.

"Nee, if you follow your recipe every time, there is no need to taste every batch. If I did that, I'd weigh as much as my horse and buggy!"

"But you didn't follow a recipe, so how do you know it is *gut?"*

Benjamin winked at her. "The recipes are part of me. I know them like I know my own heart."

Ach, you're full of whoopie pie filling!

"Besides," he continued. "I saw the look on your face when you tried it, so I *know* it's *gut."*

Bethany shrugged. "It wasn't anything special. I've tasted a lot of whoopie pies in my day, and if you've tasted one, you've tasted them all."

She was hoping to make him think he'd done something wrong so he would taste the filling, but he didn't fall for it.

"I suppose if I hope to impress you with my baking skills, I will have to try harder."

Bethany scrunched up her face. "Why would you try to impress me?"

Benjamin winked at her a second time and smiled warmly. "What would be the point if I couldn't use my confections to gain your affection?"

His smile was the sweetest smile, and it caused Bethany to swoon—just before guilt flooded her heart.

CHAPTER 17

Bethany arrived late to Sunday service at the Widow Yoder's home. She'd dawdled over Libby's letter she'd been too tired to read the night before. After a long day at the bakery, she'd fallen asleep and hadn't read past the first line. This morning, however, she was so excited to read that her best friend would be home in the middle of next week, she was nearly beside herself.

When she walked in through the kitchen so as not to interrupt the service, she wasn't so distracted that she didn't see the widow arranging the casseroles and deserts that would feed the community after the service. Her heart did a somersault behind her ribcage when she spotted the cakes she'd frosted at the bakery just yesterday—the same cakes in which she'd added egg shells to the batter. Her eyes scanned for the whoopie pies until she set her gaze upon them at the far end of the counter.

Bethany froze, unable to move or think or breathe.

What am I going to do? I can't let anyone eat those. I put pepper in the filling—a lot of pepper!

"H-how did those get h-here?" she stammered.

The widow looked up at her face that must have been as pale as the snow. "Your *daed* picked them up this morning from your bakery. The entire community has been anticipating the first treats from the bakery ever since they heard it was reopening. Your *daed* thought this would be a *gut* preview and might draw in some business for you."

Bethany was numb to the widow's ramblings. All she could think about was the Bishop biting into one of those whoopie pies and shunning her for such sinful behavior. But not before her father took her behind the widow's barn and gave her a sound lashing—most certainly within earshot of Benjamin.

What was she to do?

If she disturbed the service to tell Benjamin, the Bishop and her father would dole out a punishment that would certainty not be anything she could live with. Not to mention Benjamin's reaction to her childish prank. The widow, on the other hand, was right here. Could she trust the old woman with her secret? It would seem she had no other choice.

"What's wrong with you?" the widow asked. "You look like someone just died."

Bethany swallowed hard the lump of fear in her throat. "Or is about to!"

"What on earth are you talking about?"

Bethany began to shake. "I messed up. I did something really *narrish,* and *mei daed* is going to have *mei* hide if I don't fix it."

The widow steered Bethany to a nearby chair.

"It can't be all that bad, now, can it?"

Tears welled up in her eyes. "Worse. But I only did it because I wanted Benjamin out of *mei mamm's* bakery."

The widow sank into the chair across from Bethany, eyes wide. "This already doesn't sound *gut.* Does this have anything to do with the cakes and whoopie pies your *daed* and Benjamin brought over here this morning?"

Bethany raised an eyebrow. "Benjamin came here with *mei daed?"*

"Jah, they have become close in the past two weeks. Your *vadder* talks very highly of him. I think it does him *gut* to bond with Benjamin. He offered him your *bruder,* Daniel's, loft apartment yesterday."

Bethany gasped and shook her head, feeling more confused than ever. Her father had changed so much since she and Lavinia had run off to live at the B&B, and then even more after Lavinia's impromptu wedding. A lot had changed. But for her father to bond with Benjamin and allow him to use Daniel's loft when he wouldn't even allow his own daughters

402

to live in it—that just didn't make any sense. If he had become this close to Benjamin, it was more vital than ever that she get rid of the tainted baked goods to avoid blame against Benjamin—not because she felt he deserved anything from her after the way he'd betrayed her, but because her father would surely take *his* side in the matter, and *she* would end up with a sound lashing.

Bethany jumped up from the chair and crossed to the counter where the cakes sat neatly decorated. She had really done a nice job on them once Benjamin showed her how to make swirls along the edges by putting frosting on a piece of wax paper and rolling it up to make a tube for decorating.

What did it matter when the inside of the cake was ruined with egg shells?

Bethany picked up the cakes one-by-one and dumped them into the trash can.

The widow jumped up from her chair. "What are you doing? Jacob is going to wonder what happened to the cakes he brought in."

"We will have to think of an excuse to tell him because they are not edible." She crossed to the other end of the counter and began to do the same with the neatly-wrapped whoopie pies.

The widow grabbed her arm to stop her. "Why are you throwing all of this away?"

Bethany yanked her arm away and resumed her tirade with the whoopie pies. "I crushed up egg shells into the cake batter, and I poured a lot of pepper into the whoopie pie filling."

"*Ach,* that *is* a problem," the widow said as she grabbed the remainder of the whoopie pies and put them into the trash bin. "But tell me why you *really* did it."

Bethany slumped back into the kitchen chair, discouragement clouding her thoughts. "Because I'm a fool."

"I won't argue with you there," the widow said, chuckling. "I thought you liked Benjamin. I thought you were sweet on him."

Resting her chin in her hands, elbows propped on the table, Bethany blew out a discouraging sigh. "I was—I mean, I am."

"Then I'm going to have to ask you again why you did it."

"Because I'm a fool," Bethany repeated.

CHAPTER 18

"We have time to replace the whoopie pies," the widow said. "But I'm not so certain we can do anything about the cakes. Not to mention, I don't have enough pans or ingredients to make all of that."

"But what about the fancy wrapping? Benjamin will notice they aren't wrapped," Bethany said nervously.

"We'll say we unwrapped them. As for the cakes, you could say you dropped them!"

"*I* dropped them? Why me?"

The widow furrowed her brow. "Would you rather admit you put eggshells in them?"

Bethany thought about it for a minute. "*Nee,* but how can I explain dropping *four* cakes?"

The widow chuckled heartily. "Not my problem. You got yourself into this mess; you get yourself out. I'm only going along with it to keep your *vadder* from embarrassment."

Bethany hadn't thought about what this would do to her father's reputation in the community, especially how it would make him look to the Bishop. She hadn't thought about anything or anyone but herself. Shame flooded her heart, making it difficult to breath.

The widow put a hand on Bethany's shoulder.

"Now is not the time to panic. We have just under three hours before the service is over and everyone will be expecting to eat. Let's get the whoopie pies made so you don't have to explain that one too."

Bethany's expression fell. "But I don't even know how to make them. I did a lot of watching and not enough baking because Benjamin didn't trust me."

"Do you blame him?"

Shame washed over her again. "I suppose I don't."

The widow sighed heavily. "Well, let's not worry about that now. You're going to have to listen fast and do everything I tell you. I'll make one batch and you can make the other. Do everything I do and it should turn out just right."

"Should?"

"Jah," the widow assured her. "Don't worry. You worry too much. That's what gets you into so much trouble—all that *thinking* you do."

The widow quickly pulled two mixing bowls from the cupboard and gathered up eggs, flour, butter, and various small ingredients and tossed them onto the counter.

This did nothing but overwhelm Bethany.

"Now, pay close attention," the widow warned. "Because I'm going to move very fast. Whatever I mix in my bowl, you do the same in yours and we should be alright."

"There you go throwing out the word *should* again. Don't do that because you're making me even more nervous."

"Well, then I suppose you're just going to have to trust me."

Bethany had no other choice but to trust the widow, and that worried her more than ever. If this backfired on her, there would be no turning back. Her mistake in judgment would be exposed, and there would be no way to salvage her father's trust. It could even cause her to lose her mother's bakery after all, and that scared her more than anything at the moment.

By the time they had the first batch in the oven, Bethany still had no idea how to make a whoopie pie. She was so nervous and so worried about mirroring the widow's actions that she couldn't remember one ingredient from the next, or one step from another. If the widow had asked her to repeat the process, she'd not trust herself to get it right.

"Do you remember what he put in his filling?" the widow asked.

"*Nee*—except cinnamon. He asked me to put in a pinch of cinnamon, but I added a handful of pepper instead."

The widow clicked her tongue in disgust, causing Bethany to hang her head.

"You make me wonder how you'd treat him if you *loved* him. If this is how you treat him when you like him, how much more would he suffer from your love?"

If the widow was trying to make her feel guilty, it was working. But she was right. She had already begun to fall for Benjamin, but then, suddenly everything went wrong—especially with her thinking. How had she managed to let things get this far out of control? Was she losing her focus so much that she'd forgotten what was truly important in all of this? She wished she knew what advice her mother would give her in this situation. Lavinia would most likely tell her to let go of everything except Benjamin. Only problem was; she didn't know how to do that.

Once again, they'd made the filling, and Bethany was still oblivious as to how it had been made. They took the first batch out of the oven and set them by the kitchen window, which the widow cracked open, so they would cool faster. Once the second batch was tucked away into the oven, the widow tested the first batch and declared they were ready to fill.

That was the easy part. It was tedious work, but manageable for Bethany because it was a mindless task. Right now, she wasn't capable of much of anything that would require any kind of real thought. She couldn't stay on task despite knowing her life practically depended on it. Before she realized, they had finished the whoopie pies and had even managed to clean most of the dishes.

They'd made it in time. Now would be the real test— getting by her father and Benjamin without having to explain what had happened to the cakes.

From the other room, Bethany could hear the familiar sound of hymns being sung from the *Ausbund,* and she knew the service was coming to an end. How had the time gone so fast? She'd always struggled to sit through the long services, but this morning, the time had somehow passed without her even realizing it.

CHAPTER 19

"I'm curious about something," Benjamin leaned in close and whispered in Bethany's ear. "Why do you suppose these whoopie pies taste so different from the ones we baked yesterday?"

"I didn't notice anything different," she fibbed nervously.

He was right. She'd relished the taste of the filling Benjamin had made yesterday, and she'd never tasted anything like it. If she had to describe the taste, it would almost be like cotton candy. Light and fluffy, and airy like the clouds. The filling she and the widow had made was pasty and thick, and sticky.

"You're not going to get away with this," Benjamin warned.

Bethany smirked. "It seems to me I just did!"

"It's all going to catch up to you, Bethany. Don't expect that I will be around to catch you when you fall—and fall you will."

Bethany gestured to her father who was across the large sitting room conversing pleasantly with the Bishop while they each seemed to be enjoying their whoopie pies.

"See *mei daed* over there? Right now, he's proud of me—for the first time in my life, he's proud of *me.*"

"*Jah,* but how proud would he be if he knew the truth about whatever it was you did with the whoopie pies and cakes we made yesterday?"

"I accidently dropped them on the floor, that's all. I couldn't very well serve desert with dirt on it. So, I had to make new ones, and I didn't do too badly if I do say so myself."

"Dropped them on the floor? Don't you mean whatever else it was you did to sabotage this? Don't you see this was your chance to make an impression on the community so they would become customers of your bakery?"

"And I've accomplished that," Bethany said through gritted teeth. "Look around you. Everyone is enjoying their whoopie pies."

"They're mediocre at best. And I'm certain the widow made them—not you! Mine were spectacular and you know it. I think you threw them away because you are jealous of me because I can bake and you can't."

411

"Nee, you have that all wrong."

"Do I? I think you did something to the cakes and the whoopie pies, but you didn't count on your *vadder* wanting them so he could show off your new skill to the Bishop. *Jah,* he's proud, but only because he doesn't know the truth. But you and I do!"

"You know nothing, Benjamin Schrock! You're wrong about me!"

He leaned in and whispered in her ear, lingering; his warm breath making her regret ever trying to sabotage him. "I think I know you pretty well, and I'm not so sure I like what I know."

That stung. But she could see by the look in his icy blue-green eyes that he knew just how much he'd hurt her with the comment.

Bethany bit her bottom lip, attempting to suppress the tears that threatened to spill from her eyes. She turned her back on him and focused on her father. He turned to her and held up his whoopie pie, a wide smile crowding his face.

The man never smiled.

He had never been proud of her, but now, it seemed, he was proud *and* happy.

She scanned the room and locked her gaze on the widow, who flashed her a sympathetic smile. She'd really messed things up. She had no idea how to fix the mess she'd caused.

What was she to do now?

Bethany stepped out the back door of the widow's house and walked across the snowy landscape to a nearby tree. She leaned up against the tree intending to have a good cry, but Benjamin had followed fast on her heels.

She turned around angrily. "Why did you follow me? So you could insult me some more?"

"Nee. So I could make you understand," he said gently.

"What's to understand? You've made your feelings for me very clear."

He and the Widow Yoder were both disappointed with her, and her father held fast to a false sense of pride over her accomplishment as a baker.

Now she would surely have to eat crow.

She would have to swallow her pride and learn from the two of them to make up for lost time. That is, if they would even agree to teach her after the way she'd behaved. The widow had been kind to her, and didn't deserve to be put in the middle of her mess just for sake of keeping her father from being embarrassed by her childish actions. As for Benjamin; he'd made it clear to her that he was both ashamed of her and uninterested. She'd lost any chance she had of marrying him, and she dearly loved him already.

Now it was too late.

Or was it?

She turned back to Benjamin, who held contempt in his eyes for her. "Please give me another chance. I promise I will listen to everything you say and will pay attention to your instruction. And no more dirty tricks."

"As long as you realize that by sabotaging *me,* you are only sabotaging yourself and your bakery!" he said sternly.

Bethany hadn't really thought about it that way. He was right. This was *her* bakery, and she needed to do everything she could to make it a success. If she failed at this, she would never be able to hold her head up in the community. It was bad enough they all knew about her getting let go from the B&B.

"So, does that mean you'll give me another chance?" she asked meekly.

"*Jah,* but it goes against my better judgment."

Bethany flung her arms around Benjamin and pulled him into a hug. "You won't regret this, I promise you won't."

Benjamin peeled her off of him. "There'll be none of that. I've made my position very clear to you about our relationship. It will be strictly business from now on, understood?"

Bethany nodded, though she hoped she would have the chance to change his mind about that.

CHAPTER 20

"Your *vadder* is coming up the lane," Benjamin warned. "You prop open the back door to let out the smoke, and I'll dump these burnt muffins into a trash bag."

Bethany scrambled to the door and flung it open, swinging it open and closed a few times, hoping to force in the fresh air and fan out the smoke. She couldn't have her father seeing what a mess she was making of her mother's bakery. Not now that she was actually trying to make it work.

The grinding of the buggy wheels against the gravel drive and the clip-clop of her father's gelding drew closer. She went to the counter and tossed the scorched pans into the large, stainless steel sink and squirted soap over them and then turned on the water. If they could get rid of the evidence of her newest mistake, she might stand a chance of meeting her father's approval.

Before she knew it, her father stood in the doorway of the kitchen, a stern look in his eye.

"Benjamin," he bellowed. "I would like a word with you outside."

Bethany jumped. Her father had a way of putting fear in her without even trying.

Benjamin nodded, worry creasing his forehead.

The two men walked out to her father's buggy, and Bethany tip-toed to the doorway and leaned into the wall, hoping not to get caught eavesdropping. She desperately needed to hear the conversation between the two men, despite her father making it very clear to her that it was not any of her business.

"Before I picked you up on Sunday," her father said sternly. "I dropped off one of the bakery cakes and half a dozen whoopie pies to a *familye* who have been struggling and haven't made it to service in a while. When I went over there to check on them today, I was surprised and more than a little disappointed to hear that the food I took to them was inedible. *Frau* Fisher said she crunched on egg shells in the cake, and the whoopie pie filling made her *kinner* cry because it was so peppery. Correct me if I'm wrong, but I don't think pepper is an ingredient in whoopie pies."

"*Nee,* it isn't," Benjamin said quietly. "I will stop by the Fisher place after we close today and offer the *familye* a fresh cake and bread that is edible, along with my apologies. We have had a few setbacks in training, but I assure you we have things worked out now."

Bethany clamped her hand over her mouth to muffle the gasp that escaped her lips. Why was he taking full responsibility for *her* mistakes?

"What I don't understand," her father continued. "Is how the whoopie pies that were served to the community were not damaged."

"Bethany discovered the mistake when she arrived at the Widow Yoder's *haus,* and they corrected it by making a new batch of whoopie pies. Unfortunately, the cakes had to be thrown away. I take full responsibility and promise you it won't happen again."

"See to it that it doesn't happen again," her father warned sternly. "Or I'll have to ask you to find employment elsewhere."

"I give you my word," Benjamin said, humbly.

Bethany choked back tears as she ran to the bathroom. How could her father be so intolerant? Benjamin hadn't done anything wrong, but he stood to lose his job because of her. He hadn't even tried to defend himself.

Staring at herself in the mirror above the sink, she watched the color drain from her face. Shame washed over her as if a storm cloud hovered over her head, pouring down heavy rain. How could she ever make up for what she'd done to Benjamin? It was no wonder he wanted nothing to do with her. She had done absolutely nothing to deserve his kindness, yet he'd given it to her freely.

Just outside the door, she could hear pans rattling in the kitchen. Benjamin had returned from his conversation with her father. How was she going to face him after what she'd heard? She could barely face herself. Her own reflection disgusted her. She'd become so out of control, she barely recognized herself anymore. She'd always been way too reckless, according to Lavinia, but this was too much, even for her. There was nothing else she could do but commit herself to learning, no matter how hard it was. She owed everyone that much—her parents and Benjamin, but most of all, herself.

Benjamin watched Bethany exit the bathroom, her red-rimmed eyes indicating she must have heard her father's threat to relieve him of his employment. Was it possible she felt remorse for putting him in such a predicament? He hoped it was so, but he wouldn't be so quick to trust her. If he wasn't so enamored with her, he'd have walked away and let her suffer the consequences of her mistakes on her own. He didn't need this hassle. He had a family bakery where he could go work, and he'd be appreciated there.

Gazing at Bethany as she busied herself dusting the tops of the whoopie pies with powdered sugar, he wondered if she would ever really learn her lesson. It seemed she had made the decision to do what was needed, but only time would tell.

If she was unwilling to learn what was needed to run her own bakery, he certainly wouldn't think she would ever be able to run a home or raise children. No, it would seem she was not the one for him, but he hoped she would make some sort of progress that would change his mind about her.

Bethany crossed the room with the tray of whoopie pies and set them in front of Benjamin. He picked one up and hesitated before tasting it. Seeing his distrust, Bethany picked one up and stuffed it in her mouth, biting off more than she could chew.

She raised an eyebrow when it touched her palate. "Mmm, this is actually *gut!*"

Crumbs sprayed from her lips, and she giggled.

Benjamin took a small bite, and as the taste registered, he took a larger bite.

He nodded and smiled.

Bethany swallowed the treat, smiling back at Benjamin. "I'm sorry," she said, humbly.

CHAPTER 21

"I have to run into town to pick up some supplies," Benjamin said. "Are you sure you can handle this by yourself?"

"Of course, I can," she assured him.

Famous last words, he thought to himself.

Benjamin hesitated before leaving the kitchen, making note that all she had to do was to pull the bread out of the oven, and she'd done it with perfect timing all week. He had to admit, she had improved. Her skills were still nowhere near what she needed to run the place on her own, but he was certain by the time winter was over she would be ready for any season. In the meantime, they still had Christmas to get through, and he knew it could pose a challenge for her.

Bethany sensed his hesitation. "Go! Lavinia will be along shortly, so if I have any trouble, she can advise me."

"I'll be back before closing time," he promised. "Don't forget the bread. You remember I'm taking most of that to the Fisher's. They have all those *kinner* to feed, and they could use the bread."

"They will get their bread," she reassured him. "Now go. We need those supplies to start practicing on the Christmas treats. I'm very excited about that."

Benjamin smiled warmly. "It's *gut* to see you so eager to make this work. You had me worried only a few days ago."

She cringed at the mention of her bad behavior. She wished he'd stop bringing it up, but she supposed it would be a while before he trusted her. She couldn't blame him for that.

"I won't be long," he repeated as he grabbed his hat from the peg by the door.

With his navy, wool coat buttoned up, she couldn't help but reflect on the first time he'd picked her up in his buggy. She'd been so cold, and he'd sheltered her in his arms. He'd protected her the same way he'd protected her from her father's anger over the mistakes she'd made regarding the bakery. Was it possible he still cared for her? His smile offered possibility, even if his words did not. He hadn't even made another attempt at kissing her—just as he'd promised. He'd kept things strictly business between them. Now that his kisses were missing in her life, she craved them more than ever.

Bethany listened to the clip-clop of the horses' hooves until they became too faint to detect. He'd actually left her in charge of her own bakery for the first time since they'd opened.

Suddenly, she felt nervous and pressured. What was she to do? Glancing at the timer, she noted it was nearly time to take the bread out of the oven. She looked around, deciding she would get a head start on cleaning the kitchen, since they'd only had one customer all day, and she didn't anticipate seeing anyone this late. She figured she had enough time to get the mop water ready. The entire floor needed a good sweeping and mopping.

By the time Benjamin would return, she would have the entire kitchen cleaned and ready to close after the inventory was put away. The bread would be perfect, and he would be proud of her. Certainly, that would turn his head toward her.

She stepped into the small utility room and turned on the water in the mop sink on the floor. As she reached for the cleaner, the wooden mop handle fell away from the wall where it had been propped, and hit her in the head.

Anger mixed with pain as she felt the knot already forming on her scalp.

Benjamin had promised to put up hooks for the broom and mop so they weren't always in the way. He'd also promised to replace the knob that had fallen off the door so it could be opened without the use of a screwdriver, but it was still propped open with an empty bucket, just as it had been all week. He expected perfection from her regarding the bakery, yet he'd slacked off his promises because he was always too busy hovering over her.

If he'd mind his own business, he'd have gotten these little things taken care of. But he thinks he needs to watch over me like I'm not capable of taking care of my own bakery. I've learned enough to handle it by myself, but he's never going to trust me!

Her anger getting the better of her, Bethany picked up the mop and flung it behind her out of the door of the utility room. She heard it make contact with the bucket propped against the door. As she turned around to see where it landed, the door swung around and slammed shut.

She was trapped!

CHAPTER 22

Panic welled up in Bethany as she realized the door had slammed shut and she was alone in the bakery.

"Stay calm," she said aloud.

It was too late for that. She knew that even if she screamed, no one would hear her. She was already shaking so much that she couldn't think straight. Looking around, she searched for something she could use to pry open the door, but there was nothing.

It would be more than an hour before Benjamin would return, and her only hope of being rescued would be if Lavinia were to show up as promised.

Bethany slid to the floor and began to cry. She'd messed everything up, and now she'd trapped herself because of her short temper. A sudden thought forced her up from the floor, panic suffocating her.

What if Benjamin's trip into town took longer than he anticipated and he went home afterward instead of returning to the bakery? She'd be trapped in here all night. Bethany shook almost uncontrollably as she frantically searched the tiny room for anything that would help her get the door open.

All she found was a wooden paint stick, and that would never help her.

Glancing up at the tiny window above her head, Bethany wondered if she'd be able to get any more than her head through the opening. She upturned the mop –bucket and dumped the water out of it. Then, she set it upside down below the window so she could stand on it and test it.

Once she was eye-level with the window, she realized she would be hard-pressed to fit her head through, much less the rest of her.

Suddenly, Bethany sensed something was wrong.

She sniffed the air.

That's smoke! Something is on fire—mei bread!

Bethany coughed.

The smoke was getting thicker!

Dear Gott, please don't let me die in here!

Bethany choked back tears. There was no time to waste crying. She had to get out of the bakery somehow.

Bethany coughed again.

She pulled in a ragged breath, choking on the smoky air.

How was she going to get out?

Panic took over her as she imagined joining her mother in the *great beyond,* and she wasn't ready for that yet. She wanted to marry Benjamin, and have lots of *kinner.* She wanted another chance to make up for all the things she'd said and done to hurt Benjamin. She loved him, and now she might never get a chance to tell him.

Bethany sank to the floor, dizziness taking over.

Please Gott, don't let me die in here.

She leaned into the wall, feeling defeated, when a broom handle swung down and hit her in the head. She rested her hand on it only for a moment before she jumped up from the floor and jabbed at the small window with the end of the broom handle until she broke a hole in the glass. Using the wooden handle, she traced the outline of the window to remove the rest of the glass from the frame.

Bethany climbed back up onto the mop-bucket with shaky legs. She breathed in the fresh, crisp air from outside. Several breaths, until she no longer coughed when she drew in deeply. Snow blew in making her shiver, but at least she was alive—for now.

"Help!" she cried weakly.

Poking her head out the tiny opening, Bethany could see the empty parking lot behind the store. Her gaze followed the long path to her father's house, and her heart nearly skipped a beat when she spotted the man in the yard near the barn.

"Help, *Daed,* help," she screamed with all her strength.

The force of her plea made her cough. But she was determined to yell as much as it took to get her father's attention. For the next several minutes she yelled and coughed repeatedly, until finally, her father turned his head.

"O-ver here," she screamed. "Help! Fire!"

Relief washed over her as she watched her father sprint down the road toward her. Tears forced their way up through her throat.

He was going to rescue her.

She would not die today.

"Hurry!" she cried. "I'm stuck in here and it's getting harder to breathe."

"I'll be right there." Her father hollered as he rounded the building quickly. She could hear from the jingling of the bell on the door that he'd entered through the front.

A knock to the utility room door startled her, but filled her with hope as she jumped from the bucket and rushed to the door.

"Bethany…"

She could hear her father coughing. "I need to open the back door and find something to get you out of there. I'll be right back."

She waited for what seemed like half an hour before he returned with tools to open the door.

When the door burst open, Bethany flung herself into her father's arms. "I'm so glad you're here. *Danki* for getting me out of there."

"Let's get you outside and into some fresh air."

He guided her out the back door and sat her on a tree stump they used to tie their buggies up to. She watched him run back into the kitchen and pull open the ovens.

Mei bread!

Her father dropped six bread pans one-by-one into the deep, stainless steel sink, and then walked back out to where he'd left Bethany.

"Where is Benjamin?" he asked gruffly.

Bethany coughed. "He went into town to get supplies."

"He left you here alone?"

"Jah."

"Well, then I suppose I'll be letting him go."

"You mean you're going to fire him?" Bethany shrieked.

"Jah," her father replied firmly. "He's fired."

CHAPTER 23

"Bethany, go up to the *haus,* and stop arguing with me. This is for me to take care of, not you."

Her father was being unfair and unreasonable. It was *her* fault the bread burned—not Benjamin's. If she couldn't keep her father from firing Benjamin, she would *never* have a chance with him. He would leave, and she would probably never see him again, and that was not something she could live with.

"But *Daed,*" she attempted a second time.

"Not another word from you, *dochder,*" he warned.

Bethany turned on her heel and marched up the lane intending to pack her things and go back to the B&B. She would rather go back begging Jessup King for her old job than to have to live under her father's authority for another minute. With Benjamin getting fired, she would surely be losing the bakery. That would leave her with no means of support, and no means to move out of her father's house. Her father didn't trust her, and with good reason. Her reputation for learning the business was not what it should be.

She reflected on her short career at her mother's bakery, realizing she'd made every mistake she possibly could have—right down to losing the man she loved. How would she ever recover from it?

Looking back over her shoulder, tears welled up in her throat as she watched Benjamin pull his buggy into the parking area of the bakery. She wanted to run to him, to warn him before her father had a chance to ruin everything. She'd hurt him, and there would be no taking it back. There would be no forgiveness for her from Benjamin, she was sure of it. And she would certainly never get another chance to kiss him—much less to marry him.

By this time, Bethany was bawling uncontrollably. Her life was in shambles, and she was doomed to live with her newlywed father and his bride for the rest of her life. She would become a lonely spinster and would never know the love of a man or the satisfaction of blessing him with children. While her father had been fortunate to find love a second time in his life, she was doomed to never experience it.

Gott, please help me to find a way out of this mess I've created. Forgive me for hurting Benjamin and for being so rebellious. Please, Gott, put forgiveness in his heart for me.

Bethany meant every word. For the first time in her life, she knew what it felt like to think of someone other than herself. She only hoped it wasn't too late for it to matter.

****

Bethany cast her line to the middle of Willow Creek and stared into the clear depth. Ice had formed along the edges of the creek bank, and snow had built up in drifts from the recent wind storm they'd had. She shivered a little, but mostly, she was numb. It was more of a state of mind than physical. Fishing was the only thing she knew to do to take her mind off Benjamin being fired. Knowing it was unlikely she would catch anything, she stared into the water and let her mind go blank. She was helpless in every way.

Anger filled her heart, leaving very little room for understanding toward her father. She had tried so hard to make it work, and now she was about to lose everything that was dear to her—including her father. She didn't believe she would ever be able to forgive him for firing Benjamin. And although the blame rested on *her* shoulders, she couldn't let go of the way her father was treating an innocent man.

"I thought I'd find you down here," Benjamin's familiar baritone startled her.

She had been so lost in thought that she hadn't heard him approach. If she hadn't had her feet firmly planted in the deep snow, she might have ended up in the middle of the creek with her line. Turning around, she looked him in the eye, guilt causing her to avert her gaze immediately.

"I'm sorry," she offered without looking at him. "I tried to stop *mei* father from firing you, but he wouldn't listen."

"It's probably for the best," he said soberly. "You didn't want to learn to bake any more than your *vadder* wanted to give you the bakery."

"That's not true," she shot back. "I admit I let my anger get the best of me in the beginning, but I've been working this last week so hard to get everything right. Now because I accidentally locked myself in the utility room, *mei* father fired you and has taken the bakery away from me."

"I don't think you have to worry about losing the bakery," he told her. "Your *vadder* seemed pretty determined to get someone to teach you properly—someone other than me."

"There is no one better to teach me than you! No one I'd *rather* teach me than you." Bethany cried.

Benjamin looked her in the eye, noting the sincerity there. For the first time since they'd started working together, he could see the change in her, and it was a good change. A change that put hope in his heart for their friendship that he'd hoped could blossom into more.

"I'm afraid it's too late to change your *vadder's* mind. I wish you the best of luck with your bakery, and I pray that it's everything you hoped it would be."

His tone was genuine—even now, after all she'd done to hurt him. She didn't want him to leave, but it was too late.

Too much had happened. Too many ill-spoken words had come from her mouth like fiery darts aimed at his heart.

Now, it was *her* heart that was broken.

CHAPTER 24

"I came to you for help, Lavinia, I didn't come to hear a lecture," Bethany complained.

"You have brought this all on yourself, dear *schweschder*. If you had learned what you needed to learn while you were young instead of always running off with Libby, you would already have the skills needed to run that bakery."

Bethany kicked at the snow-drift, spraying snow up in her face from the sudden shift in the wind. She sputtered and swiped at her cold, wet cheeks, anger making her tantrum worse.

"I'm not entirely to blame. You should take some of that blame yourself. *You* let me get away with it."

Lavinia shook her head with unbelief. "I can't believe you would even suggest such a thing. If you had the skills you needed, and didn't always try to scheme your way through life, *Daed* would never have had to hire Benjamin in the first place."

Bethany blew out a discouraging sigh. "I know I wasn't as welcoming to him as I should have been when *Daed* first hired him, and I know I messed a lot of stuff up, but I think I love Benjamin, and I don't want him to leave."

"Perhaps you should have thought about that before you started acting like a spoiled *boppli,*" her sister scolded her.

"Please don't say that," Bethany said, breaking off an ice sickle from the porch rail of the bakery and nibbling the end of it. "I don't want to lose the bakery, but I would be even more heart-broken if I lost Benjamin."

"The way I see it," Lavinia advised. "You have only one choice here. You have to tell *Daed* the truth."

"I already tried that and he wouldn't listen to me. He fired Benjamin anyway," she said, tears in her eyes. "You could talk to *Daed* and get him to listen."

Lavinia shook her head. "I'm an adult and married. I have a responsibility to *mei* husband now, and I don't think he would want me getting in the middle of your problems with *Daed*. Perhaps the Widow Yoder could be of some help. She is about to marry *Daed*. Surely she knows how to handle him by now."

The two of them giggled, Bethany swiping at tears that still fell.

"If she doesn't, she's in for a long end to her life."

"*Jah,*" Lavinia agreed. "That is for sure and for certain."

****

Bethany stood on the widow's porch, her hand mid-air, as she considered leaving before she knocked on the door. She knew if she didn't get this talk over with, she might lose her nerve. She also knew it was a long-shot to involve the widow, but the woman had already helped her once for her father's sake. Perhaps she would be a better ally than Bethany thought at first. Because her father could be harsh at times, she wanted someone on her side. Lavinia used to be, but now that she was married, she'd left Bethany behind to fend for herself.

Before Bethany had a chance to change her mind, the door swung open and the widow welcomed her in. "I was expecting you," she said.

Bethany sighed. "I forgot *mei vadder* tells you everything!"

She followed the woman into the kitchen.

"That isn't always a bad thing," the widow said. "I think it could benefit you to have me as a buffer between you and your *vadder.*"

"*Jah,*" Bethany agreed. "Which is exactly why I'm here."

437

Bethany sat down at the kitchen table and pulled off her mittens while the widow put on the tea kettle.

"I need to tell *mei vadder* the truth about what happened, and I might need your help with that. I already tried to tell him and he wouldn't listen to me. I need to clear Benjamin. Everything that went wrong with the bakery was all *my* fault."

The widow sat down across from her and smiled. "I'm so happy to hear you take responsibility for your mistakes. It shows you're growing up."

"Jah, I'm too grown up to live with *mei vadder* and his new bride. I certainly don't want to be there when Benjamin moves out of *mei bruder's* loft. But I've lost the bakery, which was my only hope of getting out on my own."

"As for the bakery," the widow began. "I have no idea if your *vadder* intends to give you another chance. And I'm not certain I can do anything to help with Benjamin. But as for your feelings about living with us after we are married, I've discussed an option with him that he agrees with."

Bethany widened her gaze on the widow, trying to decipher what she was trying to tell her, but couldn't figure it out. "Is he going to let me take over the loft when Benjamin leaves?"

The widow smiled. *"Nee.* I wanted to save this until your *vadder* and I were married, but I'd like you to have *mei haus.* I never had any *kinner* of *mei* own since *mei* husband passed away only a few years after we were married, so I have no one to pass it on to. I know you're too old to need a new *mamm,* but I'd like it if you would consider me part of your *familye."*

Bethany couldn't believe what she was hearing. She looked into the widow's eyes and saw the kindness of a friend—of a mother. It was something that had been missing from her life since she was too young to remember. Tears welled up in her eyes. Perhaps her life wasn't ruined after all. Perhaps some good was going to come from all of this. She felt suddenly grown up. She was going to be responsible for her own home, and if she was lucky enough, she'd have her own bakery too. Bethany nodded, accepting the widow's offer on both accounts.

CHAPTER 25

Bethany rolled over and stuffed her head under the feather pillow to block out the sunlight that had just started to peek through the lace curtains. She'd spent most of the night tossing about in the old, creaky bed in the guest room at the widow's house. In a heated tantrum, she'd packed her things and left her father's house before he'd come in from the barn for the night. She didn't want to be there to witness Benjamin moving out of the loft apartment above the barn.

In a few days, after the widow married her father, she would move her things into the larger bedroom downstairs where the older woman now slept. It would be *her* house. But until then, she would rather sleep in the guest room at the widow's home than to stay another night in her father's house, with whom she was very angry. She was certain the widow had already informed her father that she had moved into her house, and she hoped that he would get the hint of just how mad she was at him.

In the meantime, she did not intend to get up until the widow had left to take her father his afternoon meal, as she had been doing since they'd become engaged. She had no intention of going anywhere near the happy couple. It wasn't that she wasn't happy for her father, but her anger toward him for firing Benjamin had clouded her ability to reason.

A knock sounded at her door, causing her heart to race. If she answered, she would have to face the widow, and she wasn't in the mood for any lectures about giving her father another chance. He hadn't given one to Benjamin, and that was all that concerned her at the moment. Deciding to ignore the second knock, Bethany closed her eyes and tried to calm her breathing in case the widow should let herself in.

"I'm leaving early to go into to town so I can run a few errands before I go feed your *vadder,*" the widow said from the other side of the door. "I'll be back later this evening."

Bethany didn't respond, but instead, listened for the footfalls that let her know the widow had left. She let out a heavy sigh of relief. She would have the entire day to herself to think. With her housing situation now taken care of, the biggest dilemma on her mind was to find a way to change her father's mind about her mother's bakery.

Unable to sleep, Bethany crawled from beneath the warm quilt and placed her stocking feet onto the cold, wooden floor. She shivered a little as she pulled a knitted throw around her shoulders. She dressed quickly after washing her face and brushing her teeth. The day had already gotten a head start on her, and she wanted to explore her new property a little more in-depth. She hoped the excitement over that would take her mind off Benjamin.

Grabbing a hot cup of coffee, Bethany sipped as she looked out at the snowdrifts that had swept up around the house like a cocoon. The house was quiet—too quiet. Bethany missed the chatter between herself and Lavinia in the mornings. Lavinia was a morning person, and enjoyed talking early in the morning, while Bethany preferred the quiet. She never let up until Bethany participated in the conversation. She missed that now. She even missed the deliberate footfalls of her father down the stairs when he was too tired to begin his chores in the mornings.

Hoping the loneliness would pass, she shouldered out into the wind, her scarf flapping lightly. She blinked away thick snowflakes that landed on her lashes as she strained to hear the trickle from Willow Creek, despite the snowfall muffling the sounds of the earth around her.

Stepping around the large drifts, Bethany set her course for the creek. She wished she'd had the mindset to have packed her fishing pole, but for now, she would have to do without it. Perhaps later she would ask the widow if she had a fishing pole to lend her.

When she reached the creek, she was surprised to find her father there. She wished she would have seen him earlier so she could have turned around and gone back to the house. It was too late now. He'd already seen her and had nodded toward her.

It wasn't fair that he'd ambushed her.

He knew the creek would be the first place she would want to explore of her new home. And there he was—waiting for her.

"*Frau* Yoder told me what really happened with Benjamin," he began. "I came to tell you that I offered him to return to his job at the bakery, but he turned me down."

Bethany's expression fell.

"Why would he do that when everything was *my* fault?"

Her father looked out over the creek as if deep in thought. "He told me he doesn't believe you're serious about running the bakery. Perhaps when you're a little older and have settled down from your *rumspringa.*"

"*Nee,*" she denied. "I haven't taken *mei rumspringa* yet, and I hadn't intended to take it because I hoped I would marry Benjamin."

Bethany knew it was a bold confession to make to her father, but she had failed so miserably at everything lately that she felt she had nothing more to lose by continuing her antics. She figured it wouldn't hurt to give the truth a try for a change, and let the chips fall where they may.

"I had no idea the two of you were so close," her father said cautiously. "But dear *dochder,* you have been on *rumspringa* ever since your *mamm* passed from this world."

"But *Daed…"*

Her father held up a hand to stop her mid-sentence. "*Nee,* let me finish. I blame myself for this. I should have put *mei kinner* first, instead of hiding behind my own grief. If I'd taken better care of the three of you, I would have been the one fixing the fence the day Daniel died."

Bethany looked into her father's eyes, seeing a deep remorse she'd never seen there before. She'd had no idea he'd been carrying around such guilt for so many years over the death of her brother.

His jaw clenched and his face grew red, as if he would burst into tears at any moment. Bethany closed the space between them and hugged her father for the first time since she was young.

"I love you, *Daed.*"

He bent toward her and hugged her back.

"I love you too, *Bethany.*"

CHAPTER 26

Bethany waited at the edge of the road in front of the bakery—her bakery. Libby had come in on the afternoon bus from Nappanee, and she could hardly wait to see her. She had so much to tell her, she felt as if she would burst if the girl didn't show up soon.

Then, her thoughts turned to Benjamin.

Oh, how she wished she had news to share with her best friend about Benjamin. If only her father had been able to convince him to stay on at the bakery and teach her. Now, she would have to remind Libby of her promise to run it with her. She'd talked to her father well into the day, and he'd complimented her on her progress in learning. It was Benjamin who had told him she was ready to run the place on her own—Benjamin, who'd convinced her father that she had a talent for baking if she could only have enough confidence in herself. At the conclusion of their talk, it was her father's declaration that he was proud of her that had given her the courage to accept the bakery, knowing that Benjamin was right. She knew how to bake, and it was all because of his generosity and patience with her that had done it.

Bethany tipped her chin up slightly and smiled.

Danki, Lord for blessing me with the ability to bake. I pray that you will help me to carry on mei mamm's legacy with her bakery so she can be proud of me when she looks down from Heaven to watch over me. Lord, if it be your will, please bless me with Benjamin for a husband.

She knew her father would probably scold her for such a prideful prayer, but she just couldn't help but hope that God was as proud of her as she was of herself.

The familiar clip-clop of horse's hooves filled her with excitement. Libby would finally be home after such a long stay with her cousins, and the two of them could finally do what they'd always said they would do, from the time they were young; run the bakery together. It had been Bethany's dream for so many years, and now, it was about to come true.

As the buggy neared, Libby waved. Bethany walked swiftly toward her, unable to contain her excitement any longer. Adam stopped the buggy and let his sister out to prevent her from jumping from the seat. Practically jumping into Bethany's arms, they giggled and hugged as if the time between them had been years rather than weeks.

"I've missed you so," Bethany managed around the laughter. "I have so much to tell you."

"Does it involve a beau?" Libby asked excitedly.

Bethany's expression sank. "*Nee,* I'm afraid it doesn't, but *mei daed* finally gave his permission for the two of us to run the bakery. *Kume,* see how nicely it's been fixed up."

"I saw it from the road, and couldn't believe how much it's changed. Are you certain he's going to let the two of us run it by ourselves?"

Libby looped her arm in Bethany's as they walked toward the bakery. "Tell me, since there isn't a beau in your life yet, are you ready to consider settling down with *mei bruder?* I want you to be *mei schweschder.*"

Bethany practically choked on her friend's words as she thought of Benjamin. She hadn't told Libby about him yet—mostly because there wasn't anything she could say about him that wouldn't cause her complete embarrassment.

"*Nee,*" Bethany finally answered. "He's always been in love with Melody Stoltzfus."

"*Jah,* but Melody doesn't seem interested in ending her *rumspringa,* and *mei bruder* isn't getting any younger."

"If he loves her enough, he will wait for her."

Bethany reflected on Benjamin again, and wondered how long she would have to wait for him. Would he ever forgive her, or would he move on and find someone else that wasn't as difficult to love as Melody likely was for Adam?

The two stepped up onto the porch of the bakery and walked inside. Libby freed herself from Bethany and wandered over to the front counter. The glass had been replaced, and doilies lined the shelves, where trays littered with crumbs boasted a working bakery.

"Everything is so clean," Libby said with a smile. "It all looks so new."

She walked over to the stainless-steel prep table and ran her hand along the freshly washed surface. Bethany could see that her father had cleaned up and removed the burnt loaves of bread from the sink. Or had he? She took a closer look around, noting how neat and clean the place was. The widow was more likely the one who'd cleaned the mess—especially since Benjamin had rejected the offer of employment from her father. Bethany concluded that the woman must have offered to clean so her father could come and speak with her at the creek.

What a blessing it will be to have her as a new mamm, Bethany thought.

"Your last letter to me said your *vadder* hired Miriam's *bruder* to teach you how to bake. He must have taught you very well for your *vadder* to let you take over on your own."

Jah, he was a *gut* teacher," Bethany said sadly.

Libby ignored her as she looked around the bakery, a far-off look in her eyes. "Who would have thought such a handsome *mann* knew how to bake?"

Bethany felt her heart skip a beat.

"Your letter said how difficult it was for you to get along with him, and how much you disliked him. I can't imagine that. He was so nice at Miriam's wedding."

I never said I didn't like him. I said I didn't like having to work with him as mei boss.

"Well, I think he's worth pursuing," Libby continued, ignoring Bethany's sudden change in mood. "I think I shall set *mei* aim on him. He would make a *gut* match for a husband. Ain't it so?"

Bethany couldn't answer. She was suddenly filled with too much regret over not sharing her feelings for Benjamin.

CHAPTER 27

Bethany took in a deep breath, enjoying the aroma of fresh-baked bread. Bread that she, herself had baked, without the help of anyone. A sense of pride filled her as she heard the jingle of the bells on the door of the bakery from just outside the kitchen door.

Their first customer had arrived.

With Libby behind the counter that was already filled to the brim with the first batch of bread and whoopie pies, along with various cakes and cookies, that the two of them had spent the morning baking, Bethany sighed with relief. Success was just around the corner, as would be the words she'd longed to hear from her father. Soon, very soon, he would tell her how proud he was of her, and the thought of it made her smile.

Her smile quickly turned to dread as she heard Benjamin's voice in the lobby. Bethany tossed the linen towel in her hand across the counter with a slap. She would not let him ruin her first day on her own in the bakery. The day she and Libby had been dreaming of nearly most of their lives.

Before she could push through the swinging door that separated the kitchen from the lobby, Bethany overheard Libby offering Benjamin a *taste* of the cookies they'd baked.

It's a sample, Libby. I've told you a million times to offer customers a sample—not a taste.

Still standing behind the door, Bethany suddenly realized why Libby had called it a *taste.* She was flirting shamelessly with Benjamin.

Bethany could feel her blood boiling.

Before she could aim her anger toward her life-long friend, she remembered that she had never told Libby of her feelings for Benjamin. But Benjamin knew of her feelings, and he was being a little more cordial toward Libby than she was comfortable with.

Bethany pursed her lips and exited the kitchen door, intending to get rid of Benjamin so she could tell Libby everything.

"What can I help you with, Benjamin?" she snapped.

He looked up, his smile melting away all her aggravation. "I stopped in to see how you were doing, but by the looks of things, and the *wunderbaar gut* aroma coming from the kitchen, I'd say you have things well in hand."

Bethany twirled her index finger toward Benjamin, inviting him to follow her into the kitchen.

"Can I speak with you for a minute?"

Libby shot her a look that let her know she understood the connection between her and Benjamin. They'd been friends long enough that they knew each other's habits well, and Libby thankfully got the hint.

Benjamin walked over to the bread cooling on the far counter. "You really have outdone yourself."

"*Danki*. I owe it all to you. You were a *gut* teacher."

Benjamin winked at her. "And I thought all that time you weren't listening to a thing I'd taught you."

She smiled. "I heard every word."

"I knew you had it in you all the time," he complimented her. "That's why I refused your *vadder's* offer to come back to work here. I knew it was a dream of yours and Libby's."

"*Danki.*"

He reached into his coat pocket and handed her a small notebook. "I wanted to give you this. It's all my favorite recipes—in case you might want them. I even reveal my secret ingredient for my whoopie pie filling."

Bethany giggled, happy that he would trust her with such a secret. "*Danki*. I hope you'll come in and see me from time to time—in case I need some advice or something."

Benjamin smiled. "Of course, I will. Your *vadder* asked me to stay on in Willow Creek. He is letting me stay in the loft above the barn. He even asked if I would help him on his farm. He said something about wanting to retire now that he's getting married."

Bethany laughed at the sound of it. She wasn't certain if she would ever get used to the changes in her father. She liked the changes. More than that, she was delighted that Benjamin would be staying close-by. With him just up the lane from the bakery, she hoped it would give her ample opportunities to *drop in* and visit with her father and the widow. If it just so happened that Benjamin was there too, well, then that would be an added benefit.

"Well, I should get back to the chores your *vadder* has for me."

They exited the kitchen as Libby was finishing up with an *Englisch* customer. She handed Benjamin a small bag with cookies in it.

"I thought you might like to take some with you," she said sweetly.

"*Jah,* I would like that very much." He smiled at Bethany and tipped his hat to Libby just before exiting the bakery.

Libby sighed. "That *mann* has stars in his eyes for you, Bethany."

"He does not," Bethany corrected her. "You're seeing things!"

Libby shook her head. "From what I can see, you feel the same way about him."

Bethany frowned. "I'm afraid it's too late. I messed things up with him."

"From the look in his eyes, I'd say he's over it—whatever you did."

She hoped Libby was right about Benjamin. She also hoped her friend would never ask her what she'd done that was so wrong. It was something she intended to put behind her and never repeat such a mistake as long as she lived.

CHAPTER 28

Bethany finished covering the trays of leftover cookies from the day, while she took in the sound of sleigh bells from a distance. The clip-clop of horse's hooves mixed with the jingle bells, and her immediate thought was that her father had taken his sleigh out to fetch the widow. But it couldn't have been her father, or surely, she would have heard him leaving some time ago. Peering out the window, she swiped at the condensation that clouded the glass from her warm breath against the cold window.

It was Benjamin.

Adam had picked up Libby a little early because he was in the area making a delivery to a neighbor, and had left Bethany alone to finish the last of the dishes and cleanup. They'd had a good first day together. Bethany even thought they'd made a decent profit.

Her father would be proud.

Benjamin stopped the sleigh in front of the bakery, giving Bethany's heart a jolt of excitement. Was he, perhaps, there to take her for a sleigh ride? She certainly hoped it was so. It was a bit early in the season for a sleigh ride, but they'd already had such an accumulation of snow, the weather had certainly made an accommodation for it.

She busied herself taking the empty trays back to the kitchen. She wiped them down and put them on the shelf just as the bells on the door alerted her Benjamin had entered the bakery. He called her name from the lobby.

Bethany poked her head through the swinging door. "In here. Just finishing up."

He followed her into the kitchen, watching her hang her soiled apron across the sink.

"What brings you here so late?"

She didn't want to jump to assumptions, but she couldn't wait around for him to ask her. She was too anxious to find out.

Benjamin raised an eyebrow and smiled sheepishly. "I was hoping to convince you to go for a sleigh ride with me."

"I don't know about that," she said with a smile. "A sleigh ride could give a girl the wrong idea. You said you wanted to keep our relationship strictly business."

Benjamin smirked. "That was before—when we were working together. We aren't working together anymore."

"We certainly are not," Bethany agreed, trying to hide her smile.

"It looks like you have everything under control here. Shall we leave?"

Bethany looked around, making a mental note of her closing checklist.

The back door was locked.

Her father had come by an hour earlier to remove the majority of the cash.

Ovens were off.

Everything was washed and put away.

Adam had taken out the trash before he'd left with Libby.

"All is done!"

"I can see that. Your *mamm* would be very proud."

Tears welled up in Bethany's throat. "Do you really think so?"

He pulled her into a gentle hug. "Of course, I do. I'm proud of you too. You were an exceptional student."

"Exceptionally rotten," she said, sniffling.

He chuckled. "*Jah,* you really weren't a very *gut* student, but the point is, you learned despite all of it."

Tears fell from her eyes. She didn't want to leave the comfort of Benjamin's arms, and she didn't want to lose him

457

again. "I'm sorry for sabotaging you. I didn't mean to hurt you. I let my own selfish wants get in the way of being the sort of person that deserved to be treated as well as you treated me—even when I was at my worst."

"I have a confession to make," he said.

Bethany wiped her eyes. "What could *you* possibly have to confess?"

"Well, I suppose I have *two* confessions to make."

Bethany stared into his mischievous eyes. "Now you're making me a little nervous."

"Nothing to be nervous about. But I have to tell you that the tricks you pulled made me laugh."

He let out a chuckle, and Bethany joined in with a hearty laugh. "*Mei vadder* didn't think it was very funny."

"*Jah,* I suppose that's why he fired me," he said, laughing so hard his eyes filled with tears.

They both laughed as they exited the bakery, Bethany turning the key in the front door. All was secure, and her first day was a complete success, right down to the very moment Benjamin walked in the door.

Benjamin assisted Bethany into the sleigh and offered her a double quilt of red hues and floral patterns. It reminded her of Christmas, as did riding in a sleigh. Before her mother had passed on, her father used to take the family on regular sleigh rides. She was happy to see her father had dusted off the sleigh and decided to use it again to take the widow out courting.

Bethany pushed aside thoughts of her past and set her mind to the present and all it had to offer. Benjamin slid onto the seat close to her and pulled the quilt over his lap. Picking up the reins, he set the horse into a slow trot, the jingle bells adding a little romance to the air.

He slowed the horse as he neared the creek bank at the far end of her new property. Moonlight glistened across the ripples in the water as is flowed by, rushing over rocks and under fallen branches. The trickling of the water and the sound of distant owls filled the cool air. The moon was nearly full, and it lit up the snowy landscape with a bluish tint. She couldn't have asked for a better setting.

Benjamin turned to her and cupped his hands around her cheeks, pulling her gently toward him as he closed the space between them. His lips touched hers, and instant warmth filled her from head to toe.

She suddenly pulled away from him. "You never told me what your second confession was."

Benjamin smiled. "I was only going to confess my love for you."

Bethany giggled nervously, knowing how much she loved him too.

She couldn't believe she'd been so foolish as to nearly lose Benjamin. That was all in the past. Now, she couldn't imagine her life without him.

CHAPTER 29

Bethany hurried to finish making the special breakfast she'd promised Lavinia she'd prepare so the two of them could spend the morning with their father on his wedding day.

Lavinia pushed her way through the kitchen door, the wind catching the handle from her grasp and slamming the door against the wall. Snow blew in, swirling about the floor as her sister struggled to get the door closed before the entire snowstorm blustered in through the opening. Bethany dropped the last piece of bacon onto the large platter and rushed to the door to help her sister.

"It's a *gut* thing Benjamin offered to fetch the widow in the sleigh," Lavinia stated. "I believe the entire community will be using their sleighs to attend *Daed's* wedding."

Bethany peered out the window at the swirling snow hitting the glass with little icy *pings*.

"*Jah,* but I'm worried some of them won't make it in this weather, and that would disappoint *Daed.*"

"*Nee.* Adam and Nate have their sleighs out of the barn as well, and have gone to fetch a few community members who don't have them. They will make certain everyone is in attendance for *Daed's* sake. I'm certain when Benjamin returns with the widow, he will join them to make sure everyone who is able to be here is in attendance."

Bethany was pleased to hear that.

"I'm sure you're right about that."

She crossed to the other side of the kitchen and grabbed the dishes from the cupboard to set the table.

Lavinia watched her sister work. "You've come a long way since I've left you to marry Nate. Who would have thought that *mei* little *schweschder* would grow up to be such a fine young woman?"

Bethany blushed. "I suppose I did learn a few things working at the B&B. Most of what I know I learned from you and Benjamin, though."

Lavinia pulled the lid off the scrambled eggs and hash, breathing in the aroma with a heavenly smile.

"You worked very hard for this, now don't mess it up dear *schweschder.*"

"I won't," Bethany said. "I only wish I'd have learned sooner that everyone was not out to get me. I was the only one working against myself the whole time. By trying to sabotage

462

Benjamin, I nearly sabotaged myself. I had become my own worst enemy."

"It's *gut* to hear you talk this way, Bethany," her father's deep baritone sounded from the doorway of the front room.

Startled, she assumed he must have come in through the front door to add firewood to the already large pile to keep the guests warm during the service and the wedding. It had been a while since they'd hosted a service in their home, and Bethany had forgotten the amount of work it entailed.

Soon, the counters would fill with dishes of food brought by the women in the community. The cake she had made for the wedding already graced the counter like a trophy.

It didn't go unnoticed by her father.

He walked toward the cake and admired it.

"Your *mamm* would be proud to see such a cake made by the hands of her *dochder*. I'm very proud of you too. You have carried on your *mamm's* legacy in a special way to honor our *familye*."

"*Danki, Daed.*"

He sniffed the air. "Let's eat. I've worked up quite the appetite already and the day has only begun."

Lavinia and Bethany brought the breakfast to the table for this very special day. It would be the last meal they would take together before everything changed.

Change is gut, Bethany thought to herself as she sneaked another peek at the cake.

She was proud of herself for turning out such a flawless creation. She only hoped it would taste as good as it looked.

CHAPTER 30

Bethany looked for the widow in the kitchen, hoping to catch her before all the women-folk crowded in to serve their families. She found her admiring the cake she'd made for their wedding.

She stood back for a moment and looked at the woman from the doorway. She was no longer a widow; she was married to Bethany's father. What was Bethany to call her now that she was married? She supposed *Frau* Miller would work, but it seemed too formal. She would never dream of being so disrespectful to her elder by addressing her by her given name, unless the woman was to permit that.

As she watched the prideful smile fill the older woman's face as she admired the special cake, Bethany decided that none of those titles meant as much to her as having a mother would.

She approached the woman and hugged her.

"I didn't see you come in," she said to Bethany.

"I think you did a *wunderbaar* job making this cake. It would seem as if you never needed my help at all; from the look of this cake, I'd say you have a natural talent. Most likely an inheritance from your *mamm*. She would be proud if she could see what you have made in her honor."

"I didn't make it in honor of *her*. I made it in honor of *you*—as *mei* new *mamm*."

"*Danki,*" the older woman said, tears filling her eyes. "It would be an honor to be your new *mamm*."

Bethany hugged her again. "You're wrong about one thing, though."

"What about?"

"I do need your help," Bethany admitted. "I still need you to teach me how to make that shoofly pie. I believe I'm finally ready."

"I believe you are," her new *mamm* said.

Bethany could hardly wait.

THE END

READ ON TO THE NEXT BOOK

Amish Brides
of Willow Creek
Book Four: Snowflake Bride

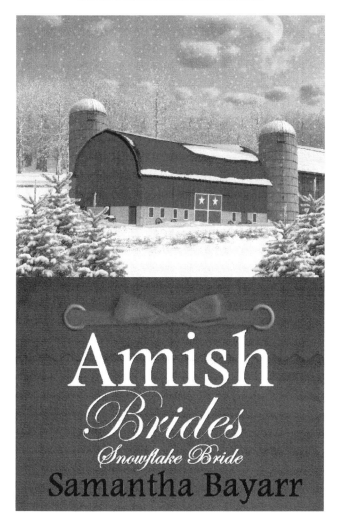

Table of Contents

[CHAPTER 1](#)

[CHAPTER 2](#)

[CHAPTER 3](#)

[CHAPTER 4](#)

[CHAPTER 5](#)

[CHAPTER 6](#)

[CHAPTER 7](#)

[CHAPTER 8](#)

[CHAPTER 9](#)

[CHAPTER 10](#)

[CHAPTER 11](#)

[CHAPTER 12](#)

[CHAPTER 13](#)

[CHAPTER 14](#)

[CHAPTER 15](#)

[CHAPTER 16](#)

[CHAPTER 17](#)

[CHAPTER 18](#)

[CHAPTER 19](#)

[CHAPTER 20](#)

[CHAPTER 21](#)

CHAPTER 22

CHAPTER 23

CHAPTER 24

CHAPTER 25

CHAPTER 26

CHAPTER 27

CHAPTER 28

CHAPTER 29

❧Snowflake Bride❧

CHAPTER 1

"Am I dead?" Libby heard herself whisper.

No one answered.

Libby felt no pain. Only weightlessness, as she beheld snowflakes fluttering toward her. She could no more blink them away, than she could move. No sound reached her ears except the steady rhythm of her own heartbeat, and even that was subdued by the gentle breeze that propelled wispy snowflakes to and fro. The grey sky, endlessly populated with flurries, blanketed her in a tranquil haven, devoid of all reasoning.

"Am I dead?" she repeated.

The wailing of distant sirens invaded her sanctuary from reality.

The warmth of a hand slipped into hers and squeezed lightly. A faint and gentle baritone spoke calming words she struggled to comprehend. If not for the tone, they would have instilled panic in her.

Did she know that voice?

Snowflakes swirled overhead, their slow-motion dance carrying her away.

Another squeeze of warmth against her hand brought her back. "Stay with me now, Darlin'," the smooth baritone pleaded.

Was there a face that went with the voice?

Libby averted her focus away from the downy snowflakes long enough to gaze into a pair of golden brown eyes.

"There you are, Darlin'," the soothing voice spoke near her ear. "For a minute there, I thought you were going to leave me."

Do I know you?

Sweet, brown eyes crinkled slightly at the corners, a bright smile aimed hospitality toward her. Whoever he was, Libby thought he was quite handsome. She focused on the kindness of his eyes. Sunlight peeked through the clouds behind him, making him appear almost angelic.

"Don't leave me, Libby."

The handsome face smiled brightly, kindness emanating from him.

Libby lost herself in his gaze, until pain interrupted her thoughts. She closed her eyes tightly, wincing against the pain that seemed to press against her skull like the weight of a horse. Tears slipped from her eyes, and panic overcame her. It rushed through her like the force of an ice-storm, crippling her with fear.

Trying to raise her head, Libby opened her eyes long enough to witness everything around her spinning out of control. Bile burned her throat as she heaved the contents of her stomach. What was happening to her?

"Libby," someone was saying. "Hang in there, we're taking you to the hospital. Everything is going to be okay."

"Just relax and let us take care of everything," someone else was saying.

Take care of what? What's wrong with me? Why can't I move, and why do I hurt so much?

"Can you hear me, Darlin'?" the kind voice asked her.

Libby tried to nod, but couldn't.

"We need to get her into the ambulance."

She looked around at the gathering crowd of people she didn't recognize. They were moving in slow-motion, and the sounds coming from them seemed muffled. She could no longer comprehend their movements or their words.

What was happening to her?

Libby tried to move, but everything hurt. She could feel herself being lifted and moved. Her eyes wide, the sky moved swiftly away from her. The snowflakes disappeared, bright lights replacing them.

"Am I dead?" she cried?

No one answered.

The handsome face faded.

It was the last thing she remembered before everything went black.

CHAPTER 2

"They tell me my name is Libby," she said to the nurse, who was resetting her IV.

"Yes," the nurse said kindly. "It's Libby Troyer."

"Is that short for anything?" Libby asked, fighting a feeling of wooziness.

"Your family didn't say," the nurse answered.

"*Mei familye?*" Libby asked. "*Ach,* you mean the Amish ones? I don't think they're kin to me."

"What would make you say that?"

"Because I'm an *Englisher,* and *mei* name is Liberty."

"Liberty *Troyer?*"

"*Nee,* just Liberty," Libby said.

"Do you remember the accident?" the nurse asked.

"The doctor told me I was ice skating and hit my head on the ice."

"Your family said you're quite the skater. Your mother told me you've been skating since you were two years old, and that you give lessons every winter to the younger kids."

"But I don't even know how to ice skate," Libby protested. "Come to think of it, I don't even know me *mudder.*"

The nurse pushed a vile of medicine into Libby's IV. "This will help you to get some rest. Maybe when you wake up, things will be a little less confusing."

Libby agreed that she did feel confused. The medicine relaxed her, and soon she'd drifted off to sleep.

****

"When will she regain her memory?" *Frau* Troyer asked the doctor.

"I'm afraid there's no guarantee on that. The memory is a delicate, yet tricky aspect of our brains. She could regain all of it within the next twenty-four hours, or it may take weeks. At least until after the swelling goes down completely, we can't know for sure. Either way, there is no telling if she will ever regain all of it, or only select things. What concerns me most is the fact she seems to have invented an alternate identity for herself. Is this a game she may have played as a child? Perhaps someone she knows outside of the community?

If we knew the source, we might be able to unlock it in her mind."

"Jah," her *mudder* agreed. "I've never heard her speak the name before. But for her to think she is an *Englisher,* and she doesn't recognize her own *familye—ach,* that is worrisome for sure and for certain."

The doctor offered a weak smile. "We'll know more in the next twenty-four hours or so. In the meantime, all we can do is pray."

He left *Frau* Troyer in the hall just outside Libby's hospital room with an uneasy feeling.

CHAPTER 3

"Of course, you can move in with me, Libby," Bethany conceded. "But what about your *familye?*

"They're not *mei familye,*" she protested. "And *mei* name is Liberty!"

Bethany rolled her eyes. How was she going to get used to calling her lifetime friend by another name? But she would have to for the sake of Libby's health. Her doctors had advised them to go along with anything she said, no matter how out-of-character it was, just for sake of not putting more confusion in her than she already felt.

"Alright, *Liberty,* you can move into *mei haus* with me for as long as you need to, but your *familye* will want to see you."

Libby ignored her. Though it annoyed Bethany, it was an old trait of Libby's that wasn't such a bad thing at the moment. In all their years as friends, any time Bethany would say something Libby didn't agree with, she would ignore her and change the subject. She'd done a lot of that during their discussion of Jonas. Before the accident, Bethany had tried to encourage Libby to give Jonas another chance, and Libby would not participate in the conversation after that point.

Now, her dear friend would have to come to her own conclusions of her family, and Bethany might just have to take a back seat concerning Libby's home-life for the time being. It wasn't in her nature to do so because she cared so much about her friend, but she would do whatever it took to keep Libby happy under the stressful conditions that were now her life.

"I know *mei mamm* has been here the whole time with me, and I'm grateful for that, but my mind struggles with it. I know she's *mei mamm,* but I don't know how our relationship was before—before I hit *mei* head."

Bethany knew what it was like to have no knowledge her own mother, but only because she hadn't been with her since she was a toddler. To have spent an entire lifetime with a mother and not remember her was a mystery to Bethany that left her with confusion too. She couldn't imagine what poor Libby was suffering.

"I will help you fill in some of the memories if you'd like, but I do know you were close." she offered.

"*Jah,*" Libby said quietly. "I would like that. It seems *narrish* that I could forget *mei* own *familye.*"

I think I would be terrified, Bethany thought.

Bethany looked at the clock on the wall and excused herself to Libby, knowing she needed to intercept an impending visitor.

****

Bethany stood outside of Libby's hospital room waiting for Jonas. Adam had told her Jonas had sent word that he was coming to see her. He'd not been told of her accident yet, and Bethany suspected Adam and his father would tell the poor fellow. But since Bethany knew the most about Jonas' relationship with Libby, she was probably the best buffer between the two of them when he made his visit.

Before long, a tall Amish man appeared at the end of the long hall and began to walk toward her. He was just as Libby had described. Aside from the look of worry in his kindhearted, brown eyes, she'd have probably known him anywhere. Libby had described his features to Bethany in such detail, that she even knew his mannerisms right down to his stride as he approached her.

He tipped his hat. "I'm Jonas Graber from Nappanee. Is Libby in there?"

Bethany held up a hand to him as he gestured toward the door behind her. "Wait a minute. You can't just barge in there without knowing what is going on."

He tipped his hat again. "Her *vadder* and *bruder* told me she has memory loss, but surely she will remember me— I'm her betrothed!"

479

My, he is polite, but persistent.

"Not anymore, you're not," Bethany argued. "She broke it off with you before she came home from her visit in Nappanee. And she doesn't even recognize her own *mamm,* so what makes you think she will know you?"

"Our love is as strong as a mule," he said with confidence.

And you seem as stubborn as one!

Bethany couldn't help but snicker. "Well, I hope you're in for a mule-sized kick to the head because she thinks her name is *Liberty*, and she thinks she's an *Englisher!"*

Jonas furrowed his brow. "She thinks she's an *Englisher?* Her *familye* didn't tell me that."

"I'm sorry to be the one to have to tell you, but she asked me if she could live with me because she doesn't feel comfortable living with *those people,* as she calls her *familye* now."

His face drained of its sun-kissed color. "Surely she remembers her own *mamm!"*

"Jah, but very little, and her *daed* and *bruder* are strangers to her, and that scares her."

"Mei poor Libby," he said as he hung his head.

Bethany smirked. "That's another thing. You'd better get used to calling her *Liberty* because she won't answer to anything else at the moment!"

Jonas' expression fell, and Bethany couldn't help but feel sorry for him, even more than before.

CHAPTER 4

"I will *not* help you trick Libby," Bethany argued. "She's like a *schweschder* to me."

"I'm not asking you to trick her," Jonas pleaded. "I still love her and I came here to tell her that I changed *mei* mind about moving to Pinecraft. I still want to marry her, and if the only way I can get her to know me again is through skating, then I have to try."

"If you hadn't chickened out yesterday instead of visiting her, then you would have already known if she remembered you," Bethany scolded him.

Jonas blew out a discouraging breath. "I needed time to think this through and how I would handle it if she didn't recognize me."

Bethany pursed her lips. "I think you're a coward, but if she fails to recognize you, I will introduce you as a skating instructor. But I don't know what *gut* will come of it. She's already told me she's afraid to go back out onto the ice because she can't skate."

Jonas tipped his hat to her. "You won't regret this. We both know she is *gut* enough to compete professionally. She just needs to remember her love for it—and for me."

Bethany shook her head and leered at Jonas.

"*Jah,* it seems you have prideful reasons for doing this, and it will come back on your head if you aren't careful."

"I don't intend to hurt her, and I don't intend to lose her again," he said.

Bethany felt sorry for him. She knew from having conversations with Libby that she still loved him too, but she had felt she had to break things off with him because he was so set on moving to Florida. She hadn't wanted to leave her family or Bethany to move so far away to another community. Her fears drove her to leave Jonas, but she'd not stopped loving him; Bethany was certain of that, and it was the *only* reason she agreed to help Jonas.

"I'm only doing this for Libby because I know she still loves you too, but if you hurt her, she will never trust me again because I helped you, and I'm not certain I can live with that."

He tipped his hat again. "I give you my word I will not do anything that will hurt her. I only want a chance to remind her of our love."

"I don't know how you think you can get her back on the ice, and that's even if the doctor lets her."

"If you fall off a horse, you get back on and ride. Libby always had that attitude about skating—at least that is what she taught her young charges. I think I can apply the same principles with her, and help her to remember."

"I wish you luck with that," Bethany said.

"You are her best friend. You could try being optimistic instead of sarcastic for Libby's sake."

Bethany rolled her eyes. "You mean for Liberty's sake!"

"More sarcasm?"

Bethany planted her fists on her hips. "What am I supposed to say? That this is normal?"

She swallowed down the lump that clogged her throat. Even though Bethany knew Libby was just in the next room, it seemed as if she was gone. That she'd somehow not survived the accident and would never return. She supposed that was what it would be like if she never regained her memory. Bethany wasn't even certain she would be able to embrace *Liberty* in the same manner. She'd lost her best friend, and she feared she would never get her back.

Jonas sighed. "Of course, it isn't normal, but it's what we have to deal with for now. At least until she gets better."

"And if she doesn't? Will you want to marry *Liberty? Ach,* what if you do and she doesn't want to marry you because she truly thinks she's an *Englisher.* What then?"

Jonas wasn't able to think that far ahead. "I suppose I won't know the answer to that question until I meet *Liberty.*"

Bethany sighed deeply and gestured toward Libby's hospital room. "Are you certain you're up to this? Or will you chicken out again today?"

Jonas took a few steps away from the door. He was certain God had put Libby and him together, and wasn't about to give up on her. He loved her. But did he love her enough to marry her as an *Englisher?* What if she rejected him again? Could his heart take the stress of losing her all over again if she chose not to take him back—or worse—if she didn't even remember him?

"I suppose there is only one way to find out, and it won't happen with me standing out here in the hall waiting for it to come to me."

Jonas took a brave step toward Libby's door and breathed a faint prayer for God to bless him with strength. He couldn't be certain, but he suspected he was about to need an extra dose of it.

CHAPTER 5

"Get out of here!" Libby shouted. "I don't want a skating instructor. I don't want to go back onto the ice where I fell because I obviously don't know how to ice skate!"

Jonas backed away, not knowing how to deal with Libby's sudden mood change. Only moments ago, they were getting along just fine, but the mere mention of skating and getting back out onto the ice had caused her to snap. It frightened Jonas that he could love someone so much who had no idea who he even was.

Tipping his hat, Jonas excused himself from Libby's hospital room and waited in the hall for Bethany to come back out. When she did, she flashed him an *I told you so* look, and Jonas didn't appreciate it one bit.

"I warned you," she added.

"Don't add insult to injury," he said sadly. "Perhaps there is another way I can talk to her. The direct approach never hurt anything. I should have just asked her to take a buggy ride with me."

Bethany swished her head back and forth with a tsk, tsk. "Try telling her the truth! Tell her you *used* to be her beau, and see what happens."

He shook his head vigorously. "I can't tell her that because then she will know she broke it off with me and I'll never get another chance with her."

Bethany rolled her eyes impatiently. "She's going to remember eventually, and then she will be upset with both of us for tricking her.'"

"I already told you," he said. "I'm not trying to trick her. I only want a second chance with her."

"Then get it honestly or don't get it at all. From now on, you're on your own. I'm not deceiving my best friend."

Jonas raised an eyebrow. "Even if it's all to make her happy?"

Bethany pursed her lips. "I won't help you anymore, but I won't tell her who you are either. That is up to you to tell her the truth about who you are, but I'm not getting in the middle of it anymore. That is between you and her."

"Danki," he said respectfully. "Just so you know, the last thing I want to do it hurt her. I love her."

Bethany patted his arm. "I believe you do."

She walked down the hall, hoping Jonas would be brave enough to go back in Libby's room and try a different approach. One that didn't involve lying.

She passed the dinner cart and nearly gagged from the smell. She felt sorry for Libby having to eat the hospital food. When she returned, she would bring her something from home. The bakery had been closed for the past two days since her accident, and Bethany wasn't certain how long she would have to keep it closed to the public while waiting on Libby's recovery. In the meantime, she'd kept up her orders from the surrounding folks in the community, especially the Fisher family, who counted on the daily donations from the bakery.

Jonas stepped cautiously into Libby's room, aware that her new temper could meet up with him before he could manage to get a word in. Still, he took a chance that she might have calmed down since he'd left a few minutes before. Barely in the doorway, Jonas turned around when he heard a male voice greeting Libby.

"There you are Miss Liberty," he said, and then turning to Jonas, he said, "You must be family, how is she doing?"

Jonas wanted to blurt out to the smooth *Englisher* that he was Libby's betrothed, but he held his tongue.

"He's not *familye,* he was just leaving," Libby said through gritted teeth. "I've already told him I don't want a skating instructor, but he doesn't want to take *no* for an answer."

"Actually," the stranger interrupted. "A skating instructor might be just the thing to help you."

The man suddenly had Libby's full attention.

"I'm not sure if you remember me or not, but I'm Logan Carter, a medical student, and I was doing a ride-along with the paramedics on the ambulance service the day you were brought here."

Libby smiled at Logan and fluttered her eyelashes in a flirting manner. Jonas stood by, fuming at her brazen behavior.

"Do you have a few minutes so I can explain why I'm here?" Logan asked.

Jonas started to excuse himself.

"No, please stay," he said. "What was your name?"

"I'm Jonas Graber, and I'm not *familye...*"

"I know," Logan interrupted. "You're the skating instructor."

Jonas wanted to argue, but decided against it. There was no point. This man was a smooth *Englisher,* and at the moment, his betrothed thought she was an *Englisher* too, and gave the smooth-talker the advantage.

"With your permission, I'd like to study you because I'm in the middle of writing my dissertation on memory loss, and methods of retraining your memory. I believe your case is unique, and I'd like the opportunity to shadow you for a little while to compare your case with my research."

Libby looked at him starry-eyed. "I'm not certain I understand."

He ran a hand through his thick, blonde hair. "Mostly, I would study your medical records and the treatment methods of your doctors, but I would also like to see if you truly have forgotten how to ice skate, or if you only *think* you've forgotten. That, and other things you may not remember fully, such as your family."

"I don't know how to skate at all," Libby stated. "And I still don't even know what I was doing out on the ice to begin with."

"The spectators all witnessed you giving a skating lesson, and your student accidentally tripped you," Logan said.

"That's what Bethany told me, but I just don't know what to make of that."

Logan looked between Libby and Jonas.

"Who's Bethany?"

"*Ach,* she's *mei* best friend. We've been friends all our lives. In fact, our *mamm's* used to put us in the same cradle together."

"That's a good sign," Logan said. "That means that your long-term memory seems to be intact. It means you remember from back as far as early childhood."

Libby shook her head. "I don't remember *mei* own *familye.*"

And you don't remember me, Jonas grumbled under his breath.

CHAPTER 6

Bethany hurried to make a pot of coffee for Libby's homecoming. Did she still like coffee? She had to admit there was a lot she didn't know about her life-long friend anymore. The past few days had been taxing, to say the least, and she wasn't certain if the two of them would even get along under the same roof for too long. But for Libby's sake, she was willing to give it a try.

Looking out the kitchen window, Bethany shivered at the heavy snow that fell in thick clumps, and had already formed a white shadow on the windowsill and along the branches of the maple tree closest to the house. The wind whistled through the cracks of the windows that were in need of replacing.

It was one of a long list of repairs that Benjamin had already compiled to make once they were married. He'd begun a few of the items, but said he would have more time to complete the many small things once he was living on the property. But until then, they would get things done as he had the time after long days of working her father's farmland. His intention was to continue working for her father, and in return, they would receive a portion of his land each year in addition to a fair wage.

For now, the whistling wind was a comforting distraction to calm her anxiety and impatience in waiting for Adam to bring Libby. On a plate, she arranged fresh banana muffins, warm from the oven, and slathered butter over the tops, then, rearranged the table to make it special for the first girl-talk she and Libby would have since her accident.

Muffled clip-clops and the grinding of buggy wheels against the gravel drive alerted her that they had pulled into the long, narrow path that led to her home. Bethany fidgeted, worrying how her friend would act, what her mood would be like, and how her speech would be away from the hospital and the prying eyes of her family. She was already strange to be around when they had been together at the hospital, and things were even more strained when her mother was with them.

Bethany hoped Libby would be more relaxed now that she was free from the disconnected, sterile environment of the *Englisch* world. It did worry her that Libby still insisted she was an *Englisher* herself. She hoped that the slow environment of the farm and getting back to the bakery would jar Libby's memory back to what it was.

A sudden knock at the door startled Bethany out of her reverie. How long had she been standing at the window lost in thought? She knew it took a horse five long minutes to pull a buggy up the narrow driveway in the snow, so it had to have been at least that long. She cleared her throat, determined not to be too anxious about Libby's stay with her. After all, they'd been friends all their lives, and Bethany was one of the few people she remembered. It was Bethany that Libby remembered the most, even compared to her own mother.

Bethany crossed the kitchen and opened the back door, greeting her friend as normally as she could possibly manage under the circumstances.

"*Gudemariye,*" Bethany said as cheerfully as possible.

By the expression on Libby's face, she'd say she was a little too cheerful.

Libby dropped her suitcase at the door and crossed to the table, picking up a muffin and mumbling the words *real food* before stuffing it into her mouth. She turned around and faced Bethany, who stood with the door still wide open, her mouth agape.

"Close the door or you'll let that blizzard in here," Libby barked, spraying muffin crumbs from her mouth when she spoke.

Bethany shivered and closed the door with an automated shove, while Adam moved out of the way, looking equally stunned by his sister's behavior.

Bethany turned to Adam. "Won't you stay and have a muffin and some *kaffi* with us?"

Adam purposely let his gaze trail to his sister.

"*Nee,*" he said, smiling. "You two have fun. I'll bring *mamm* over tomorrow to see her."

Bethany shot him a pleading look to stay while Libby plopped down in a chair at the table near them, oblivious to anything but the muffins and coffee, which she continued to stuff into her mouth as if she hadn't eaten in weeks.

Bethany and Adam stood there for some minutes, watching Libby devour one muffin after another, each not really believing what they were seeing with their own eyes.

Finally, Adam picked up her suitcase and asked where he could put it.

"First door on the right, at the top of the stairs," Bethany instructed.

Meanwhile, Bethany brought another plate of muffins to the table. She barely had time to set the plate down, and Libby was reaching for another one. Adam had returned by this time and had witnessed his sister's terrible manners. Bethany could tell by his expression he wanted to reprimand her, but his look softened, letting her know he'd changed his mind. She couldn't help but feel as forlorn as Adam looked. What was she to do with poor Libby until she was back to her old self again?

What if she *never* came back?

The thought put a shiver down Bethany's spine. She pushed back the thought, realizing it was going to take a lot of prayer and patience just to get through each day, let alone to wait for Libby to return to normal.

Adam excused himself and walked toward the door after Libby ignored his farewell to her. Bethany followed him and let him out into the whirlwind of snow.

"Gut luck," he whispered before walking out. "I think you're going to need it."

CHAPTER 7

"He *is* quite handsome—for an Amish *mann,*" Libby agreed. "But it doesn't change the fact he's Amish and I'm an *Englisher.*"

You are not!

Bethany held her tongue, fearing if she argued with Libby it would slow her healing process. It was frustrating to hear her speak of Jonas as being Amish in the sense that meant something was wrong with him.

"How do you *know* you're an *Englisher?*"

"*Ach,* there can be no other explanation for the fact that *those people* are not *mei familye.*"

"But, Libby, I know they're you're *familye.* We grew up together. We've been friends since we were born. You've been like a *schweschder* to me."

Libby tied her apron around her narrow waist and leaned against the stainless-steel counter of the bakery.

"I know we've known each other since birth, and that is why I trust you, but hearing you call me Libby makes no sense to me. And even though I know *mei mamm,* I don't know her as a *mudder.* Does that make sense to you?"

Bethany sighed as she placed four large baking sheets on the counter. "I suppose I would be pretty scared if I was in your head right now. But you know you don't have any business dating an *Englisher.* What would your *daed* say if he knew? You know how strict he is."

"That's the problem. I have no idea how he would react. All I know is that Logan is very handsome—I agree, not as handsome as Jonas—that Amish *mann,* but I *have* to see if what I believe in *mei* own mind is right. Dating an *Englisher* just makes more sense to me right now. Please understand, and don't judge me. Be a supportive friend just like you've always been, and let me find my own way in all of this."

Bethany tried to put herself in Libby's situation, wondering how she would react in the same circumstances. Though she didn't agree with her friend, she needed to let her live her own life, free from judgment from her best friend. After all, Libby depended on her to see her through this difficult time in her life.

"I can do that much for you," Bethany relented. "I give you my word. I won't try to make you see things *my* way, and I won't give you any advice unless you ask me for it."

Libby threw her arms around Bethany.

"*Danki.* I promise you I'll be careful. Besides, the *Amish one* will be tagging along the entire time. And it isn't really even a *date* with Logan—it's more like research. He said he wants to observe my skills on the ice. No matter how much I told him I can't skate, he's convinced I can, based on some study he's doing in school. That is why he wants Jonas to help me on the ice. He said something about it proving that my subconscious mind knows how to skate even if I can't remember. I'm not sure I understand that, but I'm not going to question him if he wants to spend so much time with me."

Bethany dropped whoopie pie batter onto the baking sheets while Libby began a fresh batch of dough for afternoon bread. "It sounds very interesting. But I have to say, as your friend, it seems as if his interest is strictly medical, not romantic."

Libby smiled dreamily. "That doesn't mean I can't change his mind."

"Won't that be awkward with Jonas right there the whole time?"

Libby rolled her eyes. "That's *his* problem, not mine. I don't know him, so I don't owe him anything other than what he will be paid for the skating lessons. I can tell he's interested in me, but I am not interested in dating an Amish *mann.*"

"*Ach,* Libby, you can't really know what you want until your memory returns, and it wouldn't be fair to either of them for you to date one of them until you are well."

499

Libby pursed her lips. "Please stop calling me Libby. It sounds foreign to me. I've told you several times *mei* name is Liberty."

Bethany shook her head, struggling to concentrate on dropping batter onto the baking sheets.

"Liberty sounds foreign to *me!*"

"*Ach,* it does to me too, Bethany, but not as much as Libby does."

Bethany scrunched up her face. "Are you really going to *force* me to call you Liberty?"

"*Nee,* I suppose not. Perhaps Libby could be short for *Liberty,* but only for you. I think everyone else should have to call me Liberty."

Bethany blew out a sigh of relief. "*Danki.*"

"*Jah,* I suppose it's the least I can do for you since you took me into your home and kept me on at the bakery even though I didn't remember working here. It's amazing I still know how to bake."

"The doctors said you needed to stick to your normal routines as much as possible to give you the best chance of bringing your memory back. I have to admit, though it does seem sort of random the things you seem to be blocking out. It's almost as if…"

Libby stopped mixing and stared at her friend nervously. "As if what?"

Bethany paused before placing the whoopie pies into the oven. "As if most of your memory loss is centered around your return to Willow Creek."

Libby shrugged. "I don't see what that has to do with anything."

"Perhaps something happened in Nappanee that has you blocking out everything since you took that trip."

Libby waved a hand at Bethany, hoping she'd leave her alone. She didn't like the direction the conversation was taking. If something did go wrong with her trip to Nappanee, she wasn't ready to face it, and she figured her mind was protecting her for some reason or another. That is, if that was the case.

"Then why don't I remember *mei familye?*"

"You said yourself that you remember them, but the memories are not strong enough for you to feel comfortable around them. But you have me wondering if that was just a convenient way of getting your *daed* to let you move in with me. He's been forbidding it ever since I got the *haus,* and you've been asking him just as long."

Libby glared at her. "Now what are you trying to say?"

"It just seems strange to me that you remember everyone except…"

Bethany stopped herself before she exposed Jonas' true identity to Libby. She was caught between loyalty to her friend and loyalty to her word. She'd given Jonas her word, and it was not going to be easy to keep it if Libby continued to question everything she said.

"Remember who?" Libby asked.

CHAPTER 8

"He's here!" Libby squealed as she looked out the window at the dark grey sedan traveling slowly down the lane toward the house.

Bethany worried that Libby sounded a little too anxious for her meeting with Logan—especially since she claimed it was not supposed to be a date. It didn't even seem to matter to Libby that Jonas had steered his buggy in right behind Logan.

"Will you stall him? I'm not ready yet."

Her sense of urgency irritated Bethany, especially since, in her opinion, Libby looked plenty ready to go.

"What could you possibly have left to do?"

Libby smiled mischievously. "You'll see."

That doesn't worry me at all, Bethany thought sarcastically.

While Libby flitted off to the upstairs bathroom, Bethany opened the door to Jonas and an *Englisher* she could only assume was Logan.

"Welcome," she said as they entered. "It's *gut* to see you again, Jonas."

Bethany didn't think Libby was going to be too happy to see Jonas, and she wasn't certain how she felt about it either—especially since the tension was even too much for her. How did Libby manage to get herself two *dates* for the same day? She might be claiming that neither of these men were her date, but from the looks on both of their faces and the amount of tension between the two men, they each thought they had a date with Libby, and each wanted it to be exclusive. Bethany had to wonder what would become of such a date.

Excusing herself from the awkward tension between the two men, Bethany was all too happy to check on Libby's progress. They were making her feel uncomfortable in her own home, and she didn't like it very much.

At the top of the stairs, Bethany knocked lightly on Libby's door and waited for an invitation into the room. She opened the door, and was shocked to see Libby looking so much like an *Englisher*.

"What are you wearing?"

Libby shrugged. "Just a pair of jeans and a t-shirt."

Bethany closed the space between them, but could not seem to close the gape of her mouth.

"Those pants are so tight, it looks like you've painted your legs blue!"

Libby smiled. "They look that *gut?*"

Bethany shook her head wildly. "*Nee,* they don't look proper at all. What would your *mudder* say?"

Libby leered at her. "I no longer have a *mudder!*"

"*Ach,* Libby you should not talk that way about your *mudder.* She loves you."

Libby brushed out her long, flaxen hair, and then hung it down her back in loose tendrils. "That may be true, but for now, I am free from the strict rules of the Ordnung."

Bethany narrowed her eyes at Libby. If she didn't know better, she'd think the girl was faking.

"Surely you will be putting your hair up in your *kapp,*" she advised Libby.

She smoothed a hand down the back of her hair and smiled at herself in the mirror. "*Nee,* I like it this way. Besides, it isn't as if you haven't used your hair to catch the attention of a *mann.*"

Bethany rolled her eyes. "*Jah,* I did let *mei* hair down only for a minute for Benjamin, who is about to be *mei* husband, but I would *never* wear it that way in public."

Libby powdered her face and studied her appearance longer than she ought to be without being accused of vanity.

"Where did you get all this stuff—the clothes, the makeup?"

She shrugged. "I don't know. Wait…I got it when I was in Nappanee. *Mei* cousin, Mary, has begun her *rumspringa,* and she took me shopping. It was a lot of fun."

Bethany lowered herself onto the bed and watched Libby admiring herself in the mirror. "You remembered something new?"

"*Jah.*"

"*Ach,* perhaps that should prove to you that you're not an *Englisher* after all."

Libby shook her head. "That doesn't prove anything except that I went shopping with a cousin."

"Don't you see, Libby, you said yourself your cousin began her *rumspringa,* so perhaps you got a taste of that rebellion while you were there. It's a clue."

"The only clues to be found will be for the *mann* waiting downstairs for me."

"Correction, Libby. *Menner!*"

Libby gasped. "The *Amish* one is here too?"

Bethany jumped up impatiently and crossed to the frosty window and looked out at the snow. "I wish you'd stop saying that like it's a dirty word."

"I have mixed feelings about Jonas, that's all."

"Why do you suppose that is?"

506

"I don't know, but it's almost as if he reminds me of someone."

Bethany turned back and watched Libby paint her lips with a light pink lip gloss.

"He's from Nappanee," Bethany offered boldly, hoping to get a reaction out of her. "Perhaps you've met him before and you don't remember."

"I think I would have remembered him if I'd met him."

Bethany raised an eyebrow. "What makes you say that?"

"Because he's very handsome."

"What about Logan?" Bethany teased.

"They're both *gut* looking, *jah?*"

Bethany was uncomfortable with Libby's question. "They're all the same to me now, and it makes no difference because I only have eyes for one *mann,* and that's Benjamin."

"*Ach,* Bethany, you're impossible."

Funny, but I was just thinking the same thing about you, Libby.

CHAPTER 9

"I must insist you bind up your hair and change into some clothing that is approved within the rules of the Ordnung." Jonas reprimanded calmly.

"Who are *you* to tell me how I can dress? You aren't the Bishop!" Libby shot back.

Jonas pursed his lips.

"*Nee,* but I'm your—your…"

He wanted to claim her as his betrothed. He wanted to claim her as his own, to declare his right as the head over her, but unfortunately, he was not yet married to her.

Bethany could see the strain in Jonas' eyes, and she almost felt sorry for him.

Libby, however, raised an eyebrow and leered at him. "You think because you are Amish and you're teaching me to skate that I have to follow some sort of dress code?"

Jonas clenched his jaw. *"Nee,* but I believe that you should dress with propriety and stick to the rules of the Ordnung."

Libby laughed at Jonas, causing heat to rise in his face as if it had been badly sun-burned.

"That might apply to me if I was Amish, but since I'm an *Englisher,* I am free to do as I please."

Bethany studied Libby's expression, noting the defiance in her eyes. She'd known Libby all her life, and she knew there was something not right about the way she now spoke. Her tone was deliberate, and her words were chosen carefully, as if rehearsed.

Jonas plunked his hat on his head, his expression clouded with defeat. "Shall we go then?"

As they exited the side door, Benjamin was already outside checking the harnesses, making certain the horses were securely fastened to the sleigh. Jingle bells adorned the harnesses, and hung decoratively around the horse's necks. They snorted impatiently, rolling surges of icy air billowing from their nostrils with crystalized vapors. Their hooves lifted from the snow in anticipation of pulling the sleigh.

Bethany certainly couldn't wait to get underway. The sooner they made it through this day, the better she would feel. She and Benjamin were along as chaperones, despite Libby insisting she wasn't in need of one. Bethany prayed that Logan's experiment with Libby's memory would return her to normal because she wasn't sure how much more she could stomach from *Englisher-Liberty.*

Tipping her head behind her, she glanced back at Libby, who sat inappropriately between Jonas and Logan. Each was equally doting on her, trying to ensure her warmth. It was almost sickening the way she played them against each other. Had she really forgotten how much she loved Jonas? Upon her return from Nappanee, Libby had shared with Bethany her doubts over breaking it off with Jonas, but here she was, flirting shamelessly with another man—an *Englisher,* and she was doing it right in front of Jonas. Bethany thought it was almost cruel the way Libby was behaving.

Libby nestled in between two handsome men, both of them appealing enough to catch her attention. Though she feigned annoyance with Jonas, his concern for her well-being did make her heart sing just a little. Logan, on the other hand, was very smart and worldly, and that was a plus for her right now. If not for Logan, her destiny was certain to end with her settling down with an Amish man like Jonas, and that wasn't what she wanted at the moment. She had a real hunger to explore the world outside of the community, and the only way she could do that was to steer clear of Jonas' advances, no matter how tempting they may be.

Warmth emanated from each man, sending equal surges of excitement through Libby. Though her attraction to Logan was more out of curiosity for the *Englisch* world than anything else, it did help that he was nice to look at. If not for the fact that she was more than a little nervous to be on the ice in front of two very handsome men, she might have been able to enjoy this outing. But as it were, she feared more than rejection from Logan at the present moment. She feared she would fall and make a fool of herself, but most of all, she feared getting hurt again.

Bethany turned in her seat. "It's so cold out here, I think we might sit inside at the B&B and watch from the window while you skate—if that's alright with you, Libby."

"*Ach,* I don't blame you. I don't know why you would want to be on the ice in that dress. It's just too cold."

Bethany scrunched up her brow. "You used to wear a dress whenever you gave lessons. Don't you remember?"

Libby tipped her head as if to give the matter some thought. "*Nee,* I don't remember being able to skate—no matter how much you might try to convince me."

"I know you would wear Adam's broad-fall trousers when you figure-skated, but nothing like the blue-jeans…"

"Enough about my clothes," Libby snapped.

Bethany faced front, and Benjamin clenched her hand. She felt helpless to save Libby from herself, but that didn't mean she wouldn't keep trying. If she had simply been acting out for the sake of her *rumspringa,* Bethany would probably be less inclined to worry, but given the fact Libby didn't remember who she was made her more uneasy than she could say.

When they arrived at the pond, Logan jumped down from the sleigh and held a hand out to Libby, who was eager to put his theory to rest.

"Let's get this over with," she said with a heavy sigh. "So I can prove to you that I can't skate!"

Jonas dragged himself from the sleigh, unable to stomach watching his betrothed flirting with another man even for another minute without hurling the contents of his morning meal across the ice.

CHAPTER 10

Libby wobbled onto the ice, holding tight to Jonas. Snowflakes landed on her lashes, obstructing her view of the pond, but she had to admit, there was something strangely familiar about the setting.

"Don't let me fall," she begged as she blinked away heavy snowflakes.

"I would never let you fall."

His gentle baritone struck a familiar cord in her.

What was it about him that both irritated her and intrigued her at the same time? She looked into his soulful, brown eyes. There was a kindness there that put her at ease. She trusted him. But how could she know that? They'd only just met.

Libby looked deep in his eyes, allowing him to lead her around the pond. Thick snow whirled about, melting on her warm cheeks. She lowered her lashes against the falling snow, breathing in the crisp, December air. Feeling weightless as she twirled and spun, Libby flew across the ice with ease. With Jonas at her side, she could do anything—even skate. He was her rock, the steadying force that drove her—that drove her mad!

I know you, don't I? Libby thought. *Perhaps we were even quite close, but I get the feeling we didn't part on such gut terms.*

She took another look into his kind eyes. She felt at home there. So, what was the nagging thought that crept into her mind? Was her mind still playing tricks on her? Jonas was a kind man, Libby could see that in his eyes. A hint of sadness lingered there too. He looked at her with the sort of sadness that made her wonder if his mood had something to do with her.

"Have we met before?"

She couldn't help but ask the question, but by the look on his face, she now wished she could take it back.

"In a manner of speaking," he said softly as he whisked her around the far end of the pond.

She studied him for a minute, noting his clenched jaw and the tension that furrowed his brow.

He was awfully handsome.

Keep your mind on task, Liberty, she scolded herself. *He's Amish, and there is an equally handsome Englisher waiting for me on the other side of the pond.*

"Either we've met before or we haven't. Which is it?"

Jonas wasn't certain how much he should reveal to her. If he told her how well they knew each other, it could ruin his second chance to win her heart. His gaze trailed over her golden locks that hung from beneath her knitted hat. He wanted to run his hands through her hair. He wanted to pull her to him and place his lips against hers again. He longed to be near her. He'd missed her so much since she'd left Nappanee just a few short weeks ago.

"We do know each other," he said cautiously.

"How *well* do we know each other?"

Jonas could feel his heart slam against his ribcage. Libby's doctors had warned them not to upset her in any way, and he feared a reminder of their breakup would be just the thing to send her over the edge of permanent memory loss.

He couldn't be responsible for such a thing.

The other side of that could give him the opportunity to remind her of their relationship, leaving out the part about them breaking up. But that could backfire on him later.

That left him with only one option.

"We were friends in Nappanee," he said wearily.

"You must have been my skating instructor then?"

515

"We did skate together quite often."

She flashed him a half-smile. "Did we *date?*"

She could tell she'd caught him off guard, and that he had no intention of answering her question. What was he hiding from her? Whatever it was, he was suddenly having trouble looking her in the eye.

"Good job, Liberty," Logan called to her, breaking the spell. "I knew you could do it!"

His sudden outburst broke her concentration, sending her feet into a slippery whirlwind. Jonas caught her by the arm to steady her until her feet stopped flopping around.

Logan was suddenly at her side, a spray of ice arched across the pond from his quick stop. "You were skating! You proved my theory."

Libby wobbled and tightened her grip on Jonas' arm. "I can't skate. Didn't you see me almost fall?"

"Yes, I did, but before I startled you, which I'm very sorry for, by the way, you were skating."

"He's right," Jonas added.

She leered at Jonas. "I was distracted, that's all."

Logan shooed her with his gloved hands.

"By all means, continue. I need to observe you skating by whatever means it takes to conclude this theory I have."

Libby didn't want to skate anymore, but she relented for the sake of pleasing Logan. She watched him skate to the edge of the pond and sit on one of the benches. Caught between exploring what her *friendship* status was with Jonas, and seeing where it *could* go with Logan, Libby was quite unsure of herself at the moment. She was suddenly more confused than she had been since she'd woken up in the hospital.

Jonas happily pulled Libby away from Logan, hoping to resume his conversation with her—hoping to jar her memory of at least the good parts of their short-lived courtship. They'd fallen into it almost as fast as they'd fallen out of it. He hadn't stopped loving her, and he prayed that she still loved him, but only time would tell. Unfortunately, with Logan in the way, he didn't have any time to waste.

"Are you going to answer my question?" Libby asked when they were out of earshot from Logan.

Jonas sighed.

She wasn't going to let him off the hook.

"I'd prefer if you remembered on your own," he answered gently.

Libby swallowed hard. She knew that when a person didn't want to answer, it was usually because the answer was yes, and that made her more nervous than Jonas looked at the moment.

CHAPTER 11

Jonas stood by, helplessly watching Libby and Logan drive off toward town to have their first *date*. It took every bit of strength he possessed to keep from forbidding her to go, but he had no claim to her anymore, and if Logan could make her happy, who was he to stand in her way?

Snowflakes whirled around him as he stood on the porch with Bethany and Benjamin. He sensed their pity, and it grated on his nerves like the sting of porcupine quills. He didn't want to let her go, but at the moment, he had no choice. She'd made her choice. Really, she'd made the choice for both of them, and it felt somehow unfair that she held that much of his own future in her hands.

Defeat filled him as he watched the car disappear onto the main road. He stepped off the end of the porch and onto the slippery walkway with several inches of accumulation awaiting a snow-shovel to clear it away. He kicked at the snow as he made his way toward the barn for his horse. The sooner he hitched Gallup to his buggy, the sooner he could go home. He needed to throw himself into his chores so he could take his mind off Libby and her date with the would-be-doctor.

"Leaving so soon?" Benjamin called after him.

"*Jah,*" he said over his shoulder. "I've got to earn my keep at the Troyer's farm. I suppose the least I can do is to help Libby's *familye*—even if she doesn't want me to be part of it."

Bethany watched Jonas walk to the barn, his head lowered in defeat. She felt sorry for him, realizing he really loved Libby. She considered her friend very fortunate to have someone like Jonas who was willing to put her first—even if she wasn't aware of it.

Inside the warmth of the barn, Jonas patted his horse. He hated to bring his gelding back out into the snow when he looked so content in the stall, but he needed to leave this place hoping it would remove the memory of Libby and Logan that was practically etched in his brain. Gallop whinnied and snorted, bobbing his head toward Jonas, and then nuzzled his arm affectionately as if he knew the woes of his human caretaker.

Jonas looked deep into the soulful eyes of his horse, wondering what the animal was thinking. Normally, Jonas didn't think too much about the horse in such a personal light, but he was the only thing in Willow Creek of any familiarity besides Libby, and she was disconnected from him at the moment. He felt lost in a snowstorm of emotions. He was usually tougher than this, but Libby held a soft spot in his heart that left him weak at the knees.

After hitching the horse to the buggy, he pointed Gallop toward his temporary home and his borrowed family, wondering what *they* really thought of his intrusion into their lives. Libby's mother had been more than accommodating, hoping he could somehow bring Libby's memory back. For Jonas, helping Libby to remember left him with mixed feelings. He wanted more than anything for her to be well again, but if she remembered him, she would certainly recall breaking up with him. That was something he wasn't yet ready to face. It would be like losing her all over again, but in reality, he didn't really have her now any more than he had when he'd shown up to lay claim to her.

Jonas reflected on his time on the ice with Libby, realizing he had some hope. She'd remembered him, but more importantly, she knew how to skate. Skating was always something of great importance to Libby, and he hoped she would continue to trust her instincts and keep skating. If only he could find a way to keep her interest in him and in skating. Perhaps when he saw her again tomorrow he could try to work on her memory of him a little more.

Thinking of the look on her face when he told her he wanted her to remember him on her own caused him to frown. A little of the Libby he knew came out in that look. He'd seen it before. She'd given him that same look the day she broke up with him. It was a look of disappointment he hoped he would never see in her again, but today he had.

Regret filled him as he thought of how he might have handled Libby's question differently. He would get another chance to change it tomorrow, and he needed to rethink the situation so he didn't make the same mistake with her next time. Keeping the status of their relationship from her seemed to cause her a bit of anxiety, so he would have to find the right words to reveal it without ruining the opportunity to have a second chance with her.

Oh, what he wouldn't give to have a second chance at winning her heart. To be able to take back the words that were spoken so harshly the night they'd broken up. He knew that if he could get that chance, he'd do everything in his power to change things around so neither of them would get hurt again. He loved her, and he intended to tell her just as soon he could.

Jonas looked down the icy road, blinking away heavy snowflakes so he could see the person walking toward him.

It was Libby, and she was alone.

Jonas couldn't help but smile.

It looked as if he was about to get that second chance sooner than he could have hoped for.

CHAPTER 12

Logan turned his car into a narrow drive off the main road and pulled up toward the bank of Willow Creek. Libby knew the place well. It was the spot where the youth would gather to hang out with others that were enjoying their *rumspringa*. Some would smoke or talk on cell phones, but most would spend private time in the backs of buggies kissing, and doing other things that were always talked about in hushed tones.

The area was heavily wooded, and at the present time, quite abandoned. Her heart quickened its pace at the thought of Logan trying to kiss her. It was an exciting thought, but she wondered if she would be able to go through with it.

To the best of her recollection, she'd not yet been kissed, even though if she had to be honest with herself, she had to wonder if she'd kissed Jonas at some point. She tried to put Jonas from her mind. She was with Logan, and had no intention of dwelling on what might have been or was in the obvious past with Jonas—no matter how much it nagged at her.

"Why are we stopping here?" Libby asked Logan as he turned off the engine.

He shifted casually in his seat to face her. "I thought it might be nice to just sit and talk a little—get to know one another a little better."

Libby had thought they would do that at the restaurant, but she supposed it wouldn't hurt to get the awkwardness out of the way without the added stress of being exposed in the public eye. For some strange reason, she knew what it was like to be stared at and whispered about, but she wasn't sure why. Perhaps it was because she had a lot of Amish friends, but no, that couldn't be it.

Shaking off the feeling of uneasiness she suddenly felt, Libby turned toward Logan and smiled.

"*Jah,* that would be nice. We could walk down to the creek, if you'd like to."

Logan nodded as he opened his door.

Libby got out eagerly. She loved this time of the year. If she had her way, it would snow year-round just so she could spend every moment skating.

Logan held a hand out to her and she took it.

"I just had a strange thought," Libby said.

Logan squeezed her hand as he led them down the creek bank. "What's that?"

"I had the feeling I actually miss skating."

She looked down at the creek, the edges of the bank covered in ice. Water rushed over and around the ice formations, bringing strange thoughts to Libby's mind. Flashes of twirling on the ice entered her mind's eye. She was happy, but how could that be? Though her first instinct told her she was an expert skater, she couldn't help but wonder where her sudden aversion to it had come from.

"From what I've heard from everyone, including Jonas, you're quite the skater." Logan offered. "I got to see a little bit of that today."

The mention of Jonas pricked her attention.

"What did Jonas say about my skating? He doesn't even know me!"

Logan looked at her curiously. "I got the impression the two of you used to date."

Libby's face heated at his comment. "That isn't even possible since I don't know him."

Logan raised an eyebrow. "Do you think you could have forgotten him the way you *forgot* how to skate?"

Libby's heart rolled against her ribcage hard enough to knock the wind out of her. She knew from today's experiment that she hadn't forgotten how to skate. Was it possible that she'd also not forgotten Jonas and her relationship with him?

He had seemed familiar to her, and it now worried her to think they could have dated at one time.

"Surely I would have remembered if I'd dated Jonas—wouldn't I?"

"Maybe the two of you broke up."

"Nee, the Amish don't usually do that. They court one person until marriage."

"You know a lot about the Amish."

"Because I'm—I'm."

Libby couldn't finish her sentence. She was confused about who she was. She *knew* her family was Amish, which would make *her* Amish, but she honestly didn't think she *could* be Amish.

"Because you're Amish," Logan finished for her.

"Jah, I mean—I don't know what I mean anymore!"

Logan pulled her into an unexpected hug.

"Don't try too hard. It will come to you."

Libby gently pulled away from Logan. It wasn't that she didn't like the closeness between them, but she had more important things on her mind at the moment.

"We should go," she said. "It's getting late."

Logan took her hand and led her back to the car. He turned over the engine and cranked up the heat to warm them up quickly. Then, he leaned over and tried to kiss Libby.

She turned her head and backed toward the passenger side door, her head bumping the window.

"I can't kiss you?" Logan asked.

"Not yet," she said shyly. "It's too soon. Maybe after we've had a few dates—then, maybe."

Logan smirked. "You thought this was a date?"

"If it wasn't a date, why would you try to kiss me?"

"I just think you're pretty, that's all."

Libby folded her arms in front of her and pursed her lips. "Perhaps we should just go into town and eat like we planned."

Logan distorted his face. "I didn't really want to go into town either."

"Then just *what* was your plan with me?" Libby asked angrily.

"Not to go into town with you."

Libby leered at him. "Just what is that supposed to mean?"

"Well," he stammered. "You're *Amish*. What would my friends say if they saw me with you?"

Libby pointed to her jeans. "Do I *look* Amish to you?"

Logan shrugged. "Well, your long hair and the way you wear your makeup does make you *look* Amish, but more than that, you *talk* like the Amish."

"But you said I was *pretty!*" Libby argued.

"Yeah, but—I—I."

"You what?" Libby demanded. "You thought I was pretty enough to kiss, but not pretty enough to take on a date in front of your friends? You will *not* take advantage of me this way—I won't let you!"

Libby opened the door of Logan's car and got out, pointing her feet back toward her temporary home with Bethany. It would be a long walk back in the cold, but at least her virtue would remain intact, as would her dignity.

CHAPTER 13

Libby's anger kept her warm as she walked down the icy road toward home. The last thing she wanted was to run into Jonas, but he was riding toward her in his buggy, and she was certain he'd already seen her. It wasn't like there was anywhere for her to turn off the road, but even if there was, she'd have probably taken a turn rather than face him at the moment. She would surely suffer ridicule from him for not listening to his warning about going out with the *Englisher* in the first place. It wasn't what she needed to hear right now. All she wanted to hear was how Logan was in the wrong—not her.

Jonas pulled his buggy up alongside of Libby. Though he was tempted to ask why she was walking when she was supposed to be out on a date with Logan, he decided to let her off the hook. It was obvious by her expression that the date had not gone well. That, coupled with the fact she was walking and alone, made him wonder what kind of man would do such a thing to a woman. Jonas had taken her home the night she'd broken up with him, and though his heart was breaking at the time, he knew it was the right thing to do.

"Hop in," he offered. "You look freezing."

"Danki," she said quietly.

She climbed up inside the buggy beside him without a word.

"I'll have to go up the road a ways to the turnoff so I can turn around and head back—unless you're hungry and would like to join me in town for some food."

Libby thought about it for a minute. "You wouldn't be embarrassed to be seen in public with me?"

Jonas slighted his eyes from the road long enough to assess her expression. "Why would you ask such a question?"

Libby stared out at the snow. "Answer the question and I'll tell you."

Jonas smiled. Even if she was distraught, she was acting like her *old self.* "Alright. I would not be embarrassed to be seen in public with you. Now will you tell me why you want to know the answer to such an odd question?"

"Because of the way I'm dressed."

"What about it?" he asked casually.

"Logan said I look Amish!"

Jonas wanted to remind her that she *is* Amish, but he held his tongue. "You look like you're enjoying your *rumspringa,* that's all. But why would you think it would embarrass me?"

Libby blew out a discouraging sigh. "Logan told me he was embarrassed to be seen in public with me."

"*Englischers* can be cruel. I'm sorry he said such an unkind thing to you."

"*Danki,*" she said, nudging against him.

It put a lump in his throat. He missed her so much, and he wished more than anything that he could slip his arm around her, but he didn't want to scare her any more than she might have been by Logan's actions.

"So tell me," he finally said. "Why is it that I found you out here walking all by yourself? He didn't leave you, did he?"

Libby shook her head. "I got out of the car after he tried to kiss me."

Jonas clenched his jaw, but kept his gaze forward so she wouldn't see the fury he was certain would show in his eyes. He was a forgiving man, but it grated down his nerves to think of another man putting his hands on Libby. He breathed a quick prayer, thanking God that she was able to get away from him unharmed.

"You are lucky to have gotten away from him before something more serious happened."

As soon as the words left his lips he regretted saying it. The last thing he wanted to do was frighten her or cause her anxiety.

"I'm sorry, I shouldn't have said that. I was so worried for you when you left with Logan, and now I know the reason I had such a bad feeling."

Libby looked at him curiously. "I thought you were just jealous. I didn't think that you could be worried about me since you don't know me."

But I do know you! Jonas thought. *And I was certainly jealous!*

"That isn't entirely true," he said.

"Which part?"

"Well," Jonas began. "I suppose if I was being honest with myself *and* with you, I'd have to admit truth to all of it."

She giggled. "I *knew* you were jealous!"

Jonas nudged her back playfully. "I am not!"

"Are you ever going to tell me how we know each other?" she asked.

Jonas smiled at her. "I think I might make you work for it."

Libby raised an eyebrow. "What is that supposed to mean?"

"It means that if I told you, there wouldn't be any fun in that. As long as I keep it a mystery, I can keep your interest."

"Well I do like a *gut* mystery, but you already have my interest."

Jonas winked at her. "I was really hoping you'd say that."

"I'm not sure why, but I have a feeling you won't disappoint me," Libby said.

"I'll try my best."

They both laughed, and to Jonas, it felt a little bit like *old times*.

CHAPTER 14

"We could eat here," Jonas offered, pointing to the family restaurant on the corner of Main Street. "They serve breakfast all day."

Libby smiled and nodded. "I could eat breakfast all day long."

Jonas knew this about her, but didn't dare let on how well he really knew her, fearing it would scare her off.

"It's settled then," he said as he pulled the buggy into the parking lot.

After assisting Libby out of the buggy, Jonas tied up the horse.

Libby tipped her head back, watching the snow swirl about overhead. She loved the snow and wouldn't mind at all if it stayed winter year-round.

Lost in the magic of the snowfall, Libby didn't hear Jonas when he called her name. He closed the space between them and touched her arm, hoping not to startle her.

Libby lowered her head slowly, looking at Jonas. A flash memory of him entered her mind just as quickly as it left her. She blinked and shook her head. Was she seeing things? Perhaps not, she reasoned with herself. After all, he was standing right in front of her.

Jonas held his arm out to her. "Shall we go inside where it's warm?"

"You know, I don't mind the cold," she said as she looped her arm in the crook of his elbow.

"*Jah,* I know," he said with a chuckle. "You could stay out on the ice for hours, but I don't want to turn into an ice sickle out here."

She tightened her grip on his arm. "I wish I knew how you know so much about me. I'm guessing we were at least friends."

He winked at her as they walked through the door of the diner. "*Jah,* we were *gut* friends."

She leaned in and whispered to him so the hostess would not hear her. "I had a feeling we were."

Jonas patted her hand that hung from the crook of his elbow, thinking he'd much rather hold her in his arms, but that just wasn't possible yet.

When the hostess showed them to a booth, Jonas gestured for her to sit before he did.

"Here you are Darlin'. This looks like the best seat in the *haus.*"

Libby looked at him curiously before she slid into the booth. Where had she heard that before? From Jonas, perhaps? Either way, it was strangely familiar.

The server handed them a couple of menus and left them to get their drink order. Neither of them picked up the menus.

"Do you know what you want?" Jonas asked after an awkward moment.

"*Jah,* I always get the same thing."

He smiled, knowing what it was she always ordered. "Me too."

She smiled back as the server showed up with their drinks.

"What would you like, Miss?" the server asked.

Libby raised an eyebrow at Jonas and smiled.

"I would like hard-scrambled eggs, bacon, potato wedges, and two pieces of French toast."

"Are you really going to eat all of that?" Jonas asked her jokingly, knowing he would end up eating what she couldn't finish, just as he had when they were a couple.

"*Jah,*" she said with a giggle.

He paused for a moment, thinking how much he missed that giggle.

"Well, in that case, I will have hard-scrambled eggs…" he paused again, looking for the change in her expression.

She didn't disappoint him.

She'd noticed he'd ordered his eggs the same way she had.

He set his focus back onto the older woman waiting for his order. "I'll also have bacon, hash browns, and…"

"Toast instead of pancakes," Libby interrupted him.

He winked at her, pleased that she'd remembered.

The server smiled as she picked up the menus.

Once she was gone, Libby narrowed her eyes playfully. "I'm guessing we've eaten here together before."

"*Jah,*" Jonas admitted, wishing he could tell her it had been quite often.

Dishes clanging helped to fill the awkward silence between them, but Jonas was determined to offer up a few more reminders to Libby about their relationship. As long as he could avoid the question of why they'd lost contact a couple of weeks ago, he figured he would do alright.

He looked out at the snow, gesturing to Libby to follow his gaze out the window. "The snow is best seen when you're lying on your back on the ice. From that angle, it seems to just float around, and you can't tell where the snow starts and the sky ends."

"You like to do that, too?" she asked.

"*Jah,*" he said with a smile. "Ever since you first showed me."

Libby put a hand to her chest. "I showed you that?"

"*Jah.* Before you pointed that out, I'd never looked at snow from that angle."

She smiled.

"You also told me that each snowflake is different. You said that you'd read it in a book at the library that no two snowflakes are alike."

Libby tipped her head to the side, looking deep in thought for a minute. "I remember going to the library with my cousin in Nappanee, but I don't remember telling you that about the snowflakes—although I do remember reading about it in a book."

Jonas felt a little frustrated, wondering what he could safely say to jar her memory.

"We spent more than an hour one afternoon catching the large snowflakes on our gloves and trying to see if we could tell the difference in them."

"Did we?"

"*Nee,* but we laughed a lot while we tried."

Libby lowered her head. "It sounds as if we had a lot of fun playing in the snow. I wish I could remember it."

"I do too," Jonas said sadly.

CHAPTER 15

Libby hurried to dress herself. She was actually looking forward to the invitation from Jonas to skate with him at the pond today. Funny how just yesterday she was looking forward to skating with Logan again, and hoping it would be their second date, but after the way he'd treated her, she didn't ever want to see him again.

Pulling on a pair of cable-knit stockings, she wondered if she should rethink her attire. She'd chosen her favorite blue dress, hoping it would turn Jonas' head. In reality, though she *knew* it was her favorite, it didn't keep her from feeling foreign in the dress.

Studying her appearance in the bathroom mirror, she had to admit she looked awfully Amish in the dress, even if her untamed tresses didn't. Surely, she should pull her hair back. After all, Jonas had kindly reminded her yesterday that she should wear it as was fitting per the rules of the Ordnung.

They weren't a part of the strictest of Ordnungs, but she was required to keep her hair pinned back and tucked away behind a prayer *kapp.*

Libby breathed out a heavy sigh as she looked at herself in the mirror. Had she always been this plain? With makeup on and her hair down she was certainly prettier in her own eyes, but she knew that beauty was in the eye of the beholder. She believed her mother had most likely told her that. If not, she'd surely heard it somewhere from someone who obviously cared a great deal for her, and that was all that mattered to her.

Satisfied she wasn't going to get any prettier no matter how long she stared into her reflection, Libby stepped away from the mirror and headed down the stairs to where Bethany was eagerly waiting for her.

"*Ach,* you look so much nicer today," Bethany told her.

Libby distorted her face. "I look plain and dull."

"*Nee,* you're as beautiful as always, but don't tell anyone I said that."

They both giggled and Libby hugged her.

"*Danki,* I really needed to hear that. I'm feeling a little awkward in this dress. Did I really skate in a dress before the accident?"

"*Jah.* And don't worry about Jonas. I have a feeling he's going to be happy to see you in that dress."

Libby crossed to the window when she heard his horse coming up the driveway. "He should. He practically sent me to my room when he saw me in those jeans yesterday!"

Bethany giggled. *"Jah,* he wasn't very happy to see you dressed that way."

Libby turned around, a sense of urgency in her expression. "Do you know what my relationship with Jonas was like before the accident?"

Bethany raised an eyebrow. "What did Jonas say about it?"

Rolling her eyes, Libby watched out the window as the buggy drew nearer to the house. "He wants me to remember on my own."

"It will come to you. Isn't that what you want?"

"I really like him, Bethany, but I don't know if I liked him before, or if he liked me, and if it was more, and why we aren't together now. I have so many *what-if* questions that I need answered, and it doesn't help that my feelings for him are conflicted."

"What do you mean?"

Libby checked the window again before answering. Jonas was almost to the house.

"I mean that I think I could *love* him, but I know it's way too soon to have such *narrish* thoughts about this *mann* when I've barely just met him. And only yesterday I thought I wanted the *Englisher!* But now, I'm conflicted."

Bethany crossed the room and stood by the window with Libby, watching Jonas pull his buggy close to the house. "Perhaps it is a *rekindled* love you are feeling for Jonas."

Libby sighed. "If I loved him before, why do I get the feeling that I *stopped?"*

"Ach, only you and Jonas can answer that."

"What if I can't answer that for myself? Jonas has made a *game* of not telling me details. If I don't figure it out on my own, he's not going to tell me."

"Try to let go of the past, Libby, and just go with what you are feeling now. It might surprise you in the best way possible."

Libby sighed again. "I hope you're right."

Jonas tied up his horse and walked up to the porch and grabbed the shovel that leaned against the side of the house. He began to shovel the steps and the front walkway that led to the driveway. What was it that made Jonas so appealing to her? Was he more appealing than the *Englisher?* Certainly, in so many ways.

Confusion gripped her heart as she watched him. He was obviously cleaning the walkway for her. She was certain Logan would not have done such a thing for her—something that was so apparently automatic in nature for Jonas. She was conflicted by her attraction to both men who were such opposites. Perhaps her attraction to Logan had stemmed from the rebellion she was fighting regarding her Amish heritage.

She couldn't deny who she was any more than she could deny her feelings for Jonas.

The only thing still bothering her was the past. If they'd had a past, why couldn't she remember? Perhaps it was not very memorable to begin with. If so, why would she have such strong feelings for him now? She wasn't certain at this point if she should fight those stirrings within her, or give in to them. She couldn't deny, even to herself, that she loved Jonas, so what was the point in fighting it?

Libby couldn't help but admire him from the window, where he had no idea he was being watched. Jonas was truly a kind man—a man most worthy of consideration.

CHAPTER 16

"What are you doing here?" Libby asked Logan through gritted teeth. "Didn't I make myself clear to you yesterday how I felt about you?"

"I suppose you did, Liberty, but I'm not through with my research."

"Don't call me *Liberty!*"

"That's your name, isn't it?"

"*Nee,* I'm Libby, and I'm *Amish.* You got a problem with that?"

Jonas squeezed her elbow. "I'll handle this," he said to her under his breath.

Logan stepped forward. "What are you going to do about it? She already signed the release so I could observe her for my research, and I'm not leaving until I get it. My dissertation could get me placement in a good hospital, and

I'm not about to give that up or all my hard work because you're jealous that I took out your girlfriend last night."

Jonas smirked. "I heard that didn't go too well for you."

"She's just a tease, that's all," Logan said.

"I can't imagine you being a very *gut* doctor because you don't have any respect for your fellow *mann,*" Jonas said, shaking his head.

"Why, because I don't live my life back in time the way you all do?"

Jonas could feel his jaw clench. Not only had he insulted their heritage, he'd insulted Libby in a way that no woman should be insulted. By this time, Benjamin had shown up with Bethany and was at his side. Adam skated over to them as well, bringing two of his cousins.

Logan backed away and held up his hands.

"Hey, I don't want any trouble. I don't need the Amish Mafia after me or anything."

"We are a peaceful community," Jonas said.

"I'll bet that's what the Amish Mafia said to their victims right before they started fighting with them."

Benjamin chuckled. "I think you watch too much TV."

Adam stepped forward. "If Libby gives her consent, you can observe her skating so you can finish your paper, but while you're here, you will be respectful of the community. Understood?"

Logan's expression fell. "I give you my word."

Logan turned to Libby. "I'm sorry for what I said—and for the way I treated you yesterday. If you let me stay I will be completely respectful."

Libby nodded her consent. Then she pulled Jonas by the arm onto the ice. She looked him in the eye and smiled. "Let's give *him* something to be jealous of," she whispered.

Jonas smiled back, turning her around and skating backward while he held her hands. Though she was still a little wobbly, she was almost as perfect a skater as she'd always been—as long as she kept her eyes on him.

Snowflakes drifted from the heavens as they twirled around the pond together. As long as Libby kept her focus on Jonas, it was almost as if they were all alone on the pond. The rest of the world did not exist as she gazed into his eyes—it was just the two of them.

Libby faltered a bit as she let her gaze leave Jonas, her focus drifting toward Logan. She was glad that he'd apologized, but it wasn't enough to turn her head back toward him. So why couldn't she seem to keep her concentration on Jonas all of a sudden? She was doing so well. Her mind reeled in more thoughts than she could process at the moment. Even though he'd seemed remorseful for his actions, she was certain Logan's sudden change in attitude had more to do with fear of getting into a fight and selfishly wanting to finish his research than it did with genuine sorrow for what he'd done. Nonetheless, he was being respectful, but she wasn't comfortable with having Logan watching her and Jonas skate any longer.

She wanted to be alone with Jonas, and those feelings grew stronger the more they skated together. His light touch at the small of her back sent tingles down her spine, and the warmth of his hand against hers could be felt even through her homemade mittens.

Out of the corner of her eye, she could see Logan leaving—without saying goodbye.

What a relief, she thought.

Jonas slighted his eyes to the right, noticing Logan's sudden departure. He was pleased that he had won Libby over—against an *Englisher*. He hoped the man would not return to Willow Creek, or try to bother Libby again. He would certainly not welcome Logan's company again, no matter how many times he apologized. His behavior toward Libby had been nothing short of inexcusable. Jonas was a peaceable person, but he had been prepared to defend Libby's honor.

With Logan now gone, Jonas would try to work his way back into Libby's heart. Skating beside her, Jonas pulled her closer to him with his right arm at her waistline, while his left hand held steady with her left. He couldn't think of anything more graceful and romantic than skating with her.

After trolling the pond a few times, she suddenly let her hand go limp from his while her ankles started to wobble. If not for his quick reflexes, she'd have fallen on the ice. He held her close as he brought her to the edge of the pond and sat her down on a bench.

Libby's eyes drooped, and Jonas gripped the sides of her face. "Stay with me, Darlin'."

"What did you say," she asked weakly.

"Don't go passing out on me, Darlin'."

Libby widened her eyes as best she could, trying to ignore the dizziness and tunnel vision. This very scene had played out before her eyes once before. She'd heard that voice—when she'd fallen on the ice.

Had it been as real then as it was now?

She pulled off her mitten and reached up to touch Jonas' strong jawline, his freshly-shaven skin felt warm and smooth under her fingertips. Closing her eyes, her hand still touching him, she felt his lips touch hers. Fear gripped her as she dared not open her eyes to see if what she was feeling was real. Libby decided she would keep her eyes closed if it meant she could enjoy Jonas for just a few minutes longer.

CHAPTER 17

"Go up to the B&B and call for an ambulance," Jonas begged. "She needs to go back to the hospital."

Adam ran across the long stretch of snow-covered lawn that separated the B&B from the pond so he could use the phone there.

Libby lay outstretched in the snow, going in and out of consciousness next to the bench she'd been sitting in only minutes before.

Benjamin put a hand to Jonas' shoulder. "I see Logan's car up there in the parking lot. Should I get him? He might be able to help."

Jonas clenched his jaw, his heart rate accelerating at the thought of having to ask Logan for help, but his feelings didn't matter right now. Libby was his first priority.

Jonas nodded slowly while he held Libby's hand. "*Jah, get him,*" he said quietly.

Benjamin followed the same trail in the snow that Adam had just sprinted across to get his sister some much-needed help, while Jonas continued to stay close to her side.

Libby opened her eyes and stared up into the swirling snow above her.

"Stay with me, Darlin'," a familiar baritone spoke to her.

"I love you, Jonas," Libby whispered to the snowflakes.

Jonas squeezed Libby's hand and leaned in close to her ear. "I love you too, Darlin'."

Libby turned her head slowly toward Jonas and looked him the eye. "It was you," she whispered.

Jonas put a warm hand to her cold cheek. "Just rest, Darlin'. Don't try to talk. There's an ambulance on the way."

Libby blinked away light snowflakes, her eyes drooping. She could feel Jonas pulling her head into his lap, his comforting touch soothing her and making her feel safe.

Logan ran toward them, stopping just short of Libby to catch his breath. "What happened?"

Jonas answered without looking up. "She said she felt dizzy, and before I knew it, her legs became wobbly and she started to fall before I could get her to the edge of the pond."

"Did she hit her head on the ice again?" Logan asked.

"*Nee*—no. I was able to catch her in time."

Logan bent down and grabbed her wrist, checking her pulse against his watch. "Her pulse is strong, and her breathing seems fine. This may have been a little too overwhelming for her, and she could be suffering from exhaustion. We'll know more when we get her to the hospital and run some tests."

Logan patted her hand repeatedly. "Liberty, can you hear me?"

He kept it up until Libby's lashes fluttered.

"I thought I already told you, my name is not Liberty—it's Libby! Ain't it so, Jonas?"

Jonas held fast to her other hand and gave it a squeeze. "That's right, Darlin'."

Logan's eyes darted between Libby and Jonas.

"*Darlin'?* Since when did the two of you become a couple?" Logan asked.

"Since he asked me to marry him two months ago in Nappanee." Libby said weakly.

Jonas' eyes widened at her comment and his heart did a flip-flop behind his ribcage. If she remembered they were engaged to be married, surely, she remembered she'd broken it off with him. Was she just putting on an act and stretching the truth so Logan would leave her alone? Jonas hoped it wasn't so.

"Wow, you Amish sure do move fast! I don't understand why you went out with me last night if you were engaged to *him*." Logan said, pointing to Jonas, disgust dripping from his tone.

"We broke up that's all, but now we're back together," Libby said.

She does know, Jonas thought with worry.

Jonas patted her hand. "Now don't go giving away all our business, Darlin'." Jonas said nervously.

Libby looked up at Jonas. "*Darling*—I feel fine now. I think I want to just go home."

Was she teasing him, or was she trying to keep Logan from getting any funny ideas about the two of them? Whichever one it was, Jonas wasn't going to miss the opportunity to enjoy his new *relationship* with Libby whether it was real or not.

Before he could answer, the sirens from the ambulance broke the spell between them.

Logan briefed the paramedics of Libby's history and current condition while they lowered a gurney next to her. Then he turned to Adam and Jonas. "If you fellas want to ride with me, I'll get you to the hospital right behind the ambulance."

"I want my fiancé to go with me," Libby told the paramedics.

One of them looked up. "Which one of you is her fiancé?"

Jonas smiled proudly. "That would be *me!*"

Logan rolled his eyes at Jonas as he beckoned Adam, Benjamin, and Bethany toward his car at the B&B.

Bethany grabbed Libby's hand as they were wheeling her into the ambulance. "We'll be right behind you, and I'll be praying the whole way for you."

Libby squeezed Bethany's hand gently.

"*Danki,* but I'm not worried. I'm in *gut* hands."

She smiled weakly toward Jonas, causing his heart to jump behind his ribcage.

Once inside the ambulance and they were on their way, Libby pulled Jonas down toward her so she could whisper to him while the paramedics put an IV in her other arm.

"I hope you don't mind that I told Logan a fib about us," she said quietly.

Jonas swallowed hard. She hadn't remembered their relationship after all. He almost wished she had because all the wondering and waiting was torturing him.

"No problem," was all he could say in response.

"I hope you understand, I only wanted him to leave me alone, so I figured if he thought you and I were engaged he wouldn't bother me anymore. It scared me to see him taking care of me just now."

Jonas forced a smile, wondering how she knew when they'd become engaged if she'd really told him a fib about their relationship. "I'll do anything for you, I hope you know that."

She smiled back at him. "I'm beginning to."

CHAPTER 18

"You need to get better so you will be out of here for my wedding on Thursday," Bethany told Libby.

Libby blew out an impatient sigh. "No one wants me out of here more than I do. If for no other reason than to get away from Logan."

"How does Jonas feel about him being here?"

"I can tell he doesn't like it," Libby admitted. "But he has no *real* claim on me. We aren't *really* engaged, but I think he's enjoying putting on a show for Logan's sake."

"And how do *you* feel about that arrangement, Libby?"

"To be honest, I don't like it at all."

Bethany crossed to the window and looked out at the snowfall. "I thought you were beginning to like him."

"I am, and that's why I don't like it. I just wish it could be real."

"*Jah,* but Jonas seems to really care for you. Give it some time, and perhaps he might surprise you."

"I'm not sure we have much time. Surely he has a life he needs to return to in Nappanee."

Bethany looked over her shoulder at Libby, who rested upright in her hospital bed. "There is another thing to consider."

"What is that?" Bethany asked.

"Did you forget that Jonas is Amish?"

"I haven't forgotten," Libby said. "But I've tried not to think about it too much."

Bethany sat down on the edge of the bed and faced Libby. "Why is that?"

"Because I feel lost, like I don't really belong anywhere. Like I'm caught between two worlds."

"You don't still think you're an *Englisher,* do you?"

"Don't look at me like that, Bethany. I'm just not certain I believe in the Amish ways."

"I've never heard you talk about such things," Bethany said. "Where do you suppose these thoughts could have come from?"

"I spent a lot of time with my rebellious cousin in Nappanee, and when *mei mamm* learned of it, that is when she sent for my return home."

Bethany smiled. "That is a breakthrough! You didn't know about that yesterday, did you?"

Libby shook her head. "I don't think so."

"What else do you remember?"

Libby closed her eyes and thought about it for a minute. In her mind's eye, she saw snowflakes falling toward her, and she could hear the smooth baritone that belonged to only one man. Jonas.

"Jonas was there with me when I fell on the ice."

Bethany shook her head. "*Nee,* he was not. He was in Nappanee, and didn't know anything about your accident until he arrived here to see you."

Bethany clamped a hand over her mouth, realizing she'd just let it slip out that Jonas knew her before the accident.

Libby laughed. "You should see your face right now! You look as white as a sheep."

"I'm sorry, Libby. I didn't mean to tell you about Jonas."

Libby narrowed her eyes at Bethany. "Why can't you tell me about Jonas?"

Bethany threw her hands up. "Don't get mad at me, but Jonas asked me not to tell you."

"Tell me what?" Libby asked.

"I can't tell you. I promised him I wouldn't."

Libby huffed. "What about your loyalty to me? We have been friends all our lives."

"Libby, you are not going to guilt me into telling you. While it's true, we have been friends all our lives, it is because of that friendship that I will not tell you anything about Jonas."

"Why not?"

"Because…"

"Because he told you not to," Libby interrupted and finished Bethany's sentence.

"And I told him I wouldn't, and I intend to keep my word."

"Keep your word to a *mann* you don't even know?"

"Don't question me like that, Libby. It is for your own *gut.*" Bethany said firmly.

She raised from the corner of the bed and went to window again to stare out at the snow as if it intrigued her in some way. Truth be told, she and Libby could not be more opposite in their love for the seasons. While Libby could live forever in winter, Bethany preferred the summer months, unable to bear the cold weather the way Libby could. She didn't enjoy ice skating or sledding or any of the delights that came with the winter months that kept Libby the happiest she would be all year round. Although Bethany had to admit she had not ever enjoyed riding in a sleigh until this season with Benjamin, and sitting in front of a roaring fire with him was also romantic, the rest of it—the cold and the snow, she could stand to do without all of it.

"I cannot believe that you could be so cruel as to keep a secret from me. We have shared all our secrets over the years. Why stop now?"

"You are not going to wear me down with guilt, Libby, so stop trying. I'm not telling you anything about you and Jonas, and that is that."

"That's alright, I already know."

Bethany shook her head at Libby, who was smiling. "You do not, or you wouldn't be wearing that silly grin on your face."

"But I *do* know!"

Bethany sighed. "Then you tell me, because I'm completely lost now."

"When I passed out yesterday on the ice, I saw Jonas."

"He was there with you," Bethany informed her.

"I know that he was with me *this* time, but I'm talking about when I fell and hit my head."

"But he wasn't…"

"I know he wasn't there that time," Libby interrupted. "But I saw him and heard him as though he was there. I felt his presence and *knew* that I loved him, but I only just remembered this yesterday when I passed out. So, I know now that we have a past, and that I loved him very much. What I can't figure out is why we weren't together the day of my accident."

Bethany looked out the window feigning interest in the heavily falling snow.

"You know, don't you?" Libby demanded.

Bethany turned slowly to face her. "*Jah,* but I…"

"But you promised not to tell," Libby interrupted.

CHAPTER 19

"You are over-exerting yourself and you need to rest or you will not recover," the doctor scolded Libby. "Most of your recovery depends on you taking it easy. You need to stop trying to force your memories to come back to you and just wait for them to return on their own. I can't stress to you enough that you should continue in your normal routines— without the ice skating, and *that* will help to restore your memories sooner."

Libby nodded acceptance to the doctor's orders so he would let her out of the hospital to be an attendant for Bethany's wedding. It had always been their plan to have a wedding together, but Libby was not ready for marriage yet. She couldn't be certain if she had ever even considered marriage, though she suddenly found herself daydreaming about it a lot.

"I'll make certain she takes it easy and sticks to her normal routine as much as possible," Bethany said.

Libby suddenly wished her mother was there with her, but she'd been unable to make it. She would be moving her things out of Bethany's home and moving back with her parents, so her mother had needed the extra time to prepare her room. Unsure of how she felt about that, Libby tried to push the worry from her mind and enjoy her time with Jonas.

Logan popped his head in the door of her room just then. "Hey are you decent? I'd like to talk to you."

Libby nodded. "*Jah,* come in."

Bethany excused herself while Jonas moved closer to Libby, ready to give the would-be doctor a final run for his money. If the man wanted to be competition for Libby's heart, he was going to get competition in return from Jonas. He truly loved Libby, and wasn't about to lose her again—especially not to an *Englisher.*

"I see the two of you are cozy as ever," Logan said with a condescending tone.

With Jonas standing close to the edge of the bed, Libby slipped her hand in his and gave it a squeeze. "We are as happy as ever, and eager for me to get out of here so we can get back to planning our future together."

Logan opened her chart and browsed, his jaw clenching. "We are waiting on a few of your tests to come back, but I'm certain that if everything comes back normal, I don't see why your doctor wouldn't let you out of here as soon as tomorrow."

"Just in time for the wedding," Libby said happily.

Logan's expression fell. "What wedding—surely not *your* wedding?"

Libby tightened her grip on Jonas' hand. "*Jah,* it is. Bethany and I had always planned to have a double wedding, and that is exactly what we are doing. We are all getting married at the same time."

Logan nodded, defeat showing in his eyes. "My sister and her best friend did the same thing. I suppose that is more of a *girl-thing* because us men don't really care about that stuff, am I right, Jonas?"

Logan sounded a bit nervous and desperate, but Jonas suspected it was more about pride and preserving his dignity after what he'd done and the rejection he'd suffered because of his actions.

"Normally I might agree with you, Logan," Jonas offered. "But with my Libby, I don't take anything for granted anymore, and her life is more important to me than my own, so her needs will always come before my own."

Logan blew out a heavy sigh. "It seems I have a lot more to learn about life than what I've learned from books and school, because I don't know if I will ever understand that kind of love—the kind of love you have for *Libby.*"

"Ach, you will meet someone that will become so much a part of you that you won't know how you ever lived your life without her."

"I hope you're right, my friend."

Logan extended his hand to Jonas, and the two shook hands.

When he left the room, Jonas turned to Libby. "I hope you don't think because I shook his hand and he called me *friend* that we are now friends. I could not make friends with a *mann* who is so selfish and prideful. I hope you know that."

She squeezed his hand. "I do. It seems he's finally given up on me. *Danki."*

"Ach, I'd do it all over again if it meant I could hold your hand some more."

Libby smiled shyly, keeping a tight grip on his hand. "You can hold my hand any time you want to."

Jonas smile back. "I'd like that. But what I would like even more is you getting better so I can take you for a sleigh ride in the snow."

"And that is the quickest way to my heart, Jonas Graber. *Ach,* I remembered your last name! I wonder what else I will remember as we spend more time together."

Jonas could feel his heart slam against his ribcage. He hoped it would take her a little longer to remember the breakup so she could fall in love with him all over again. He knew it was a selfish thought, but he loved her too much to let her go again.

Libby felt satisfied that she'd finally shaken off Logan, and she was delighted that Jonas had asked her for a sleigh ride. She could see the differences in the two men more clearly now, realizing the shallowness of Logan against the kindness and pure intentions of Jonas. He truly seemed to have her best interest at heart, and for that alone she would give him a chance. She certainly hoped he'd meant everything he'd said to Logan. If truth be told, Jonas was easy to love, and she would not deny those feelings in her anymore.

CHAPTER 20

"Why do I feel like I'm moving backward by moving back into my *parent's haus?"*

"You worry too much over silly things, Libby. This is progress, and you have to look at it this way. A week ago, you would have nothing to do with your *familye,* and now, you are going to be closer than ever with them."

"Just because I am moving into their *haus* does not make them any less foreign to me. I must admit I'm a little scared."

"They are nothing to be afraid of," Bethany said. "They are your *familye.* Your *mamm* is the kindest woman I know, and without her in my life over the years, I would have felt a very big void. She's been like a *mamm* to me just as you have been like a *schweschder."*

"What about Lavinia? Don't let her hear you talk like that. It might upset her and feel like she's been replaced."

"Ach, Lavinia knows how I feel about your *mamm."*

Libby looked up from the box she was packing.

"She does? And it doesn't hurt her feelings?"

Bethany shook her head.

"But Lavinia *was* a *mamm* to you for your entire life."

"She knew I needed both," Bethany said. "That is why she never got after me for spending so much time at your *haus* instead of my own."

Libby stopped packing and crossed the room to look out the window. "I can't believe you are getting married tomorrow."

Bethany giggled. "It's hard for me to believe too."

Libby stared out at the snow with a sigh. "I always thought we would get married on the same day. It kind of breaks my heart that we won't be."

Bethany closed the space between them and pulled her lifelong friend into her arms. "It will happen for you dear *schweschder.* I promise you it will."

Libby began to cry. "I'm sorry to break down like this. Please don't think I'm not happy for you. I just feel so overwhelmed by all of this. I don't understand why some things I remember as though they were yesterday, but some things have a lot of parts missing."

"Like what?" Bethany asked. "Maybe I can help fill in some of the gaps."

"I don't understand why I can't remember much about *mei* own *mamm*. You would think she would not feel like a stranger to me. I only remember a few small things about her, like the way she loves the crisp smell of the sheets after they have dried on the clothesline, or the fact she shared five generations of cooking secrets with me, and the way she used to brush my hair for hours when I was younger. Adam, I remember the most, but *mei vadder* might as well be someone I've never met before because that is how I feel about him."

Bethany pulled her tight for a moment and then let her go. "I have a feeling it will all be crowding your mind sooner than you want it to. Just remember what the doctor said and don't try to push yourself too hard to remember, or the memories could remain lost forever."

Libby sniffled. "That is what I fear the most. What if they are lost forever? What if I never remember?"

Bethany smiled. "Then you will make new memories with the people who love you most."

"But that is part of the problem," Libby complained. "I'm not even certain who I love anymore. Or who I *used* to love…"

She let her voice trail off as she stared out at the snow. It was the one thing that she was sure of in her life. She loved the snow and everything about winter. Beyond that, she couldn't' even be sure of who she was anymore.

Bethany put the remaining few items in Libby's box and closed the top flaps. "What do you mean?"

"I'm not sure I have the right to love Jonas when I don't know what role he played in the past. I am certain I must have loved him before because the feelings are so strong, but I just don't know how long ago it was. I can only assume it was while I was in Nappanee, but for all I know, I was running around with *mei* cousin pretending to be *Liberty* the *Englisher.*"

"*Ach,* I hardly think Jonas would have taken an interest in you while you were in Nappanee if you had been living as an *Englisher.*"

Libby sniffled again. "What if I've been living a double life? I've blocked out most of the time I spent there. What if I did something *narrish* while I was there?"

Bethany smiled weakly. "Then perhaps it is better if you *don't* remember it."

"I don't think that's the right plan for this. I am about to go for a sleigh ride with him tonight, and that could establish us as courting. So, if there is something between us that needs to be settled or talked about, it should probably be done before we go, don't you think?"

"*Ach,* but what if talking about it ruins everything with him?" Libby continued. "Do you think it's better if I keep my mouth shut of the subject and don't speak of it at all?"

Bethany raised an eyebrow. "I think you need to just relax and have fun with Jonas, and see where the night leads you. If you end up courting when the night is through, then what is the harm in that?"

"I suppose you're right about that. And I certainly don't want to say or do anything that will drive Jonas away. I really think I love him. He could be *the one.*"

"*Ach,* are you sure?" Bethany begged to know.

"*Jah,*" Libby said with a whimsical smile as she stared out at the snow. She could hardly wait for her first sleigh ride with Jonas.

CHAPTER 21

"Are you certain you want to go for a sleigh ride with Jonas?" her mother asked.

"*Jah,* why wouldn't I?"

"I suppose I thought it might be too painful."

Her mother went back to peeling the apples for a pie. "Never mind. I've said too much."

Libby picked up a firm, red apple and bit into it.

"You haven't said too much!" she said around a mouthful of apple. "You haven't said *anything* at all."

Sprinkling cinnamon in the bowl of diced apples, the woman tried her best to avoid eye contact with Libby. "Perhaps I should stay out of it, and let you make that decision on your own."

It doesn't matter what you say, Libby thought. *I won't take your advice anyway. At least Bethany was happy to hear I was seeing Jonas. If you are really mei mamm, you would be happy for me too.*

There had been an awkwardness between them since she'd walked in the door, but now, her comments about Jonas had put a wedge between them. If forced to choose, Libby would choose Jonas over a family of strangers every time.

Libby set the half-eaten apple on the table. "I'm feeling tired. I think I will take a short rest before the meal is finished."

Disappointment showed on her mother's face as she shooed her out of the kitchen. "I will come get you when it's time to eat."

As Libby dragged her feet up the stairs, she felt guilt tugging at her heart over her conversation with her mother. The woman hadn't given her much of a choice. She'd backed Libby into a corner with her concerns over her big night with Jonas. This would be a special night for the two of them. It would be the deciding factor in whether they would begin courting or not, and her mother was seemingly trying to put doubts in her mind about Jonas. Libby would have no part of that, even if it meant defying her mother.

Once she was safely in her room with the door closed, she looked around for anything that looked familiar. When she'd packed her few belongings the first time so she could stay with Bethany, she hadn't been able to identify a single thing in her room that meant anything to her. Had she lived such a dull life here that she had nothing that stood out as special? In the corner of the bureau, her gaze fell on a single, dried rose. Her first thought was to toss it in the trash, but for some strange reason unknown even to herself, she felt a sense of kinship to the dead rosebud.

Drawn to the rose, she went to it to examine it more closely. Picking it up, she closed her eyes and put it to her nose, a hint of fragrance still clinging to it. It had been picked recently, that much she remembered, but from where? Instincts told her it came from a greenhouse, but whose? She pressed it to her nose and breathed in deeply once again, hoping the fragrance would bring back the memory and tell the tale of its presence in her life.

In her mind, she could hear faint laughter. Hers, perhaps?

I sell the different flowers to several florists in the area so they have flowers year-round, the familiar baritone said.

"Jonas!" she said aloud.

He must have given me the rose when I was in Nappanee.

She breathed in again feeling the softness of lips on hers. Her eyes popped open suddenly, her heart skipping a beat. She hadn't allowed Logan to kiss her, so that meant only one thing.

Jonas had kissed her!

He kissed me when he gave me the rose.

Her fingers instinctively reached for her lips where they lingered as she remembered a very steamy kiss from Jonas. Why had he kissed her so passionately, yet now they were apart?

Had Jonas broken it off with her and now regretted it? Was that why he pursued her so intently? If so, should she give him another chance? After only a moment of thought, she decided it was worth giving him another chance. She had no idea what really happened between them, unless there had been another woman involved, but Jonas just did not fit that profile. She could already tell he was an honorable man, a man most worthy of her love.

Feeling a little tired, Libby tucked the rose in her apron pocket and pulled back the quilt on her bed. She knew she had time to get in a short nap, and she was certainly in need of one. Tucking the quilt over her, she snuggled into the soft bed, sinking into the feather pillow. She was exhausted to say the very least, and would need to rest if she was to enjoy her outing with Jonas.

Libby stared at the ceiling, suddenly unable to sleep. Shivering, she pulled the quilt up to her neck, her finger catching in a tear at the top edge.

Mamm was supposed to fix this for me. I wonder why she didn't.

Libby sat up suddenly, examining the quilt a little more closely.

She remembered the quilt!

She and her mother had made the quilt when she was only twelve years old. It was her first experience with quilting since she'd been such a tomboy up until then. Funny thing was, even knowing she had made the quilt with her mother didn't help her to have an emotional attachment like she thought she should.

What was it that had happened to her mind when she'd fallen? Panic gripped her and didn't want to let go. It was the sort of fear that was accompanied by a feeling of impending doom. Had she misplaced more than her memories? Yes, she had lost her whole life. Not in the physical sense, but mentally, emotionally, and possibly even spiritually.

CHAPTER 22

"Jonas is here," her mother said quietly from the other side of the door.

Libby opened her bedroom door to greet her mother, hoping it would not end up in a confrontation. She needed peace before she went out with Jonas to set the mood for the evening. She wanted to have some fun for a change, and she wasn't up for her mother's condescending remarks about her time with Jonas.

"It's not too late to change your mind about going out tonight if you're not up to it."

"Why wouldn't I be up to it?" Libby snapped. "It's not like I don't know about the breakup, but I've decided to give Jonas another chance."

"I had no idea you knew," her mother said.

Libby was only challenging her. She had no real idea that they had broken up, but her mother's confirmation was enough for her. She only wished she knew why they had broken it off. She couldn't just come out and ask her mother why, she had to be strategic about it so the woman would be none the wiser as she was giving up precious information she had no idea she was giving up.

"Of course, I know. Why wouldn't I know? But I had no idea *you* knew."

"You told me all about it when you returned from Nappanee," her mother said. "I didn't think you were ever going to stop crying. I was worried about you that whole week."

I cried for an entire week? Libby thought to herself. *Jonas must have been the one to break it off.*

"Well, it doesn't matter because I'm over it and Jonas and I are back together."

Her mother's expression fell. "I suppose this means you've changed your mind, then."

Libby had no idea what her mother was talking about, but she was already too deep in the conversation to back out now and admit she was lying to her mother, so she had no choice but to go along with it and finish the discussion.

"*Jah,* I suppose I have," Libby said.

"It sounds like you have your mind made up then. Jonas will have to break the news to your *vadder*. He isn't going to take the news very well."

What news?

Libby wished so much that her mother would just come out and say what it was so it wouldn't be a mystery to her. It would be a challenge to get the information from Jonas as well since he seemingly enjoyed the game of *cat and mouse* he was playing with her. What was the big *mystery* behind their breakup? Was it possible there had been another woman in the mix? If so, Libby wouldn't dream of entering a relationship with such a man. Somehow, she had to find out the truth, even if it meant keeping up with the lie of making others think she knew everything of the breakup, and that included Jonas.

Libby pursed her lips and stepped through the doorway, forcing her mother to step aside to allow her passage. "We will deal with that later. As for now, I'm going for a sleigh ride, and I'm going to have a little fun for a change. All this memory loss is wearing me out."

Her mother pulled her into a light embrace.

"Have fun. You are young and healthy. We will let the rest worry about itself."

Caught off guard, Libby didn't think to hug her mother back until the woman had already let go of her, and then it was too late. Regret filled her as she momentarily mourned the loss of her mother—not in the physical sense, but by the fact that she simply could not remember too much about her. It was just short of frightening to think that her own mother was a stranger to her, but that was her new reality, a reality that had become too difficult to live with.

As she walked down the stairs, her mind was reeling. How was she going to get Jonas to tell her why they had broken up?

She still had too many questions that nagged at her. Why had Jonas returned to her life? What had he done that was so awful that he needed to keep it from her, and why would her father be upset with her sudden *change of heart* where Jonas was concerned.

What did Jonas have to hide?

That was the biggest question weighing on Libby's mind.

As she reached the landing at the bottom of the stairwell, Libby spotted Jonas standing alone at the hearth, warming his hands against the flames. He was seemingly deep in thought. She half-expected to see her father or brother with him, perhaps even lecturing him, but there he stood. Alone.

Was it enough that she loved him? She'd remembered being in love with him before, which only intensified those feelings. But was it enough to overlook whatever he had done to lose her in the first place? Had he lost her trust? He was, in fact, deceiving her now by not telling her what had happened between them, or what had caused the breakup.

Was it such a terrible offense that she'd blocked it out as a way to protect herself, or was it such a minute problem that her love for him could overlook it to where it didn't matter?

Whatever it was had broken them up. That fact remained etched in her mind, but her heart could not let go of the love she felt for him. One of them had severed the ties that bound them, but for some reason that no longer mattered.

Libby went to Jonas and put her hand in his.

"I'm ready for whatever is in store for us."

He gave her hand a little squeeze and smiled. She trusted him, and for that reason alone, he would not let her down a second time.

CHAPTER 23

Jonas assisted Libby into his open sleigh, the warmth of her hand permeating her mittens. He'd left his own gloves off just so he could feel her warmth. He slipped them on before grabbing the lead-straps.

"I was surprised your *vadder* didn't greet me," Jonas said.

Libby's heart thumped. He'd opened the conversation for her to broach the subject of their breakup. She breathed in deeply, knowing she wanted only to put that behind her and not think about it again. Just knowing they'd broken up didn't sit well with her, but she was determined not to think about it anymore.

She knew she might not get another window to find out what had happened between them, but she'd made up her mind that she didn't want to know, and she needed to stick to that.

"*Mei vadder* probably isn't eager to deal with my change of heart about you and me."

"You know about the breakup, don't you?" he asked, the color draining from his face.

"*Jah,* I do," was all she would say. She didn't want him knowing she didn't remember the details. They didn't matter. All that mattered was her love for him. The rest, she prayed, would take care of itself.

Jonas could feel his heart tightening. How was it that she knew, yet here she was out with him like it had never mattered in the first place? She'd made such a grand exit from his life over not wanting to leave her family behind while he moved her to Florida. Perhaps she'd really had a change of heart like she said she did. Either way, if Libby was on board with leaving, he would make the arrangements for their immediate departure. Though he knew it would not be possible to join Bethany and Benjamin for their wedding tomorrow, he hoped she would agree to keep their original wedding date, which was the following week.

"I can't believe you changed your mind," he said quietly. "Does this mean our wedding is still on for next week?"

Libby's heart skipped a beat. "N-next week?"

"*Jah,* that was the plan—until…"

"I will marry you next week," she interrupted. She wasn't about to give *him* a chance to change his mind. She knew he was a good match for her, and she knew she loved him enough to marry him. The past didn't matter, and she took the mindset that what she didn't know could not possibly hurt her.

Jonas stopped the sleigh in front of Willow Creek. He'd cut across the open field at the back of her parent's property, the full moon reflecting off the snow illuminated the way. Stars lit up the heavens creating an indigo backdrop against intermittent cloud cover. Occasional wispy snowflakes fluttered around them, making for the perfect romantic setting. Add the flux of the creek coursing over the rocks and ice patches along the bank, and they didn't lack any resource for romance. It was even in the crisp air they breathed in.

Jonas turned to Libby, thinking how beautiful she looked in the moonlight. "Are you cold?"

Libby giggled. "Of course not. You know I could live outdoors in the winter."

Truth be told, she was a little chilly, and now chided herself for not admitting it. That truth could have landed her in his arms, but she was so nervous she wasn't thinking straight. She'd just told him she would marry him, and suddenly things turned a little awkward. Perhaps it was because they were both pretty shy, and they had moved things along rather quickly between them.

Thankfully, Jonas pulled her into his arms regardless. He tucked the lap quilt closely around the two of them, and Libby did not object. He was certainly a considerate man.

The comforting thought in all of this for Libby was the fact they'd shared a past that was reconcilable. Without that, she would not have been so agreeable to let things advance as quickly as they had. The fact they'd already set a wedding date meant a lot to her.

But what of their wedding night? They were practically strangers. She barely remembered kissing him. It was something she greatly desired, and she feared if he didn't kiss her soon she would faint from the anxiety of it.

No sooner had she resolved herself to the disappointment, than he leaned in and pressed his lips to hers. His breath was warm against her cold mouth. Pulling his gloves off, he placed his warm hands on her cheeks and deepened the kiss. Drawing her closer, Jonas whispered to her in-between kisses.

"I've missed you," he said.

She wished she could say it back to him, but she wasn't sure if she missed him because she hadn't felt the gap between them the way he had.

"I love you," he whispered.

This, she could reciprocate.

"I love you too," she whispered.

Jonas deepened the kiss further still, making Libby warmer than she thought possible in the twenty-one-degree weather. After several minutes, Libby slowed down the return of his kisses.

"What's wrong," he asked.

"Maybe we should talk about our future plans. Where we will live, and what role we will play in the community."

"We already decided that—at least I thought we did. That is until…"

"Until we broke up," Libby said, wishing she hadn't said it just as soon as it left her lips.

Jonas didn't want to rehash the past. He was enjoying the possible future with Libby, and had every intention of making things work right here in Willow Creek if that was what it would take to keep her happy.

"I can set up greenhouses here if that is what you want me to do. I can work from wherever. I'm guessing you want to stay near your *familye.*"

"Nee, I don't," she said, surprising him. "I was hoping you'd take me far away from here."

Jonas looked at her wide-eyed.

What had just happened?

CHAPTER 24

Jonas looked at Libby as if she'd just grown two heads. Did he dare mention the huge fight they'd had before she'd left him and come back home to Willow Creek? She'd made such a point to let him know she was not interested in leaving her family to move to Florida, yet here she was telling him she'd changed her mind.

Was *this* the *change of heart* she'd mentioned at the start of their date? They had been on two separate sides of the fence on this subject, and now it would seem they still were. He'd come to tell her that he was the one to change his mind, and now she had completely turned opposite of him. He thought it best to keep quiet and let her have her say without his input. He didn't intend to do anything to clash with her idea of how she saw their future unfolding.

Libby stopped talking, realizing she'd said something terribly wrong. From the expression on Jonas' face, she could tell she'd made a mistake. Now, she decided to remain quiet and let him make the final decision for their future.

As her future husband, she would respect Jonas' decisions and his wishes, rather than acting like an unruly woman he would not want to marry. If she wanted peace in her life with Jonas she would have to learn the art of submission before it was too late. She wasn't trying to go against him, she just wasn't up for living so close to a family she didn't know, but she would do whatever was necessary to keep Jonas happy.

"I didn't mean that the way it sounded," she said, trying to retract her harsh statement. "I *love* them. I just don't have the same feelings about them since the accident. It's odd but I feel separated from them. Sort of how I felt about you right after the accident."

"I suppose the next question is; how far away do you want to live from them?" he asked cautiously.

Libby thought about it for a minute. Was this a trick question? As far as she knew, there were only two options. Willow Creek or Nappanee, and neither place was so far from the other that it wouldn't accommodate frequent visits.

"Where else is there?" she asked.

There it was.

The wedge that had pulled them apart.

Was she setting him up for another argument?

He was not in the mood for a debate, but it was something they needed to resolve. If they could do it amicably, they could salvage this dilemma and keep both of them happy, but he insisted on getting his way like he had last time they'd discussed it, and that would never work now. So, he relented and decided to let her make the final call. He knew he would essentially be happy wherever they were as long as it was with her.

"I'll be happy wherever you are," she said.

That was what he needed to hear from her the first time they'd discussed this—when they'd broken up in a heated argument. But now, well, now he needed her to be truly happy.

"Are you sure about that?" he asked.

Libby looked at Jonas curiously. What was it he was trying not to say to her?

"I only want you to be happy," she said. "I will be happy wherever we live as long as it's with you."

Why couldn't you have said that last time? He thought to himself.

He didn't dare continue with this conversation. He wanted to get back to kissing. He'd missed holding her in his arms. He'd missed the love between them, and right now, that was all he could think of. If he could think past the kissing, they might perhaps resolve the difference of opinion, but he didn't want that time to be tonight. Not when the moon and stars shone so brightly in the crisp, winter sky just for them.

Jonas pulled her back to him. "I don't want to talk about this now. I only want to kiss you."

Libby smiled. "I like the sound of that."

He smiled back at her, pressing his lips to hers.

"Your lips are cold," he said playfully.

Libby pulled the lapel of his woolen coat. "Then warm them up."

She kissed him softly, repeatedly, warmly. And to think she'd nearly passed up this man for an *Englisher*. Thankfully, she'd come to her senses before it was too late. She'd have missed out on this, and she couldn't even imagine living without this man now.

Libby blinked away snowflakes. The wind began to pick up, sending shivers through her.

"I thought you could live out here all winter," he teased.

Libby's teeth chattered. "Normally I c-could. I d-don't know wh-what's wrong w-with m-me."

Jonas pulled her close, tucking the lap quilt all the way around her. He pressed her face in the crook of his neck to shield her from a sudden gust of wind.

"Maybe we should get you home."

"*Nee,* just a little longer," she begged. "I'm not ready to go home yet. Not to a *haus* full of strangers."

"Have you thought about taking the time to get to know them all over again?" Jonas suggested.

"I hadn't really thought about that, but I do have to wonder if there isn't a reason that I've blocked them out of my memory."

She'd blocked him out too, but Jonas wasn't about to remind her of that. If there was one thing this night had taught him, keeping quiet about the past was probably for the best.

Jonas pressed his lips to hers once more, breathing in the night air.

Something was amiss.

Pulling away from Libby, Jonas sniffed the air and looked for what he feared he would find. "We have to go," he said, grabbing the reins.

"Why?" Libby asked. "I told you I wasn't ready to go."

"Don't you smell that?" he asked. "Something is on fire!"

CHAPTER 25

Jonas could see smoke coming from the direction of Libby's family home, but he tried not to alert her to his suspicions. He prayed it wasn't their home that was on fire as he pressed his horse to pull the sleigh a little faster in the deep snow.

As they rounded the curve of the creek toward the clearing, Jonas spotted fire. From what he could tell it wasn't the house that was burning, but more likely the barn, but it was definitely Libby's family farm that was in danger.

It was too late to spare her the reality of it. From out of the clearing they could see her property easier.

Libby gasped. "Hurry, Jonas. *Mei familye* is in trouble!"

She felt a sudden urgency to go to them, anxiety over the last words she'd spoken to her mother replaying in her head. She'd all but told her to keep out of her dealings with Jonas. Told her that it was none of her business. She'd been disrespectful to say the least.

Libby felt her throat constrict as she thought of her family getting hurt. What would she do without them?

"Can't you make your horse go any faster?" she shrieked, panic overtaking her. "I can almost walk faster."

Libby knew that wasn't the truth. The snow was far too deep for her to walk through, but it didn't change the anxious feeling that brought bile to her throat.

"Nee," he said. "He's going as fast as he can in this deep snow. We'll get there."

Tears welled up in her eyes as they neared, partly from the thick smoke in the air, but mostly because she had no idea where her family was or if they were safe. They were still too far away for her to see from that distance in the dark. The moon had dipped behind thick cloud cover, and heavy snow had begun to swirl and blow, bringing the visibility to a minimum.

The jingling of the bells on the horse's bridle drowned out communication between them, but Jonas concentrated on the jutted path that had brought them to the creek, hoping it would get them to the house more quickly.

"Hurry," Libby begged him.

Jonas could hear the sense of urgency in her voice, anxiety clouding reality for her.

Libby choked back tears, the cries catching in her throat. *Lord, please keep mei familye safe.*

It was the simplest of prayers, but it was all she had in her.

As they approached the edge of the farm, they could see more easily that the roof of the barn was engulfed in flames. Jonas' horse whinnied and snorted as he weaved back and forth across the path, protesting drawing the sleigh nearer to the burning building.

Jonas pulled on the reigns realizing he would not get any closer with the horse. Jumping down from the sleigh, he helped Libby down quickly and held her hand as they sprinted across the yard toward the barn.

"Don't get too close," Jonas warned as they ran.

As they neared the corral close to the barn, Libby could hear the horses' high-pitched whinnying, panic in their cries. But there was another cry that Libby had not expected. To the side of the corral, Libby's mother paced and cried out to God to spare them.

Spare who?

Her mother spotted Libby and ran to her, pulling her daughter into her arms.

"What happened, *mamm?*"

"I don't know," her mother answered with a desperate cry. "Your *vadder* and Adam are in there getting the animals."

"You stay here," Jonas warned. "I'm going in to help."

"*Nee,*" she begged between heavy sobs.

She watched Jonas put a hand up to her as if to let her know he'd be right back. She grabbed at the air toward him, but her mother held fast to her, holding her back to allow Jonas to leave her side.

Libby suddenly couldn't breathe. The sobs in her throat choked her more than the smoke that billowed from the top floor of the barn.

Just then, the barn door burst open and her father and brother met Jonas at the entrance. Two of the horses ran from the open door, as the three men disappeared behind the smoke to get the rest of them.

Libby held her breath as she waited with her mother, both women praying furiously, while the animals trailed out of the barn one-by-one. Unfortunately, there was no sign of the men that meant everything to her.

Libby's horse, Daisy, suddenly burst from the barn door, a trail of smoke following her out. The horse had gotten old and slow over the years, especially given the fact she was already quite old when her father had purchased the horse for her. It was her first horse, and her father had spent many hours teaching Libby how to properly ride the horse. She'd been only five years old, but Libby remembered it like it was just yesterday. Her father had been very patient with her constant complaining that the horse was too slow, and her persistent begging to ride a faster, younger horse.

Libby buried her head in her mother's neck and sobbed. "*Mamm,* please tell me they're going to come out of there alive."

Her mother stroked her hair and stifled her own cries to pray over her daughter. "I love you."

Libby lifted her head from her mother's shoulder and looked her in the eye. All her memories of the woman suddenly tumbled into her mind like the force of the flames that heated her face. "I love you too, *mamm.* I'm so sorry for the way I've been acting."

Her mother forced a weak smile around the tears that welled up in her eyes.

Soon, Butterball, their milking cow came strolling out with a protesting *moo,* followed by several squawking chickens flying out the open door. Libby was smart enough to know that as long as the animals were being pushed out the door, the flames had not gotten to the men in her life she cherished so much.

A sudden creaking added to the already noisy crackling of the fire. The creaking became louder until the right side of the barn began to collapse.

Libby's sobs came out in a scream as she pulled away from her mother's grasp and ran toward the barn.

CHAPTER 26

Libby ran toward the barn intending to go in and rescue the three men in her life she knew she couldn't live without. As she reached the door, her father stumbled out coughing and choking. Libby threw her arms around him, sobbing tears of gratitude he was alive.

There was still no sign of Jonas or Adam.

Her mother rushed to her husband's side, helping him toward the split-rail fence that enclosed the horse corral.

"I'm going in after Adam and Jonas," Libby cried.

Her father coughed as he grabbed her arm, barely able to catch his breath. "You stay here. After I get a little air, I'll go back in to look for them."

"Please don't make me stand here helplessly while they're in there in danger. Let me help," Libby begged.

The barn roof creaked loudly, sending Libby's heart racing so fast her legs felt shaky and weak. "I love you, *Daed,* but I have to save them. Let me go!"

Sobs caught in her throat as the creaking yielded to the flames, sending another section of the roof into the second floor of the barn. If they didn't come out of there soon, they would perish, and to Libby, that was not an option.

Pulling away from her other parent's grasp, Libby ran toward the barn a second time. Adam suddenly burst through the door, choking and falling to the ground.

Libby rushed to his side, bawling. "Where's Jonas?"

"I—don't—know," Adam barely got out between coughs.

As if under a spell, Libby raised from the ground and stepped through the open doors screaming for Jonas, and sobbing uncontrollably. Her father caught her arm just as she was about to enter the smoky barn.

"I'll get him. You stay here," her father scolded her.

She looked him in the eye for only a moment.

"Please save him," she begged.

"I will," he said over his shoulder, and then disappeared behind the thick smoke.

Libby paced and prayed outside the barn doors, choking on the smoke that billowed out, and not caring that the heat from the fire was so hot it made her sweat. With every creak and fallen board into the flames, Libby prayed harder and more desperately. She could hear her mother tending to her brother behind her, but she could not think past the danger her father and Jonas faced.

She *had* to help.

She *had* to save them.

Lord, help me, Libby whispered as she entered the smoky barn. Smoke burned her lungs as she stumbled a few feet. She called out weakly to her father and Jonas, unable to breathe. She choked and coughed, heaving in smoke instead of air. Blackness encompassed her as she fell to the floor. Her eyes closed, and her will to move escaped her.

CHAPTER 27

"Come on Darlin', stay with me," the muffled baritone spoke to her. Libby felt weightless as she drew in cool air. Reaching up to her nose, she fingered the plastic tube that brought her fresh air. Her thoughts were weak, but never were they as clear as they were at this moment.

"*Daed,*" she called faintly.

"He's in the ambulance behind us, Miss," a voice said to her.

Libby's lashes fluttered. Sirens assaulted her ears, and she felt the motion of the moving vehicle beneath her lifeless body. She could not move, but she could think.

She was in an ambulance.

She was alive.

Someone had saved her.

Feeling a squeeze to her hand, she let her gaze follow the blurry path to a face she recognized; a face she trusted.

"Jonas," she whispered. "I thought—you were—dead."

Jonas pulled the hand he held to his lips and placed a soft kiss to the back of it. "I'm right here, and I'm not leaving you."

"How did you...?"

He squeezed her hand tightly. "I kicked through the feed hatch of the chicken coop on the other side of the barn."

"What about *mei daed?*" she asked weakly.

"Your *daed* followed me out. Since he went in after me, he breathed in a little more smoke than I did, so they are taking him to the hospital too. But you—you shouldn't have gone into the barn. By the time we realized you'd gone in there, it was almost too..."

Jonas couldn't finish his sentence.

Libby could hear the emotion in his voice. She tightened the grip he had on her hand.

"I'm sorry I worried you, but I thought you and *mei daed* needed help. I was trying to save you."

Jonas bent to kiss her on the forehead. "I need saving, but not from a burning barn. I need you to save me from having to spend the rest of my life without you as *mei fraa.*"

Tears welled up in Libby's eyes. "I can do that."

"I almost lost you three times in the last month, and I don't think *mei* heart can take anymore. Promise me you won't ever do anything like that again."

"I promise," she said with a cough.

The ambulance stopped and the back door flung open. Paramedics wheeled her out into the cold air. Snowflakes cooled her cheeks as she looked over and saw her father being wheeled from another ambulance. Paramedics pushed her through the doors of the emergency room, but she called out to her father.

He held up a hand, and made eye-contact with her only for a moment, but she knew he was alive, and that meant everything to her.

For now, everything was going to be alright.

CHAPTER 28

"It's only two days," Bethany said to Libby. "I can't get married without you. I can wait until you get out of the hospital, and surely Benjamin can wait two more days for me."

"I don't want you to wait on my account."

Libby's throat was sore and her voice hoarse.

"You know I remember everything now, Bethany." Libby admitted.

Bethany looked her in the eye hesitantly. "Even about Jonas?"

"I know why I broke up with him, *jah.*"

"*Ach,* what are you going to do? Are you going to break up with him again?"

Libby could see the genuine concern in Bethany's eyes, but she intended to squelch her fears.

"*Nee,* I will have to move to Florida if that is what he wants. He is to be *mei* husband in less than a week, and I already promised to marry him—not that I would take back such a promise, but I love him enough to go wherever he goes."

Bethany smiled. "You won't have to. He came here to tell you he changed his mind about Florida."

Libby sat up in her hospital bed. "You knew this the whole time and you didn't tell me?"

"Quiet down," Bethany scolded her. "I bet they heard you all the way to the nurse's station."

Libby leered at her. "You and Jonas betrayed my trust. You both lied to me and led me to believe I was meeting Jonas for the first time. But then when I remembered, it was admitted that we indeed had a past, but not the past you both fed me. Was I going to marry him and not find out until it was too late that he was moving me to Florida?"

Bethany put a hand over Libby's arm. "Calm down. We never meant to deceive you. We were trying to spare you too much because of the accident. The doctors told us not to upset you."

"Didn't you think *lying* to me would upset me?"

"We weren't trying to lie to you. We were trying to spare you the pain of knowing you'd broken up with him for

603

nothing. You love him and he loves you! And he intends to marry you and keep you here in this community, and *that* is why he came to Willow Creek right after your accident. It broke his heart that you didn't remember him, and that is the *only* reason I went along with this."

Libby turned toward the window, exposing her back side to Bethany.

"Don't turn your back on me, Libby. Life is too short to spend it angry over things you can't change. You almost lost your *daed* and Adam and Jonas last night, and we almost lost *you* too!"

As tough as it was for Libby to admit, she could not deny the truth Bethany spoke. The important thing was that she and Jonas were back together, and she remembered her family finally. Jonas no longer had intention of taking her away from her family or her community, and they would start a life together here.

CHAPTER 29

Jonas held fast to Libby's hand as they skated around the pond one more time before rounding the curve where their family and friends waited for them at the B&B for their wedding meal.

"Just one more time around the pond," Libby begged her new husband.

"How can I resist such a sweet request?" Jonas said with a proud smile.

He whisked her around the pond illuminated by the lanterns that lined the perimeter. Snowflakes fell from the heavens, and the moon occasionally peeked through a gap in the clouds. She couldn't have asked for a more romantic setting for her wedding.

She was the happiest she thought she could ever be at this moment. She could stay out here skating with him for hours, but their families waited for them so they could share their special day.

Libby tipped her head up to the swirling snow remembering how much it had played a part in the return of her memory the day of her accident.

She had not forgotten Jonas.

He was the love of her life.

She'd heard his voice floating on the snowflakes that day. It had kept her from slipping away into the darkness that had tried to overtake her.

Even when she was lying on the floor of the burning barn, she'd remembered the snowflakes that tied her to her beloved Jonas. It was on the ice that they'd fallen in love, and it was on the ice now that they celebrated that love.

THE END

JOIN ME ON FACEBOOK

Please enjoy sample chapters

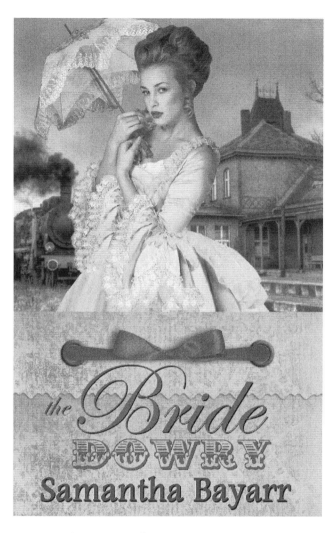

Bride Dowry

THE BRIDE DOWRY: Maddie Hawkins answers an advertisement posted at the General Store for silver mine shares being given away to women.

When she arrives in Tombstone in the spring of 1885, she is informed the only way she can collect those shares is to marry one of the miners in town, due to a shortage of women in Arizona Territory.

Broke, Maddie is unable to return home, so her only choice is to marry a complete stranger. Calamities unfold as a result of her decision, and she soon regrets putting her signature to the contract.

When all the available suitors meet her at the Founder's Day picnic, she is appalled by the choices, and the only man suitable is already promised to another bride.

Wanting to marry for love, Maddie fears her dreams of a happy married life will not come to pass if she accepts the conditions of the Bride Dowry.

The Bride Dowry
Book One

CHAPTER 1

Tombstone Arizona, 1885

Maddie Hawkins stood on the platform in front of the mining office and crumpled the advertisement, stuffing it angrily into her reticule. It boasted shares in the silver mines to women who should come to Tombstone to help populate the town, but little had she known there were conditions upon the collection of those shares.

She'd been unsure of what they'd meant by *populate* the town.

She knew now!

"What do you mean I have to marry one of the miners in order to collect the shares?"

Her tone resonated across the mining yard, where several workers looked up at her outburst.

"In other words, the *man* gets the shares in the mine if I marry him, not the other way around."

Maddie felt like she'd been tricked. Lured by a false advertisement.

"We prefer to call it a bonus in pay for your new husband," the man behind the barred window said with a snicker.

She sneered at him, biting back tears.

"What did you say your name was, Miss? I don't see you on the list," the man said.

"List?"

"Yes, Miss…who did you correspond with?"

Maddie gulped. "Well, you're the first one I've spoken to about this."

"You were supposed to correspond with one of the eligible men, and then meet him at the Founder's Day picnic this Saturday."

Maddie lowered her gaze, hoping to avert his attention from her pinked cheeks. Reaching into her reticule, she smoothed out the advertisement and read the fine print at the bottom of the page. She had been so anxious to get out of Texas Territory that she had not read those lines before planning her trip to Tombstone. She'd been so consumed with leaving her uncle's home and getting away from her cousin, she hadn't paid the proper amount of attention to the details of the offer.

Now she wished she had.

She lowered her gaze once again to the page in her hand. Sure enough, there were the instructions, plain as day. But what was she to do about it now? The trip had cost her every bit of the money she'd put aside from being a governess to the Wexler children for the past four years, minus the portion she'd paid to her uncle for room and board.

"You're here a little earlier than we expected, but the others will be here by the end of the week."

"Others?" she asked curiously. "How many women responded to this trickery?"

The man bit down on the cigar in his mouth, clenching it between his teeth as he perused the list. "I have twenty-three on my list who have their husbands lined up because they took the last three months to correspond like the notice says."

She couldn't help but feel humiliated, as if he was questioning her intelligence, but judging by his appearance, she didn't suspect him of having as high an education as she'd had.

"If you're still interested, you can attend the Founder's Day picnic on Saturday, and one of the fellas who haven't already been paired up with a bride will pick you."

"Pick me? You mean I can't do my own choosing?"

"No, Ma'am," he said with a smile. "It's the men who do the choosing."

Maddie fanned herself with the lace fan that matched her dress as she held her parasol closer to her face to shield her cheeks from the sweltering, afternoon sun.

"In the meantime, here is a voucher for the hotel in town."

Maddie looked at the slip of paper with the hotel logo on it as he slid it under the bars.

"Just sign here, and you can be on your way."

Maddie took the fountain pen mindlessly from the clerk's hand and grazed over the short document in front of her. Was this what her life had been reduced to? Marrying a complete stranger for a place to stay? She knew how few coins she had left in her reticule, and it was not enough to cover the train fare back home, let alone room and board.

But where was home for her anyway?

She'd lived with her uncle on her mother's side since her mother's passing four years ago, and she'd been considered a burden the entire time. This trip had been a source of hope to start a new life for herself away from the control of her uncle, and out from the shadow of her overbearing cousin.

Since she was ready to be out on her own and settle down, she was too eager to travel to Tombstone, thinking what better way to start off a new life than with a little nest egg, and the shares in the silver mine had mesmerized her attention away from reality.

Now, it seemed, she would have to relinquish control of that to a strange husband, and trust that he would not waste it on immoral means.

She no more wanted to find a husband in haste than she relished the idea of wiring her uncle and begging for passage back to Texas Territory.

Maddie had snatched up the notice without thinking it through. The moment she heard it from her friend, Willa Mae, whose father was the post master and owner of the General Store, Maddie thought it was her destiny.

"I thought you would want to know about owning your own silver mine shares since your wedding with Carver is off," Willa Mae had said that day. "I didn't want that *fancy-*

pants cousin of yours to get her hands on it. This is your ticket out of here."

"That wedding was never *on*. Besides, Abby isn't so bad," Maddie said, more to convince herself than Willa Mae.

To wit; Willa Mae promptly reminded her that Abby had stolen her beau, Carver Jennings. In the end, he'd left Abby for another woman soon after they'd begun dating, so Maddie had let the matter drop, having been grateful that her cousin, for once, had done her a kindness through her horrid behavior.

Now, it seemed she had to stomach another choice made against her will, and hoped it, too, would come out in her favor.

Maddie blew out a discouraging sigh and let go of her pride long enough to accept the voucher for the hotel as she reluctantly signed her name, agreeing to the terms of the offer.

CHAPTER 2

Hoss Tucker ambled across the boardwalk in front of the hotel, looking to see if his *mail order bride* had arrived on today's stage. But how would he even know which one she was?

What had his brother and sister-in-law been thinking when they'd written to some poor, unsuspecting woman pretending to be Hoss? How could they have done such a thing to him? He'd told his brother time and again he wanted to marry for love. He'd told him several times that he wanted no part in sending away for a bride. After all, he was still young and mighty handsome according to their ma, and he wasn't about to settle for a loveless marriage to a stranger. Call him a romantic, but he wanted all that falling in love would give him. He'd never been in love before, but he'd heard plenty from his brother while he was courting Emily, and it put a mighty appealing desire in his heart for the same.

Surely his brother understood that Hoss wanted the same thing he'd been lucky enough to find with Emily. Only thing was, he didn't want a mail order bride, Hoss wanted to do his own choosing.

It didn't matter now.

Thanks to his brother's meddling, he was stuck in a legally-binding contract with a stranger. He hoped she would let him out of the contract once he explained to her what had happened. He prayed she would not want to enter into a marriage with him after she discovered it hadn't been him that had written the letters to her. He'd even offer to pay her passage back to wherever she'd traveled from.

He was *that* desperate to get out of it.

Maddie strolled sadly across the boardwalk in front of the General Store, wishing it was Willa Mae's family store back in Texas she was in front of instead of the reality that now slammed around in her mind. Clenching the hotel voucher in her fist, she wondered if she could sneak away on tomorrow's stage and get away without consequence for putting her signature to that contract at the silver mining office. The long walk back to the hotel had given her time enough to think that she should not have been so hasty in signing—even though it had meant a roof over her head for the night.

But what else could she do? She didn't have enough money to get herself home.

What had she been thinking?

Was she so desperate to escape Texas Territory that she would sign her life away this easily? Perhaps if she'd thought more about it, she would have saved enough to get herself back home, in case it was necessary. If only she'd known about the details of the contract *before* she'd set off on such a half-thought-out adventure, she would have willingly accepted it was her destiny to stay in Texas and become a spinster in her uncle's home.

Maddie stiffened her lips that quivered with fear, and threatened to let a cry escape them if she should continue to wonder if she'd done the right thing. If there was one thing her ma had taught her, it was that life could sometimes present you with some really exciting surprises when you least expect them.

Determined to see what good God could bring out of her hasty decision, Maddie picked up her head and walked past the General Store and toward the hotel that would be her *home* for the next few days—until she was wed to a stranger.

Her breath caught in her dry, dusty throat as her gaze fell upon the tall, handsome man walking toward her same destination.

If that was the sort of man that would choose her at the Founder's Day picnic, she might reconsider her woes.

The man swaggered toward the hotel entrance and paused, leaning against the wood frame of the building. He crossed one leg over the other, his spur clicking against the wooden boardwalk.

Maddie slowed her walk just to drink him in a little more. She was parched from the travel along the dusty trail to Tombstone, and she couldn't think of a better way to quench that thirst than with that tall drink of water standing in front of the hotel aiming his gaze upon her.

Hoss looked up just in time to see the most delicate little filly he'd ever seen sauntering down the boardwalk in his direction. Her blue dress and full skirts sashayed over the boardwalk as if she was floating toward him. One dainty hand held fast to the parasol that rested on her milky shoulder, the other struggled with an oversized carpetbag that flounced against her skirts with every step she took. The delicate lace that encircled her neck and wrists fluttered in the warm breeze that seemed to carry her down the stretch of Allen Street with the sort of sweetness that Hoss admired so much, it etched a place in his heart for her.

Remembering his manners, he lifted himself from the side of the building and approached her, stretching an arm toward her bag as he tipped his Stetson with one finger and nodded.

"Let me get that bag for you, Miss."

Maddie let the man take her bag as she mindlessly followed him into the hotel. She was too tired to worry about whether he worked for the hotel, and he was too handsome for her to resist anything he might offer her. He led her to the desk and set her bag down as she handed the hotel voucher over the counter to the proprietor.

Oh, Lord, let this sweet woman be my mail order bride.

"Are you here to check in with the rest of the mail order brides?" the man behind the counter asked.

Maddie swallowed hard against what she deemed to be a derogatory term for her.

"Yes, Sir," she said quietly, feeling suddenly embarrassed in front of the man who'd brought in her bag. "I'm Maddie Hawkins, and the man at the silver mining office told me that voucher would get me a room free of charge."

Hoss felt his heart clench behind his ribcage when she'd given her name. He stepped away from the counter with a tip of his hat toward her and exited the hotel, feeling discouraged that *Maddie* was not the bride he was contracted to marry.

END OF SAMPLE

Please turn the page to view the next sample

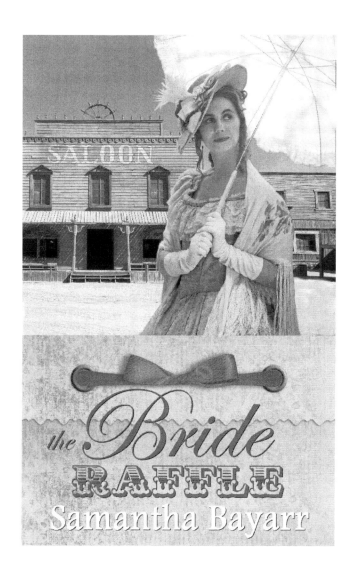

Bride Raffle

THE BRIDE RAFFLE: When Belle Calhoun steps off the stage into Tombstone Arizona in the spring of 1885, she never dreamed she'd arrive just in time to witness a hanging, get into a tussle with a saloon owner, have to borrow a dress from a saloon girl, or attend a stranger's funeral, all within her first hour in town.

When her circumstances suddenly find her without her intended mail order groom, Belle has a hard time staying out of trouble when his brother threatens to raffle her off to the highest bidder.

Dalton, who has vowed to protect her, can't do that when he gets himself into some trouble of his own with the new deputy in town.

The Bride Raffle
Book Two

CHAPTER 1

Tombstone Arizona, Spring, 1885

Belle Calhoun stepped off the stage and into the crowded streets of Tombstone. The sweltering heat of the afternoon sun added to the ruckus of the crowd that gathered around…

"Oh my!" Belle clamped a gloved hand over her mouth to cover the unexpected cry that escaped her lips.

The town-folk had gathered around the courthouse, and Belle had arrived just in time to witness a hanging.

"Jedidiah Griff," a man called from the platform of the gallows. "Do you have any last words?"

"No!" Belle screamed barely above a whisper.

She could feel her breath catch as she ran to the front of the crowd to reach the gallows, where a man stood with his hands bound behind his back, a noose around his neck.

"Please, Sheriff," she cried, turning the crowd's attention onto her. "I—I came all this way! I need to talk to Jed before you—before…"

It was too horrible for her to push the words from her mouth, much less, to think about what she was about to witness.

"What business do you have with the prisoner?" Sheriff Daniels asked.

"I'm his—his *mail order bride.*" She said, choking back tears that caught in her throat.

The words sounded suddenly pointless, even to her.

"Justice, will you escort your brother's *bride* to the platform," he said to a man standing behind her.

The sheriff was obligated to uphold the law, but everyone in town knew he was also a fair man.

Belle felt a strained grip on her arm as she was led up the wooden steps by a man who smelled of saloon and cigars. She didn't turn to see his face; she didn't want to look him in the eye.

Belle shook as she stood next to the man about to be hanged.

"May I s—see his face?" she asked quietly.

Sheriff Daniels lifted the feed sack from the man's head, while Belle held a hand over her mouth, fearful of the cry that waited in her throat.

Green eyes squinted, but didn't look her way. His light, thick hair still bore an indentation from his Stetson that lay at his feet; his chin lifted as if in defiance.

She touched his arm lightly, unable to speak.

He turned to look at her. "You're just as beautiful as I imagined, Belle."

His eyes glazed over with moisture, but he clenched his jaw to keep in the tears.

"Justice," he said, turning to his brother. "Promise me you'll marry Belle and take care of her, and that you'll stay out of the saloon. Give her Ma's ring. It's in my trunk. Please do everything you can to clear my name—even after I'm gone—to keep from shaming Ma."

His lips quivered, but his words never faltered.

Belle wanted to protest, but she wouldn't deny him his last wish—even if she had no intention of honoring it.

"I'll pray for your soul," she whispered as she lifted herself to kiss his cheek.

"The letters I wrote to you," he whispered back. "Read them again. You'll know who I am."

She agreed, even though she didn't understand what he meant.

Justice nodded to his brother soberly, and then clenched Belle's arm, pulling her back down into the crowd.

Sheriff Daniels replaced the sack over Jed's face and nodded to the hangman in the corner of the platform.

Belle's scream rent the air as the lever was pulled, snapping the line that held fast to Jed's noose.

His head went limp, his feet twitched.

Then, it was over.

Her mail order groom was dead.

End of sample

Bride Duel

THE BRIDE DUEL: When two brothers send away for a mail order bride for domestic reasons, they find themselves with more trouble than they bargained for, and each will do anything they can to get out of marrying her!

Lizzie Ramsey traveled to Tombstone on her last dollar and a promise. When she arrives to find her dream is nothing more than a domestic nightmare, she sets out to teach the Bodine Brothers a lesson they won't soon forget.

The Bride Duel
Book Three

CHAPTER 1

Tombstone Arizona, Summer, 1885

Lizzie Ramsey stepped off the stage, looking for her intended groom. But after several of the town folk passed her by without one man fitting the description of the man she'd travelled to meet, she decided it was time to look for him. The sun was high in the sky, making the heat so intense, it nearly choked her to take in a breath.

She wondered how people managed here without falling over dead from the heat.

Strolling into the General Store, her spurs clicked across the wooden floor planks, announcing her presence like a local. Hoping to find some solace from the warmth of the street, and to see if her *betrothed* might perhaps be waiting for her in there, she walked to the back of the store and stepped up to the counter.

"Excuse me," Lizzie interrupted the woman behind the counter. "I'm looking for Sawyer Amos. I was supposed to meet him today when the stage came in. Do you happen to know where I might find him?"

The woman snickered and looked at Lizzie for a minute, studying her as if she was trying to decipher if she was serious or not. "I think you must mean the Bodine brothers!"

"Brothers?" Lizzie asked. "No, I'm only looking for one man—Sawyer Amos."

"Then you're looking for Sawyer *and* Amos Bodine!" the woman corrected her.

Lizzie's eyes widened at the store owner's remark, pausing just long enough for it to sink in.

"You mean it's not just *one* man?"

The older woman planted her hands on her hips and furrowed her brow. "Now just what have them two boys done this time?"

"*Two boys?*" Lizzie repeated angrily. "Just how *old* are these two *boys?*"

The older woman smirked again. "Oh, they're plenty old enough to get themselves into trouble that would involve a pretty girl like you, but not mature enough to get themselves out of it. Did they try to sell you something, Miss?"

Lizzie was growing angrier by the minute. "No, they didn't exactly *sell* me something, except perhaps a future of lies!"

"I can only imagine what they said to get you to come here! What was it?"

Lizzie slapped a stack of letters on the counter that she'd had tucked under her arm. "One of them—Sawyer, I'm guessing—made me an offer to be his mail order bride!"

The older woman's face curled up. "Sawyer is the older of the two. I might expect that from Amos, but not from Sawyer. I thought he had more sense than that."

"Apparently he doesn't," Lizzie said.

She was furious by this time. Her hands rested on the six-guns strapped at her waistline, anger boiling in her. "Where can I find those two so I can straighten them out?"

A smile crossed the old woman's lips. "Oh, they've got a real nice place just outside of town. You can't miss it if you head east. It's a big house with its own barn. Their folks didn't lack for money, but those two had the notion they were going to come out west and be cowboys, but neither one 'em can shoot a gun to save their lives! They have a few chickens, but even those are disappearing because they just don't know how to care for 'em properly. Coyotes are getting 'em. They don't even do their own laundry; they bring it into town. The last time I paid them a visit to bring them a pie, the house was so filthy, I could barely walk through the place, and the dishes are piled up, though I don't know why because they don't cook. They take most of their meals here at the hotel restaurant."

What had she gotten herself mixed up in?

"That still doesn't explain why they would send away for a mail order bride by pretending to be one man."

"I'm guessing they want someone to take care of them because I refused to do it. I'm betting that's why they sent for you. I suppose they thought if one of them had a wife, she'd cook and clean and take care of both of them!"

"Well, if they think that I came here to take care of a couple of spoiled men who act like boys, they've got another thing coming to them."

"Them two boys came out here a year ago after their ma passed away, and they've been nothing but trouble ever since they got here. I'm Etta Mae, and I was friends with their ma in our school days, and so I made a promise to her on her death bed that I'd look after them for her. Little did I know she'd spoiled them to the point they can't do nothing for themselves, and they come up with one scheme after another! Well, neither of them boys are mature enough to handle themselves, much less, a wife."

"It sounds to me as if they need to be taught a lesson!" Lizzie said. "I didn't come all the way out here to be a caretaker for two spoiled boys. I came out here to get married to a responsible man, and I aim to get just that, even if I have to force one of them to grow up!"

Etta Mae raised an eyebrow at her. "If you get tired of trying with them two, you come see me, but I have a feeling you might be just what those two boys need!"

"It would have been proper if they'd at least met me at the stage when I came in. I have baggage and a trunk."

"There ain't much proper about them two boys, and they likely forgot you were coming in. Have the stage driver bring your things in here. You can leave them with me until you get out to their place and hog-tie one of 'em into bringing the buckboard to fetch your belongings."

Lizzie snatched up the letters from the counter.

"They certainly didn't forget to write to me twice a week!"

"I'm surprised Mabel didn't tell me they were corresponding with you. She's the biggest gossiper in this town. I'd have certainly put a stop to those boys and their lies before things got out of control. I'm sorry they brought you all the way here for nothing."

"They promised me a husband," Lizzie said. "And one of them is going to have to own up to it!"

"I wish you luck, Miss…"

"Elizabeth Ramsey, but I go by Lizzie."

"Well, Lizzie, I certainly wish you luck with them two boys," Etta Mae said.

Lizzie tugged on a strap that hung from her shoulder, a Remington, double-barrel shotgun swung from around her back. She held it confidently in her right hand, pointing the barrel toward the ceiling of the General Store. "This is all the luck I'm going to need!"

Thank you for reading sample chapters of

Wester Mail Order Brides

Newly Released books
99 cents or FREE with
Kindle Unlimited.

♡ LOVE to Read?
♡ LOVE 99 cent Books?
♡ LOVE GIVEAWAYS?

YOU MIGHT ALSO LIKE:

Amish Weddings Collection

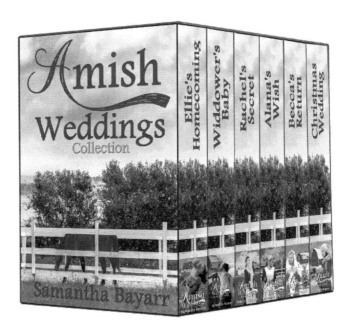

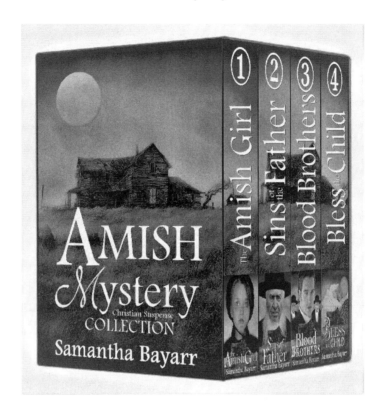

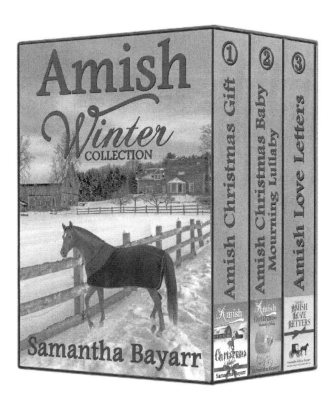

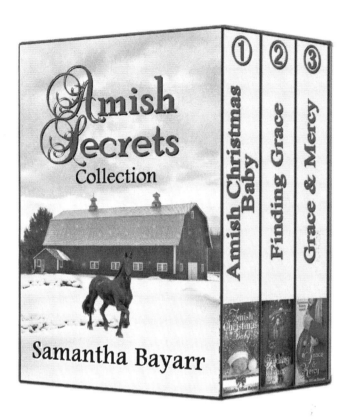

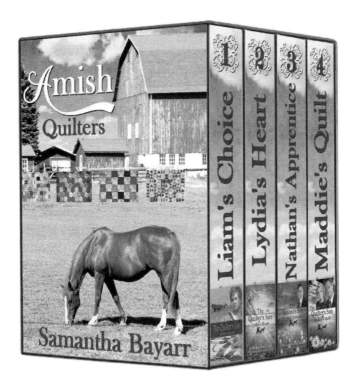

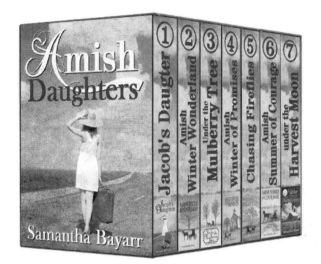

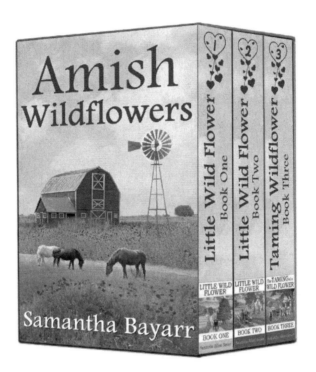

Made in the USA
Monee, IL
12 October 2020